SHEEHAN'S DOG

BOOKS BY LES ROBERTS

Milan Jacovich Mysteries
Pepper Pike
Full Cleveland
Deep Shakeer'
The Cleveland Connection
The Lake Effect
The Duke of Cleveland
Collision Bend
The Cleveland Local
A Shoot in Cleveland
The Best-Kept Secret
The Indian Sign
The Dutch
The Irish Sports Pages
King of the Holly Hop
The Cleveland Creep
Whiskey Island
Win, Place or Die
(with Dan S. Kennedy)
The Ashtabula Hat Trick
Speaking of Murder
(with Dan S. Kennedy)

Non-Fiction Memoir
We'll Always Have Cleveland

Saxon Mysteries
*An Infinite Number
of Monkeys*
Not Enough Horses
A Carrot for the Donkey
Snake Oil
Seeing the Elephant
The Lemon Chicken Jones

Dominic Candiotti Novels
*The Strange Death of
Father Candy*
Wet Work

Stand-Alone
The Chinese Fire Drill

Novella
A Carol for Cleveland
(later made into a play by
Eric Coble for the Cleveland
Play House holiday season)

Short Stories
The Scent of Spiced Oranges

LES ROBERTS

SHEEHAN'S DOG

DOWN&OUT
BOOKS

Down & Out Books
3959 Van Dyke Road, Suite 265
Lutz, FL 33558
DownAndOutBooks.com

The characters and events in this book are fictitious. Any similarity to real persons, living or dead, is coincidental and not intended by the author.

Cover design by JT Lindroos

ISBN: 1-64396-247-7
ISBN-13: 978-1-64396-247-4

To Holly Albin—
Half this novel and all its soul is hers

CHAPTER ONE

When one is born and raised into an Irish Catholic family on the rugged west side of a rough-edged Rust Belt town like Cleveland, Ohio, one doesn't grow up dreaming about elegant things rich people had, like expensive cars and an elite homestead with a swimming pool and a tennis court, or a roomy boat that cruised the waters of nearby Lake Erie with a crowd of other rich friends, hanging over the side and drinking liquor whenever the weather was nice.

It was hard enough getting through elementary school without getting one's head knocked off in the adjoining playground, or cringing in the office of a stern and terrifying assistant principal to answer why a suspension for selling weekly college football cards to other kids and maybe going home with two extra bucks or so, or—and this was the real biggie—being hauled into the local precinct by one of those red-faced Irish cops for "borrowing" another kid's bike without permission, or walking out of the corner drugstore with an unpaid-for comic book stuffed under a shirt.

That was a fairly accurate description of the first eighteen years of the life of one Brock Sheehan. Then he got smart, got tough, snared a job that any Irish kid in the neighborhood would have happily killed for, and started putting away most of his salary, plus bonuses, to eventually score some of those sumptuous opulent toys the big boys played with when they were rich.

The Harbor Lagoon in Vermillion, Ohio on the southern shore of Lake Erie is where Brock Sheehan lived for more than half the year since he'd turned forty-five years old. In the wintertime, the lake was a living, breathing menace, often flooding US 90 east of downtown Cleveland, wind-driven waves crashing over no man's land between the water and the highway. This was mid-September, though, so early in the evening he was enjoying his second Bushmills Black relaxing on the deck of his houseboat, a roomy river and lake yacht that slept six, especially if all six were very good friends.

The trouble was that he didn't have many friends—not anymore. He spent much of his time aboard since he had retired quietly ten years earlier from what had been his adult life's work in Cleveland and moved a bit westward. Late afternoon sun painting his rugged face with orange hues, he wore long khaki pants, deck shoes with no socks, and a white Irish cable-knit sweater over a flannel shirt, while he sipped his Bushmills Black. A true Irishman right down to his toes, he preferred drinking Irish whiskey to anything else.

In the summer, the location was a delight of sorts, especially for water lovers, and often during weekend days there was much socializing aboard in what's been dubbed Harbortown, with bikini-clad women thirty years younger than the boat owners, bringing sinuous class to the neighborhood along with all-day-long champagne. Not for Brock Sheehan, though. He preferred his privacy.

Sheehan owned his boat outright, but had never paid a nickel for it, nor declared it on his income tax—and no one had ever asked him to. He'd only become a boat owner when he retired, due to a fortuitous gift bestowed on him by his longtime boss. He never became a devout sailor, though. His boat trips were relegated to occasional visits to the islands north of Ohio, where there was not much more to do than drink and carouse.

It was just three weeks past Labor Day—he wondered if

2

anyone remembered why a Monday holiday was given that particular name. Back in the early and middle twentieth century, the blue-collar hardworking middle class and the union guys used to be called "The Labor Force," and maybe someone decided they should get a holiday in September. But laborers in the twenty-first century were rushing pell-mell toward the sad extinction of the dodo and the passenger pigeon, thanks to national politics. Sheehan knew the too-wet, too-cold weather would arrive quickly and with a vengeance, as it always did in the fall; Ohio summer was just about over. Within the next few weeks, he would put the houseboat in dry-dock and head west to ride out the winter in more clement weather—probably to Arizona or New Mexico—a longer trip than the annual escape to Florida of the Ohio snowbirds, and always by car. But he had no use for the American south. He was not able to understand strange southern accents, like "Hah yew?" and "bidness" and "all y'all," in a climate where humidity alone could kill you.

Besides, many rebels still fight what they insist on remembering as the War of Northern Aggression, and persist calling anyone not born below the Mason-Dixon line a "Yankee," a sneer curling their upper lip. The last thing Sheehan wanted was to get into another civil uprising, despite the most famous Grant-Lee surrender in the history of world warfare that hadn't really stopped hatred down in Dixie within the last hundred and fifty years.

He despised even more the northeast winters in which he'd been raised. Within a short time, the lake would be frozen solid for several miles out. Even moving from a boat to a mainland apartment meant dealing with blizzards and brutal winds from November to April. He vaguely remembered one recent year in which recorded Cleveland snowfall happened in nine of the twelve months. Only June, July, and August that year that didn't call for sweaters and hoodies and padded parkas.

Brock Sheehan was broad-shouldered, with big, powerful hands, grizzled gray hair always in need of a barber, and a muscular physique that had gained only fifteen pounds since his

3

teen years, despite his aversion to any adult exercise more exhausting than climbing on and off barstools. His eyes were blue, green, or in between, depending on the lighting and his particular mood. Under this setting sun, they appeared hazel.

He'd turned fifty-eight years old on his last birthday, which he didn't celebrate or even think about it. He'd received no congratulatory cards, flowers, gifts of any kind, or a birthday party—even a small one—nor had he expected them. He explicitly ignored birthdays as he considered them a yearly tap on the shoulder reminding everyone that they were growing old whether they liked it or not.

His extended Irish relatives were either deceased or very distant from him, and he had few friends—only acquaintances. He'd never revealed his age or birthdate to any of them. The job from which he'd retired had required a certain privacy and secrecy, which had put him at odds with anyone else in the Sheehan family, so he'd learned to keep his cards close to the vest from everyone he knew.

Now, two years away from the Big Six-O, a milestone birthday that is no longer called "middle age," he'd outgrown his usefulness. At top form, he'd been on the highest rung of danger guys for the Cleveland Irish Mafia, one step below the so-called godfather who for forty years ran the west side of Cleveland, leaving the east side to Italians, the near west side to Puerto Ricans, and downtown and its environs to African Americans. Several years into voluntary retirement, Sheehan had become a quiet, thoughtful man who lived on his boat seven months out of twelve, read two books each week from the local library, and drank Irish whiskey neat, even though it kicked up his stomach ulcer.

He bothered no one.

Unmarried, childless, and tiptoeing toward "golden years" which are not golden for anyone, he recalled being shot twice during his heyday, stabbed once, and arrested four times on suspicion of murder—once in Erie, Pennsylvania, once in New

York City, and twice in Cleveland—but never indicted. Not being the actual leader, he'd mostly been ignored by the cops, the press, and other Irishmen who had no mutual criminal tendencies. He'd never served in the military nor donned a uniform of any kind, not counting the white shirt and black tie he was forced to wear to a Catholic high school.

Living under the radar in historic Vermillion, a New England-style town right on Lake Erie, midway between Cleveland and Toledo, he was relatively unknown to fellow residents. He maintained a polite detachment from summer tourists, or those who visited their own harbored boats on warm weekends. He'd thought of selling the houseboat—or exchanging it for a much smaller one—to put down home roots on a nearby island. But South Bass—known for the raucous Put-In-Bay—or Kelley's Island, or Rattlesnake Island were all super-rich enclaves charging much more than they should for real estate. He was more secure on the mainland. Doctors and hospitals guided Cleveland's fortunes, an hour's drive away, as one of the best medical cities in the world, and Brock Sheehan wasn't getting any younger. His joints were sore and stiff in the mornings, and when he walked too fast, or carried something heavy, he had to stop momentarily and catch his breath. He was comforted, though, knowing many superb doctors at the Cleveland Clinic were within driving distance.

Sheehan was lonely most of the time, as many older people are. But for most of his adult life, he'd had everything he wanted at his fingertips—money, women, power, and best of all, respect. A big, good-looking man who terrified those within his bailiwick, he was invisible for all intents and purposes, quietly repaying the world for his good years.

He'd learned early—nobody rides for free.

Far from being broke, he spread more than three hundred thousand dollars in cash over several Ohio savings banks, and he owned stocks and bonds worth three times that. His fifty-four-foot houseboat had been a gift, bilked from an Italian mob money launderer and given to him as a goodbye remembrance by the Irish godfather who treated him like a son, and whose tax lawyers figured out how not to let the IRS know who really owned the boat.

In his younger days, Sheehan engendered affection and often fear from everyone who knew him. Women found him fascinating, but he'd stopped hunting them five years earlier, not jazzed by those close to his age, and uninterested in any enduring relationship with a twenty-five-year-old, as he had no idea how to handle one sporting tattoos and metal face piercings. Aging gracefully, one-night stands were too much trouble, and hookers—no matter how classy and expensive—were skanky to him and had never been part of his lifestyle. "Aloneness" is what he'd chosen.

Aloneness granted him a generous dollop of security.

As far as power was concerned, he still had that well in hand, should he ever need it again. He simply had no desire to do so.

The breeze had turned chilly this autumn afternoon, and he took another healthy Bushmills gulp to warm his insides. Now wavering between agnosticism and atheism, he'd grown up a previously devout lace curtain mick, and his fascination and need for anything Celtic came easily to him—food, booze, clothes, and Irish music and literature.

A sudden wind gust from the lake rocked the boat—Mother Nature's preview of weather as fall crept toward winter. He shifted in his deck chair for comfort, and noticed someone walking down the dock toward him, a large dog trotting at his side.

The young man had reddish-brown hair and a certain swagger, but he didn't look tough—just a kid who *wished* he were a tough guy. The round Irish face topped a body like a track athlete's, probably a hundred-yarder. He didn't seem to be a football player or heavyweight boxer—too slim to last long in hand-to-hand combat, and had about him an ambience of innocence and purity.

With narrowed eyes, Sheehan watched the kid's approach

ahead of the orange sun that made him a silhouette—vaguely familiar, though he couldn't quite place him. The brindle dog was about eighty pounds of solid muscle with a head like a battering ram.

Sheehan put down his drink, setting his feet under him so he could rise quickly if necessary—something he'd learned long ago, as remaining seated made one an inviting target. He kept his face neutral—not welcoming, but not threatening either.

The young man stopped at the end of the plank. The dog sat on the dock, ears up and alert, the quiet marred only by the gentle sloshing of water beneath the boat.

Sheehan broke the silence. "Afternoon. Fine-looking dog you got there."

"Thanks." The man ran his hand through his hair, tossed by the lake breeze. "Mr. Sheehan?"

Sheehan didn't like strangers knowing his name. It was uncomfortable for him. Not nervous; he never got nervous—just suspicious. "What about it?"

"You don't recognize me. It's been ten years. I'm Linus Callahan—your nephew."

Sheehan took a moment to put that all together in his mind. Then, with a lightness in his voice that even surprised him, he said, "Linus Callahan? You're Fiona's son? My sister Fiona?"

"Good to see you again, Uncle Brock. Permission to come aboard, sir?"

Sheehan stood up, faintly smiling. "This isn't the Navy. No salutes necessary." Linus beamed as he trotted down the plank and stepped onto the boat, the dog at his heels, and shook hands with his uncle. An awkward moment, naturally, as neither even recalled what the other had looked like. Eventually Sheehan said, "Damn, it's good to see you, son. Jesus, Mary, and Joseph, you've grown up. How's your family?"

"They're okay. My sister Maeve just started Hiram College, majoring in political science. Dad retired from the carpenters union after forty years. He doesn't feel great, but he's okay." He felt foolish standing there. "We all still miss Mom, you know."

Sheehan lost his older sister Fiona to cancer almost ten years earlier, and it ground his insides that they'd never been close, not even as children—and adulthood had turned them both into antagonists. Fiona had disapproved of his profession from the start. A three-masses-per-week Catholic girl who knelt each night for a pre-sleep prayer, not knowing or understanding violence, of hurting people—a perfect description of what her baby brother did for a living.

Fiona wasn't quiet about it either, and it wound up with every Sheehan in Greater Cleveland ignoring and shunning the existence of financially successful Brock, who was within the embrace of the West Side Gaelic Society—thus the rupture of Brock's clan, and its after-church brunches, Thanksgiving and Easter dinners, or crowding around the spinet to sing Christmas carols. Days long gone, replaced with aloneness again, sharp and painful.

"Pull a chair over so we can talk," Sheehan said, trying to keep the meeting light. "Want a drink? Coke? Lemonade?" He raised his glass. "Something stronger?"

Linus moved the extra chair so he and Brock were opposite each other. "That's okay," he said. "I don't need anything. Sorry."

The dog stretched across Linus's feet, and Brock asked, "Is your friend thirsty?"

"No. I keep water in the car for him, and dog treats in my pocket. He goes almost everyplace I go. His name is Patton."

Patton, Sheehan thought, was one hell of a name, honoring the legendary World War II tank commander, General George S. Patton. It fit the dog perfectly, as he looked as if his head could blast through a brick wall like a tank. "A pit bull?"

Linus nodded. "Mixed with something else. He was abandoned—probably was a pet, too, and not a trained killer, thank god. I rescued him about two years ago. I saw on Facebook that he only had one day left before the shelter moved him to the city dog pound where he'd be put down. They do that all the time to pit bulls. It broke my heart. I drove down there first thing in the morning to adopt him, and wound up working at the no-kill shelter, too—full-time." He tried not to puff out his chest with pride.

"I only had one dog in my life, an Irish wolfhound." Brock indicated his late dog's nearly waist-high height. "I always took him downtown for the St. Paddy's Day parade—and he got more attention than the marchers. That's the hell of it, though—big dogs have shorter life expectancies than other dogs. I lost mine when he was seven. Brain tumor."

"Sorry," Linus said. "Patton is about six now. I'm hoping he has lots more time."

"Is it okay if I pet him?" Sheehan reached down and scratched Patton on his neck, then patted him firmly on his side, evincing a thumping, bass drum sound from his solid body. Sheehan enjoyed it, knowing that patting a tiny Yorkshire terrier or a Chihuahua that hard could be fatal. "Good boy," he said, their eyes meeting. "He likes me." Facial expressions of animals touched him even more strongly than those of humans, and Patton seemed to be smiling. Dogs are loyal. They don't cheat you or betray you the way people do. "Why'd you adopt a dog anyway?"

"I'm an animal person. I rescue abused or neglected dogs and cats, and take them where they can get the attention and medical treatment and care they need until they're fostered or adopted."

"Good for you, Linus. That's a brave thing." Brock moved his chair so the sun wouldn't be directly in his face. "So how the hell did you find me, anyway? I'm pretty much off the beaten path."

"Not many people knew where you were. I asked around until I ran into my cousin Sean. He said he thought you were living in Vermillion on a boat."

"Sean?"

"A distant cousin on my dad's side. So anyway, I drove here from Cleveland and stopped by the dock master's office to find out where your boat was."

"And he told you right off?"

"No, not right away. I had to convince him you're my uncle."

Sheehan valued his privacy and wanted no one to take advantage of it, and had so informed the dock master when he moved in, along with a bottle of Bushmills. He'd left his born and raised hometown for a reason, along with the sports teams, neighborhood bars, and the quirky vibrancy of Public Square. There was no hit out on him, though he'd made more than one enemy in his day—but he was haunted by too many recalls.

"I didn't think anyone could find me just by asking."

"I bet no one searched for you in a long time." Linus took a quick look around. "This is one hell of a boat. Beautiful. I wouldn't mind living on one of these myself." He hoped for a guided tour, but no offer was forthcoming.

"It floats." Sheehan folded his arms across his chest, the breeze turning chillier by the minute. "Linus—you didn't go to all this trouble just to say hello."

Linus bobbed his head. "I'm afraid you got that right." He chewed on the inside of his cheek, feeling clumsy. "I'm in deep shit, Uncle Brock."

Oh, hell! Sheehan thought. He hadn't seen the kid for a decade, nor remembered his name—and now Linus was badly agitated and showing up unannounced, with a pit bull at his heel. Was he here to ask for money? Or did he want a tough guy like his vintage uncle to beat up somebody for him? "That doesn't sound good."

"I didn't do anything wrong—but I might be a murder suspect."

"*Murder?*" Brock Sheehan's mouth went dry and he took another hasty swallow of whiskey. He hadn't even heard the word murder in a decade.

Linus took a moment, putting his thoughts together. "You heard about Kenny Pine, right?"

"I don't read papers or watch news. Who's Kenny Pine?"

"Oh. Sorry. A few years ago, Kenny Pine was a college basketball star at Ohio State—he'd led them with points and assists all the way to the National Championship game against Duke—and he won that one for them, too. Every pro team wanted him—they said he could be the next LeBron James." Linus looked uncertain. "You know who LeBron James is?"

"I know who LeBron James is. I don't live at the bottom of a coal mine."

"Sorry, I didn't mean—"

"Finish your story."

"Okay, sorry."

Sheehan gritted his teeth. If Linus said "sorry" again, he'd toss him overboard.

"Well, about three years ago, one week before the NBA draft—and Pine was up there in the top three choices—he got arrested."

"Arrested? Why?"

"For running a high-profit dogfighting business just outside Youngstown. Pit bulls, mostly—or mixes, like Patton here." He reached down and rumpled the dog's ears. "So brutal! They torture these dogs, beat them, starve them, make them vicious, and then throw them in with another abused dog to fight to the death. Pitties are the nicest dogs in the world, but when those dogfight cocksuckers get hold of them and train them to kill, they're dangerous enough to get banned in quite a few cities. In fights, they get all chewed up, especially around the face, even if they win! And if they lose—well, there's no profit in feeding a dog gamblers won't bet on. So instead of Kenny Pine choosing a vet to put them down, he electrocuted them, drowned them, hanged them by the neck with a rope or a wire and watched them die—or just strangled them with his own two hands. Personally!" Linus's eyes grew moist. "You believe that?"

"Sounds bad," Brock said, "but what are you telling me?"

"Okay, okay. Sorry. Anyhow, Pine got arrested and convicted for animal cruelty and illegal gambling, and went to jail for almost three years. But when he got out, all the pro teams went after him like he'd never done anything wrong and he could be another major superstar. He just signed with the Denver Nuggets—three years for twenty-eight million dollars!"

Sheehan shook his head. "That's no surprise. Profits are more important in this country—in sports and everything else."

Linus Callahan's face twisted. "He should die of hunger in the fucking gutter, not get to be a multimillionaire."

Brock Sheehan was quiet. Though he'd never been jailed, lots of his friends had, but Pine might not have gone through seven circles of hell during his incarceration, being big and strong, and famous to fellow inmates who ever bothered reading a newspaper.

"He didn't learn anything in jail. There's no law keeping him from owning another dog!" Linus leaned forward earnestly. "Other people get out of prison and can't even find a job! This guy woulda got paid millions."

"Those Kardashians get millions, too—and they don't do a damn thing for it. At least Kenny can sink hoops."

"Not now," Linus said, looking around furtively to see if anyone on the dock or a nearby boat could hear him. "A few days ago, Kenny Pine was murdered."

Sheehan blinked hard. "You're kidding."

"They found him on the east side of the Flats in downtown Cleveland—near the Flat Iron Cafe just around the corner from the swinging bridge." The kid tore his eyes away from Sheehan's and stared out across the lake, his hand dropping to stroke Patton's head. "Someone cut his throat."

Neither man spoke. The only sounds were the gentle lapping of waves against the boat's lee side and the pleasurable groan of the dog, Patton, as he rolled over onto his back and closed his eyes.

Then Sheehan said, "I dig that you're not grief-stricken—but I still don't get it why you're here, Linus."

Linus Callahan's weary sigh was broken, uneven. "I'm here, because according to the Cleveland cops, I'm the number one suspect for killing him."

Ninety-three hours earlier

It was a fall Sunday evening, shortly after eight o'clock. The Cleveland Browns had played their first home game of the season that afternoon—losing to the Kansas City Chiefs in the last ninety seconds—but that never kept fans from celebrating. Downtown was busier than usual, mostly with young people who, like many locals, lived and died over whatever game was played with a ball. Football, basketball, or baseball—it made no difference. Any sporting event was a good excuse to head toward Public Square or the East Flats to a crowded drinking hole, speak very loudly, order beer by the pitcher, and work diligently on getting more than halfway smashed.

On lucky game days, sports fans might run into a professional athlete who garners more attention, adulation, and free drinks from their suddenly devoted sports nuts than astronauts, politicians, creative artists, news giants, actors, writers, and composers who don't have to wear jockstraps to work.

Linus Callahan was no aficionado, but he and his girlfriend Maureen Flanagan took advantage of the mild weather, donning lightweight jackets to first walk around Public Square, spruced up at a price tag of several million bucks for the 2016 Republican National Convention held four blocks away, and then find a lively bar to mingle with well-dressed tourists, and gawk at the homeless citizens who lived right on the street. Eventually they repaired to a jumping saloon on West 6th Street for a drink and perhaps a few laughs. Together for two years since Maureen had volunteered at the animal shelter where he worked, they were fairly happy, as are most relationships that go up and down when the seasons change. In his heart, though, Linus secretly loved having such a pretty woman on his arm so others would grind their teeth in envy. They found seats at the crowded bar, as all tables were reserved at four thirty that afternoon, right after the game, for regular weekend drinkers and big-time gamblers.

Maureen sipped ladylike on her second mojito, and Linus worked on his third Jameson, when commotion and cheering near the front door got their attention. Kenny Pine had entered. At six foot seven towering over everyone in sight, glowing in glory from his top-money contract signing with Denver, and hoping, like all athletes do, to be patted on the back, told how wonderful he was, and doubtless get laid by whichever woman caught his fancy. Narcissism hung over him like an invisible force field.

Of course, he'd showed up at the Browns game that afternoon and was introduced to the crowd as "the superstar of The Ohio State basketball team, and the newest member of the Denver Nuggets."

There was a smattering of boos from the crowd, probably from animal lovers, but most were thrilled to death to see an OSU grad who made it to the big time so easily.

Linus Callahan's back stiffened. He'd never seen Kenny Pine in person before, but his photos had been in the newspapers so often—both in the crime section and on the sports pages. Linus hated him bitterly. He thought of his dog, sleeping at the foot of his bed, and sent gratitude to a god he didn't believe in that Patton had never been goaded into becoming a killer dog, especially at the brutal hands of Kenny Pine. Patton was safe.

Dressed in a scarlet-and-gray Buckeyes shirt and Denver Nuggets cap, thereby ignoring the unwritten law that one doesn't wear clothing promoting two different teams at the same time, Pine worked his way through the throng gathered about him like hungry seagulls hoping someone drops a crumb from their hot dog bun, accepted the cheers and the applause, getting high-fived by the young males, and embraced and sometimes kissed by the females, none of whom imagined their great good fortune to drink in the same room as a lionized VIP like the recently-released celebrity felon.

The bartender, sporting a man-bun and Miami Vice-style stubble, proceeded to ignore everyone else in the place, calling out Kenny Pine's name as if he were sitting ringside during the final three minutes of a close game. When Kenny ordered vodka on ice and reached into his pocket, the bar guy said, "Your money's no good here, Kenny," and poured him a double shot.

Linus wondered why a man who just signed a twenty-eight-million-dollar sports contract was given drinks for free while everyone else who worked forty hours a week at a shitty job had to dig up the price of booze. But that was hardly the reason he loathed Kenny Pine.

His pit bull could have been one of the tormented dogs, perhaps "bait," who lost too many fights in Pine's stable of killer-trained animals and would have been executed in the most horrible fashion, like hanging by the neck or holding the head under water until the dog drowned. To Linus, anyone who abused and maltreated an animal occupied a level of infamy far below that of whale shit.

Pine was moving from table to table, hugging, handshaking, groping women, and answering stupid questions about the team he'd yet to play for.

"Prick!" Linus said under his breath.

"Who is he, anyway?" Maureen whispered. She wasn't a sports fan, either.

"Hotshot Ohio State basketball bullshit artist who just signed with the Denver Nuggets. He took the Buckeyes all the way to the final."

"How does that make him a prick?"

"He served nearly three years in prison for running a dog-fighting business," Linus hissed, "and the cruel way he treated and killed them. Now he's a multimillionaire. Cross your fingers he doesn't make it down to this end of the bar."

Overhearing, the bartender's head whipped around, glaring at Linus. "How does that make it your business?"

"I work at an animal shelter," Linus replied, not taking his eyes off Kenny Pine. "Anybody who hurts and kills animals is my enemy."

The bartender shook his head, disgust and contempt flashing behind his eyes and the turned-down corner of his lip. "What a tight-assed dick you are!"

"Don't start anything, Linus," Maureen warned. "He's twice your size."

But Kenny Pine wasn't about to miss one to flirt with—and catching a glimpse of the pretty redhead sitting with Linus Callahan, his eyes opened wider and his grin grew more appreciative. He decided Maureen would be his ultimate destination.

Sucking up the veneration, he finally stopped behind Maureen and put his huge hands on both her shoulders. "And who," he asked, bending close enough to audaciously sniff her shampoo, "is this sexy redhead I can't stop staring at?"

Linus half-turned on his stool. "Keep your goddamn hands off her!" he snarled.

He said it loudly enough to quiet the place down immediately. Tension quickly conquered joviality, replacing it with worry on every face. Kenny Pine was more shocked than anyone, as no one had spoken to him like that since he first picked up a basketball at twelve years old. He left his hands where they were on Maureen's shoulders. "Whoa, easy there, Ace."

Linus was on his feet now—eight inches shorter than Pine, but fists clenched, looking up his nose. "I'm not your ace, asshole. Get away. Go electrocute another dog."

That stirred a few oohs and aahs from the onlookers. Pine stretched his body as tall as he could. "You're too small to fuck with me, man." Then he grinned down at Maureen, his hands on her shoulders again. "Why stay with this dumb fuckwad anyway, gorgeous? Why don't you and me go away and have some fun?"

Linus didn't give a second thought to start a fight with a man who he knew could take him apart within seconds. He slammed both open palms into Kenny Pine's chest, pushing him away. "Take a hike, bastard!"

Pine stumbled a few steps backward, surprised. Then his eyes squinted in rage and he bared his teeth. Linus was in for a beating, as Pine's on-court fury to players of the opposite team had been legendary. Luck had it, as several male onlookers came forward to pin Kenny Pine's arms to his body and pull him away from the stare down. They were all smaller than Pine, some smaller than Linus, too. They appeared to be medium-sized coyotes trying to take down a water buffalo. But they did outnumber and outweigh him, and that stood for something.

One of the men said, "Hey, Kenny, be cool. Otherwise you might kill him."

"Not if I kill him first!" Linus growled.

Another stuck his face right into Linus's, their noses almost touching. "Why you start a fight with a local hero, asshole? You a Michigan fan or something?"

Linus struggled to get around him. "One stray dog is worth fifty of him!"

"Yeah?" The bartender plopped Linus Callahan's tab in front of him "You're eighty-sixed, motherfucker. Pay up and pound sand. I don't tolerate trouble in here!"

Linus threw his MasterCard on the bar, hatred shooting out of him toward the tall, gawky basketball star scowling back at him with contempt. Maureen was already bent out of shape, feeling she'd caused the problem in the first place.

He signed the credit card slip with anger and resentment, grasping his girlfriend firmly by the elbow, and stormed out the door into the night.

He didn't leave a tip, either.

CHAPTER TWO

The temperature dipped about eight degrees while Linus Callahan told Sheehan his story. Now his uncle sat with arms folded and shoulders hunched against the Lake Erie wind, taking several moments to put this tale into perspective. Then he said, "The police found you through your credit card?"

Nodding, Linus ran his hand over his face as if to wipe away his shame. "I'd never even been in a police station before."

Sheehan couldn't help chuckling. "Really? I know half the Cleveland cops by their first names—or used to, anyway. It's been a lot of years, and I'm yesterday's news. They never nailed me for anything." He glanced at Patton. "You really started the shit with Pine because you're an animal lover?"

"No other reason," Linus said. "I don't give a damn about basketball millionaires one way or another."

"Did they cuff your hands behind you?"

"No. I wasn't arrested. They knocked on my door two days later, invited me to come downtown with them, kept me on the hot seat for almost four hours, asking me about Kenny Pine, and then sent me home after telling me I was a 'person of interest,' and not to leave town. If I tried leaving, they'd bust me."

"You got that right."

"The same questions—over and over again, waiting for me to make a slip so they could throw me in jail."

"Arresting people is what they *do*. Their motto is *'To protect and serve,'* but cops aren't promoted for protecting and serving. The percentage of arrests is just as political as presidential campaigns every four years. And by the way, you are now in Vermillion—which effectively means you've left town—Cleveland. You're two whole counties away." Sheehan licked his lips, and took another sip of his Bushmills. "But they finally let you go."

"I would've called you, Uncle Brock, but nobody had your phone number."

"Your mom—and I loved her to pieces, don't you ever forget it—your mom didn't approve of me. I've pretty much kept away from the rest of you."

"Why's that?"

Brock hesitated. Then he inhaled deeply and let it out. "You know what I did for a living for thirty years. The rest of the Sheehan clan didn't like it—so I had to make a choice. Stick with lower-middle-class shanty Irish who work for the city and buy generic food at the supermarket—or live on a boat and tuck away more than a million dollars in savings? Not much of a choice." He stood and walked a few steps to the edge of the deck, leaning on the railing to enjoy the orange and purple sunset hues in the sky, breathing what was northern Ohio's cleanest air and wishing he were out on the lake right now, where all was quiet and peaceful. No stress. "So you found me—but I don't know what you want."

Linus stammered, then took a deep breath and said, "Help me."

"Help you with what?"

"If they don't get another suspect soon, a small army's going to come after me."

"So you want me to...?"

"Find the guy *for* them."

"Guys who run dogfight clubs?"

"That'd be a start. I can't think of anyone else who'd want him dead."

19

"I like animals, too," Sheehan said, "but I don't go batshit crazy about it. As for solving a murder case, I'm no detective. I wouldn't even know where to begin."

Linus chewed on his lower lip. Then he said, "Talk to your—well, your people."

"My people," he said softly, and a surprisingly sharp stab in the heart awakened his abandonment. "I don't have *people* anymore."

"Your mob guys."

"There's no *mob*. I left Cleveland long ago, and most of the friends I had—the mob guys, as you call them—are dead."

"You got mob ties. Everybody knows that."

"I did belong to the West Side Gaelic Society—which is a social and cultural club—or maybe I still do—but I haven't talked to any of them for years."

"Gaelic Society my ass!" Linus was getting angrier than he wanted to, but he couldn't help himself. "Don't jerk me around. I wasn't born yesterday. Those guys all know somebody—who knows somebody who knows somebody."

"Not in the dogfight business!" Brock was breathing heavily, and took a moment to calm down. "Gambling. Whores. Money laundering. Controlling certain industries in Greater Cleveland. Pulling local political strings. That's who they know, not those mouth-breathing snotlickers who run dogfights. Call it a mob if you want; we call it something else."

"I heard a lot more crap about you than how you pull strings."

"Then what you heard is your problem, Linus."

"That's not my problem!" Linus's voice nearly became a whine. "I don't want to fry for something I didn't do. Help me, Uncle Brock! You don't do anything but sit on this boat getting shitfaced every night, like right now!" He pointed to the drink in Sheehan's hand. Forcing himself calm, he stood and joined his uncle at the rail, squinting out at the setting sun. "You're the only one in the world I can turn to. You're—*family*."

Brock Sheehan pondered that. When he was the right hand at the Gaelic Society, they were indeed *his* family, the only one left to whom they could turn. But eventually his tough guy reputation caught up with him, the Sheehan family more or less disowned him.

Thus the move to a houseboat in Vermillion.

"Well," he told Linus, a weary burnout rendering his voice low and hoarse, "I guess I'm *distant* family."

Sheehan stayed on deck long after his nephew left, pouring himself two more drinks and consuming them slowly. The older he got, the more he drank. Back in the day, he was often told that while not an alcoholic, he was a "heavy hitter" and could put away more booze than most people on any given evening. Was he really becoming a dangerous imbiber? He hoped not, nor would he *join* anything; to stand and announce his name and his alcoholism at AA meetings so they all could say "Hi, Brock" terrified him. Yet nearly every night, he drank quietly and alone on his boat as the late afternoon turned to twilight and then to darkness.

His mind turned dark, too, with memories of longtime boss of the Irish mob, Rory McCurdy, and of a man named Liam Hannigan, who had betrayed McCurdy by squealing a big-deal-in-the-making to the Italian mob back in the eighties. The Italians had paid Liam Hannigan ten thousand dollars, and the blown deal cost McCurdy nearly half a million. Being disloyal to Rory McCurdy was not a good idea, and Brock Sheehan was sent to his first lethal assignment.

He met Liam coming out of an Irish bar in Cleveland Heights, and followed him out to the parking lot at two in the morning. A single punch sent him into a coma; then Sheehan loaded him into his car and drove down to Summit County. By the time they slogged through high grass, weeds, and bramble bushes to get to the deepest part of the woods near the Akron gorge, Hannigan was almost conscious, half-realizing what was happening as Sheehan held the side of his head with one hand and his chin with the other, then did a short snap sideways, breaking his neck. It took little energy, and was quick and efficient, much faster than even one deep stab with a keenly honed knife. But there was no mess, no blood—only a small moment of moaning and groaning before the spirit left the body and rose into midair as the eyes rolled backwards in the head.

Sheehan left the body on a slope at the bank of the Cuyahoga River, and felt bad about it for less than five minutes. He'd shared laughs and drinks with Liam Hannigan in the past. He'd never taken a human life before, but he vividly remembered beatings and arm-breakings and the worst fear of all he could throw into his opponents—the warnings.

He had skillfully learned about threatening. Several Irish lives were saved by his warnings of ghastly retaliation, as the targets gave back the most sincere of promises and apologies, and even handed over fistfuls of money.

Were there any old-time Cleveland cops left—the ones who heard his name every day and looked at his face several times each year—who recalled the dangerous life he'd led, the support he always welcomed from the Irish mafia? Whenever he was arrested and held on suspicion of something or other—too often whether he'd done anything wrong or not—the one phone call allowed by law was not to a lawyer or relative, but always to the Gaelic Society boss man, Rory McCurdy. Within a half hour, the city's best lawyer, Gowan Scully, was at downtown headquarters to get him released. Scully's only weapons were his nimble tongue and a great knowledge of the law.

Sheehan had done plenty wrong, but never had a moment worrying about it. He'd always been nurtured by those who shared his Irish culture, despite the relationships that were often more sad than happy. They always had his back, and that made him secure.

He'd had little correspondence with any of them since moving west to Vermillion, and he knew out of sight meant out of mind, especially on the fringes of the underworld. He wondered if the Gaelic Society would remember him, or was he now just nebulous shadows of memory—like the monsters his mother warned him were under his bed in case he didn't attend catechism every day after school?

Hungry, he went below deck to fix dinner. He tore up fresh romaine lettuce from the local Giant Eagle market the day before, topped it with fresh sliced mushrooms, green pepper slices, hummus, and olive oil dressing, which he ate with cocktail peanuts instead of croutons. He also broiled a pork chop—just one. Even though retired, the last thing he wanted to do was put on weight, and he steered away from eating meat as often as he could. In his youth, pinching flesh at his waist was nothing there to grab onto. As time tumbled past, an apron of love handles appeared—a calling card of unstoppable age and unwilling deterioration. Sheehan hated it, doing thirty sit-ups each morning on the deck. When he moved to Vermillion, he'd promised himself a daily two-mile beach run to keep fit and trim, but running in the sand was exhausting and breath-robbing, and now it no longer occurred to him to do so.

After dinner he buried himself in a book for more than half an hour, this time a fairly up-to-date political scandal, although he mostly preferred fiction—especially crime fiction. His reading had fallen off in the past few years, especially during the good months he was on his boat. Fading eyesight accompanied by too many drinks had made getting through a book a duty, not a pleasure, even when he wore reading glasses he bought at the drugstore. On this particular night, after Linus and Patton had departed, thoughts of what he'd do the next morning bounced around inside his brain like a soaked pair of canvas shoes making a lot of noise in a dryer.

What did he hope to accomplish? Investigation was new to him, and Linus might as well ask him to become an instant brain surgeon or a rocket scientist. He had no idea how to prove homicidal innocence of a kid he didn't even know anymore.

Brock's only sister, Fiona, Linus's mother, was long gone from ravaging colon cancer, the only family member he got along with, despite relentless reprimands that eventually pushed them apart like two volumes on a tight shelf making way for a third book in the middle. Fiona was a multiple confessor to the priest at Saint Colman's, though Sheehan had wondered what on earth she'd had to confess in the first place. She probably never knew about the killings, but was well aware her big, handsome Gaelic brother paralyzed anyone with fear who came in contact with him. She hammered away at him daily, even after he'd moved into his own apartment about eight blocks away, and threw bad shade at him to anyone connected to the Sheehan clan. He was shunned—as if he'd been a formerly devout Mennonite who'd bought a sixty-inch TV and a muscle car, and put TV antennae on the roof of the home he'd just electrified.

If he tried to name all the Sheehan family who wouldn't even speak to him—nephews, cousins, in-laws—it would take days. Other than a love for Celtic literature and a galloping Irish thirst, he was no more a Sheehan any more than a Shapiro, a Luczkowski or a Gandolfino. He was just a lonely old fart on an expensive boat with no loose ends except for a long-ignored and unexpected nephew with one hell of a big problem.

He went to bed early, tossed and turned, finally wrapped himself in a blanket and went back out on deck to look at the moon. The homes, built close together and filling up each side of the crowded harbor, were dark, and closing time for all the bars and taverns had come and gone. There was no one to talk to.

All right, he thought finally. For his big sister Fiona, who'd beaten him up almost daily when they were kids, he'd try his damnedest to dig his nephew out of a deep dark hole that might send him to prison for the rest of his life. Pine had been a VIP athlete. If a bona fide suspect wasn't found quickly, his Ohio State idolaters might invade Cleveland with pitchforks and flaming torches, demanding justice, or that Linus be turned over to them for a lynching.

Brock's eyes eventually closed, his chin dropping to his chest as he fell asleep on the deck. He awoke at six o'clock the next chilly morning with a stiff neck, aching back, and sniffles. Making coffee, he had no idea where to begin his search for the killer of Kenny Pine—a name he'd never heard until five o'clock the previous afternoon.

He donned chinos and a casual shirt, throwing a sports jacket on at the last minute. He locked everything onboard under a bright blue canvas, climbed into his 2015 Honda Accord, and drove up onto I-90, heading east.

It was less than an hour's trip to Cleveland, but first he needed a solid breakfast. He selected an independently owned diner run by a married couple in Elyria, Ohio. He'd never been there before, but one hard-and-fast rule of his was to never eat at a corporate restaurant—member of a franchise one could find in any city in America.

The upper middle-aged waitress came by the table when he was nearly finished, holding a pot. "More coffee there, honey?"

He had to smile. When he was younger, coffee shop waitresses always called their clients "honey," and this one had obviously been in the business forever. Things have changed—no one was ever supposed to refer to someone of the opposite sex as "honey" unless they shared a serious romantic relationship.

He said, "Sure, please," and waited as she filled his cup. "I need to find an internet cafe around here. Do you happen to know of one close by?"

She frowned. "A whatkinda cafe?"

"A place where people who don't have the right technical device with them, like a computer or an iPad, can go in, pay a small fee, and look things up on the internet. There must be a place like that here in Elyria somewhere."

She chewed on her upper lip. "I don't know. Lemme go ask." She disappeared into the kitchen, coming out moments later followed by a man in a chef's apron and hat.

"Hey, there," the man said, "You're looking for an internet cafe?"

Sheehan nodded. "Yes—someplace to let me use a computer for half an hour."

The chef said, "The public library has computers all over the place you can use—no charge. It's not far from here."

Libraries had always pleased him. Once he found the nearby Elyria branch and went inside, the reference librarian was pleasant and helpful, and took the time to show him how to use a computer and get on the internet. As a young kid, all he knew was that librarians' main job was shushing people who talked too loudly. Big as he was, he couldn't remember anyone shushing him after he was about eleven years old.

It took him five minutes to learn about Kenny Pine.

Born, 1994 in Cleveland. Played in a youth basketball league when he was twelve. Easily made the high school team at thirteen, dazzling all with towering height, scoring, and rebounds. Scholarship offers from many universities in the Midwest and east. Eventually Kenny Pine accepted a generous invitation from The Ohio State University.

Only Ohioans knew the proper name of the school was *The* Ohio State University. Sheehan couldn't think of any other major state university that was a *The*.

Reading on, he discovered Kenny Pine, who had pocketed "expense money" from some alumni—names not disclosed— had invested in a large farm in Mahoning County not far from Youngstown, where he installed a vast section of kennels, and remodeled a large barn into a fighting ring for dogs, complete with bleachers for fans who paid a handsome sum to get in. During non-basketball months, coaches carefully constructed his academic program so his attendance was minimal. He worked the farm tirelessly, betting on fights, skimming a healthy share of the profits, and destroying the loser dogs in the worst and most violent ways possible.

Law enforcement didn't find out about it until after Kenny

led OSU to the national championship game against Duke, winning by six points. Arrested before he had a real opportunity to pose all over the place holding the championship cup, he was convicted on several counts of abusing animals and running an illegal sport. He spent nearly three years in federal prison in Leavenworth, Kansas. A superstar on the intermural basketball team, he kept constant contact with his sports agent to peddle his ass to the most generous NBA team as soon as he was released.

After serving his sentence, Pine was treated like the prodigal son returning, and nearly every team in the NBA approached him with a huge offer—big profits and high game points overwhelming the disgust at particularly brutal dog killings. He was once more in the papers and on local TV until he hungrily accepted the Nuggets contract, and spent his free time in hometown Cleveland before heading to Denver for socializing in *their* downtown taverns and ready himself for preseason training, expecting his fans to fawn on him and tell him how wonderful he was.

That's when he met Linus Callahan.

Of course, the internet didn't say anything about Linus—yet. Sheehan decided he would stop that from happening—if he could.

He got back into his car and proceeded east toward Cleveland.

The little bar on West 65th Street was quiet during lunch hour. They supposedly served food—they had a kitchen approximately the size of what small studio apartments used to call a "kitchenette"—but nobody ever ordered any food other than a trail mix or a bowl of stale popcorn. Saint Colman's Catholic Church, about three-quarters of a mile south, was mobbed on Sundays by several generations of mostly Irish people to hear the Mayo County priest's sermon. Early mass was attended by those living within walking distance of the church, though on afternoon weekdays, the neighborhood was more or less deserted.

Brock Sheehan entered the tavern carefully, having not been

in there to drink since he relocated to Vermillion, but he found no surprises. No cartoon leprechauns or four-leaf shamrocks tacked onto the wall or Scotch-taped on the mirror behind the bar that would make any bar look phony-Irish—just a framed photograph of John Fitzgerald Kennedy, the only Irish-American president. This place was West Side Gaelic Society home base for serious drinking because the club had never applied for an on-premises liquor license.

Squinting from the bright sun, Sheehan took a moment to reacclimate himself. A newer, larger, skinnier TV replaced the old cathode ray set with the rabbit ears that had droned behind the bar for a generation, but in midmorning it was silent. The vintage jukebox was gone, replaced by a video game no one ever played, and put there by some invisible mob group whether the owners liked it or not. He recognized the odor of stale beer, stale piss, and months-old cigarette smoke. Even the clanking air conditioner was the same. As ever, the men's room wasn't cleaned more than twice per month. On this early afternoon only two daytime drinkers were in attendance at the far end of the bar, coddling two beers and a bowl of trail mix between them.

The bartender had aged since Brock last saw him. The hair had grown gray-white and thinned out a lot, there was a double chin where there never was before, and the bags beneath the eyes were twice as big.

"Well, I'll be double goddamned!" he said, coming out from behind the bar and enveloping Sheehan in a hug. "Holy crap, Brock, I swear the last time I saw you, George W. was the president of the United States. Where the hell you been, my friend?"

"Around. Not in town much anymore."

"Well, sit. Sit! You still drink Irish?"

"Never stopped, Eddie." Sheehan shook Eddie's hand. It felt old, dry, tired, not the strong clasp he remembered. Eddie used to be able to kick ass, mostly with a Reggie Jackson baseball bat hidden behind the bar, accessible at a moment's notice. Sheehan climbed onto a stool, as far away from the other two men as he could get.

Eddie went back behind the bar, reaching up on the highest shelf to take down a bottle covered with light dust, turning his back to blow most of it away so it didn't get into Brock's face. "This one's for you, Brock. This here they call Tyrconnell—ten years old with a sherry cask finish. It costs twenty bucks a shot. I don't serve it to just anybody, I save it for special occasions. And you showin' up after all these years is sure as hell a special occasion."

"Never tried Tyrconnell, or even heard of it. But it's early in the day for me."

Eddie shook his head. "Screw that, it's six o'clock somewhere in the world." He overfilled a double shot glass and pushed it toward Brock. "Now don't shoot it down in one gulp, cuz it's expensive as hell. Sip it."

Sheehan slowly savored the smoky taste on his tongue. "Damn good stuff," he said. "I wouldn't think a joint like this carried such an expensive brand. Aren't you going to join me?"

Eddie made a backhand gesture as though shooing away a fly. "I'm on the wagon. Six years now. You can't spend your whole life behind a bar and not get drunk every goddamn night—so I quit."

"AA?"

"Nah. I started there, but I quit before the Second Step. The whole Bill Wilson thing was too religious for me." He came back around and took the stool next to Sheehan. "So, Brock—what you been up to all these years?"

"Staying quiet."

"You ain't been in prison, huh? They never had nothing on you that stuck."

"No. I just—retired—you know, from the Society."

Eddie nodded, frowning. "When you walked out, it broke the Old Man's heart."

"He was pissed off, I suppose, but he understood. When you

reach a certain age, a certain point in your life, it's time to maybe do something else."

"He's a lot older than you," Eddie observed. "He must be in his nineties, now—and he didn't quit."

"If I were him, I wouldn't quit, either, Eddie. But he's a businessman. He knows how to run things, how to negotiate. I stink at business, always have. He kept me around because I was a muscle guy."

"You're still a muscle guy. You ain't changed much. More gray in the hair, but otherwise about the same." Eddie grinned. "You need a goddamn haircut, Brock."

They sat quietly, Brock commenting on the Tyrconnell. Then he said, "Are any of the guys around, Eddie? They all got old, like me. Are they still around?"

Eddie lifted his shoulders and then dropped them. "A few. Some moved away or even went back to Ireland. Some died. Like everything else, people change. Things change, too."

"How about the Old Man? Has he changed?"

Eddie put his hands on his hips. "He don't come in much no more—maybe once or twice a month. This was his home away from home for a lotta years, but he hadda quit drinking, quit staying out late. Now he's got around-the-clock visiting nurses. He turned all the upstairs rooms in his house into spare bedrooms for them, even his own bedroom, cuz now he sleeps on a hospital bed right in the middle of the living room. I know he forgets sometimes—names and stuff. So yeah, he's changed some."

Sheehan flexed his right fist—not from anger but because arthritis attacked that part of his anatomy. Flexing eased the pain—and on days when it was real bad, he'd squeeze a rubber ball for an hour at a time. "Does he still go to the Gaelic?"

"Oh, yeah. That's his office, that's where he gets things done—with other guys around to make sure he don't go off the deep end. When he's at home, he just sits and watches the TV crap during the day. You watch the *Today Show* anymore, Brock? It's awful. Four people gettin' paid millions of bucks every year, sitting around, laughing and giggling, all talking at once so you can't understand what anybody's saying."

Sheehan said, "Eddie—if I went over there, would the Old Man talk to me?"

Eddie looked perplexed. "Maybe—if he recognizes you."

"Is he that far gone?"

"You can't tell from one day to the next. Sometimes he don't even know it's Tuesday. Other times he'll chew you up and spit you out because he's sharp enough to notice you fucked up. There's still guys from the old days hangin' around because they don't have nothing else to do. Somebody's gonna remember your name."

Sheehan took the final sip of the Tyrconnell and raised his glass into a salute to Eddie before pushing it away from him. "This was nice. Appreciate it."

"Welcome home, Brock," Eddie said. "This was a celebration for me. Now, don't be a stranger."

Brock Sheehan got back into his Honda Accord. *Don't be a stranger?* Too damn bad, because after all his absent years, he was one, whether he liked it or not.

The West Side Gaelic Society headquarters was in an ancient building near what once was a slaughterhouse, further south on West 65th Street—almost as big a stockyard area as the one that used to be in Chicago. Hundreds of thousands of cattle wound up there—abused, murdered, butchered, and shipped all over the country. The underground sewers had been too narrow to handle the overflow of blood, so local residents weren't surprised by an escaped cow galloping down the gory streets, employees in hot pursuit.

The gutters of West 65th Street were still running cattle blood red when a group of feisty Irishmen, disgusted with the signs of the day reading "No Coloreds, No Italians, No Irish, No Dogs Allowed," posted everywhere, bought the building, refurbished it, and turned it into a private club. They didn't mind posting signs of their own at the front door. "Members Only" and "Private Property. Trespassers will be Violated." Brock Sheehan was one of few who understood that intended pun.

To the present day, no trespassers were ever violated or prosecuted, though during the Society's early history a few were shot dead, and several others disappeared, never to be seen again.

Brock stood before the steel door, staring up at the vidcam. Videos exposing one's privacy was a new techie quirk for him, added to the front entrance after he left. It bugged the hell out of him.

Change never sat well with him. He read the warnings again, wondering if he were still a member in good standing. When he'd risen to one rank below the Old Man himself, he'd owned a rare key to the door, but along the way he'd lost or misplaced it in what he called the "black hole" in his home, wherever he lived at the time. He hadn't resigned, exactly. He'd said goodbye to the Old Man, and left without leaving a mailing address.

He leaned on the doorbell, the door so thick he could barely hear the buzz inside, and glanced up once more at the camera. Eventually locks clicked, and the portal opened. A large young man—flushed Irish face, freckles, small piercing eyes the color of rabbit pellets—examined him with suspicion. "This place is for members only. Didn't you read the signs?"

Sheehan nodded. "I read them. I am a member, or I used to be."

The kid inhaled, seeming to stretch himself up even taller, his chin jutting out like the prow of a Viking ship. "Yeah. Who are you, then?"

Someone who can rip out your lung with his bare hands, Brock Sheehan thought. He told the young man his name, and was surprised to see his face change completely. The kid's mistrust turned into something close to idolatry.

"You're Brock Sheehan? Holy shit! I've been hearing about you since I was born. I'm honored to meet you, sir—really honored." He pumped Sheehan's hand, almost but not quite bowing. "I'm Niall Grogan. Junior, that is. My father knew you very well."

Sheehan nodded. "He and I were good friends for a long time. How's he doing?"

Junior's face fell. "He passed away about three years ago." He tapped himself on the chest. "Heart attack."

"I hope he got to heaven before the devil knew he's dead," Brock said, quoting an old Irish saying. Why, he wondered, weren't there any *new* Irish sayings? Did they all stop being amusing the day James Joyce died?

"Thanks, sir," Niall said. "My mom's okay, though. She'll flip when I tell her you're back."

"I'm not back, exactly. Just passing through. But I hope to see Rory McCurdy for a few minutes. Is he in?"

Junior nodded. "He's always in—during the day, anyway." Then he lowered his voice to a near whisper. "Go easy with him. He's not so young anymore. He forgets things. He don't have that Oldtimer's Disease or nothin'. He's—well, old I guess."

Oldtimer's disease. Not Alzheimer's—Oldtimer's. Irishmen living in Ireland are voracious readers—Sean O'Casey, Oscar Wilde, Brendan Behan, George Bernard Shaw. Now Irish Americans only know the obituaries in the local newspaper each morning—the Irish Sports Pages. Sheehan said, "A brain is like a computer. You put so much in that computer that there's no room left. It's the same with the brain. He's around ninety, isn't he?"

"More."

"Okay, I'll be gentle with him."

Junior let his voice return to normal. "You want me to tell him you're here?"

"That would be nice," Sheehan sighed.

Left alone for a moment, he braced himself. The godfather had treated him like a son, gifted him with the houseboat and hugged him goodbye, telling him he was always welcome, because he always obeyed orders to the letter—even ones that rubbed him the wrong way.

As he looked around the room, he recalled being dealt most of those orders right where he was standing, or in the inner office behind a closed door. One assignment in particular bothered him the most, because Rory McCurdy had a colorful imagination.

McCurdy understood disagreements between people, especially those of other gangs in the general vicinity, and often he preferred a broken kneecap as a punishment rather than a more violent condemnation. The only thing, however, he could not accept—nor forget—was betrayal.

For instance: Hugh Dockerty had been a Gaelic Society underling for decades, so dedicated to making sure the Old Man felt good that sometimes McCurdy was disgusted with him. He was little more than a coffee fetcher and occasional tough guy at McCurdy's fingertips all the time, especially since his salary was minuscule.

But McCurdy couldn't help notice Dockerty wearing expensive suits, driving a Lincoln Continental instead of a clunky old Ford Fairlane, and showing up with overblown, sexy-looking "exotic dancers" on his arm. He asked Niall Senior to investigate, follow Dockerty around discreetly and figure out where he was getting all the money.

It took Grogan eight days, most of which were boring as hell until his undercover snooping hit paydirt. Hugh Dockerty—born into poverty in County Mayo and brought to America in his early teens, sporting an Irish brogue he never got rid of—was meeting weekly in Little Italy where Don Giancarlo D'Allessandro, the Italian godfather, made decisions and issued orders. Dockerty always parked several blocks away, in University Circle, and walked up the incline until he was in solid Italian territory—not the most careful place for a mick to visit, but then he was no genius, either.

The Italian and Irish mobs had coexisted in Greater Cleveland for eighty years, quietly tolerating each other, moving in different circles without stepping on toes—but the Italian gang had more money to spend, and perhaps the don was thinking of taking control of some local unions run by the Irish. Thus they found Hugh Dockerty hungry, willing, and able to report the Gaelic Society's doings each week, making D'Allessandro smile.

No smiles came from Rory McCurdy. To stop the leaking and punish high treason, he turned to the large, powerful man just under him who made *everyone* nervous.

On a Friday evening in chilly March at the Gaelic club, Brock Sheehan accosted Hugh Dockerty and told him he was interested in meeting one of Dockerty's strip-dancer girlfriends. He bought Dockerty a tasty dinner at a solid Irish restaurant, and when they returned to Hugh's almost brand-new Lincoln Continental and headed toward an east side strip club on Saint Clair Avenue, Sheehan forced the driver into a quiet alley, where he busted all five fingers on Dockerty's left hand, one by one, and broke his wrist as well until he disclosed everything that had gone on between him and D'Allessandro, including setting up a secret meeting between the don and one of the more powerful Irish labor leaders on the west side.

Sheehan's orders from McCurdy had been to find out everything he could from Dockerty—and if it sounded bad, Dockerty was to be eliminated. It took only a moment's hesitation before Sheehan broke Dockerty's neck.

Pulling him over into the passenger seat, Sheehan drove back to Little Italy and dumped the body, headfirst, into a Dumpster behind one of the area's famous restaurants, only feet and legs showing above the rim. Then he drove the Lincoln all the way out to Lake County and parked it in the lot of the Great Lakes Mall. He went into a bar-restaurant in there and phoned Niall Grogan Senior, who came out and got him as he was drinking his second Irish bourbon, dealing with his own brutality and guilt.

That was early in his career. At last the beatings, arm-breakings, and even worse eventually took its toll on Brock Sheehan's soul—if indeed he had one. He'd given up church shortly after his mother's death, scolding and screeching from sister Fiona notwithstanding. Eventually he chose voluntary retirement from the Gaelic Society, and never mentioned to anyone that he just couldn't take it anymore.

His departure had rubbed the Old Man the wrong way, and he knew it, although there was a semi-affectionate goodbye and naturally the gift of McCurdy's houseboat. He'd never heard a single word from him after his leaving, and he was certain the years since had abraded his temperament even further.

Then the inner door opened, and Rory McCurdy entered the room, moving slowly, Niall Junior guiding him, keeping him from falling over on his face. A briar cane thick as a shillelagh was in his right hand. His face was pale and sallow, and most of the color had drifted down from his cheeks to his jowls. His John Lennon-type glasses were tinted slightly gray, as if too much light bothered him.

Rory—an old Celtic name that translated to "Red King"— pushed away from the younger man and moved steadily toward Brock Sheehan. When he got close enough to kiss him, he stopped, raised his head back, and examined him as though he were some sort of space alien who wound up on the face of the earth by mistake. "Lord love a duck!" he said

McCurdy had aged like everyone else, but he'd done some extra-hard living. He'd lost most of his hair; the dirty gray ones remaining were combed over. His wrinkled skin looked like gift wrapping a day after Christmas, ripped open by a feisty child. Brown spots on his forehead were new, and his formerly broad chest had lowered its bulk and breadth into his stomach. He licked his lips often.

"Where the hell you been?" he croaked. No hug, no handshake, not even a twinkle in the eye. No hatred, either. *Nothing.* "Nobody knows where you been all these years."

"I've been here and there, Rory."

"Here and there, eh? What a pile of shite! Get inside!" he ordered, moving into his inner office. Niall Junior backed away quietly, closing the door behind him.

How often had Sheehan been in this office? A thousand times, probably more. The lemon wall paint, the walnut paneling and carefully crafted crown molding, the high stained-glass window depicting a Celtic cross which McCurdy had ordered from a Dublin church about to be destroyed, personally paying for it forty years earlier. Yellow shag carpet from the sixties had been replaced with more shag, this one on the tan side. The green-shaded reading lamp was on one edge of the big desk, which was scarred with a thousand cigarettes that had fallen from the ashtray. The small bathroom was off to the side, the toilet gurgling constantly as it always had. Visitors' chairs scattered all over the room were the old-fashioned schoolroom type with a built-in writing surface, probably bought from an overstocked truck warehouse during the 1970s.

The Old Man lowered himself into an executive chair, groaning as if putting down a great weight he'd carried around with him all his life. "Don't tell me I look good after all these years. I look like shite, which comes with age. When you're old, everything changes. I got no more hair on my head. If someone farts loud, three inches from my face, and I can't smell the stink because I lost my sense of smell. I can't see. I can't hear. I can't walk. I can't fuck—and half the time I'm pissing blood. My nose and my ears all of a sudden got bigger and sprouted lots of hair I never had there—and my dick got smaller! I got no use for it any more except to piss through."

Sheehan nodded knowingly, though he had many years before becoming another Rory McCurdy. He was in relatively healthy shape for a guy who drank too much, and he knew he looked quite handsome, though rugged, and athletic indeed.

Except for his ass. He hardly had any ass. The rest of his body was fearsome, even though as a kid he turned down all the offers from his high school to play football, saying he didn't like getting hurt. The truth was that because of his own personal and private vanity, he knew that in his tight football pants, everyone in the stands, especially the girls, might remark too loudly that he didn't have an ass.

McCurdy inhaled deeply, then leaned back in his chair and folded his hands across his belly. "Back from the dead, Brock? Or back from wherever the hell you been? You were the best guy who ever watched my back. How many years in this place for you? Twenty-five? Thirty?" He sucked loudly on his dentures—a hissing sound they'd always made, as Rory had lost all his teeth at a young age. No one ever dared ask him why.

He'd been youthful and innocent when emigrating from County Mayo, arriving in Chicago after the end of World War II, seventy-three bucks in his pocket and dreams costing a thousand times more than that. Chicago was a Gaelic town, then. All the city big shots were Irish—the mayor, the aldermen, and their relatives and cronies filling the jobs that kept the city running, most living on the west side in what was called "Back of the Yards," close to the enormous, foul-smelling Chicago stockyards.

Rory's older cousin was a Chicago police detective first class on the North Side, willing to get Rory on the force and be his "Chinaman," a nickname for a high-up Windy City cop who'd take on a kid, mentor him, and make sure he earned his stripes the easiest way possible.

Rory, though, wasn't interested in law enforcement. There were too many people spread out all across the shore of Lake Michigan, too many mob guys shooting at each other in the street. His ultimate goal was to be a big fish in a small pond, a fish everyone would respect and adore and listen to and ask how high when he told them to jump. He was no reader—he'd not gotten past the fifth grade—but through research he discovered there was another city, not too far away, in which Irish politicians more or less shared power with the Italians. So he worked for a year or so at lousy jobs, lived in a tiny fourth-floor apartment over a bar on the Near North Side, and subsisted on macaroni and cheese and as many tacos and tamales as he could steal from the hand-pushed street carts that fed half the downtown workers their daily lunches. He saved most of his earnings, only spending recklessly twice a month on any five-dollar hooker he could find on North Dearborn Street.

Then he moved to Cleveland.

He went to work for the West Side Gaelic Society and Michael Deegan, who from prohibition in the1930s ran the organization with an iron fist. Rory rose from janitor and errand boy to perform the jobs he eventually hired Brock Sheehan to do.

He was much smarter than Deegan. When he caught his boss doing something completely illegal and immoral to the Irish community, he offered him two choices—pack up relatives and underlings and move out of town, preferably back to the Emerald Isle, or be quietly turned over to the police, which would put him in the state prison in Mansfield for the rest of his life.

There was a third choice, too, Rory McCurdy didn't mention to Deegan—the elimination of him, his family, and all the whining toadies who'd sucked around after him for the last forty years. Michael Deegan was no fool; within a month, he returned to County Mayo, where he lived a few more years in anonymity and then died of a massive stroke. Most of his loyal second-level employees left town as well, winding up in places like Memphis, New York, Boston—one knew a friend of a friend who knew Whitey Bulger—and Providence, Rhode Island.

The Deegan gang who chose to stay in Cleveland mostly disappeared during the following twelve months, or else were found floating in the Cuyahoga River, or in dark alleys behind tall buildings from which they had either jumped or were pushed. In one particular case, a Gaelic man who'd found himself without a job and had somehow hooked himself up with the Italian mob on Murray Hill in Little Italy. Pieces of his body were distributed into three east side parks, a trash can at Euclid Beach, and the head atop an Italian's gravestone in a small cemetery across the street from what is now the Indians ballpark, Progressive Field, with his flaccid penis inserted between his lips.

Eventually, McCurdy developed a reputation that was sure

to land him in prison. Now that he had the power, personal violence was becoming dangerous to him, so he looked around for a "hit man," until he became aware of a large, tough sycophant with a certain charm and a sharp mind, who could fill the role of "enforcer."

That was Brock Sheehan.

Sheehan worked closely with Rory, even though he frowned on old-time brutality. He didn't like killing, never carried a gun. But his necessary beatings were infamous—and though he was arrested four times for murder, he was never tried in a court of law.

He was the number two man in the Irish mob for almost twenty years until he'd had enough, and quietly left the organization and moved away from Cleveland.

Rory had loved Brock Sheehan—but hated his turning away and disappearing into the ether. He let Sheehan go with warm wishes and a magnificent gift of a houseboat—but never quite recuperated from losing his right hand.

Now, in his nineties, McCurdy looked Brock in the eye for the first time since his retirement, and shook his head sadly. "You walked out—not even a goodbye or a look over your shoulder." He closed his eyes for a moment. "I never forgave you for that. You were a shite to leave me, Brock. A complete shite."

"I just got tired of it, Rory."

"We're all tired—but that don't mean we lay down on the floor and wait for birds to fly in and cover us with leaves." McCurdy narrowed one eye, pointing an aged finger across his desk. "I've got enough on you to put you in prison for the rest of your life if I want to."

Sheehan nodded. "We'll share a jail cell, then, because I'd take you right over the side with me. I could've done it years ago, but I cared too much for you."

"Then why didn't you stay?"

"I needed—a change of scenery."

The Old Man said, "You could've stayed and married my

daughter like I asked you to. She was crazy about you."

"I was very fond of Rosemary," Sheehan said, "but I wasn't in love with her."

"You don't have to be in love to have a good marriage."

"I'm—not the marrying kind."

McCurdy sounded bitter. "She married a Hungarian instead. A Hungarian, for the love o' Jesus! Hungarians turn mean when the goddamn weather changes!" He coughed, not bothering to cover his mouth. "What are you doing, sniffing around here again after all these years? You want your job back? I got no job for you. I don't got no disloyal people around me."

"I've always been loyal, Rory, and I never once screwed you over—but I don't need a job. I need help. Family help."

"Family?" Rory McCurdy said. "*Your* family? The Sheehans—what's left of 'em—they don't even remember your name."

"Somebody does. You knew my sister Fiona, didn't you?"

"Ah, a lovely girl. She married a Callahan—who'd never go anywhere, had no ambition. At least he brought his paycheck home every two weeks." Sadness shimmered behind his watery eyes. "He was good to her."

"They had a son," Sheehan said. "Linus Callahan."

Rory frowned, thinking hard as too many reminiscences were bouncing around in his head, and he had trouble picking out the one he was looking for. Finally, frowning, he nodded. "Linus. Yes! I was at his christening. So were you."

Sheehan nodded. "Linus came to me yesterday. He's in trouble."

Rory McCurdy glanced up at the pounded-tin ceiling, of which he was very proud. Many Cleveland bars sported tin overheads, which gave them a vintage look—but Brock thought them tacky, a corny architectural entity from another era, another century. "How did he find you?"

"Maybe he knows more about me than I thought. Do you know who Kenny Pine is, Rory? The basketball player?"

"He played for Ohio State. I follow sports, even if you never did. Isn't he the one who got his throat cut the other night?" He drew his index finger sideways along the front of his neck and made a noise to illustrate it.

"That's him. He was convicted for animal abuse—holding dogfights and killing off the losers. He got out of prison a month ago, signed a huge contract with the Denver Nuggets, and got murdered a few nights back. Then the cops hauled in Linus Callahan—as a so-called person of interest."

"Why is Linus Callahan a person of interest?"

Brock leaned forward, arms resting on thighs, and hoped McCurdy would listen as he told him Linus's story.

When the tale was finished, the Old Man rubbed his cheeks and squinted, then tapped his spread fingertips on both hands together. "You don't kill a perfect stranger," he said as if it were an effort to talk, "who makes a move on your lady-love. Only in bad movies."

"Men hit on Linus's girlfriend all the time because she's pretty, only that doesn't light his dynamite wick. But a dog lover like him? That's a different kettle of fish."

"Dog lover, hey? You used to have a dog. Irish wolfhound, right?" Rory laughed one short burst that turned into coughing.

"A long time ago. I loved him to pieces—but sadly, the bigger the dog, the shorter the lifespan. When he died, I never got another one."

"And this Linus loves dogs so much that he kills for them?"

"He works at a no-kill shelter. And he has a dog of his own—a pit bull."

"Jesus," Rory said, his jaw pointing straight at Sheehan as though he were aiming at it. "He loves dogs so much that he cuts the throat of a man that abused them and then paid for it in prison?"

"I don't think Linus killed him."

"You don't even know him!"

Sheehan shrugged. "Call it a gut instinct."

"A hell of a lot that'll do you. You know about cops. Once

they set their sights on a suspect, they forget about everyone else and hammer away until their guy crumbles."

"Linus won't crumble." Sheehan sat back in his chair. "I know my family—or at least my sister."

"Your sister never got leaned on by the cops."

"No—but I did, more times than I can count. For *you*." Recalling with shocking clarity his many trips to the Second Precinct on West Twenty-fifth Street, knocking heads with cops who half the time wanted to lock him up and throw away the key and the other half wanting him to do them a favor.

Both men were silent for more than a minute. Finally, Sheehan got to his feet. "I've wasted your time. Sorry I bothered you."

"Bothered me for *what*?" Rory McCurdy looked as if he might stand up, too, but achingly stiff knees didn't make it worthwhile. "What help can I give you?"

Sheehan paused, then sat down again. "You know everyone in this town worth knowing. Every cop, lawyer, crook, bagman—even every Irish drunk."

"And every bartender, too—at least I used to. I don't gallivant around every night like I once did."

"Then introduce me to a bartender who's almost as smart as you."

"You already talked to Eddie today," Rory said.

"I'm impressed. Word gets around."

"Word always gets around. For a long time, that word was from you. You were an extension of me. You kept this organization running. When you left, it took a lot of worry and misery to put it back together again."

Sheehan shook his head. "You give me too much credit. I was a negotiator, that's all."

"If that's all you were, I could've picked up the phone and hired twenty guys to do the same thing. You were smart."

"Not anymore."

"Don't fuck with me."

Sheehan was startled enough to take a quick breath, trying to think if he'd ever heard Rory McCurdy use that word before, though everyone else did so in his presence. Probably that one shard of true Catholicism had stuck with him.

"God knows why," McCurdy said. "You're totally out of what happens in Cleveland."

"Will you help, then?"

The Old Man angrily wiped at his face as if being tormented by mosquitoes. "I'm in my goddamn nineties. What do you want from me?"

"Give me a place to start."

"Places? I'm a Clevelander who's old and tired. I hardly ever go to the suburbs."

Another hunk of silence—then: "I have a lawyer—sharp as a tack. A young guy, maybe forty. His name's Garrett Lavender."

"You're kidding! What happened to Gowan Scully?" Sheehan had unforgettable memories of Gowan Scully, Esq., longtime personal attorney of Rory McCurdy who'd represented Brock every time he was busted—four-for-four, all arrests being dismissed.

"He's gone, God rest his soul," Rory said, "only two years younger than me. His heart quit on him like that—" and he snapped his fingers in Sheehan's face. "Nobody knew anything was wrong with him. One morning he woke up, had breakfast in his own kitchen, and all of a sudden he stopped breathing." His sigh was heavy, and nine decades of sorrow came with it. McCurdy fumbled in a drawer to find a tattered business card. "Lavender was Gowan's junior partner—doing small-time crap for us. But when Gowan died, he took over the business, but kept Gowan's name on the door along with his own."

Sheehan glanced down at the card. *Scully and Lavender, LLP,* it said, Garrett Lavender's name at the bottom, followed by *Managing Partner.*

"He knows everything these days," Rory said, "whether it's the best restaurant in Greater Cleveland that makes boxty potato pancakes, or the cleanest men's room to take a piss in when you're in Tuscarawas County."

"Next time I need to piss in Tuscarawas County, I'll call him."

"You'll be a bigger fool than you are already if you don't contact him," Rory told him. "I'll say to expect your call."

"For when?"

"For right now."

"What if he's busy?"

"He won't be busy if I tell him you'll be in touch."

McCurdy, geriatric or no, still called the shots on the Irish west side. Sheehan said, "That's good enough, Rory, and I appreciate it. The law could hold Linus Callahan in the joint for seventy-two hours, not charging him with anything—any time they feel like it."

The Old Man rubbed his eyes with his thumb and middle finger. Sometimes he felt he'd spent more time in court or in police stations than he had on the job, which made him as famous as the Italian godfather in Greater Cleveland the last half of the twentieth century. Now, his fame was ancient and weary as he—and those remembering him at all were simply waiting for him to die.

"That's cops for you," Rory McCurdy said.

CHAPTER THREE

Lawyer Garrett Lavender no longer occupied the dinky offices of the late Gowan Sullivan, once located in an old building on West 65th Street and Detroit Road, which was rundown and threadbare as the rest of the area. Now that stretch of Detroit Road has upgraded to gentrification and a new name, Gordon Square. Lavender hadn't hung around, though. He moved his headquarters to an elegant glass skyscraper on Superior, two blocks from Public Square. Brock Sheehan, noting modern, soulless office furniture and hideous black and white carpet, and a sleek receptionist who could have been a supermodel who stalks Paris and Milan runways looking enraged with the entire world, none of whom were half as beautiful, figured Lavender earned more money than Scully ever dreamed of, or else lived in a one-bedroom apartment in a lousy neighborhood, eating Ramen noodles for dinner, and driving a fifteen-year-old Chevy Malibu in order to afford the new business space.

Reigning supreme in his sixteenth-floor corner office, blocks from the courthouse, Lavender wore a dark blue, totally unwrinkled suit. Since the sun rose behind his desk, it was hard to ascertain whether he sported makeup, but his skin was flawless—not a bump or mark. His hair was sprayed stiff so no random cowlick might appear. Thinking of him with Rory McCurdy was too much for first-time visitor Brock Sheehan to assimilate.

"According to Mr. McCurdy, one of your family is a murder

suspect," Lavender said to begin the conversation. "What I need to know is, did he do it or not? I don't give a damn one way or the other, but the answer will give me a certain way to build my case."

Sheehan told him, "I'm guessing he didn't—but I don't know him very well."

"You're just guessing?"

"Yes." Every story, often retold, gains its own rhythms and excessiveness each time out. Once again, he explained Linus's surprise meeting with Pine, and tried not to further embellish it.

"He wasn't arrested?"

"No."

"Dragged into police headquarters and questioned?"

"He wasn't dragged, exactly. He was asked to show up there. I only talked to him once."

"Fine—and then he was let go?"

"Yes."

Lavender extended his hands, palms up. "What do you want from me?"

"Advice."

"What am I? The guru on the mountaintop?"

"Rory McCurdy said you were the best in town."

"Did McCurdy happen to mention my fee is four hundred dollars an hour?"

Sheehan didn't flinch. "A halfway decent call girl earns more than that."

"I'm more than a halfway decent call girl," Lavender lied easily. "Have you talked to the police?"

"No—I only heard about this whole thing yesterday."

Lavender swung his chair around momentarily to look out the window at the lake, giving Brock Sheehan the back of his head, and then half-circled again to face him. The chair was his own private little amusement park ride. "A nephew you haven't laid eyes on since his adolescence is crapping his pants because cops brought him in for pushing a guy in the chest who's twice his size and earns more in one year than he does in ten lifetimes—and a few days later the push-ee gets his throat cut. Now you're paying me four hundred bucks for—what is it again? Advice?"

Brock conspicuously looked at his wristwatch, making sure Garrett Lavender saw it was a Patek Philippe. "I've got ten times four hundred bucks worth of your advice right here on my wrist, so I can ask you any goddamn thing I want. Do I make myself clear?"

"Still a tough guy." Lavender nodded in reluctant appreciation. "I've heard stories about you, Mr. Sheehan. You're a legend. Are you here to break my kneecaps?"

"I'd love to, but I wouldn't want to wrinkle your suit."

"Fair enough. All right, then—let's think this through." He stood up, walked to the window, and looked out again. "Let's say your nephew is two baby steps away from being a saint, and he didn't slice open Kenny Pine's throat—and you want to know how you can keep his shoes from getting scuffed." He turned around, leaning his ass against the windowsill. "Pine did prison time for dog fighting, right?"

"Almost three years."

"It wasn't just a flea-bitten farm where they raised fighting pits. It was the center of a very big business that crossed state lines."

"I didn't know that, no."

"Several hundred grand a year passed through Kenny Pine's circus—illegally supporting the lifestyle to which he was accustomed while he bounced balls for OSU."

"You know this," Brock said, "since Rory McCurdy called you an hour ago?"

"I got my bachelor's degree at Ohio State. I've always been a college basketball fan. I know about Pine's on-court talent, and I read all the stories when he got busted, so this is no breaking news to me."

"You're talking a hell of a lot of money in the pocket of a college kid."

"Legally or otherwise, the alumni took care of him while he

played," the attorney reminded him. "Rich alums are big gamblers, especially when their own college plays football or basketball."

"What does that have to do with Kenny Pine?" Sheehan asked.

Lavender's shrug was masterful. "I haven't the vaguest idea. Just giving you background, Mr. Sheehan—the least I can do for four big ones."

"What did Pine do to make someone mad enough to slash him to death?"

"It's probably not for feeling up your nephew's old lady. Maybe it was about him getting even richer. The minute they let him walk out the prison gates, the NBA teams were all over him like white on rice. He did just fine with the Denver Nuggets. Too bad he didn't live long enough to enjoy it—all because your nephew hated him for abusing dogs."

"Lots of animal lovers in the world hated him, Mr. Lavender."

"Enough to kill a guy who'd already gone to prison and paid his dues?"

"Maybe the same business people were so pissed at his success," Brock suggested, "they might have iced him as soon as he got out."

"Barely possible—but it's a good place to start."

"Where? I don't know shit about dogs. I won't know where to find anybody in the dogfighting business."

"Neither would I. But there's a place where they breed killer pitties—just blocks from Lake Erie, inland off Lake Shore Boulevard on the east side, just north of Bratenahl."

Sheehan took a ballpoint pen and a small spiral notebook from his jacket pocket. "What's the address?"

"How the hell would I know? It was more than a year ago anyone even mentioned dogfighting to me. Cruise the neighborhood until you see lots of dog kennels."

"And then what do I do? Walk in there and blow the place up?"

Lavender rubbed his right eyebrow as though a headache was starting. "It's your ballgame. The West Side Gaelic Society won't come to your rescue—and due to your past reputation, cops will be after your ass, too, before your gun cools off enough to put back in your pocket."

"I don't carry a gun."

"Your angel wings actually fit under that jacket? Whoopee." Garrett Lavender flapped his arms like angel's wings. "Go talk to the police first."

"I don't do well talking to cops."

"Find the homicide dick who corralled Linus in the first place. If they recognize your name—and most of them won't because you haven't poked your head out of your rabbit hole for ten years—they'll want to learn something they don't know. If you're smart as you think you are, you'll learn plenty from them, too."

"What's the name of the homicide cop?"

"Linus didn't mention it?"

Sheehan shook his head. "If he did, I missed it."

Garrett Lavender wrinkled up his nose as if he'd just smelled a ten-day-old corpse. Swinging his chair around again so his back was to Sheehan, he dialed his personal cell phone to reach a particular working police officer in Cleveland. He spoke quietly into the mouthpiece, then mumbled his thanks and hung up. Turning back around, he pulled a white pad toward him, scribbled down a name, and handed the top page to Sheehan.

"The he is a she. Detective Sergeant Tobe Blaine, Homicide Division—and if you get over there pretty quick, she's still in her office."

"Should I mention your name?"

"If you do, I'll have to kill you. Write me a check."

"I don't have a checkbook." He dug into his pocket for a fat roll of bills, counting four Benjamins off the top and dumping them on the desk. "Is cash all right?"

Garrett Lavender's face brightened. He scooped up the bills

and stuffed them into his pocket. "I love getting cash I don't report to the IRS. I think I'm going to like you, Brock Sheehan."

Crowded in late afternoon by people wearing older, unfashionable clothes and scuffed shoes with rundown heels and who'd rather be anyplace else than the building housing the courts and the police headquarters, Sheehan joined them to file beneath an electronic arch similar to those at airport security points that buzz loudly if anyone tries to carry anything dangerous, like two nickels in their pocket. At least he wouldn't have to take off his shoes and belt this time, nor throw away his shampoo.

Stepping off the elevator, he was once more subjected to a search, this time emptying his pockets into a plastic tray. The security cop, months from retiring and too broad in the beam to chase bad guys down the street on foot, demanded to know why he was there, whom he wanted to see, and on what subject.

"Tell Detective Sergeant Blaine," he said, "that I'm here about Linus Callahan."

The cop didn't react one way or another, but made a phone call, turning away so Sheehan couldn't hear. Then he hung up, stepped aside, and said, "Fourth door on your right, down the hallway."

Sheehan knew he'd been in this same corridor more than once. In offices on either side, cops were in ties and shirtsleeves, all gabbing on phones and scribbling on yellow legal pads. He didn't recognize any faces because most were *young* faces. After years poking into grisly murders, some mature cops not yet retired had requested transfer to a department not as gruesome or emotionally shattering as the Homicide Division.

A completely glassed-in cubicle with a sign stenciled on the door, *FLORENCE McHARGUE, Lieutenant*, dominated the hallway. The woman inside was African American, in her early fifties, her hair sprinkled with gray. The facial expression she probably wore even in the shower made everyone think twice before messing with her.

The fourth door on the right was the same as the rest of them on the floor. No stencil, but a plaque to the right of the door read *Detective Sergeant Tobe Blaine.* The door was wide open, but Brock Sheehan wisely chose to knock.

Blaine looked up, frowned as he announced himself. She was also black, a decade younger than Florence McHargue. Stunning, with short curly hair, dark chocolate eyes, and a full, sensuous mouth, she was not beautiful, but a truly handsome woman. There are few women Brock would describe as "handsome."

"Mr.—" She looked down at the name she'd scrawled half a minute earlier. "Mr. Sheenan? Come in and sit down, please. You want to see me about Linus Callahan?"

"It's Shee-hahn. Just one *N.* Linus Callahan is my nephew. You brought him in for questioning in the Kenny Pine murder."

"That's right."

"He didn't do it, Detective Sergeant."

"Gosh," she said. "That makes my life a lot easier."

"I doubt that."

"He says he's innocent? Not many murderers run around confessing."

"I have a feeling about it."

"A feeling? Really?" She laughed a phony laugh—nothing behind it other than suspicious eyes. "That's how we do police work, huh? Feelings?"

"I know the Sheehans, Detective. They're honest as the day is long."

"You're a Sheehan, too—so that makes you prejudiced. You live with them?"

He took a beat before answering. "I live—out of town, sort of. Vermillion."

"Sort of? Define *sort of.*"

"I live on a houseboat."

"During Ohio winters?"

"No. During the winter, I travel—to places that aren't quite so cold and snowy."

"But you drive in to have dinner with your own clan every Sunday, right?"

He didn't respond.

"What do you do for a living, Mr. Sheehan, when you're not heaping praise on your family?"

"I'm—retired."

"You look young to retire. From what, may I ask?"

Crap! Sheehan thought. This Detective Sergeant knew exactly where and how hard to push to cause immediate discomfort that took a long time to go away. "I was an—adjudicator. I negotiated things between parties and then acted as a referee, so to speak."

"So to speak. Like in a boxing match?"

"No."

Blaine nodded. "What company did you work for?"

"Freelance."

"In Cleveland?"

He nodded. "In other places, too."

"I see." Blaine leaned back in her chair for comfort, and Sheehan noticed she wore slacks and not a skirt. "You're here today to 'adjudicate' me—is that right?"

"No, Detective—I'm here suggesting you might look elsewhere for your perp."

She lifted her eyebrows. "My *perp*? Well, *that's* cop talk."

He shook his head. "TV cop talk." He wanted to lean forward and put his hands on her desk, but wisely thought better of it. "There are always guys in bars who push other guys for coming on too strong to their ladies—a hundred times a night somewhere in this county and twice as many on weekends—but it's not usually a prelude to murder."

"You've seen lots of preludes to murder, have you?"

"I haven't been a monk who swore a life of silence."

She cocked her head. "I wish I knew more monks who swear a life of silence. Now, set me straight. You were at the same bar at the same time Sunday night? Or not?"

"Not."

"So how do you know what it looked like? Yeah, yeah—feelings." Tobe Blaine waved her hand dismissively. "I had Callahan in here for hours. Did you think I wouldn't ask him what he does for a living?" She rushed on, but Sheehan wasn't about to interrupt. "He works at a no-kill animal shelter because he loves animals. And Kenny Pine just got out of prison for killing animals."

"Most inmates love dogs."

"How would you know that? Were you an inmate?"

"No—but I've known a few who were."

"Nice friends, Mr. Sheehan. My guess," she said, "is Kenny Pine did light time. He's too big and strong to have been anybody's candy-ass—and too Ohio-famous to be fucked with. Your baby-boy nephew, though, sings a different tune."

"Why?"

"His last words to Kenny Pine were, and I quote, 'Go electrocute another dog.'"

"Where did you get that from?"

Tobe Blaine opened a file in front of her and sifted through the papers. Then she said, "From eight witnesses standing right there ogling their dribbling idol graciously deigning to have a drink with the peasants and probably get laid in the process. These witnesses heard it all—including the bartender."

"I see the way you cops are," Sheehan said. "If a subject looks halfway good, you stop everything and bust your butts to prove he's guilty. Saves you a lot of extra work."

"If we had other suspects, we'd be leaning on them, too."

"Why aren't you looking for one?"

Blaine closed her eyes for about five seconds, then opened them and glowered. "Are you hanging around here all day being a pretend cop?"

"What if I look around for another suspect? Freelance?"

"We'd throw you in the joint for interfering in a police investigation—and lose the key for a month."

Sheehan got to his feet. "Then I'm afraid I wasted my time."

"You sure as hell wasted mine." Tobe Blaine ripped a sheet from her yellow pad and pushed it toward him. "Write down your phone number and address, in case we have to get in touch with you."

"No land line." He took out a business card and passed it across the desk. "This is my cell number. Thanks for seeing me, anyway."

"It's been charming," she said.

Not quite a hard-ass cop, Sheehan thought, but incisive and quick. She probably had a glittering gold arrest record. He knew their hello-and-goodbye would not be the last time their paths crossed. He was in the elevator on his way down before she looked at the card again. The phone number had a 216 code, which meant Cleveland—yet his home address was a dock slip at the Harbor Lagoon in Vermillion.

Tobe Blaine thought about him being an adjudicator. At least that's what he told her. He was too young to retire—rich, or at least comfortable, living on a houseboat in an upscale harbor city. She needed a bit more information on him than a ten-minute meeting.

She walked down the hall to a larger room where seven other homicide detectives had their desks, approaching Jamal Washington, recently elevated from uniformed traffic cop to plain-clothes detective catching murderers.

"Do me a favor, Washington," she said, noting that even while sitting, he snapped to attention when a detective sergeant walked through the door. "Pull up whatever you can on a fifty-ish guy named Brock Sheehan. He once lived in Cleveland and belonged to the Irish dynasty he never talks to anymore. I want everything about him—including his whole life history, from the year one AD to five minutes ago. Tell me what he has for breakfast, what kind of car he drives, if he watches Netflix or Hulu, and when he takes a shower, what does he wash first? His armpits or his ass?" She thoughtfully put her thumb to her lips. "Don't ask me why—but this son of a bitch interests the crap out of me."

Patton, the pit bull, was stretched out in front of the sofa where his master sat. Maureen Flanagan, on the other side of the room, barely sipped her beer, watching her live-in boyfriend, Linus Callahan, scarf down the pizza he'd just brought home. She'd taken only one piece, nibbled a few bites and then pushed it away. She wasn't hungry—too jangled, too much on edge to be hungry. She never ate the crusts anyway, but Linus thought the crust was the best part—one of many contrasts in their relationship.

Her pretty red hair was in a ponytail, but at her day job it was worn loose to her shoulders. Like most redheads, she hated being called "Red," or even worse, "Ginger."

But her hair color didn't bother her on this particular evening. Linus did.

"How can you eat?" she finally said.

Linus kept on munching pizza—everything on it except anchovies. He'd prefer a root canal to eating anchovies. "If you don't eat," he said between mouthfuls, "you die."

"If you get convicted of murder, you'll die too, you little shit."

"I'm not accused of anything. They haven't put me behind bars."

"Not yet."

"Don't close my coffin, okay."

"Don't blame me," she warned. "I'll be out of here so fast it'll make your head spin."

"I'm not blaming you!" He reached down and ran his hand over the head and back of Patton, who moaned in ecstasy. "I blame Pine for what he did to dogs."

"He did his time!"

"That won't bring back the dogs he tortured and murdered," Linus reminded her. "You know how I feel about that. I'll get out of this shit somehow."

"You can't fight this alone, Linus."

"I don't have to. I've got family."

"Half the time, your father can't even remember to zip up his fly."

He tried not allowing that remark to sting too badly, but failed. His father was prematurely senile, forgetting the names of his close family relatives and unable to recite his own telephone number, so Maureen's remark cut Linus Callahan deeply. The truth was that the only entity he really cared about was his dog, who lifted his head to listen, alert and on guard, when either Linus or Maureen raised their voice.

Linus searched for an answer, found none. Eventually he said, "I have other family besides my father."

"Second cousins," she scoffed, "who work in the sewer department!"

"I've got an uncle I haven't seen since I was about twelve years old."

"Some family," she said, and took another pull at the beer bottle, thinking Linus not nearly as much fun as when they'd met more than two years earlier. Within months of that first date, they found a place to share—this apartment, in a red brick century-old complex on Clifton Avenue, close to Edgewater Park and Whiskey Island.

Still young, although nearly a year older than Linus, she eventually realized that mad, wild sexual relationships always transmogrify into something else—best possible case being solid friendship and not much physical intimacy, or at least not the kind she remembered. The worst possible case? Get-the-fuck-out-of-my-life, you creep!

Even before Linus was hauled in for questioning, their relationship was slowly fading into the mist like Brigadoon.

"You slugged this Kenny guy just for trying to feel me up?" she demanded.

"I didn't 'slug' him, I pushed him. And he didn't grope you, even though he was working up to it."

"What happens to me when they lock you up? We share the rent on this place, and the groceries too!"

Linus Callahan didn't answer, figuring she'd probably find a new boyfriend within three weeks of his being sent to prison. She was more concerned about her own existence than of him being convicted for a murder he didn't commit. Life with Maureen wasn't nearly as terrific as it once was.

One slice of pizza remained. He said, "You sure you don't want this?"

"Knock yourself out." She arose and went into the bedroom, the suddenness of it making Patton sit up and stare after her. She turned on her TV, loud, as usual—one of those "romantic reality shows" with beautiful people thrown together on a desert island. Linus never had the stomach to watch.

He petted the dog's neck and thumped his muscular side. He knew Maureen liked dogs—that was how they met in the first place—but she wasn't crazy about Patton. Like most people, pit bulls frightened her. She'd be far more entranced with a Chihuahua or Yorkie she could tuck into her big purse. No one, however, would attempt picking up the hefty Patton.

Not interested in the last slice of pizza, Linus closed the box and put it in the trash bin, glad there were no dishes or silverware to wash. In Chicago, he'd heard, everyone eats extra-thick Sicilian pizza with a knife and fork. Not in Cleveland.

He never understood relationships, anyway. Most Sheehans surrendered any ideas of romance they had before getting married, allowing themselves to sink knee-deep into the Irish Catholic morass of resigned acceptance. He had no idea of what a great marriage *was*. His parents had barely tolerated one another, even before his mother's untimely passing.

Then there was Uncle Brock, who'd never been married. He'd rarely brought a girlfriend around for corned beef and cabbage in his youth because he rarely dated Irish women—the only kind his family wished to meet. Linus heard many stories about Brock Sheehan since he was a kid—arrests, redemptions, and crimes he might or might not have committed, of which none would speak above a whisper. He was a big, powerful man, a quiet one compared to the rollicking Sheehan family who, at the drop of a hat, would get into fistfights with each other about football (all of them were Browns fans), religion (Catholics, fighting about who attended mass too often or not often enough), women (which one had the biggest rack or the best ass), or even a favorite TV show.

Was it a good idea to approach him? Linus didn't know yet. Brock had said he'd "look into it," but what did that mean when push came to shove?

His shoulders slumped, as from a great weight. His distant uncle could have easily blown him off. Now Maureen was misting away, too, a puff of smoke rising into a breezy atmosphere and disappearing, never to be seen again. He felt more and more alone as the Cleveland police poked into the darkest corners of his life.

There weren't many dark corners—he'd been more or less a decent guy—but cops have been known to make some up.

Maureen Flanagan's half-finished beer was still on the table. He upended it and guzzled it down within seconds, gasping for breath, when someone rang his door buzzer. That got Patton on his feet, stalking toward the sound, his back straight, head low—loyal and suspicious.

Linus opened up without first looking through the keyhole to establish the visitor's identity. Uncle Brock's psychological physicality filled up the doorway.

"What—what are you doing here?" Linus stammered.

"You gave me this address yesterday. Since I'm still in town, I hoped you'd share a few things with me."

Linus was still overwhelmed by his uncle being anywhere near him. Brock waited a beat. "Are you going to invite me in, or talk out here in the hallway?"

"Oh, sorry. Sure, come on in."

Sheehan passed him, stepping into the living room and looking around. "Nice."

"Sit down, Uncle Brock. Want something to drink?"

"I'm okay." He sat on one end of the sofa. Linus stood there, unsure as to what he was supposed to do until he realized it was his home in which he could do whatever he wanted, so he took the easy chair opposite Sheehan.

Sheehan said, "You're guessing I haven't done a goddamn thing to help you yet."

Linus felt himself flushing. "Well—no, I wasn't thinking that."

"I've been in town all day. I talked to the Old Man at the Gaelic Society." Linus looked blank. "Rory McCurdy. The Irish godfather."

"Oh. Jesus! Is he still alive?" Immediately humiliated by asking a stupid question. "I mean, I didn't think he'd remember me."

"He was at your christening, for crysakes. He loved your whole family, even when he knew they didn't love him back."

"Why didn't they love him?"

"Because he and his crew ran this whole town. He did stuff the Sheehans hated—ordered things done that were crooked, so they shut him out." Sheehan inhaled deeply. "They shut me out, too, because I did lots of those things for him. That's why I haven't seen you all these years."

"What things did you do?"

"None of your business. You're dangling over death row by a single pussy hair right now, so let's just talk about you."

Linus started to say something when the bedroom door opened and Maureen came out wearing a multicolored polyester bathrobe supposed to look like silk, and stopped, staring at an unknown visitor. She pulled the robe tight around herself—a complete stranger in her home was more than a surprise. Her red hair was down loose around her shoulders and her bare feet were in flip-flops, bright green toenail polish twinkling. Brock's size alone overwhelmed her, but there was more to him she didn't understand. Gravitas, had she known the word—a presence that overwhelmed the room. She finally said, "Who are you?"

Sheehan stood—a gentlemanly gesture that impressed her right off the bat. "I'm Brock Sheehan. Linus is my nephew," he concluded. "And you are—?"

"I'm Maureen. Maureen Flanagan. I'm his—roommate."

Maureen—an Irish name, to be sure, Brock thought, and an apt one at that. "Maureen" means "redhead" in Celtic. He'd have to cogitate whether she was Linus's roommate. There was a vast difference between a roommate and a lover.

"If I'd known you were here," she said, batting her eyelids, "I would've put on something decent."

"You look decent—don't worry about it."

Linus said, "My uncle lives on a boat over in Vermillion."

Maureen's eyes opened wide. "You live on a boat? Wow! When are you going to take me on a boat ride?"

"It's not that kind of boat. It's a houseboat. I live there, eat there, sleep there—"

"Mmm," she purred, twinkling, "that sounds even better."

"Ease off," Linus said intensely, but that didn't slow Maureen down.

"Are you here because Linus is in trouble?" she asked. "Did he tell you he's in deep shit with the cops?"

Sheehan nodded. "I'm here to help him."

She perched on the arm of Linus's easy chair, languidly crossing one knee over the other, plenty of leg exposed. Just careless, or was she actually flirting with Uncle Brock? "Wow, that's great. Tell me all about it."

Sheehan deliberately ignored the exposed thigh. "I'm afraid it's between Linus and me. No outsiders."

"I'm no outsider, I'm his girlfriend!"

"Nice," Sheehan said, "but this is family stuff. I'm hoping you'll leave us alone for a bit."

Flirtation turned into high dudgeon. She lunged to her feet, her temper as sensitive as a filed-down trigger on a .38 Smith and Wesson. "I'm in my fucking bathrobe! Where am I supposed to go?"

"Where did you just come from?" Sheehan asked, nodding at the bedroom door. "I'm sure you're comfortable in there. Your TV is already on."

"This is my home! I'm goddamned if I'm going to move just because you say so!"

"Fine with me." Sheehan moved toward the front door. "Linus, you're on your own. I don't do pajama parties. Good luck anyway." He looked over at the woman. "Nice meeting you—considering the circumstances."

"Wait, Uncle Brock!" Linus was on his feet. "You promised you'd help me."

"I did—but I do things my own way, for my own reasons. If you and Maureen have a better idea, then Godspeed." He put his hand on the doorknob

"No! I don't have an idea—that's why I came to you."

"Well, then—" Sheehan looked from Linus to Maureen, eyebrows raised.

Linus Callahan waited only a few moments. Then he said, "Babe, why don't you go on back into the bedroom—and shut the door?"

Maureen's eyes shot daggers.

"And turn up the TV, okay?" Linus suggested. "Loud."

"Great," she said through clenched teeth. "Anything to get away from your goddamn dog and his slobbering and his farts! I'll go into the bedroom, Linus, and you stay out here on the couch—all goddamn *night!*"

She couldn't possibly have set the TV any louder than her door slam. Both men winced at the sound.

Brock hadn't had a real girlfriend for more than twenty years—a beautiful, loving, smart-as-hell woman named Arizona Skye, who'd been a field reporter for the local Channel Twelve news. They weren't together long—eight or nine months—but at the time he considered actually *marrying* her. *That* was a first.

And a last.

Rory McCurdy loathed television journalists, and had volunteered, without being asked, that he thought "Arizona" was the dumbest woman's given name he'd ever heard. Besides, he'd wanted Sheehan to marry his own daughter, Rosemary. The stress seemed impossible to live with—and eventually Sheehan was forced to make a decision.

Looking back, it was the worst choice he'd ever made—letting Arizona go. She quit her news job shortly after their breakup, and left town. Twenty years later, he wouldn't know where to find her.

"Sorry," he said to Linus, nodding at the bedroom door. "I didn't mean to cause a stink."

Linus nodded. "She's—sensitive."

"Sensitive as a pissed-off water buffalo. This is Sheehan business, Linus. I don't negotiate—not with someone else's top squeeze listening to all of it."

"Aww. Well, she's got one of those tempers—"

"I have an Irish temper, too."

"I don't know why she hates Patton," Linus said, scratching the pit bull under his chin. "I met her when she visited the shelter where I work."

Sheehan moved away from the door. "Shall I sit down again, or say goodnight?"

"Sit. Please. You know how much I need your help."

Sheehan nodded as he resumed his seat. "You need to help me, too."

Patton heaved himself off the floor, trotted across the living room, and decided that lying across Brock Sheehan's feet was his own personal space. Brock, surprised, leaned down and petted him, tickling him behind one ear. "You told me all about you and Kenny Pine the night before he died," he said. "I need to know more about you, Linus. What you do, who you do it with, where you go. I want to know more about your work—and your life."

Patton stood up, yawned, shook himself all over with spittle flying, and lay back down again between the two of them.

"How's that going to help, Uncle Brock?"

"First, knock off the 'Uncle Brock' shit. It gets on my nerves—like I'm supposed to bring you a Tootsie Pop or a Lego toy every time I see you. Call me Brock—or Mister Sheehan, if you have to. Just not 'uncle.' Okay?"

Linus shrugged.

"Where'd you go to school? Where'd you learn how to be the person you are?"

"I went to St. Ignatius."

Sheehan raised an eyebrow. "Damn good high school! How'd you get in? Play football?"

The young man laughed. "Do I look like a football player? No—I probably got in on pity—I'd just lost my mom and they felt sorry for me."

"Doesn't sound like enough."

"Well—I guess Mr. McCurdy put in a good word for me."

"Rory McCurdy?"

"He was a family friend back then."

Sheehan mumbled, "Family. Your family shut me out—mostly because I worked for Rory. That doesn't sound fair."

"My mom loved you in her heart—but disapproved of what you did for a living."

Sheehan's Irish face flushed red. "I did for Rory what he didn't want to dirty his hands with by doing it for himself."

"I have no idea what you did for Mr. McCurdy."

"Neither did your mother." Growing angry, Sheehan wanted to punch a hard fist into his opposing palm, but thought better of it. Instead he relaxed as much as he could on the sofa, resting his chin on his chest for a moment. Then: "I talked to Rory about you today. Don't look so surprised. You suggested I should get with 'my people.' He set me up with a lawyer—his lawyer—if you get into real difficulty."

Linus seemed startled. "Rory McCurdy? I haven't seen him since—"

Sheehan wiped his hand across his face as if he were erasing a blackboard in school—wiping away haunting regret over a large cadre of relatives that had deserted him. "That's what families do. So—let's hear more about you. No college?"

"I did three semesters at Tri-C."

"Cuyahoga Community College. Downtown branch?"

"West side."

"Why did you stop?"

"I dunno," Linus said. "I didn't have a career goal in mind, and I was learning a lot of shit I'd never be able to use, no matter what I did. I quit, then, and banged around for a while looking for a decent job."

"And working in a shelter is what you chose?"

Linus nodded. "For the time being. They work hard to find homes for the dogs. They keep them alive, no matter what—much better than killing them." He offered a weak smile. "They keep stray cats there, too."

"What got you into that?" Sheehan asked.

Linus Callahan shifted on his seat as though his underwear had ridden up. "Uh—well, my father. I always loved dogs—cats, too. One day I found a stray dog—a puppy. He was so cute and he looked so hungry. I picked him up and brought him home, and fed him from leftovers in the fridge. But my father said he didn't want any goddamn animals eating up his food and shitting on the carpet. Then he gave the dog one horrendous kick in the face—shut one of his eyes, probably permanently—and told me to get rid of him, or not come home that night—or any other night."

"Where did you take him?"

"I was thirteen years old, what the hell did I know? I took him to a shelter."

"A no-kill shelter like the one you work at?"

Linus hung his head. "I didn't know the difference. I took him to the city shelter—the closest one to my house."

"What happened to him?"

The boy's cheeks flamed red and he hung his head. "I—don't know. I couldn't call again, couldn't adopt him. I was a kid."

"But that turned you into an animal lover, and got you into a shoving match with Kenny Pine because of it."

"It's why work at a no-kill shelter. As for Kenny—he was a big shot athlete. He didn't need to buy into dogfighting because he'd get gigantic offers from all the NBA teams and be a multi-millionaire for as long as he lived. I figure he hated dogs from the get-go."

"Why?"

"He treated dogs like the goddamn monster he was—fighting them nearly to death. At the best of times they get their ears and noses torn off in a fight. At worst, their throats are ripped open by bigger, stronger dogs. When they don't win, there's no reason to keep them around anymore, so Pine killed them—in the most horrible ways.

Those bastards always train their fighting dogs by throwing them in with smaller, weaker dogs as 'bait.' They even tape the smaller ones' mouths shut so they can't bite the fighter back before he killed them. Pine pissed me off. He hated losers—on the basketball court, in the dogfight arena or in real life, too."

"How tall are you, Linus?"

Linus frowned, startled by the question. Finally he said, "About five foot eight."

Brock said, "Pine was nearly a foot taller than you and outweighed you by seventy pounds. What dumb-ass picks a fight he knows he's going to lose?"

"A dumb-ass who loves!" Linus was on the defensive, angry. "I tried to ignore him until he came over and put his goddamn hands all over Maureen. Then I kind of lost it." Linus slumped lower on the sofa, shaking his head sadly. "I wish I'd paid in cash at the bar instead of signing a credit card."

"What about the rest of your life? Tough guy?"

"I was a tough kid, sure. All Irish kids fight." Linus began wiggling. "Not so much now that I'm a grown-up."

Grown-up? Not nearly, Brock thought. He hadn't thought himself a real adult until he was in his early thirties, until he'd carried out McCurdy's astonishing mission—a dead man, neck broken and stuffed headfirst into a garbage can behind a butcher shop on West 65th Street.

He wasn't a kid after that. Grown up at last—perhaps too grown up.

"Losing my temper is one thing," Linus said, "but throwing a punch is another. And when somebody is cruel to animals just for the fun of it..." He dropped his arm and ran his hand across Patton's muscled neck, feeling the stored strength and power with his fingertips. "I didn't kill him, though. I swear on my mother's grave."

"Don't carry a knife?"

Linus shook his head. "I never did. I mean, cutting a guy's throat? Jesus!"

"You didn't know him before that night?"

"Just from what I read in the papers. I swear—"

"On your mother's grave, I know." Brock Sheehan stood up. So did Linus. So did the pit bull. "I've got zero connections in Cleveland these days, but I'll do whatever I can to help you. In the meantime, keep everything to yourself. *Everything!* You get what I'm saying, Linus? You don't tell your girlfriend about it, you don't inform your buddies or the people you work with! You don't even talk to the police without an attorney sitting next to you. Rory's lawyer is Garrett Lavender—write it down so you don't forget it, and call him the next time the cops hassle you." A deep breath, then words sailed out on his exhale. "You don't mention me—to anyone!"

Linus blinked. "Not even to—?"

"Nobody! Drive the speed limit. No changing lanes without signaling, even if it's the middle of the goddamn night and there's no one around for miles! You be a good boy out there so the cops don't stop you—for anything. If they do, keep both hands on the wheel while they're talking to you. Be so polite they'll think you're an actor from some British TV show." Brock's head was beginning to hurt. "And be careful about yourself."

"What do you mean?"

Sheehan closed his eyes for a moment. How could anyone be so naive—and how can he possibly help this kid who hasn't the brains to help himself? At length he walked to the front door and once more put his hand on the knob. "I mean," he said, "don't leave the toilet seat up by mistake and flush yourself down the crapper."

CHAPTER FOUR

Brock Sheehan woke up early—no one sleeps to midmorning while living on a boat. The early light, lake-fish smell, other vessels moving in and out of the harbor, and the hungry screeching of freewheeling gulls could awaken a three-day-old corpse.

He toasted a bagel and ate it with cream cheese, and brewed half a pot of coffee, wondering as he often did, why the "one-cup" marking on a pot wouldn't even half fill the coffee mug most human beings use to get their day started. He always drank it black, even when he was a kid, because Rory had told him putting a bunch of milk and sugar into coffee ruined the taste of it. On being welcomed into the West Side Gaelic Society, he quickly learned nobody stepped over a line, especially in the presence of Rory McCurdy.

Sitting in his deck chair and studying the sky and clouds, he wished for a morning paper to read, remembering sadly, as he did every morning, his kid years, waking up at six a.m., jumping aboard his bike, and delivering the *Plain Dealer* to all his neighbors on the near west side before setting off for school. His aim for a front porch while pedaling by at top speed had been nearly perfect. Now Ohio's biggest newspaper is printed three or four times each week, or only available on the internet. He wouldn't read it anyway, since they laid off most of their fine journalists for economic reasons.

After finishing the first mug, he showered, smiling ruefully that the shower head nozzle was about two inches too low for his head, making him bend his knees a bit to shampoo his hair. Maybe tall guys like him just weren't boaters. Rory McCurdy had been the original owner of the boat—and he was barely five feet ten inches.

Brock was a shower shaver, too. He wasn't bothered that most men of the twenty-first century sported some facial hair, if not a full-out mustache, beard, or goatee, at least a scruffy, forgot-to-shave look making them feel uber-macho and sexy. He'd never worn a beard or mustache, thinking the look not only messy, but very nineteenth century.

Dressed in a subdued shirt and khaki slacks, he poured himself what was left of the coffee. At twenty minutes past nine, Detective Sergeant Tobe Blaine came down the dock toward his boat. He gave her a more careful look than the day before. She seemed younger in sunshine, her hair free and casual—but after years of Brock dancing the dangerous gavotte with police departments, anyone wearing a badge, male or female, set off a shrieking warning alarm. Maybe things would be different in another lifetime.

"Apparently it's easier to locate me these days," he hailed her. "Do I have an ad in the Yellow Pages nobody ever reads anymore?"

"I couldn't find your email, or even a listing on Facebook."

"I don't own a computer. Never had one. Just an iPad. I'm— retired."

"I'm not retired, Mr. Sheehan, nor am I a barista at Starbucks." She stepped off the dock onto the boat, not asking for permission. "I'm a homicide detective, remember?"

"You can't haul me to jail this morning, Detective Sergeant, because you're out of your bailiwick. This isn't Cleveland. Besides, I haven't done anything."

"I can bust you for spitting in the lake if I feel like it. But I'm not here to arrest you. If I were, I'd have backup and a warrant."

"Then this is social? I'm flattered."

"It isn't a blind date." She briefly looked around the deck, spied the other chair, and dragged it over to Sheehan. "I found out all sorts of things about you."

"Boxers or briefs? You could have just asked me."

Tobe Blaine sat down. "Did you wear boxers or briefs back when you were Rory McCurdy's number-one leg breaker?"

His eyes opened wide in surprise. "Leg-breaker? Well, gloryosky zero! Where did you learn that? Grimm's Fairy Tales?"

She tried to hide her amusement, shaking her head. "Gloryosky zero!" she said. "Jesus!"

"From an old comic strip. My mom's favorite expressions—without the 'Jesus.'"

"What was your mother's favorite expression when Rory McCurdy hired you to kill people?"

Brock laughed softly. "How many hours did you put in doing research on my past life?"

"I had one of my third-class detectives do it for me—falling all over himself with excitement from reading about your past. He brought it in and told me all about you as if he'd just seen an advance screening of the new *Star Wars*."

"You make him water all your plants, too. Keep him busy with something really important."

"Murder is important—or should I call them assassinations?" She cocked her head to one side. "Is assassinate the right word, same as murder? Or it is only when somebody really important like the president gets killed?"

"Detective," Brock said softly, "I was arrested four times—and cleared each time before going to trial."

"But you *were* arrested. On suspicion."

"Suspicion and a buck buys you a cup of coffee at Mickey D's." He relaxed in his chair. "But *your* suspicion hauled in Linus Callahan."

"Not arrest—just a little talk. Look, he did have a fight with Kenny Pine Sunday night, and by Monday night, Pine was dead."

"It wasn't a fight, the way I heard it. It was a push."

"On the books, pushing is assault." She raised her hand. "Don't get nervous, Mr. Sheehan, I don't arrest pushers—I have a higher pay grade. That means asking questions and solving murders, whether the victim is a superstar basketball player, or the guy who rides hanging onto the side of a truck to collect your garbage."

"You're an hour away from downtown Cleveland, asking *me* questions. That makes me a suspect, doesn't it? Even though I never heard of Kenny Pine until Linus dropped by to tell me about it."

"Just one question," Tobe said, "but an interesting one." She moved in her chair so her knees and Sheehan's almost touched, leaning forward to get right in his face. "What's your business, and why is it making you a suspect?"

"Am I a suspect, too? I'm retired, as I've told you. Or do you suspect everybody? Linus Callahan is my late sister's son. I hardly know him—but he's family, so that rules out suspicion where I come from. And that means balls to the wall if I can help him in any way." He popped his knuckles—loud—a sure sign he was annoyed. "It's one of those Irish things. Y'know?"

"I'm not Irish."

"I noticed."

"All I have to look at right now is your nephew. That means if you're in my way, I'll hang your ass on the wall and use it for a dart board." Tobe stood up. "You've been out of sight a long time—since way before I came to Cleveland. Let's keep it that way."

"That confuses me, Detective Sergeant. Kenny Pine had a successful Ohio sports record, or so I hear—also a criminal conviction giving him three years laundering fellow inmates' underwear in a state prison in Mansfield. But you zero in on some half-hammered kid with a sexy girlfriend who gave Pine a little push in a downtown saloon because he was touching her tits—and you drive all the way here to give me shit one day after you never even heard of me."

"Since yesterday I know your whole life story, Mr. Sheehan."

"It'd make a lousy movie."

"I pretty much know Kenny Pine's life story, too. Want to hear it?"

"Just the highlights."

"All right," Tobe Blaine said. "Take notes if you want to." She folded her arms across her ample chest. "You know heavy betting goes on at dogfights and cockfights."

"That's why they started dogfights and cockfights in the first place."

"You also know there's big-time gambling—on college sports."

"Yeah, heavy-duty money on synchronized swimming for girls."

"Women, not girls," she corrected him. "Not as heavy-duty as on basketball."

"College games?" The corner of Sheehan's mouth tightened to camouflage a smile aborning. "That must be a dirty rumor."

"Hundreds of thousands were bet every time Kenny Pine put on a jockstrap."

"That was three years ago." He leaned forward to look at her. "Ancient history."

"Maybe," she said. "Then what do I have to do to keep you out of my life?"

"I didn't ask to hear your life story."

"This part of my life story is homicide business—not your business." She shook a finger at him like a second-grade teacher warning a kid not to talk out of turn. "Don't make me threaten you."

"Threaten?" Sheehan snickered. "Bad guys don't threaten. They just *do*. Do you really think hanging my ass on the wall is a threat?"

"If you're so damn smart, help me. If you don't, then help Linus. And when you figure out somebody else I should be looking at *besides* your nephew—I'd be ever so grateful if you'll tell me, too."

Sheehan's eyebrows lifted high. "Are you kidding?"

"Don't pull a vigilante on me and judge all by yourself. You swear you don't have a gun, so you're safe—except you kill people with your bare hands."

Brock Sheehan said, "Not since last Thursday at three o'clock in the afternoon."

"I'll take that as a devastatingly funny joke," she said without even the hint of a smile, rising and heading toward the plank. "Anchors aweigh."

"That sounds as if you want me to take you for a boat ride."

Tobe paused on the dock. "Thanks, but no thanks. I have a job. I have to go out and catch who killed Kenny Pine—before *you* do."

Bratenahl is a small, close-to-downtown lakeside suburb catering to the obscenely rich. It's only a four-minute drive through that rarely photographed luxury township until reaching a working-class section of Cleveland whose hardworking citizens ignore being just steps from one of the largest freshwater bodies in the world.

Brock Sheehan drove north and east, gaping like a tourist at the most impressive mansions anywhere between New York and Chicago. He was financially comfortable, but couldn't even afford the local taxes and heating bills Bratenahl residents shrug off.

On Lake Shore Boulevard, he parked at a do-it-yourself filling station, went inside and asked the attendant behind the counter, a young woman thirty pounds overweight with long, lank, completely straight hair hanging below her waist and a chunk of metal imbedded in her right eyebrow, if a pet shop was nearby. She looked blank, experienced only in selling potato chips, Ding Dongs, and chewing tobacco. Finally whipping out her cell phone and diddling the buttons with her fingertips, she proudly showed him her directional results to the closest establishment that sold large amounts of dog food.

He couldn't remember where he'd bought food for his Irish wolfhound, as it was two decades ago—but he'd always been a west side guy, and had no clue as to pet supply stores east of the Cuyahoga River. The Sheehans were Irish to their core, down to Gaelic first names like Linus, Fiona, Aidan, and Siobhan. Raucous Irish laughter followed by Irish moroseness and Irish tears after too much Irish whiskey, too much anger over the IRA and the Time of Troubles, battle-ready Irish temper, Notre Dame's Fighting Irish football team and its Touchdown Jesus statue in the stadium, and the worst brutality of all—Irish sarcasm.

The pet store, owned by a large corporation with locations all over the country, was in a building bigger than most ice skating arenas. No dogs were up for adoption—many pet stores have stopped buying maltreated animals from puppy mills and selling them as purebreds or adorable mongrel mixes like cockapoos and yorkiepoos. Several cats, though, were incarcerated in tiny glass-faced cages, trying desperately to charm whoever walked by into spending a hundred bucks or so to take them home. Three sad-looking rabbits were in one pen, looking as if they'd given up hope, and three super-active ferrets were in another, along with many mice, white rats, tiny fish, and crickets on sale as feeders for other animals, larger fish, and four non-poisonous snakes. A passel of finches, cockatiels and canaries were in cages too small for them—a maximum-security prison without the orange jumpsuits or dropping the soap in the shower.

The kid at the cash register, a small gold cross on a chain around his neck and a name tag reading MARV: ASSOCIATE, was one of those nearly-invisible people—young, skinny, with thick black horn-rimmed glasses so he could see more than three feet in front of him, and thin, dirty-blond hair he couldn't manage to keep combed, which would probably be gone by the time he was thirty. Nevertheless, he was paid to be cheery, and he happily greeted Brock Sheehan across the counter.

"I'm looking to buy a dog," Sheehan said.

"We don't sell dogs," Marv said solemnly, as if he were under oath saying he hadn't even puffed once on a cigarette, refused to watch porn, and never, *ever*, touched himself inappropriately in bed. "We only sell pet accouterments—and pet foods, of course."

"I was hoping you could tell me where around here I could buy one."

"There are plenty of breeders in the neighborhood, sir, depending on what breed you're looking for."

"That's the thing," Sheehan said. "I don't know what breed. A big dog—not quite as big as a Rottweiler or a Saint Bernard. I'm considering a pit bull. Doesn't have to be purebred, necessarily. I prefer a rescue-type dog."

"There are shelters."

Sheehan shook his head, trying hard to match Marv's piety. "Who knows what kind of sicknesses those dogs pick up in an animal shelter. I don't want a puppy, either—don't have the time for housebreaking. Just a big, strong, imposing dog who already knows he shouldn't poop on my carpet."

"Hmm." The young man put his thumb beneath his chin, pondering, resting his index knuckle just below his mouth. "We have a customer who, I think, has big dogs."

"You think?"

"He comes in every four weeks and buys twenty-pound bags of kibble. Sometimes he has a dog with him, looks like maybe a pit bull or a pittie mix—and sometimes he has a different dog. That sounds like a lot of dogs to me."

"Me, too," Sheehan said. "Does he sell those dogs?"

"I have no idea, sir."

"Darn." It sounded ridiculous to Sheehan when he said "darn" aloud, but he didn't figure MARV: ASSOCIATE went in for swearing. "Do you know the man's name?"

"Not off the top of my head, no."

Sheehan acted chagrined. "Doggone it," he said, and almost laughed at himself. "Is there any way you could find out? Like looking in your sales slips?"

Marv frowned, troubled. "I'd have to go back in the office

and see if I can find one. I think he was in last week."

"Could you do that?"

Marv looked around, all at once aware of his vital importance to the company, considering they paid him twelve dollars and fifty cents per hour. Then he headed toward the rear of the store, waved at Sheehan, and disappeared, to be replaced by LAKITA: ASSOCIATE, a young black woman who also wore glasses, and a green polo shirt with the store's name on it, just like Marv's. She glared at Brock Sheehan for no particular reason other than that he stood by the sales register, so he moved away and wandered a few aisles, checking out dog food brands, many of which he'd never heard.

After fifteen minutes, which left Sheehan thinking Marv had been kidnapped and flown into space for surgical tests by extra-terrestrials, the young man surfaced once more, triumphantly waving a piece of paper. "Got it, sir!" he announced.

On the paper was written *George Schmitt*. That was all.

"Thanks," Sheehan said. "Where can I find him?"

Now Marv looked bent out of shape again. "I don't know. He paid with a credit card. That's all we have on file—his name."

"Oh, shit!" That profanity made Marv gasp. Lakita noisily huffed her displeasure.

Irritated, Brock stomped outside and sat in his car for a while with the windows down. Then he took out his iPhone, shaking his head. Other than making and receiving phone calls, he barely knew what else to do with the damn thing. He'd never texted in his life and surfed the internet very rarely. It took him a quarter hour to figure out how, as his fingers were too big and clumsy. Eventually he came up with seven George Schmitts in the Greater Cleveland area—but only one of them had an address less than a mile from where Sheehan was. He hoped the damn phone wouldn't send him to Timbuktu, because he couldn't recall ever being in this neighborhood before.

He found George Schmitt's house within two minutes.

CHAPTER FIVE

The house was on a double corner lot in a lower middle-class neighborhood—close to Lake Erie, but nowhere near a beach that residents could enjoy. Not exactly rundown, but one quick glance from Brock Sheehan told him the outside paint and the slate roof should have been fixed up years earlier.

The garage around the corner was also dilapidated, and behind it was a scattering of mostly empty cages. Only three dogs were in residence—pit bulls nowhere near as big as a mastiff. One resembled Linus Callahan's canine companion, Patton. Bowls of water were in each cage, but only two dogs seemed so forlorn that neither lifted their heads to notice Sheehan without much enthusiasm. They probably hadn't been petted or played with in their entire lives.

Sheehan moved up the cracked sidewalk to the front door. A stink hung over the entire place—not dog poop, not spoiled food, not the inimical odor of a meth lab, and not even body odor from humans who forget to bathe. It was the smell of decay—of fame and hope and success that had died slowly on the vine and turned to rot.

The TV was playing inside, and as he rapped on the door, he wondered who in the world watched daytime television anyway?

His answer came when the door was yanked open by George Schmitt. He was around Sheehan's age but looking older than Rory McCurdy. He'd probably shaved about two weeks earlier and could no longer remember where he put his razor. On view were flip-flops, striped boxer shorts, and a white T-shirt so stretched out around his neck that a bison might have tried to put its head inside. A half-smoked Camel hung from one corner of his mouth as if he'd been born with it, sending stinging smoke into his right eye. People across the street could have smelled the cheap booze on his breath.

"Yuh?"

"Are you George Schmitt?"

"Yuh."

"I got your name from a guy down at the pet store. I'm looking to buy a dog."

"One o' my dogs?"

"That's a possibility."

Schmitt frowned, thinking hard as if it were a calculus problem. Then he said, "Let's go look at 'em," and pushed past Sheehan and out onto the sagging porch.

"You really going outside in your underwear, Mr. Schmitt?"

Schmitt looked across the street with contempt. "If the neighbors don' wanna see my underwear, they don't hafta look." Then he glared at Sheehan. "Does it bother *you?*"

"I'll keep my sexual fantasies under control."

Schmitt stumbled around the side of the house toward the cages. "Whaddya want with a dog, anyway?"

"Why does anyone want a dog?"

"What are you, kidding? A pit bull?" Schmitt shook his head in disbelief.

"I hear they can be very affectionate companions."

"Affectionate? Right, just after they gnaw off your dick."

Sheehan let it go. They arrived at the nearest cage occupied by a muscular tan and white male whose ears looked as if they'd been chewed on. He raised the front of his body up on his rear feet and pawed at the cage with his front ones, barking loudly to get some desperately needed attention, but his shoulders slumped. There was no movement of his tail. His eyes were dull.

"Seems like a nice dog, Mr. Schmitt. What's his name?"

Schmitt shrugged. "I never bothered to find out. Call him whatever you want. He'll come pretty quick if you got food in your hand."

"You don't breed dogs, then?"

A headshake. "I find 'em, buy 'em, then sell 'em to somebody else."

"That's how you make your living?"

"Uh—more or less, yeah."

Sheehan wandered over to the next cage. The big black dog remained quiet, chin resting on his front paws but looking up at him with yellowish eyes.

"All your dogs are male?"

"Yeah, I don't keep bitches around. They're not worth much money." He shrugged his shoulders. "All anybody wants 'em for is bait."

"For dogfights?" Sheehan couldn't hide the disgust that literally wrinkled his nose. "Ever sell dogs to Kenny Pine?"

"Shee-it!" Schmitt looked skyward, as if only the spiritual being up there could help him. "Kenny Pine ain't been in business for three years. He went to jail for it—and what I heard on TV a few nights ago is somebody iced him."

"But back in the day, he did buy dogs from you?"

"Not very often. He bought from lots a people. Dumb ass let himself get caught."

"Where'd he get all this money to buy fighting dogs? He was a college student."

"How should I know? He's outta the business, which took a big bite outa my ass."

"What about the farm where he had the fights?"

"Don't know. Somebody else owns it—but they don't run shows no more." Schmitt heaved a sorrowful sigh. "They made a shitload a money in Mahoning County. Big crowds showed up for every fight—maybe three, four hundred people, all bettors. Pine and whoever his partner was skimmed the cream off the top of every single bet."

"Where did he get the cash to invest in the first place?"

"Yo, how'm I s'poseta know? He never shared it with me, man. So—you gonna buy a dog, or what?"

"How much you want for the black one here?"

Schmitt considered it. "Eight hundred."

"Eight hundred dollars for a mixed-breed dog?"

"Okay then, make it seven fifty. I'm easy."

"So he's not a pit bull, he's a pit bull mix."

"What's the difference? He's a fighter. You can tell. Look at the ears." Schmitt took a vicious kick at the cage, close to the dog's head, which obviously startled it into standing up on all fours, head low between his shoulders, a menacing growl turning into a furious barking session. That was when George Schmitt picked up a long stick and jabbed it right through the cage opening, driving it deep into the dog's side. A loud yelp of pain, followed by snarling and trying to claw down the cage as the poor creature tried with all its might to somehow get at his owner.

"See what I mean?" Schmitt said. "You can get him to fight good, as long as you put him in the mood first."

Sheehan wrenched the stick out of Schmitt's hands and, holding it at either end, pressed it against the man's throat, pinning him against the side of the cage. Schmitt struggled hopelessly, his eyes bulging as he gasped for breath, and Sheehan knew it would take no effort to actually kill him. Just lean on the stick harder and wait until he stopped breathing. He considered it.

No, he thought. No more killing. Those days were a part of his past, but he found himself despising this shithead who was cruel to animals. Putting his face very close to Schmitt's, Sheehan said softly, "Ten years ago, I would've beat you to death with this stick. You understand? Or I'd lock you in a cage, feed you once a day out of a dirty dish, and gouge you with a stick whenever I got bored with the rest of my life. Or maybe," he continued, "I'll just lock you in that cage with *him*. You'd last about ten minutes before he tore out your throat and you bled to death."

He finally took the stick away from Schmitt's neck and broke it into three pieces over his knee, then tossed them into the cage. The dog was still growling dangerously, and Schmitt was almost on his knees, clutching at his throat trying to take a breath.

Sheehan said, "You want your stick back, asshole, march in there and get it."

He started away, trying to fight down the rage boiling inside him, but George Schmitt called after him with a voice now so raspy it was nearly unintelligible, "Hey, wait a minute, man. We can still make a deal. Six hunnert bucks and he's yours."

Sheehan stopped, turned again. "It'd cost way more than that at a hospital to have six hundred one-dollar bills surgically removed from your ass."

And he moved on.

It was too long a drive back to Vermillion without a drink or two to clear Brock's head, he thought, believing a few pops helped some think better rather than turning them into obnoxious drunks. On Cleveland's west side, he found a little Irish bar on Madison Avenue. He thought he'd been there once or twice during his Gaelic Society days, and sat on a stool at the far end of the bar away from everyone else, ordering a Bushmills Black Whiskey, neat. It wasn't as special as the Tyrconnell at Eddie's bar, but he was more used to it. It was better sipping whiskey than some of the other Bushmills varieties that were more often than not mixed with something else.

His rage at George Schmitt took longer to subside than he'd thought. Maybe he was an animal lover, too, just like Linus, but it had taken him almost sixty years to realize it. Dejected that he hadn't hurt Schmitt nearly enough, he sighed, an opportunity gone forever. Maybe when this was all over...

He heaved a sigh—devoutly to be wished.

He thought of Linus's vanilla innocence, and his unpleasant girlfriend who was halfway out the door without him being aware of it. He wondered how he could help. He wasn't in law enforcement, he was no private eye, and after ten years' absence, he hardly knew anyone in Cleveland anymore. He'd been crazy to agree to solving his nephew's problem.

The family stuff remained—the bond he could never put behind him, no matter the dysfunction that drove him away in the first place. It's not just an Irish thing, he knew. It was also an Italian thing, a Jewish thing, a Chinese thing, and hundreds of other ethnic "things." Having not seen nor heard of Linus Callahan since he'd been an ungainly pre-teen made it seem easier for Brock Sheehan, as Linus had been too young to turn his back on him and decry him as the family black sheep.

Something else bothered Sheehan, too—something he'd said to Linus that was a veiled threat: "I don't negotiate."

He'd said it more than once in his experiences, but the one time that stuck in his craw was when he sought out Charlie O'Malley more than twenty-five years earlier.

Charlie O'Malley was deeply involved in a political setup, created by Rory McCurdy to keep important local Irish politicians in their jobs. Writers and editorial commentators on TV and in the newspapers were bribed to convince people the way McCurdy wanted them to vote. If not bribed, they were threatened. So were the political opponents, quietly enduring a humiliating election without opening their mouths while watching McCurdy's favorites skate over the top during the November balloting.

But Charlie's problem was that he was about to be busted and imprisoned for something that had nothing to do with the McCurdy plan—a fraud involving, of all things, funerals. Charlie was told by the district attorney, whose cap had been set for the breaking up of the Gaelic Society and the ruin of Rory McCurdy in order to be tapped to run for the governor's seat, that his criminal record could be wiped clean, and he could walk away unscathed if he turned the tables and ratted on his best friend.

Charlie O'Malley sang like an Irish tenor crooning "Danny Boy" at a St. Patrick's Day blowout.

Almost immediately, Rory McCurdy was arrested and indicted, and after spending a great deal of money, and with the brilliance of his attorney, Gowan Scully, who made McCurdy seem like the finest Ohioan—the most generous, thoughtful, and kind—the trial jury flipped, making McCurdy completely innocent of all charges, causing Charlie O'Malley to come off looking like a goddamn fool.

There was a ten-month cooling-off period after the hoo-hah had faded from public interest. But Rory never forgot. The memory gave him daily acid reflux, caused him to drink more at Eddie's Place, and mainline fistfuls of Tums. When the time seemed right, he gave an assignment to Brock Sheehan, who dutifully went looking for Charlie O'Malley.

Charlie was on his way to a Sunday mass at St. Colman's church, walking cheerily along West 65th Street on a snappy November morning. He and Brock had known each other forever, so Charlie's greeting was friendly. But when he moved forward to embrace his old friend, he was instead rendered unconscious by one fist blow that traveled no more than six inches. Brock Sheehan knew how to throw a punch.

Charlie O'Malley didn't wake up until he was secured in the trunk of Sheehan's car—terrified, and for good reason—and driven into a large, forested preserve miles west of Cuyahoga County, between Elyria and Lorain.

There in the Sunday morning quiet, Charlie O'Malley begged. He pleaded. He sobbed and blubbered in terror of what might come.

"This isn't between you and me, Charlie," Sheehan told him quietly. "It's not a personal thing. You can't mess around with the Old Man. You're either his best buddy, his enemy, or a total stranger. Which one are you? You ratted on him, and he spent half a million bucks just to stay out of prison."

Charlie trembled, and for a moment Brock wondered if he

were going through an epileptic fit. "I was scared, Brock! Swear to God, the prosecutors were leaning on me—"

"I don't care, Charlie. Rory doesn't care, either."

Charlie's cries grew louder. He swore he'd leave town, even leave the country and return to Ireland so no one would ever hear of him again. He offered Sheehan all the money he had in the world—approximately $145,000 spread over three west side banks—to let him go peacefully.

He even—and this haunted Sheehan's mind for many years thereafter—he even promised to *give* him his own teenaged daughter, seventeen, and, he insisted, a virgin, to keep her with him for as long as he chose.

That's the first thing Charlie said that made Sheehan furious. He just said, "I don't negotiate, Charlie—and that's goddamn sick!"

Then he quickly and almost painlessly broke Charlie O'Malley's neck and left him behind a clump of bushes so no one would find him for some time—probably not until the hefty Ohio winter had come and gone and people visited the preserve again to enjoy the onset of spring.

Many wild creatures lived in that preserve—coyotes, foxes, raccoons, lynxes, feral dogs, and leafy trees full of omnivorous predatory birds, like crows, falcons, eagles, even turkey buzzards. By the following spring, there wouldn't be much left of Charlie O'Malley but bones.

Brock Sheehan drove back home in the autumn sunshine. He didn't feel guilty. He'd had nothing against Charlie O'Malley. He was just doing his job.

CHAPTER SIX

At first light the day after his dust-up with George Schmitt, Sheehan awoke with a hangover headache and a sharp pain in his on-again off-again ulcer. He brewed and drank half a pot of extra-strong coffee, showered cold, then set off on his furthest haul to help his long-lost nephew—heading down I-71 to Columbus, his GPS plugged into his cigarette lighter to tell him where to exit the freeway and what streets to drive on. Living in Ohio for his entire life, he barely knew Columbus at all. As far as he was concerned, there wasn't much to the city south of US 30, other than the state capital, a fancy neighborhood called Short North, and The Ohio State University.

The basketball enclave he searched for on campus is known as the Valley City Arena, named after the chain of cut-rate furniture stores created by Jerome Schottenstein and located in—surprise—the Jerome Schottenstein Center, which made Brock Sheehan think that if he had spare multi-millions, he wouldn't build an enormous sports complex with his name plastered all over it. Presidents do that, but sick people, needy people, hungry people, starving children—they all could use that monster amount of money.

Not basketball.

Since there were few cars in attendance on a weekday midmorning, he parked as close to the main entrance as he could, wondering if he'd even get one foot through the door before someone rushed at him waving a security badge and telling him he'd have to come back at night when the basketball team was actually playing a game. But no one bothered him as he wandered the corridors until he found the main hangout of the head basketball coach. A student secretary in the outer office explained that the coach was out of the area for the day, and asked whether he wished to talk with an assistant coach.

He did, though the student secretary's directions had evidently not been too clear. He walked around the complex for a while longer, even stumbling by accident into the main arena, usually crowded during a game but now, midmorning, empty, almost spooky as his footsteps on the court echoed off the bare walls. He stopped to glance at the seats right behind the OSU players' bench, reserved for the most fervent, vocal, endlessly loyal fans, and known far and wide as the Buckeye Nuthouse—almost but not quite as insane as the wild bedlam behind the goalposts at Cleveland's First Energy Stadium each pro football week, fondly referred to as the "Dawg Pound."

Assistant Coach Ralph Pursley looked as though he took care of himself. In his forties, with a high hairline and a healthy tan on his cheeks, his body was athletic, almost as strapping as the college-age guys he coached, and despite being not much taller than five foot ten, his hands were large and his fingers long and sinewy. He must have played a lot of basketball back in the day.

He had no secretary, so nothing stopped Brock Sheehan from marching right into his office to ask whether he could spare a few minutes.

"Sure," Pursley said, putting down the *Sports Illustrated* he'd been reading. The walls were covered with corkboard, and almost every inch of it had informational papers, charts, or news articles thumbtacked to it. "Can I see your press pass?"

"I'm not a journalist or a sports writer. I just need some information."

That took Pursley by surprise. "Oh. Well, we're not supposed to talk to anyone without a press pass."

"Who told you that?"

The coach cocked his head to one side, looking quizzical. "Jeez, I don't know. Seems like that's always been the rule."

"I'm not a spy from the University of Michigan, planning to steal away any of your players. I just need some simple information."

"There are sixty thousand students at this campus looking for information. I'm guessing you're too old to be one of them."

"Bingo," Sheehan said. "I'm checking around about a past student who played basketball here a few years back. Have you coached here for a long time?"

"Fourteen years. Is that long enough?"

"I think so. You coached Kenny Pine, right?"

Pursley's face lost most of its expression and he pursed his lips into an angry kiss. "Kenny Pine is dead."

"Everybody knows that." Sheehan looked at one of the chairs on his side of the desk. "Mind if I sit?"

Pursley took about ten seconds to consider it. Then he nodded.

"I'm writing a novel," Sheehan lied, slipping into a chair. "It's all about big-time collegiate sports. My main character is a college superstar who gets arrested right after his graduation, so when I heard about Pine, I figured I could get a little inside color to fill in some of the bare spots. The more personal stuff—like what kind of guy was he when he was off the court?"

"I don't know much about him when he wasn't playing," the coach said. "I never saw Kenny once after he graduated. I sure as hell didn't look him up after he got out of prison, and under the circumstances, he didn't swing by here to say hello to everyone—so there's nothing I can tell you."

Sheehan said, "He was more famous around here after his prison release than when he was dunking hoops."

"Because he's dead?"

"Partly, yes," Sheehan said.

"Well—*infamous* is more like it. He was a big important

campus star. He sure as hell deserved that, but Jesus! How humiliated were we, this university, by what he did with pit bulls." Pursley wiped his mouth with the edge of his thumb. "It's all been in the newspapers. Look it up in any library."

Sheehan shrugged. "I don't care about his numbers. I'm not a big basketball fan anyway."

"No?"

"I'm more interested in his life when he wasn't bouncing a ball."

Pursley shook his head. "I only knew him when he was in this building. He seemed a normal college student—with a big ego. He finished with a C-plus average."

"Did he have his own car?"

On either side of his face, where his jawbone intersected with the rest of him, Pursley's face twitched. "I suppose so. I never rode in his car."

"Where did he get the car?"

"I never asked him."

"There's a lot of gambling on college games, isn't there?"

"There's gambling, but that comes pretty much from casinos— from Vegas, or maybe Indian-owned casinos. As far as I know, no bets were laid on this campus in my memory—no big bets, the six- and seven-figure bets."

"No legal bookie gambling in the casinos here, or in Cincinnati or Cleveland?"

"I don't know. I don't get up to Cleveland very often. Cleveland's got its own rhythm, its own personality I've never been able to figure out. I'm just a Columbus guy."

"Columbus has its own rhythm, too?"

"My basketball team does, and that's pretty much all I know about. Look, there's also a lot of pinko commies getting an education here, a lot of atheists, fags and dykes, Baptist holy rollers, and people who'd revolt against the whole government and make our country a socialist commune if you gave them half a chance and a rapid-firing AK-15. But I don't know any of that shit. I'm a basketball coach. I do my job, cash my paycheck, and go home to my wife."

Pinko commies? In his head Coach Pursley could still be living in the 1950s. "Do you know anything about Pine's personal friends, coach—or his lovers?"

"All I know is he was buddies with the other guys on the team. I have no idea what happened to most of them, except maybe Cody Thacken. Now he's a publicist, I think, with Paiswell Electrics up in Cleveland. He wasn't near good enough to make it in the NBA, but he and Kenny were as close as anybody. Once they walked out of this building, I couldn't tell you what they did—and I don't care. Kenny averaged twenty-seven points per game, and eight rebounds, so that made him a pretty good friend to his coaches."

"None of you knew he ran a big-time dogfight farm in Mahoning County?"

Pursley looked shocked, as if this were the first time he'd heard of it. "We wouldn't put up with that! There are rules at this university. In our athletic department, too."

"And his girlfriends? Does the athletic department have rules against fornication during a season?"

"Oh, for fuck's sake, grow up!" Pursley glided back and away from his desk on the rollers beneath his chair. "Young athletes get laid. A lot. So do college guys who aren't athletes. You've gotta have your head up your ass not to know that. Testosterone, man—these young men lose their cool about it. It's almost like going for a walk in the hills and tripping over a gold mine. Hot-to-trot college girls drape themselves all over my boys all the time—after practice, after the games, both here and away. It's not just the big stars, it's everybody, even the ones who only get seven or eight minutes per game."

Something clicked in Sheehan's head. *Young athletes get laid a lot.* After some frustration, Coach Pursley had cracked open another door. "There's accusations of date rape on every college campus in this country," he said. "Including OSU. Did any of that involve Kenny Pine?"

Now Pursley was on his feet, angry. "I didn't ask about his sex life while he put on his jockstrap!" he snapped. "I read the sports pages—period! I check records, strengths and weaknesses of other Division 1 school teams. I cruise local high schools for players who might fit the OSU program!" Louder. "I coach basketball, and when boys graduate, I don't see them again unless they happen to live around the corner! Kenny Pine graduated from here and went directly to prison!"

Sheehan stood, too. "After he left prison, he went directly to the Denver Nuggets. How many of your basketball guys go on to the NBA?"

"I don't keep track! Gone for good basketball players is not my job!" the coach sputtered, leveling a trembling finger at Brock Sheehan. "Get the hell out of here and don't ever come back. Don't go sucking around other coaches, because I'm letting them all know what a shit you are. Whatever you're getting at, you ask pretty lousy questions about a man who died a few days ago and hasn't gone to school here for three years."

"Thanks for your time anyway, Coach Pursley. Sorry my 'pretty lousy questions' pissed you off so much."

He turned to leave, but the coach's loud voice stopped him. "Okay—now I've got a question for you. You said before you aren't much of a sports fan. Why then, I wonder, are you writing a novel about collegiate sports?"

"For the same reason," Sheehan said, continuing out the door, "some people write hard-boiled mystery novels in which characters get killed, when in real life they don't even lift their ass off the chair to swat a mosquito."

The late morning was brisk and crisp when Sheehan left the arena, a snappy breeze mussing up the hair of strolling students and teachers, blowing various hunks of paper up and down the streets. The campus foliage was turning riotous colors of bright

91

red and vibrant yellow and orange, a day making one think of hot cider and pumpkin pie. Autumn had taken up residence at The Ohio State University, which meant more than almost anywhere else in the world except New England, but frankly no leaf-peepers gave a goddamn at the moment. Fall was football time—the storied Buckeyes fighting to be the best team in the country. Saturdays were sacred here in the fall months, especially the last in the regular season when the Ohio State Buckeyes butt heads with the University of Michigan Wolverines, a rivalry more revered than the most solemn Jewish observance, Yom Kippur, the Day of Atonement, which is another High Holiday much of Columbus ignores, especially when the Bucks are winning.

After leaving the Value City arena, Brock Sheehan noticed two female students sitting on a bench, wrapped in heavy wool sweaters and working feverishly on their open laptops. He rolled down his window and asked if there was an office nearby that handled sexual complaints on campus.

One of them said, "Why? Are you planning to confess?" The other one giggled.

He was amused, too. "You must be one of the drama majors."

"Hardly. Electrical engineering. Planning to bust that glass ceiling."

"Good for you," he said, giving her a thumbs-up.

"You're looking for the Title 9 Coordinator," she said.

"What's that?"

She shook her head. "Too complicated to explain, but she's always the first one who hears about—well, you know. Sex abuse."

"That sounds right."

She directed him toward a building at the far end of the campus. Unsettled, he headed for an interview that would be awkward. In his adult life, he'd been mildly uncomfortable being with women, even Arizona Skye at the beginning. That didn't count Detective Sergeant Tobe Blaine, of course, who'd walked onto his boat uninvited, as if she were a raiding pirate.

The small office didn't have anything on or next to its door to identify itself. The woman, who presided there like a territorial warlord, sat behind a desk whose nameplate identified her as Sasha Burton. Unhappy at Sheehan's unexpected visit, she wasn't thrilled dealing with a man—any man. In her sensitive job, she listened to sexual abuse complaints every day. African American in her late thirties, she was overweight, wearing a hairstyle looking as though she cut it herself.

The meeting began badly. Sasha Burton was visibly annoyed that he hadn't phoned for an appointment, and downright angry he was neither a police officer nor a journalist, but apparently some freakazoid who got his rocks off talking about sex and rape. Sheehan recalled several arresting Cleveland police officers treating him more pleasantly.

He lied to her, too, that he was writing a novel, but her cynical downturned mouth let him know she wasn't buying it. "When strange men walk in here wanting to talk about sexual abuse on this campus, I invite them to leave in one hell of a hurry and go jack off somewhere else. Get the picture? I'm busy."

"I won't take up more than two minutes of your time. This book I'm writing is all about an athletic college VIP who was just released from prison and got murdered. I was hoping you'd help me with a little background."

Shock was written all over her face. Not many OSU athletes go directly from graduation to prison, so she knew he meant Kenny Pine and his dogfight conviction. The Ohio State was anxious to put the entire event behind them, and no one ever mentioned Kenny Pine's release from prison, nor the high-paying gig with the Denver Nuggets that he didn't live long enough to earn.

"How stupid do you think I am?" she snapped. "You've got some nerve asking about one of OSU's top athletes, especially one who's just passed away."

Passed away. Sheehan always thought that a ridiculous way to refer to the recently deceased. Why didn't people just announce that he or she died? "Like getting-your-throat-cut passed away?" he said.

"I had no use for Pine—or his teammates, either, like Barry Dalmont or Cody Thacken—two other shits just like Kenny. Still, nobody deserves to die."

"Lots of people disliked Pine, too—but good or bad, he was murdered."

She shuddered at the sound of the word. "I don't want to talk about that!"

"Ms. Burton," he went on, "I'm not really writing a book. I'm looking for justice for Pine's death. He's killed dogs. That's a fact. He also lived illegally, and high on the hog on the coattails of OSU alumni, which is also against the law, though nobody will prove it. His rat bastard reputation might mean he was involved in something sexually illegal on campus, and OSU tends to hush up things about their athletic demigods like this so no one ever hears about it."

"I don't hush anything up," she said, but it came out a whine.

Sheehan sat down without being invited to. "This is your area of expertise—following up on rape and sexual abuse of under-class women here, and probably a few male students, too. The volume must overwhelm you every day. All I want to know is if Kenny Pine's name ever wound up on your desk."

"I couldn't tell you that if I wanted to," she said. "I'd get fired—and OSU would take half a century to live it down." Her hand went to her heart as if pledging allegiance. "I love this school. I've spent half my life here. Like any other university, it's interested in protecting its—brand."

That last word hit Sheehan where he lived. It also jangled him thinking of what Sasha Burton had said: *I couldn't tell you that if I wanted to. I'd get fired.*

She probably did want to, but Sheehan doubted she'd ever talk about it, because OSU, like nearly every other college in the nation, worried about its brand. He said, "Someone close to me is being hassled by the cops as Kenny Pine's possible killer. He didn't do it, so I want to find someone else the police can investigate. I've talked around, but so far, no help. If you point me in the right direction, I'd really be grateful."

Sasha screwed up her mouth, thinking, examining him. At length she said, "I'm not sure what you're hinting at—but you look like a man who could rip somebody apart with his bare hands. Is that really what you're after? I won't help you kill anyone."

"My killing days are over," he said, hoping Sasha took it as a joke.

She shook her head. "This is an interview, if that's what you're calling it."

"Sexual abuse and harassment happens here a lot, which is why there's an office like this, and you in it. You can't give out information. I get that. All I want is a simple yes or no: did Kenny Pine's name ever wind up in your files?"

Her frown deepened, and Sheehan noticed the subtle tightening of her lips. She didn't answer for about fifteen seconds. Then: "I'm sorry, Mister, but you're outta luck."

"Why?"

"Because," Sasha Burton said with open nastiness that took Brock aback, "my job is more important to me than your ass."

Sasha Burton's non-information was as telling to Brock as if she'd spilled her guts out. Kenny Pine had been involved with a rape while busy being an OSU superstar and hanging losing dogs by the neck until they were dead.

Ms. Burton had also answered his question even while protecting the university's "brand." Kenny Pine had taken unfair advantage of a young woman.

Brock stopped into a crowded delicatessen for a take-out lunch—a Polish boy swimming in Stadium Mustard, which he was glad to see somewhere other than Greater Cleveland, accompanied by sweet potato fries, and a chilled bottle of iced tea. He ate while resting on a bench overlooking the Olentangy River, running through the campus before it's absorbed into the Scioto River. Why, he wondered, had the state of Ohio given its main rivers names, like Cuyahoga, Scioto, Olentangy, and Maumee, that no one can pronounce?

He thought about Pine's final years, slowly becoming hated or at least distrusted by almost everyone: animal lovers, gamblers, and rape survivors. Only basketball nuts seemed to think he walked on water.

Sheehan wished Linus Callahan had never discovered him in Vermillion, or that he never offered to help. Now it was turning into a big deal—and he'd avoided big deals ever since he departed Cleveland. A quiet, peaceful life was what he lived now, though it had taken time to become accustomed to the peace. No danger, no drama—just tranquil retirement.

Now he was sticking his neck out, tiptoeing through mine-fields he'd never known existed. Was his nephew that important to him?

He ate the last of his fries, washing them down with the rest of his bottled tea. Yes, he decided, Linus *was* important to him—because Linus was the son of Sheehan's dear departed sister, and that made him a relative. Rory McCurdy and his Gaelic Society were related to him as well, and now, despite difficulty already experienced talking to people who didn't give a damn about him, and what might become downright perilous, he was feeling a peculiar warmth—a reminder that after long lonely years, the idea of family was starting to comfort him again.

He deposited his lunch detritus in a trashcan, found his car, donned sunglasses, and headed through midday traffic to the nearest branch of the Columbus Public Library.

Asking one of the librarians to help him, as he was a Luddite when it came to computers and tech, he managed to figure out how to connect with the back issues of the *Columbus Dispatch*, and zip through much of the local news that happened three, four, and five years ago.

During that period, he found eleven articles regarding OSU on-campus rapes. Seven of the stories identified the rapists, six of whom were fraternity brothers, and one a maintenance employee. The students had been expelled, two arrested and now doing time. The janitor disappeared before being caught by the police, and no one knew where he was. The other villains not identified had skated free.

There was no newspaper identification of ten of the victims, which Sheehan thought a good idea. Rape was disastrous; being identified at a young age so the whole world knows about it forever is a living death to all but the most courageous of the wounded victims.

Victim number eleven's name, though, was printed in the paper. Three and a half years earlier, Meredith Oborn, a nineteen-year-old political science junior from Akron, had suffered torture-rape and humiliation at a booze party, too intoxicated to say no—or to say anything else. After six months of intense therapy, she waited until she was alone in her parents' home and hanged herself.

The name of the rapist, also an OSU enrollee, was not identified in the newspaper.

Sheehan stared at the screen without really seeing it. There must have been ten times as many rapes and sexual abuses on campus during that three-year period, but none were reported or investigated. In today's bizarre world of blame, the female victims were often assigned the fault. They drank too much, their clothes were too revealing or too tight, or they were too busty, wore too much makeup, or else were just too damn pretty. According to locally elected legislators, to some clergy and to those who believe all white males have inalienable rights that were offered to no one else, the crimes were often blamed on the survivors, not the rapists.

Rape without blame, he thought?

97

Suicide?

Most disturbing, though—no mention whatsoever of the malefactor's name.

CHAPTER SEVEN

Maureen Flanagan was tired—but at the end of a working day, most people are. Checking the office wall clock, she noted it was 4:40 in the afternoon, less than an hour until she could put her job away and head home. She wasn't looking forward to it. Who, she wondered, would be thrilled to share home and bed with a man suspected of cutting open someone's throat?

Linus Callahan was an okay kind of guy, she had to admit, and not too bad in the sack, especially during their early months together. She didn't think he murdered Kenny Pine or anyone else—but if the police believed he did, it made her want to be as far away from Linus as she could. After two years, the twice-a-day sex had dwindled down to once per week or so—almost as if they were married. Plus there was that huge, smelly, slobbering dog, Patton, who slept at the foot of their bed, snoring and moaning all night! She swore Linus loved that animal more than he loved her, as dogs were more important than sexy women. She raged at winding up in second place.

Staring at the minute hand moving at a snail's pace on the wall clock, she decided it was time to start looking for another place to live—and another person to live in it with her. Since she'd turned sixteen years old, there had always been a boyfriend in her life, one who came running at a phone ring or a finger snap—but she never stopped looking around, and another male was always "warming up in the bullpen," in case the current man of the hour grew dreary.

The apartment she shared with Linus on Clifton Avenue on the near west side of Cleveland in a building occupied mostly by the elderly wasn't all that terrific. Her gray-haired neighbors had moved from homes they found to be "too big" when all the children left the nest. Besides, in her mind, old people smelled bad, their apartments stank worse, and some of them farted in the elevator. She could say little to them beyond a curt "Good morning." She missed a neighbor close to her age to huddle with, giggle, gossip, and say terrible things to each other about their current lovers.

Finally, she left the office. She really wanted a cocktail or two at a nearby bar, but Linus would arrive home before her— wound almost to the breaking point after a grilling by a tough homicide cop—and demand to know where she'd been, who she'd been with, and why she didn't get home on time. There would be trouble a-plenty—and Maureen was in her mid-twenties, a time for fun, experimentation, for thinking about what lifetime career lay ahead of her. Twenty-somethings don't want trouble.

When she let herself into their apartment, Patton seemed overjoyed to see her, leaping up on her before she had a chance to change her clothes, drooling on her skirt and pantyhose. She pushed him away harshly with her knee, wondering why dogs seemed to like everyone who didn't like them. Cats are different— and much smarter that way. If someone disliked a cat, the animal will know it, and cat-haters will be hissed at, ignored, or clawed.

She helped herself to a beer, sipping it while she changed into her stay-at-home outfit—jeans and a T-shirt. When the doorbell rang, she frowned. Linus had a key. He wouldn't ring first, and she was not expecting visitors.

Patton following her so closely she almost tripped over his big feet, she looked through the peephole at a well-dressed woman of color in the hallway she'd never seen before. Her nerves jumped. She had few acquaintances; those she didn't know made her nervous. It was stupid, but she couldn't help it. Many who swear they aren't racist—in between insulting remarks about black people—but she couldn't imagine why a black woman was ringing her doorbell.

"Yes, what is it?" she said through the closed door.

The visitor held up a badge to her side of the peephole. "Detective Sergeant Tobe Blaine, Cleveland police."

Maureen gasped, chewing skittishly on her lower lip. Police! Why was a police officer standing in the hallway now? She hadn't done anything wrong—or she hoped she hadn't. Would she go to jail? The very thought terrified her. With a trembling hand, she opened the door.

"Ms. Flanagan?" Tobe Blaine said. "Hi. May I come in?"

The young woman was too frightened to answer. She just blinked, her breathing becoming heavier. Not quite a panic attack—yet.

"Don't worry, I'm not here to arrest you. I just want to talk."

Relieved, Maureen managed to say, "Linus isn't here."

"That's okay. I came to see you."

"Me?"

Blaine's smile was false as she moved through the doorway without being invited. "You were at the bar Sunday night when your boyfriend and Kenny Pine had some words together. I've talked to the bartender and a few other witnesses, but you were right in the middle of it, so I want to hear your side."

Patton sashayed over to Blaine and sniffed her wherever he could, especially her crotch. She patted and stroked his neck for a bit, and he quivered and happily shook himself all over. Pit bulls are big, tall, and strong, but only true dog people realize they loved to be loved. Others are certain a pit bull would tear you to pieces and eat the good parts without a thought in the world. "Good boy," she said, moving to the sofa. "May I sit down, Ms. Flanagan?"

Maureen hesitated.

"You don't have to talk to me," Blaine said. "You can tell me to get the hell out of here if you want to, and I'd go. But you're not in any trouble—and you can help me out and maybe help your boyfriend out, too. What do you say?"

"Well—I guess it's all right. Uh—go ahead, sit down. Want something to drink? A beer, maybe?"

"On duty, thanks—and I'm no beer-drinker." Patton followed Tobe to the sofa and lay down across her feet, and she had to admit it felt good. "Now, about Sunday night," she said. "Tell me in your own words what happened."

Maureen's mouth was dry. She took a big swallow of beer but it didn't help much. Licking her lips, she told the story from the very beginning, when Kenny Pine walked into that saloon and everyone made a fuss about him.

"Linus and I were at the far end of the bar," she said, "so he got to us last."

"How did you feel about Pine? I know how Linus felt, but what about you?"

The girl crinkled up her nose. "I dunno. I don't like anyone hurting animals—but damn! He was hot!"

"Hot?"

"Sexy. You know."

"Yes, I know what hot means. And then he squeezed your breasts?"

"No. Linus got pissed off because Kenny Pine put his hands on my shoulders; he was standing behind me, you know? And his hands were so goddamn big they nearly reached down to my nipples. But he wasn't doing anything dirty like you wouldn't put on television. Then he kind of asked me to go someplace with him so we could—be alone."

"Did you try to pull away from him?"

Maureen's cheeks turned bright red. "Um—no, not exactly."

Tobe Blaine leaned forward, a leopard ready to strike. "You *enjoyed* having his hands on you?"

She remained silent for almost half a minute. Then she said, "Like I said, he was really hot."

Unsurprised, Blaine leaned against the sofa back. "You

would've had sex with Kenny Pine if Linus hadn't been with you?"

"Well, damn, man—he was a celebrity! Just about anybody would fuck a celebrity if they had the chance."

"Don't call me 'man,'" Blaine warned. "Then Linus got furious over your attitude and pushed Kenny Pine. Maybe he *did* hunt him down the next day and cut his throat."

Maureen Flanagan's cheek blush suddenly faded to chalky white. "He'd never do anything like that."

"Nobody wants to kill—until they do." She crossed one leg over the other. "Did you meet Linus's uncle?"

"Just for a minute. He was rude—not wanting me in the same room when he talked to Linus. I'm his girlfriend, for crysakes! I sleep with the guy every night!"

"You're his girlfriend, Ms. Flanagan—but Brock Sheehan is *family*."

Maureen pursed her lips and dropped her head, difficult for her to even think about the home in which she was raised. Her mom was a full-time non-medical executive at University Hospital, and when she was thirteen years old, her father had run off with a much younger woman. Her only brother was nine years older than she, and they didn't have a real connection. She and Linus never spoke about it, but the Sheehan family was apparently much different than hers.

"Maureen, do you know anything about Brock Sheehan? His background, what he's all about?"

"I only met him that once, for about two minutes. If I never see him again, that'll be okay by me."

Before Tobe could ask another question, a key turned in the lock. Linus Callahan appeared in the doorway, stunned to see he had a visitor. She looked at him, a slight smile at the corners of her mouth, badge hanging on a black ribbon from the lapel pocket of her jacket. It made the backs of Linus's hands tingle in fright.

All he could think of to say was "Hi." Patton immediately

jumped up to greet his master, tail wagging.

"I was just about finished here." Blaine stood. "Interviewing another witness."

"I still say I didn't do it," he finally stammered.

"Is your Uncle Brock still on the job?"

"He's just asking questions. He's not bothering anybody."

"How much do *you* know about him?"

"Nothing." Linus was still at the door, keys in hand, as if afraid to come further into his own apartment. "I haven't heard anything about him for the last ten years."

She nodded. "And before that?"

"Before that," he said, "I was a little kid."

Troubled, Tobe wished she could tell Linus about Sheehan's suspicious past—but her heart told her that wouldn't be right. She also wished to tell him his girlfriend would have fucked Kenny Pine in a New York minute if he hadn't been there—but that was none of her business.

After the homicide detective left, there was silence, neither Maureen nor Linus moving. Finally, he put down his keys and walked toward her.

"Hey, baby," he said, putting his arms around her, aiming a kiss toward her mouth. But she turned her head at the last second, and all Linus got was a mouthful of red hair.

Brock Sheehan was on his boat, sated from fusilli he'd boiled to *al dente* and then covered with Newman's Own Marinara pasta sauce—did that movie actor really invent marinara sauce?—accompanied by sliced mushrooms, and Orlando Italian bread from a storied Cleveland baking company which he'd picked up a few days earlier to sop up the extra. Now he was back on deck, his usual evening spot, drinking. The wind off the lake was cool, and he'd donned several layers to keep him warm enough, but icy weather drew near, and it might be time to put his boat in dry-dock and head somewhere more temperate for winter, because Cleveland often begins with snow in October—or once in a while, even in September.

Despite global warming, Northeast Ohio winters were always difficult to handle. Until he was in his mid-forties, Sheehan struggled through every one of them. Now he felt he'd *earned* his winters in the sun in a place that had never even seen snow.

Earned by strong-arming people who owed Rory McCurdy money, who dared to attempt taking a piece of Rory's empire from him for profit, and beating them half to death. In one instance, Rory had instructed him: "I want the sonofabitch's hands and fingers broken so bad that he'll never be able to wipe his own ass for the rest of his life."

That was a Rory McCurdy no-argument edict, to be unquestionably followed. Sheehan had done it—but it had been a difficult moment for him.

Under Rory's direct orders, he had also disposed of two godfather wannabes—one completely disappearing and never to be found anywhere. One death was an accident, as Brock Sheehan hadn't wanted it that way, but he'd hit the victim so hard that it rattled his brain badly and sent him into a major stroke from which he never truly recovered, and he died nine weeks later.

Is that how one earns warm and snowless winters?

He'd never felt personally culpable about what he did for McCurdy. It was a job. Dog catchers, pest control workers, even butchers hacking up hunks of meat that hours earlier had been a living thing never feel guilty at what they do for a living. Just one more way of earning enough to pay their bills, like truckers or librarians or short order cooks.

He'd felt contrition about the one whose stroke he caused with a bone-crunching punch. The guy recuperated in hospital and was walking around okay, but by the time he went back home, he'd become incapable of doing the simplest things, like cutting a sandwich in half or tying his shoes. He often forgot words he'd known all his life.

Being a natural belly-puncher, it had been one of the few

times Brock hit anybody above the neck, though with the more violent cases he did some serious bone breaking. His crushing smash to the side of the head disabling Brud Kerwill had become necessary when Kerwill—almost as big as Sheehan and twice as snarky—chose to fight back. When he lost consciousness, Sheehan feared he'd killed him. Leaving Kerwill's home, he waited until he was ten blocks away before he called 911 to ask for an ambulance.

When Brud finally woke up in the emergency room of Metro Health with oxygen flowing up his nose from a plastic tube stretched across his upper lip, he swore he couldn't remember what happened to him. But he knew—and was wise enough to keep his mouth shut.

Sheehan was halfway through his third drink when Detective Sergeant Tobe Blaine showed up on the pier next to his boat. He was startled. In their two previous meetings, he found himself liking her—as much as he could like any cop. But those old feelings from danger days still haunted him, and he wished she wasn't coming after him on a chilly fall evening when he was on his way to a pleasant drunk.

"I hope I'm not bothering you when you're busy," she said, "although you don't look busy to me."

"It's getting dark out," he said. "Don't you cops ever sleep?"

"When cops get to a certain career point, there aren't any *hours*. It's twenty-four seven—especially when a murderer is walking the street."

"I haven't murdered anyone."

"Not recently." She took one step forward. "May I come aboard? You can tell me to go screw myself if you want to."

"How could I be rude to someone who's driven here all the way from Cleveland?" He stood and moved to her. "Watch your step now," he said, offering her his hand as she stepped onto his boat. "Can I fix you a drink?"

"On duty."

"Pardon the expression, but—bullshit! You're on duty every

minute of your life so you never ever have a drink anymore?" He pulled another chair over opposite his. "Don't worry, it's not one of those Bill Cosby drugged cocktails—just good whiskey."

"Bill Cosby, huh?" Blaine pondered him for a moment, trying to decide if the Bill Cosby and drugged cocktails remark coming from an advance middle-aged Irishman was racist. She decided not. "Oh, what the hell. Make it a small one—I have to drive back."

"Really?" he said, bringing a second drinking glass to the little table beside his own chair. "You're driving back tonight? You mean you're not hitting on me?"

"I'm involved elsewhere," she assured him, "and your sarcasm makes you a bad boy."

"Maybe—but not a lizard lounge." He gave her the glass and the bottle. "Pour whatever you want so you won't think I'm trying to get you drunk."

She spilled less than one finger's worth into her glass. "No ice. I drink neat."

"So do I," he said, and they clinked glasses. "We're joined at the hip now, right? Best friends forever."

"In a pig's patootie." She tasted her drink. "Nice whiskey."

"Well, what else do we have in common?"

"Not much," Blaine said, "I'm a woman and you're a man. I'm black and you're white. I'm a cop and you're a criminal."

"Criminal? Is it a crime to sit on the deck of your own boat and drink?"

"I found out about your infamous past."

"How did you do that? Ouija board?"

"You don't have the internet programs cops do," Blaine said. "You probably don't know your own history."

"I don't need a computer, Detective. I lived it."

"Arrests up the kazoo, Mr. Sheehan—four of them on suspicion of murder."

"Up the kazoo, but no convictions. Never a trial—not even one."

"That means either you're a goddamn saint, or you have one hell of a lawyer."

"My hell of a lawyer died a while back, and nobody told me about it."

"You were a leg-breaker for the Irish mafia, weren't you?"

"I was employed by the West Side Gaelic Society," he said, "but I don't remember breaking any legs."

"Bad memory?"

Sheehan put down his drink. "Sometimes people survive because of bad memory. You move into another time, another lifestyle, and you choose to forget. That's what I've done, Detective Sergeant. Otherwise you drive yourself crazy—remembering things."

"Cops can't live like that—forgetting. You bust your balls investigating a murder case, and you're this close." She held thumb and forefinger less than an inch apart. "The prime suspect is arrested and in custody. Good squeal! You sleep—and in the morning, your bad memory kicks in, you don't remember what you found out yesterday, or even what you had for dinner. Then the bad guy walks on a technical, probably to kill again. What the hell kind of life is that?"

"It's *my* life."

"Then why are you looking for answers so your nephew stays out of prison?"

"I don't know why I got involved—but Linus is the only kin I've got."

"Or maybe," she said, "you're bored living all alone in an empty shadow and not remembering yesterday." She cocked her head. "True?"

"What's the difference?"

"The difference, Mr. Sheehan, is that now I know what you were, even if you don't remember. And that means you back away from the Kenny Pine murder. This is my case. I don't need somebody like you getting under my feet."

"I'm just asking questions—seeing if I could save Linus."

"It's not your job," Blaine snapped. "It's mine. My significant other is a private investigator. Every time he gets involved in a case that's on my desk, our relationship gets shaky. I don't put up with it from him, and damned if I'll put up with it from you." She stood. "So you're out of it. Stop asking questions and bugging those you don't even know. Don't get in the way of cops who stick their necks out every day to put bad people away." She leveled a red-tipped finger at him. "People like you."

"It's not illegal to ask questions," Sheehan said.

"Really? Have you ever littered in Cleveland? Spit on the sidewalk? Jaywalked or drove your car even two miles over the speed limit? Scratch your ass in public? If you do, I'll lock you up somewhere with a three-hundred-and-eighty-pound guy who likes calling his cellmates 'Rosemary' and then forget where I put you."

"You drove all the way out here just to warn me off the Kenny Pine murder?"

She shrugged. "I had no choice. I couldn't find your phone number."

"Then get off my boat," he said easily, "before I cast off, sail all the way out into the middle of Lake Erie with you and let you swim home."

Blaine turned her body slightly in her chair and lifted the edge of her jacket to show Sheehan what she always wore around her waist. "Not that easy. I have a weapon."

"No problem," he said, almost smiling. "I could take it away from you."

She raised one eyebrow. "Are you still that tough?"

"I'm out of practice—but it's like riding a bicycle. You never forget how." He actually winked at her. Then he said, "A question?"

"You just exiled me from your boat."

"Yeah, but before you go—can I still come into Cleveland if I don't ask anybody questions? Or maybe just drive through there on my way to somewhere else?"

"You don't even have a record, and you damn well know it. So I can't do a thing about you in Cleveland."

Silence hung between them, almost visible. Then she turned to the plank preparing to get onto the dock. "Thanks for the drink."

"Any time. Just one more thing."

She sounded annoyed. "This is turning into a long Jewish goodbye."

"I'm just wondering, Detective Sergeant, who it was that got in your ear in the first place that I was hanging around asking a lot of questions?"

She started moving up the dock toward where she'd parked her car. Looking over her shoulder as she walked, she said, "Mind your own business, Brock Sheehan."

CHAPTER EIGHT

It had been a long morning for Linus Callahan. When the shelter staff had arrived, they found on their front doorstep a produce box containing five black kittens barely three weeks old, and had to figure out what to do with them besides feeding them milk through an eyedropper. They were babies, and someone had dumped them. It upset Linus more than dealing with other stray or feral creatures. Cruelty to animals was loathsome to him. Oh, well, he thought—the kittens were lucky at that. Animal-haters would either drown them or throw them into a Dumpster to starve.

At fifteen minutes before closing time, he made the rounds of the pens where the stray dogs and cats lived, stopping to look in on the kittens and passing a few words with Patti Korwin, the girl who also worked there and who'd volunteered to spend the night at the shelter looking after the newborns, feeding them milk every two hours. Pretty and blue-eyed, she attended Cuyahoga Community College, planning to advance to a four-year college to become a veterinarian. She told him she'd spend this long night catching up on her homework.

Linus always enjoyed talking to her—a young woman whose conversation, no matter how banal, was always generously laced with smiles and excitement. He suspected she mildly flirted with him, and he did give it some thought—but he was already "taken," i.e. unavailable. Still, he spent a few minutes longer

111

chatting with her than was necessary.

Before leaving, Linus spent the last moments of his workday in the dog kennels, taking extra time to talk to and pet the ones who were the most broken, including those unceremoniously thrown away by their "loving" owners because they were too old, or the family just had a baby, or caring for dogs was too time-consuming. Some dogs had spent two years or more caged at the kennel, and while workers there made a special effort to feed them treats, take them for walks, and bond with them, dog imprisonment in a roomy cage was no more than benevolent captivity.

At length, Linus headed home. His Maureen love affair had drifted into something much less wonderful in the past seven months or so, and being suspected of a crime that could land him in prison for the rest of his life wasn't helping any. Linus didn't know if she'd been with her officemates at a place where they often hung out after work, Panini's, or with a new or about-to-be-canonized boyfriend who'd replace him in her life very shortly.

At this point he didn't give a damn.

After having a beer and realizing nothing in the refrigerator could make a decent meal, he decided to go out for dinner by himself—and because those working in animal shelters usually don't smell very good, he showered first, then put on clean clothes and headed for an eatery he liked, The Root Cafe on Detroit Road—a post-hippie restaurant, very much like the latter-day beatnik hangout, Tommy's, on Coventry Road in Cleveland Heights. Most customers looked as if they'd read Jack Kerouac's *On the Road* when it was first published in the 1950s. A woman with tarot cards commandeered a front table, as she often did, telling fortunes. Linus ate dinner there frequently alone, as it wasn't Maureen's kind of place.

He wondered if their shared apartment was still Maureen's kind of place, too. When he'd met her, he'd been blown away by her sexy good looks—but after two years he'd come to realize there was little love there, and never had been. At the beginning, lust was the order of the day, but things change over time. If this relationship proceeded with its spin-dive to finality, he wouldn't be upset about it. Life goes on—except it would be nice if someone close could support him besides his own Uncle Brock. What worried him was whether Maureen would move out of that apartment, or would he?

And if he did move, would it be to a newer, nicer apartment— or to a state prison for the rest of his natural life?

He sat in The Root for an hour after he'd finished dinner, drinking coffee and looking at all the interesting people. Several attractive women came and left, but most were tattooed like drunken sailors, or had piercings and metal accouterments all over their faces that turned him off. Mostly he just sat.

Finally he zipped up his jacket against the brittle breeze coming off the lake, and made his way to his car parked on a side street, thinking he really wanted another beer or two. There was plenty at home, but he didn't like drinking in solitary. He didn't hang out in bars much anyway; sitting in a local tavern, he'd be even more alone in a crowd.

Besides, he wouldn't want to run into Maureen by accident if she were drinking with another guy. It would be too much for him in one night—too much.

He headed home, about a mile east of The Root Cafe.

He pulled into his assigned space in the long row of open garages on the side of his building, next to Maureen's. Her car was there. Good, at least she was home. It was nearly eleven o'clock. Getting out of his car, he saw three men leaning against the fence on the other side of the driveway. The one on the left, with long, shaggy hair that fell across his face with each move, was whip-thin, wearing heavy, clumsy-looking boots that probably slowed him down a step or two. On the right was a bigger man, unshaven, and balding at the crown despite his youthful appearance. The one in the middle, his hair in a Man-bun, pointed at Linus and said to his companions, "Yeah, that's the guy." They looked at each other and nodded. Pushing themselves away from the ivy-covered fence, they started across the concrete, almost moving in slow motion.

Linus didn't recall seeing them before, though Man-bun seemed vaguely familiar.

Clumsy Boots growled, "Are you Linus Callahan?"

"That's right."

"You motherfucker!" Man-bun clenched a fist. "You killed Kenny Pine!"

"You're crazy!" Linus said as they advanced toward him.

"You cut his fuckin' throat!"

"I never touched him!"

"I seen you touch him right in front of me."

Linus realized why he looked so familiar. "You're the bartender!" he said. "From Sunday night!"

"You started shit with him in my bar, and one day later he's dead."

"I pushed him! And you guys had to hold him back—not me."

"Cuz he woulda killed you, faggot!" Clumsy Boots said.

And then they were on him.

Man-bun's blow was aimed at his head, but Linus managed to sidestep far enough that it landed on his left shoulder instead, and his entire arm went numb. Clumsy Boots grabbed the other arm, and the third skinny guy drove his fist into Linus's stomach.

Pain overwhelmed him as he gasped, trying to suck air into his chest but unable to do so. His knees buckled, and Skinny smashed into his gut again, bending him over at the waist and then straightening him with an uppercut to the chin.

Linus bit the inside of his cheek very hard with the blow, and his mouth filled with blood. His chin was cut open, too.

Still, he was able to lash out with his foot, missing the genitals of Clumsy Boots but hitting the top of his thigh instead. Man-bun's kick cracked his other leg at the knee, and Linus went down. Fists and boots pummeled his head, face, chest, back, and legs, breaking two of his ribs with a sickening sound, making it even harder to gasp for air. He tried covering his face with his hands, and a solid boot crushed his ring finger. Profane insults showered down upon him as they punched and kicked, but he didn't really hear them. His pain threshold was reached—and crossed.

To Linus, it went on for hours, but only lasted about ninety seconds until they stopped. As they moved away one of them— he thought it was Man-bun—snarled, "Stay outta downtown, motherfucker, or you get more of the same. Murderer!"

One final kick, this one to the head, and then they were gone.

He lay there, half conscious. His chin and forehead were freely bleeding. He'd have a puffed-up black eye in the morning, and his damaged cheek would undoubtedly swell to the size of a ping pong ball.

His upper right eyetooth was gone. He wasn't sure whether he'd spit it out or swallowed it.

Every inch of his body hurt. After he'd gone down, most punches and kicks had landed on his back, shoulders, ribs, and stomach. The pain made him feel unreal, trapped in a bad-fantasy nightmare from which he couldn't awaken. He remembered reading that someone with a concussion should not go to sleep for a while, so he fought to keep his eyes open. He was nauseated, the shattered ends of his broken ribs grinding against each other. He didn't believe he could walk on his damaged knee for very long. The final kick, just above his left ear, had split open his scalp under his hair—and nothing ever bleeds quite as voluminously as does a scalp.

Linus wondered how long he'd have to lie there before someone else pulled in the driveway to park their car in one of the garages—but most of his neighbors were elderly, usually tucked away in their apartments by late afternoon, unless they went out to the early bird dinner at a nearby restaurant to get the senior discount. He was also unsure whether any of them could lift him.

He tried a few times to get back on his feet, but excruciating pain kept him down. Eventually, realizing he couldn't just lie there forever, he crawled the short distance to the brick wall between the garages and slumped, half sitting, waiting, wondering— *hoping*—someone would eventually notice and help him. He was not in enough control to use his cell phone.

He stayed there for more than half an hour, aching anyplace on his body that could ache. At last he was able to drag himself to his feet, unstable and weak in the knees. Clutching his broken ribs with one hand, he managed to get into the building and like a garden snake climbing a rocky incline, he wriggled up the stairs using elbows and the one good knee. He somehow found his way to his apartment and, still down on the smelly hall carpet that hadn't been vacuumed in a month, he knocked on the door, hoping Maureen had not yet gone to bed.

No answer, but he heard Patton bark loudly as though he were in another room and not in the living room. Even through all his injury, that bothered Linus. Was Maureen shacked up at this very moment with some new guy in their own bed and locked Patton in the bathroom? Hurting more than he could have imagined, he dug out his apartment key and unlocked the door.

All he could hear from the bathroom was Patton yelping, barking, and clawing at the closed door to get out. But Linus couldn't get there to release him at that moment.

Maureen was not in bed, but lying on the living room floor, blood dripping from one corner of her swollen mouth, one eye bulging over a very bruised cheekbone, and she was more than half unconscious. Her blouse and bra had been roughly torn off, and her left breast was bright pink, as if it had been slapped several times. Her thong panties had been hurled across the room, skirt raised above her hips. There was blood between her spread legs on the carpet beneath her crotch area. The only part of her moving was her head, rolling back and forth in rhythm with her moaning, which came from deep within her chest. It was the worst sound Linus Callahan could ever imagine.

* * *

The doctor in the emergency room at the Cleveland Clinic stepped back and looked at his latest patient. Linus Callahan's knee was in a brace. Three busted ribs were bandaged tightly to keep them in place. His finger was almost skinless, and in a splint. A small patch of hair behind his ear had been shaved to show sixteen visible stitches, and there were eight more stitches on his chin, closing both wounds that had drenched his shirt and jacket with blood. A butterfly bandage affixed to his forehead kept the wound from separating and causing a permanent scar. He was injected with enough painkillers to mellow out a rhinoceros.

He asked about Maureen's condition, but all they'd say was that she was resting comfortably and would sleep for the rest of the night through early morning.

"Well," the cheerful doctor said, "I'm glad you're going to live." Emergency room doctors were always cheery because they were not the ones badly injured, getting novocained and sewed up, and even Super-Glued to avoid a scar. "Make an appointment with an orthopedic surgeon about your knee, ASAP. You're a young guy, Mr. Callahan, you don't want to limp for the rest of your life."

Linus just nodded. There wasn't much else he could do at the moment.

"I'll get you a wheelchair."

"Doe wan' wee chair," he sputtered around the stitches on the inside of his cheek.

"Just to take you to the front door. Hospital regulations."

He sighed.

A few minutes later a nurse arrived with a wheelchair and insisted he crawl into it, piled dressings and bandages on his lap, tucked pain prescriptions in his jacket pocket, and rolled him down the hallway into a slow-moving elevator, and then to the lobby.

He hated it. Sitting in a wheelchair made him feel and *look like* an ancient, washed-up human being who had given up total control—and him not yet a quarter of a century old. His mouth was a razor-thin slash across his face, and he stared straight ahead, hoping no one would notice him.

Linus hadn't seen Maureen since they were both battered and broken. She was close to comatose and he had to call the EMT squad.

Bitterness in his heart hurt far worse than the physical injuries. Too recently he had come to terms, if only in his head, that his relationship with his redheaded lover was creaking slowly toward its end. The latest disaster was probably the finale.

Once back home, he had to strip off and throw away all his clothes because they were ruined, totally blood-soaked. He was too frightened to take a shower and loosen all the bandages and dressings stuck on him by the ER doctor, so he cleaned himself off as best he could with a washcloth, struggling to keep awake despite the pain meds. He slipped on clean boxer briefs and a T-shirt, and fell into bed sometime after three o'clock in the morning.

He awakened at seven thirty, his body on its way to healing, though his emotions were destroyed. Where was Maureen? Still hospitalized? Doubly enraged with the three men who beat him and raped his lover, he would easily have cut all their throats, just as someone had done to Kenny Pine—but he didn't own a knife other than the six steak knives he kept in a kitchen drawer with all his other silverware.

He felt no grief over Kenny Pine's death. But would he have killed him if he'd had the chance? Not hardly. In the bar, he'd only pushed him. He'd had fistfights as a kid, but when he'd turned eighteen, his fighting stopped. Fighting was for children.

He was a guy who couldn't quite jump-start his day without hot coffee—but drinking with his mouth stitches was excruciating, and his insides ached too much to be hungry.

He lurched into the living room and sat on the sofa with great difficulty, trying not to look at Maureen's bloodstains and torn clothing all over the floor he hadn't the energy to pick up when he first got home. He'd have to call someone in to clean the apartment. Would he have to replace the entire carpet, and would the landlord pay for it?

Patton, the pit bull, realized his master was not in good condition, so he simply lay across the room and looked soulfully at Linus, making sad noises deep in his throat.

The broken ribs and busted knee hurt Linus every awake second. Sitting and standing was now torture. He tried to watch the morning news on the station that had the prettiest women at the news desk, but even they couldn't keep his eyes open, and he dozed for a while until a cooking show with blasting opening music jerked him upright. He checked the wall clock—it was a few minutes past nine. He'd be late to work, but his pain told him there'd be no work today. His mouth was cotton-dry as he considered Maureen wouldn't be returning to her job for a longer time than that, too.

He took the phone from the side table and punched out the number of the animal shelter where he worked. It took five rings before his boss answered.

"Dave," Linus said. "Fucked up here. Can' come in today."

"You've gotta come in," Director Dave said, his voice raspy and highly strained. "We're short already, Linus. Didn't you hear what happened here last night?"

"La' nigh'? Uh-uh."

So Dave told him.

CHAPTER NINE

Brock Sheehan cursed under his breath as he drove all the way from Vermillion later that morning to Linus Callahan's apartment just west of the Cuyahoga. His phone had rung a few minutes past nine when he was still enjoying his morning coffee. He didn't get calls this early—rarely got calls at all. Obviously, his nephew had something important to tell him, but he couldn't understand a damn thing he'd said over the phone. After four minutes covering one ear to block out the harbor sound and trying to decipher what Linus was telling him and why he sounded as if his lips had been glued to the wall, he said, "Why don't I just come over to your place. You'll be there, won't you?"

"Uh-huh," was all he got.

So he dressed quickly, covered most of the deck and cabin with enormous blue tarpaulins and locks, and headed west, stopping for a full tank of gas and grabbing a tasteless pastry to keep him going.

When was it, he wondered, gas stations started selling sweet rolls and cinnamon buns? It had never been like that when he was a kid, or even a young adult. Gas stations sold gas. Oil. Candy bars and chewing gum—not stale sandwiches, desserts, and coffee. The world changes every day.

Driving east, the morning was sun-bright, and coming back west in the afternoon would be the same. Brock had four pairs of sunglasses in his car, and a few more back at the boat, so he picked out the darkest one to shield his eyes.

There are many places in the country, he thought, where sun glare isn't much of a problem. He'd been to California where the sun shone all the time, but it didn't seem to bother other drivers. Maybe at Cleveland's North Coast of the United States, the angle of the sun in late autumn caused more of a problem than in, say, Florida. That got him to thinking about winter approaching, and where he'd spend the next few months, somewhere much calmer and less hysterical. Perhaps Tucson.

Arizona.

And then Arizona Skye flashed across his memory—raven-black hair, the softest mouth, and the bluest eyes he'd ever known—the only woman he'd ever really loved. He wondered for the ten thousandth time where she had gone when she left Cleveland—maybe somewhere in the Wild West that had suggested her first name to her parents—the state in which he'd pretty much planned to wait out the Ohio winter.

The second-in-command, Brock Sheehan, was hanging around one early afternoon at the West Side Gaelic Society because Rory McCurdy had been called downtown to discuss with the county prosecutor—called the district attorney almost everywhere else in America—a real feud between the west side Irish and the Italian mob on the east side's Little Italy that had come to frantic fisticuffs and throwing of bottles and chairs two nights earlier in a venerable Flats seafood joint known as Fagan's. Several people were taken to hospitals; as it turned out, the Irish wound up at Metro Health on West 25th Street and the Italians were sent to the ER at Cleveland Clinic on the east side.

When the outside doorbell rang, it startled Sheehan. People didn't wander in and out of that place unless they had keys—or if they'd been invited. He checked the monitor showing videos of everyone coming and going, and saw an attractive young woman, and a man with a portable camera strapped around his neck and carrying a large light and a metallic suitcase that probably held a sound system. Behind them a van marked with the logo of Channel Twelve in downtown Cleveland was illegally parked at the curb.

What the hell were they doing here? Brock wondered. Someone's making a movie and no one told him about it? He went to the front door and opened it.

"Are you in the right place?" he said.

The woman answered, "We're in exactly the right place," and pushed by him. He felt her shoulder as they brushed together, and smelled the shampoo scent in her black hair—and while he normally let no one in by surprise, he certainly didn't want to kick this woman out without getting to know her.

"I'm Arizona Skye," she said, handing him her business card. "Channel Twelve reporter. This is my field producer, Andrew Lemmons."

Lemmons, a young black man with horn-rimmed glasses, just nodded—he had too much camera and sound equipment in his hands for a shake. "Hey," he said.

She looked around the outer office and pointed to one corner. "Andy, you want to set up over there? Make sure we can see the desk and some of the Irish crap they have hanging on the walls."

"Irish crap? Really? What is this all about?" Brock demanded. Ordinarily he'd get tough right away, but just looking at her stopped him, something deep inside his chest where his heart was.

"There was a riot at Fagan's Restaurant in the Flats on Saturday night," she said, "which I'm sure you're aware of. We want your take on it for the six o'clock news."

"I wasn't there."

"I don't care. What's your name, anyway?"

"Sheehan."

"Is that a first name or a last name?"

He felt his fists tightening. "Brock Sheehan."

"Okay, Brock Sheehan—would you mind sitting at the desk for me?"

"I mind like hell."

"*Why? Don't you want to be a TV star?*" *Arizona grinned.* "*Well, I guess not. If you wanted to be a TV star, you'd be a TV star.*"

He spotted that as a flirt. Whether a sincere flirt or a sneaky one, he didn't know. "*Are you offering me a job?*"

"*An unpaid job—just for this afternoon.*" Arizona took a compact from her purse, opened it, and checked herself in the mirror. "*Think I need a comb before I go on air?*"

"*You look beautiful just the way you are, Ms.—*" He looked at her business card. "*Ms. Skye.*"

"*Stow the flattery, Mr. Sheehan,*" she said, moving so Sheehan would turn his back on Lemmons setting up his equipment. "*What is it you do around here, anyway?*"

"*I throw local TV news crews out on their asses.*"

She chuckled. "*I'm not that easy to throw.*"

"*I'll remember that.*"

They chatted aimlessly for a few minutes until the video man was ready to go. She asked Lemmons, "*Do you think Mr. Sheehan needs makeup?*"

The video guy squinted through his lens. "*Maybe a little powder.*"

"*I'm not wearing any goddamn powder!*" Sheehan said.

"*Don't you want to look prettier?*" Arizona's hand moved to his face. "*Just a little bit around the mouth, here.*" Her fingers moved softly over his lips, and he tried not to show how that made his stomach flip.

"*I'm not a ballet dancer, Ms. Skye,*" he announced, "*and I'm as pretty as I want to be. Look, Rory McCurdy is the boss around here. Why don't you talk to him?*"

"*McCurdy is downtown at the county prosecutor's,*" she said, "*and another Channel Twelve crew is waiting for him there. I just suggested we talk to someone who isn't such a big shot.*"

"*Well—I'm a pretty big shot, too. Not as big as Mr. McCurdy, but—*"

"*Shh, shh, save it for when we're on the air.*"

"*I don't want to be on the air!*" Sheehan said emphatically.

"*I want you on the air, though—big handsome hunk like you.*" *She gave him that flirt look again, and then she grew serious.* "*We're not trying to embarrass you. But two nights ago there was a big blowout at Fagan's, with punches thrown—and bottles, too. Blood was spilled, and local people want to know about it. I've never been there—but I wouldn't want to get caught in a mini-riot. What started the fight? Were there bad feelings between the Irish group and the Italian group?*"

"*This is an invasion,*" *he muttered.* "*I'm a prisoner in my own bailiwick.*" *He slumped into a chair behind the desk, and Andrew looped a lapel mike around his neck.*

"*Count to ten,*" *Andrew said.*

"*Just to ten? So I don't have to take my shoes off to count?*"

"*It's a sound test, sir.*"

"*Mr. Sheehan,*" *Arizona said.* "*Be nice when we're taping this interview. If you're not, they'll just edit out everything except you being mean to me.*"

The flush of warmth in his chest and stomach made him almost smile. Almost. "*I could never be mean to—ah, forget it.*"

"*We're ready,*" *she said. Andrew Lemmons flipped some switches and a bright light went on, making Sheehan squint. Peering through the eyepiece on the camera, Andy announced,* "*And you're on!*"

The interview was short and to the point. Arizona Skye knew how to get subjects to talk openly, and within a minute, Brock Sheehan was telling her and the Cleveland TV news audience that there was never a problem between the Irish and the Italians, just as there was no animosity with any other ethnicity.

"*But people drink sometimes,*" *he said,* "*which makes them careless with what they say. I wasn't at Fagan's, but from what I was told, some guy drunkenly said something about someone else's wife, a punch was thrown, and—friends stick up for other friends. So things got a little crazy. A few black eyes came out of it—maybe a loose tooth or two—but it was nowhere near a riot. And don't think it was the start of a war between the*

Cleveland Irish and anyone else." He shrugged, smiling for the camera. "By next week, if these guys see each other at Fagan's, they'll have forgotten the whole thing, and probably buy each other drinks."

When it was all over, Sheehan had to sign a release sheet, and when he handed it back to Arizona he said, "You should get a real look at Fagan's. Let me take you there for dinner."

She cocked her head. "Are you hitting on me, Mr. Sheehan?"

"What was your first clue?"

"I get hit on constantly," she said. "That's what happens to TV newswomen. There are people who think television personalities actually visit their homes every day. Dozens of phone calls at the station, gifts, flowers, even love letters—some of them really gross. Men are creeps."

"Where do you meet men, then? At church?"

"I don't date very much."

"Well—Fagan's isn't much of a date place. Let me take you somewhere really nice. Giovanni's."

"I've been there."

"Johnny's Downtown, then," he suggested, "or anywhere else you want to go—and I promise to be a complete gentleman and keep my hands to myself."

"Forever?"

"For that evening, anyway."

She thought about it. "Well—I guess you're not really a sleazeball. So—"

"Eight o'clock tonight?"

"Tomorrow night at eight o'clock," Arizona Skye said. "Because the day after that is my day off."

And that was the beginning.

Brock parked outside his nephew's apartment building and headed up the walkway, hoping he wouldn't have to deal with the redheaded girlfriend again. He couldn't figure out why Linus had been unable to speak on the phone so that he could understand him. He punched the Callahan-Flanagan button until he heard Linus's voice through the door. "Yeah?"

"Brock Sheehan."

A harsh buzz sounded and he climbed the stairs to the third floor. He was taken aback when the door opened and the battered, bruised and limping young man waved at him to come inside. "My God, Linus," he said.

Linus turned his hands palms upward at his sides, as if that were to be the high point of his communication.

Brock sat on the sofa. "Someone beat the shit out of you." It wasn't a question.

Back in his active days, Cleveland cops beat up suspects, too. Never Sheehan, of course, because the police were too frightened of him and those he worked for. The Irish Gang, as it was called, was similar to the Italian mob, when they had more good friends in blue uniforms than not. But times had changed. Besides, today no cop would beat a suspect so badly that he limped—at least not a *white* suspect.

He said, "You better get yourself a cane of some kind, or you won't be able to walk to the john. What happened? Talk slowly, so I can understand you."

It took Linus half an hour to get through his story; Sheehan stopped him often, asking for repetitions, but the nephew left out nothing, including what happened to Maureen on the same night. Sheehan leaned toward him, better to understand him and interested that one of the men who'd attacked Linus was the bartender from the tavern in which he'd butted heads with the late Kenny Pine.

"I'll go kick the shit out of him," Sheehan said.

Linus shook his head as vehemently as he could, considering every movement sent pain spreading throughout his body, and said "Way! Way!"

It took a few moments for Sheehan to figure out he meant, "Wait."

Then Linus said, "Is more."

126

And he told him the rest of the story.

At about eleven o'clock the previous evening, Patti Korwin was disturbed at her studies by a loud banging on the locked front door of the shelter. Three young men, the obvious leader wearing a Man-bun and carrying a baseball bat, were outside demanding to be let in, despite her repeatedly telling them through the glass door that the shelter was closed and locked, and they'd have to come back tomorrow.

Man-bun said they wanted the home address of another employee, Linus Callahan. She told him the rules forbade that, but if they came back in the morning, Linus would probably be there.

But Man-bun wouldn't wait any longer, aiming his baseball bat at the vitreous door. It took five powerful swings until the glass cracked down the center, at which time the other two men kicked it in and entered the facility. The noise, shocking in the middle of a quiet night, caused a thunderous barking and howling from the dog area.

After the first swing, Patti ran back into another room with locks on the door, and dialed 911. When the intruders finally got inside, they smashed in the inner door, too, knocked the cell phone out of her hand and stomped on it. They asked her again for Linus Callahan's home address, and when she refused, Clumsy Boots backhanded her brutally across the face, sending her to the floor.

Man-bun said, "Tell us where to look for it or you're gonna be sorrier than you ever dreamed."

Patti Korwin was too shocked to answer for a moment. Then, out of her bleeding mouth, she said "No."

Clumsy Boots, who had hit her the first time bent down and did it again. Then the three began beating her very badly around the face and midsection until she was half-sentient on the floor.

At last finished with her—it was no fun to beat on her if she wasn't awake to know about it—they searched the other rooms, ripping them apart until they found the director's office and rifled through all the file drawers and the desk until they discovered a spiral notebook containing employees and volunteers' names and addresses. Making a noise more like a bear's grunt, Man-bun ripped the page out of the book and stuffed it in his jacket pocket before they left.

It took the captive dogs in the other room another twenty minutes to calm down and stop howling—but the shelter was nowhere near a residential area, so no one heard them anyway.

Patti Korwin stayed unconscious for several hours. Eventually she half awoke, one eye completely swollen shut, bloodied around the face, and the whole upper half of her body aching, but at length she managed to crawl across the floor to the nearest landline telephone to call 911. It took the police forty-five minutes to get there, since the crime had already been committed, and another twenty minutes until an ambulance arrived to take her to Metro Health, the closest emergency room.

The torn-out pages contained the name and phone number of Director Dave, so none of the cops knew who to call for several more hours, although one patrolman was left on duty at the shelter to prevent anyone else from breaking in.

When Dave finally showed up in the morning, he found the shattered glass door carelessly boarded up by the police. The five black newborn kittens, not been given milk or water since eleven o'clock the evening before, had all died of starvation.

Brock Sheehan listened quietly until the end of the story, noting Linus Callahan's difficult speech got easier to understand than when he started. Nonetheless, he was stunned by what Linus and the completely innocent Patti Korwin had endured, and by the rape of Maureen Flanagan.

"This," he finally said to Linus, "is a bigger problem than you being Detective Blaine's 'person of interest.'"

"I know."

Sheehan stood and paced the living room, stopping to look

out the window at a busy four-lane street, mostly residential, that was rarely quiet from sunrise to sunset and even beyond, and he thought to himself that his choice of a peaceful harbor town like Vermillion was the best move he'd ever made.

Then he turned back to Linus. "Are you okay?" he asked.

"Not gon' die fum a beating." The young man shifted painfully in his chair. "Bu' might feel crappy for a mont' or tho."

"You're young," Sheehan said, "and tough. You'll recuperate. I have things to do before I get you off the murder hook."

"I'll be in prison before that."

"Don't worry. I'll be back on your case before you know it." He stood and walked to the door. "For crysakes, get some sleep. Do you have Tylenol?'"

"I think tho—and Percothet."

"Then use it. Keep in touch by phone. I'm still—working for you."

"I can' thank you enough, Uncle B'ock."

"I told you, stow the 'Uncle Brock' shit."

Sheehan went downstairs and climbed into his car, wondering for a moment what he would do for the rest of the day. No point in going back to Vermillion—not when he'd have to return to Cleveland that night anyway.

Then he figured it out.

It was past noon, and he hadn't had breakfast yet. He drove over to West 65th Street, a few blocks north of Detroit Road, and had a big lunch at the Stone Mad Irish Restaurant. One reason he preferred Cleveland restaurants was that there were few Irish pubs in Vermillion where he lived. There weren't that many in Cleveland, either, but his mother had "cooked Irish" almost nightly—even corned beef and cabbage on holidays and wakes which replaced the usual boring Protestant turkeys and hams.

After his meal, he found the nearest library.

When in Columbus at the university library, he'd found a mention of the suicide of a rape victim named Meredith Oborn in the local paper, *The Columbus Dispatch*, and not a single word in the *OSU Daily Gazette*. Now here, just blocks from the West 117th Street borderline between Cleveland and Lakewood, Brock pored through the microfiche of *The Plain Dealer* and the *Akron Beacon Journal* for news stories of Meredith being raped and, later, taking her own life. There was not much in mid-Ohio papers—only that the rape occurred at a festive party in a house frequently used by the university's sports teams for meetings or celebrations.

Damn! He guessed that if any basketball or football players were involved, it made sense that Kenny Pine was somewhere in the vicinity, too, and if he were really the rapist, his sudden death might have been pure revenge, even if it were three years later.

It was now three o'clock in the afternoon, and Brock had hours to kill before that day's mission would be accomplished.

On his smart phone he zeroed in on the address he planned to visit later that night. Then he searched until he found an inexpensive motel in Lakewood. His next stop was a Lowe's hardware store not too far from the library, in which he bought several rolls of duct tape, clothesline wire, and a bolt cutter. In a nearby CVS, he acquired a box of surgical gloves along with a legal-sized yellow pad and a cheap Bic ballpoint pen—paying for them in cash.

He checked into the motel, stripped to his underwear, and set the alarm clock on the bedside table for ten o'clock that evening, not trusting any motel clerk to make a wake-up call. His sleep came quickly; he'd learned years earlier to fall asleep just about anywhere, even on a bus, train, or plane, in any kind of chair, lying on a hard floor or a lumpy ground outdoors. This time, though, he knew he'd get very little sleep.

When the subtle alarm beeped at ten, he sat up, wide awake, then jumped out of bed and splashed cold water on his face and neck. Catching a glimpse in the mirror, he shook his head sadly. He thought he'd removed himself from this particular lifestyle, but things do happen sometimes—and he saw in his reflection the hard eyes, the forward-jutting jaw, and the aggressive and angry mouth all indicating he was reverting back to being a bad guy.

Redressing, he took his hardware purchases out to his car. Not hungry enough to make a full restaurant stop, he found a Giant Eagle supermarket and purchased three "energy bars" and ate them as he drove. The manufacturers boasted that they tasted like candy, but he found no similarities, though the bars left him slightly less famished.

Once in downtown Cleveland, he looked for the parking lot closest to the bar where Linus Callahan and Kenny Pine had their first and only meeting.

Eventually Sheehan entered the just-off-Public-Square saloon, stopping inside the doorway to check out the groups, quickly ascertaining he was the oldest person there. Boy-girl couples huddled at tables, a few more groups of younger women at the bar, and a smattering of lone males looking around almost furtively, deciding if any signals looked erotically promising or inviting. The music playing sounded nothing like Sheehan had grown up listening to, and he couldn't decipher the lyrics even if he tried.

He found a seat at the end of the bar near where the Man-bun bartender worked, and ordered an Irish whiskey, neat. "How's it going?" he said to the bartender.

"Hangin' in there, as usual." The answer was pleasant enough, but there were younger sleazebags further up behind the bar to discuss the relative size of the breasts of the women in attendance, so conversation began and ended rapidly and Sheehan was left alone, only signaling when ready for another whiskey.

He drank quietly, as he frequently did when alone on his deck. He'd never been a stumbling drunk in his life, though he often found himself vaguely buzzed. He made eye contact with no one, in case he'd be remembered.

Sheehan's two drinks turned into three, until at 1:45 a.m. the bartender bellowed "Last call," and customers hurried to order their final drink of the evening. Brock sipped his slowly for ten minutes until the next cheery announcement: "Time to go. Suck 'em up and get the hell out of here," and to everyone's dismay the brighter lights clicked on, and everyone could actually see clearly whomever they were drinking with, tossed back their drinks and scrambled for the exit.

Brock didn't head for his car, but stood across the street in a doorway, slipping on a pair of inexpensive leather gloves. The neon beer signs in the tavern's windows clicked off, one by one, and twenty minutes later, the bartender came through the front door, locked it up tight, and headed for the same lot.

As he was bent over, opening his car door, Brock Sheehan came up behind him. "Hey, there, bartender," he said quietly, and when Man-bun straightened up, he threw one solid fist, weight and power beginning at his waist. His knuckles slammed into a lower jaw with sickening force.

He caught Man-bun before he hit the pavement, and throwing one arm over his shoulder, he guided the bartender to his own car as if he were assisting a drunk unable to function. He dumped him in the passenger seat, got in, and drove toward a building on the near east side he'd been in several times before, though not for the last ten years. It took him less than ten minutes to get there, during which his snoozing companion never opened his eyes.

It was a deserted old warehouse, just off Superior Avenue in the east thirties. Whatever had once been ensconced there had departed forty years earlier, so there was no sign anywhere— dusty exterior complete with illegal graffiti and an iron door no one could break into. Sheehan did have a key he hadn't used since he'd worked for McCurdy's organization, a key like others he never used but always carried with him on his overcrowded key ring, never knowing when, if ever, he might need them again.

Once inside, he switched on the only light still working in that warehouse—a one-hundred-watt bulb in the ceiling on the warehouse floor. Then he brought in the materials he'd purchased that day, setting them atop a dusty worktable. Rescuing Man-bun from the front seat, he dragged him roughly inside, locking the steel door behind them.

The guy was still unconscious, blood dripping from his mouth. Brock Sheehan quickly undressed him down to his bright red boxer shorts, and took off his work boots and white socks. Seating him in one of the chairs, he tightly fastened his hands together behind him with duct tape, then looped more tape across his neck, chest, and stomach, binding him to the back of the chair. A rope around his victim's neck connected to the leg of a heavy metal table close enough to make sure that any violent effort to escape might be fatal. Then he took off his own jacket, hung it on the back of another chair opposite him, and sat down, too.

To wait.

CHAPTER TEN

The bartender struggled himself awake forty-five minutes later, his aching head thundering like a kettledrum, the left side of his jaw swollen, a headache sending pain streaking through his neck and arms. He was shocked and confused to discover he was naked except for his boxer briefs. Even his shoes and socks were gone. Unable to move anything but his head and eyes, he could tell he was trussed up in a wooden chair in a dark, chilly place—and the temperature, just below sixty degrees, made his entire body shiver from the cold. Easily relaxing in a similar chair, a large man in shirtsleeves sat across from him, wearing leather gloves.

Their eyes met, the stranger smiling as though to an old friend, but the smile didn't go anywhere near his eyes. Man-bun was so frightened that he was almost paralyzed.

"Wakey wakey, James Janson," Brock Sheehan said. "I was afraid you were going to sleep for eight hours or so."

James Janson—Man-bun—closed his eyes tight, opened them again, and shook his head from side to side to clear his head, hoping he was having a nightmare and if he tried hard enough to wake up, the bad dream would go away. His brain rattled around in his skull, making the pain worse.

Brock Sheehan held up his hands. "You like my gloves, Jimmy? Snazzy, huh? This way, no matter what I touch, it won't leave any fingerprints." He stood up. "It's okay for me to call you Jimmy, right?" He pointed to Janson's clothes in a pile over against the wall. "You must be chilly. Well, maybe you can get dressed again later—depending."

"Depending on what?" Janson heard his own voice sounding as if he were four years old, high and fearful.

"Depending on your answers. How do you feel about that, Jimmy?"

"How do you know my name?"

Sheehan took the man's wallet out of his own pocket and opened it so it dangled. "Your driver's license is in here—pretty good picture, although it would've looked better if you smiled. Credit cards, too—MasterCard, Discover, Visa—but no American Express. Jesus, even I have one of those—a platinum one. And a condom in your wallet—like a fifteen-year-old boy?" He sighed in disgust, and pulled out a wad of cash—mostly fives and singles. "See, I didn't take your money, but I did count it—a hundred seventy-three dollars. Right? Tip money from the bar?"

"Who the fuck are you anyway?"

"Why you want to know, Jimmy? Writing a book?"

Now Janson got angry. "Untie me, goddammit!"

"Not just yet. You're taped. Duct tape—it never fails. I wrapped so many layers all over you, though, it'll take you until two weeks from Tuesday to get loose."

"What do you want from me, anyway?"

"All sorts of things. You and two of your friends sneak-attacked Linus Callahan in the dark last night, right?"

"Fuck you!"

Sheehan sighed. He crouched down so his face was inches from Janson's. "That was your one free shot, Jimmy. If you say it again, I'm going to rip off your left ear and make you eat it."

Already pale, Janson's face turned dirty gray, as though he hadn't been out in the sun for the last twenty years.

Brock Sheehan stood up straight, looming over him. "So let's start over, okay? Lying would be a big mistake—and a hell of a lot worse than lying to the FBI. Now—you and your asshole buddies beat up Linus Callahan last night, right?"

Janson wouldn't look at him, but mumbled, "So what if I did?"

"Three against one makes you a coward, doesn't it?"

"He's a murderer! He killed Kenny Pine—a goddamn great sports hero."

"A great hero who liked torturing dogs to death, which put him in the slammer for three years. But in this country everyone is innocent until proven guilty, correct? Linus Callahan is nothing more than a person of interest, so that means he's still walking around—or at least he was before last night."

Janson stuck his chin out as well as he could, being bound to the back of the chair. "I saw him start the whole thing, right there in my bar. I got a dozen witnesses who watched it happen."

"A push in the chest of a man twice his size," Sheehan said, straightening up again, "isn't quite the same thing as cutting someone's throat. So tell me—how did you find out where Callahan lived?"

Janson licked his lips, as he had no saliva left in his mouth. "I got my ways."

"Really? He doesn't have a listed number. So where *did* you get his address? From his credit card?"

"None of your bee's wax."

"Bee's wax? When were you born? 1948? Bee's wax! Jesus Christ." Brock Sheehan chuckled. "Is it also none of my bee's wax that you and your pathetic ass-buddies beat a young girl half to death to get Callahan's home address, and then gang-raped and sodomized his girlfriend in his apartment, just for the hell of it, and left her to bleed alone on the floor?"

Janson's entire face quivered, the complexion turning Ku Klux Klan white. "You—you don't know that."

"If I didn't know it, I wouldn't be here and you wouldn't be trussed up like a pig for the slaughter. So answer me. Are you or are you not a gutless, moronic rapist?"

"Fuck you!" Janson said again—just before Sheehan brought

his right boot heel down, very hard, on the top of his bare foot, hearing the bones snap loudly, even over the agonized scream.

Sheehan waited until the noise subsided a bit. Then he went to the table, put his hand inside the hardware store sack, and pulled out a bolt cutter. "I warned you, Jimmy, but you didn't listen." He clicked the cutter in front of Janson's face. "So now I'll have to cut off your ear—and shove it down your throat until you swallow it."

The terrified "NO!" went on for at least ten seconds—as long as a lonely wolf's midnight howl in the desert.

Sheehan filled his lungs with air before asking, "What are the names of the two men who were with you?"

Janson eventually stopped howling long enough to say, "I dunno."

Sheehan shook his head sadly. "Too bad." With his left hand he grabbed Janson's ear and clicked the bolt cutter again. "Okay, then," he said, and twisted.

Janson's ear felt as if it were on fire. "No! Don't—*please!*" he begged. "I'll tell you anything! Just—" He shuddered. "Just don't."

Without letting go, Brock demanded, "The names of your puke pals. Now!"

"Wait. Lemme—lemme breathe for a while."

"You have ten seconds," Sheehan said. "One. Two. Three. Four. Five. Six..."

"Okay okay okay!" Janson gagged and choked, trying to catch his breath. Finally he said, "Chuck Putka."

"Where does he live, Janson?"

"I dunno. I swear to God, he comes in my bar all the time, that's all."

"All right. Who's the second one?"

"Sandy—Sandy Homolka."

"Sandy? Really?"

"N-no. It's Sandor, I think."

"Another saloon weasel?"

"Naw. Him and me, we went to high school together."

Sheehan waited a few seconds more before letting go of Janson's ear. "Very good, Jimmy," he said. "See how much easier it is to tell the truth? Relax, now—and think about how lucky you've been. This'll only take a few minutes."

He went back to the table, sat down, and removed a yellow lined paper tablet and a pen from his sack. He thought for a while, his head tilted, clicking and unclicking the pen. Then he began to print block letters carefully, latex gloves making his handwriting difficult. Janson groaned, trying unsuccessfully to move his smashed foot, and wriggled himself as much as he could without strangling himself on the rope, but Sheehan paid him no mind.

He filled up one side of the paper, then got up and walked back over to Janson.

"I'm going to untape your hands so you can read this. Then you'll write in the names and addresses of your buddies, sign it with your full name—James, not Jim. Don't get cute when I free your hands—or it won't be just your ear I'll cut off."

"I won't do nothing. I swear to God!"

Sheehan took out his Swiss Army Knife and sawed through several thicknesses of tape on Janson's wrists. Then he handed him the tablet. "Careful with this. If I have to rewrite it, I'm going to be seriously upset."

"I'll be careful, I'll be careful," Janson blubbered, squinting to read the pad in the low light of the warehouse. His breathing grew heavy again, and more panicked as he read, and his hands were shaking like an elderly person suffering from a stroke. Finally he looked up. "I really gotta sign this?"

"You don't 'gotta,' Jim-boy—it's entirely up to you," Sheehan said, once more taking up the bolt cutter.

"No, I'll sign! I'll sign."

"Excellent judgment—and don't forget to fill in the names of your rape buddies." He waited as Janson did as directed, writing names and addresses of his two companions and signing his name across the bottom of the page. Brock then took the pad and pen away from him. "Nice big signature, too. Just like John Hancock."

"Who?"

Sheehan laughed. "Did you actually get through fifth grade? Ask somebody who'll share a jail cell with you who John Hancock was. Maybe he'll know."

"You ain't a cop!" Man-bun screeched. "You can't arrest me!"

He shook his head. "You're right. *I'm* not going to arrest you, Jim-boy." He put the pad, pen, and bolt cutter back on the table, loudly popped his knuckles, and slowly moved toward the terrified James Janson.

Officer Dennis Morgan's job for the past year and a half was to function as a guard in the lobby of the downtown Cleveland Police Headquarters during the graveyard shift, eleven p.m. to seven a.m. Boring as hell; during his tenure, no one ever attempted entering the lobby. The glass doors leading out onto the street— several inches thick and supposedly bulletproof—were locked at nine o'clock in the evening. There wasn't much of a reason for it. The entrance to the cop shop in which to make a complaint or ask for help or report a riot or a break-in or a violent crime was located around the corner and not where Morgan was assigned. There wasn't much to steal, anyway, as the whole lobby was brightly lit. The upper floors contain a city jail, the sheriff's offices, and the offices of the chief of police and the safety director. There were also courts of law, but according to most judges who preside over their fiefs like black-robed executioners, everything pretty much shut down at about three thirty in the afternoon. Dennis Morgan always figured judges were like members of the United States Congress—too much salary, too few working hours, and zealously wielding power to destroy an entire life with one pound of the gavel.

Morgan didn't like this duty, as he'd spent twenty-nine years and a hundred thirty-one days pounding his beat on foot, or later in a squad car with a series of partners, in the near-east side section once fondly called "The Roaring Third," as mob guys of various ethnicities hung out there in jazz joints and saloons during the twenties and thirties. In his lengthy and largely unexciting profession, Morgan had never drawn his weapon to point at another human being. Looking forward to a thirty-year retirement, he'd gained seventy pounds, mostly around his middle. Now, in the mostly silent night job, he half-dozed in a comfortable chair he'd liberated from a ground-level office, grateful for no longer having to run down an alley after a bad guy and losing his breath in the process—a whole lot easier for a man over sixty.

Besides, he'd married when still in his teens, and he and his wife stopped loving each other before he was thirty-five. It was not that he disliked her, but he shared with her only the certainty that the dazzling excitement of marriage invariably found a way to slither out of their home, their bed, and their lives. Now his wife had a decently salaried day job in one of the offices at University Hospital, so she was always out of the house when he was there, awake, and vice versa. After nearly a life-long marriage, they both found they enjoyed what little contact they had.

On this particular evening, he was watching an old Randolph Scott western on his smartphone. It was that, or all-night news and paid programs trying to sell him eyebrow trimmers or magical pillows for insomniacs. Sometimes on the night shift, his eyes would close whether or not he wished them to.

Then something jolted him upright—the loud honking of a car right outside the main doors. There was little or no traffic on the downtown streets in the darkest night, so any car passing police headquarters got his attention. A blasting auto horn really shook him in his shoes.

Looking out from the light into the gloom, he saw a dark

sedan—impossible for him to discern the make, model, or color, with only its parking lights on—slow down to a crawl. Then the front passenger door opened, and something large was dumped into the gutter, just beyond the sidewalk. From his angle, Morgan was unable to tell what it was.

The car roared away—and by the time the guard cop pulled himself out of his chair, crossed the lobby, and spent too much time fumbling at his belt finding the right key and unlocking the door, the driver might easily have jumped onto the nearest freeway and headed off in one of several different directions.

When he finally got the door open, he had to squint to see what had been thrown from the car—and a horrifying fright shot up his spine and through his nervous system. What if it were a *bomb*?

Dennis was no bomb guy. He feared if he got too close, it would explode, taking him—and most of the block—with it. He sucked in a ragged breath—but not much air reached his lungs, and he coughed hard.

He stood there for almost half a minute, staring out the door onto a dark sidewalk and deserted street until he got his feet moving again. He stumbled back into the lobby, relocked the door, and put in a call to the bomb squad.

Within ten minutes there were police officers shutting down intersections four blocks away in every direction. Three large men wearing bulky white suits, heavy gloves, and face masks like the villains in *Star Wars* movies circled closer and closer to the large object tossed from a passing car not slowing down enough for outside security cameras to capture the license plate numbers. Portable lights revealed the "object" as a human being, but whether that unfortunate person brought with him a bomb made them extra-cautious.

Dennis Morgan, however, had moved himself as far away from the door as he could, hiding against the wall in one of the elevator bays to protect him from most of the flying debris when the bomb exploded.

Finally a rangy African American man in a black trench coat with a police badge hanging around his neck and wearing latex gloves came around the corner of the bay and glared at him.

"Are you the one who called in the bomb squad?"

"Yes, sir," Dennis said.

The man sighed. "I'm Detective Pettigrew—from upstairs. Relax, Officer—" He peered at the nametag on Morgan's chest. "—Morgan. You're safe. It's no bomb."

Dennis sighed. "I'm relieved to hear that."

"Did you go out and take a closer look before you called the bomb unit?"

"I was too scared even to go outside."

"I see. Well, what you thought was a bomb was a—" He pulled a page of yellow foolscap from his pocket. "—a young man, unconscious, in only his red underpants, hands duct-taped behind his back and connected to his bent knees, like a hog. Barefoot, his jaw broken, his left foot smashed to bits, and gagged by stuffing his own sock into his mouth. But you called the bomb guys, huh?" Pettigrew shook his head sadly. "The only good thing I'm taking from this is that you're about five minutes away from retirement. Otherwise I'd put in a complaint about you first thing in the morning and get you the hell out of the police force for the rest of your life. Kind of a schmuck, aren't you, Morgan?"

"Me?"

"You threw this whole city into complete turmoil. Thank Christ it happened at four o'clock in the morning and not during a rainy day rush hour."

He handed the page of yellow foolscap to Morgan. "This came along with his driver's license—tucked away in the front of his underwear, so you might want to wash your hands afterward. Read it."

Embarrassed, Dennis Morgan took a pair of drug store reading glasses from his pocket and perched them near the end of his nose to read the childish printing.

I, James Janson, confess to the following crimes. Last night, after midnight, two of my buddies and me attacked, beat up and gang-raped a girl named Maureen, who's the girlfriend of Linus Callahan, at their apartment. We didn't plan to rape her—things just got out of hand. We found out who Callahan was from the cops who looked over our credit card slips from Sunday night after he attacked Kenny Pine. When Pine got killed, we got Callahan's address in Lakewood from his office where we beat up another girl. Don't know her name. Then we waited until he got home and beat the shit out of him too.

The guys with me who did all the same stuff I did were Charles Putka and Sandor Homolka. (The addresses and signature were added later, in a shaking hand.)

Sincerely yours, James Anderson Janson.

The name had been scrawled, not printed.

Sincerely yours? Dennis Morgan thought, and shook his head in amazement. What kind of a goddamn country are we living in, anyway?

Sincerely yours?

CHAPTER ELEVEN

After ejecting the slumbering James Janson from his car in front of police headquarters, Brock Sheehan was in no hurry to escape Cleveland, so did not head for the freeway, even though he'd carefully noted no one was on the street at the time when they might have seen him. Instead he drove the few blocks to Public Square within the speed limit, turned right to cross the Detroit-Superior Bridge, which is illuminated at night with bright blue lights, and went west on Detroit Road to reach his motel in Lakewood.

Thinking it over, he felt he'd done the right thing. He couldn't just march Janson into the police station himself, as he had actually tortured the confession out of him. That would have caused more problems than it was worth.

He willed himself to sleep at six a.m., and set the bedside radio alarm for ten o'clock. Four hours' sleep was not enough, but many people of advance age need less sleep than they once did. One of these days he'd allow himself eight or nine hours of shuteye to catch up. Not today, though—he had people to see and places to go.

It was Saturday, and many nine-to-fivers were home instead of at work. Sheehan showered quickly and went to the lobby lounge for the motel's continental breakfast—mostly toast, bad pastries, cold cereal, a large pot of oatmeal crusting around the edges, and plenty of coffee. Checking out shortly before noon, he managed to find an entry ramp to I-77, a freeway that would take him to Akron.

South of downtown, he passed the huge steel plant in Cleveland, which belched flames and gray-black smoke into the air every day. He couldn't imagine why anyone would choose to live just a block or two from the pollution, glad he grew up on the near west side. Driving, he kept his eyes forward, eventually exiting the freeway on Market Street in the crowded shopping district of Montrose and Fairlawn which mellowed into an upscale residential area becoming Akron, with a stretch of high-to-middle-class homes just above the street in a hilly, heavily wooded area. He checked his GPS again to make sure he had the correct address. Then he turned uphill onto one of the side streets.

On a corner where the street curved, the house Brock Sheehan looked for was large and modern, framed by a thick stand of oak, maple and black walnut trees. He pulled into the driveway, semi-circular with entrances and exits at both ends so no one would have to back out onto the street. Covered with autumn glories of colorful leaves dancing merrily in the snappy breeze, the spacious front yard grass was lush, probably needing another lawn mow or two before winter set in.

He parked, straightened his jacket, and headed to the short porch to ring the bell, then listening as footsteps approached. The door opened to reveal a casually well-dressed woman close to his age. Her graying hair was in a bun, and tired lines in her face tugged down the corners of her mouth. The sadness in her eyes was so profound that Sheehan couldn't see deep enough inside them. "Yes?" she said.

"Ms. Oborn?"

She nodded. "Yes, I'm Brenda Oborn. May I help you?"

"My name is Terry Molloy," he lied. He hadn't decided on a fake name until the door opened, and the only one he could think of right then was the *On the Waterfront* character Marlon Brando won an Oscar for playing. Great movie, he thought aimlessly—and that he'd better get his act together fast if he were to do much more of this investigating business. "I'm a reporter for the *Denver Post.*"

"Denver?" she said, frowning. "I've never been to Denver. Are you sure you have the right party?"

"Yes, ma'am," he said. "I apologize for bringing this up at all—but Kenny Pine, the basketball player from OSU, was murdered earlier this week, and—"

Brenda Oborn's skin tightened over her cheekbones and her eyes turned to narrow slits. "I have nothing to say about that man. I may never get over it. I won't talk about him—to anyone!"

"I'm just trying to find out if he was involved in—in what happened to your daughter Meredith three years ago."

Ms. Oborn's entire body shuddered. "It's old news," she managed to say. "Don't make me relive it."

While she spoke, a young man, no more than twenty, appeared behind her. Tall and athletic, his entire face was twisted in anger from overhearing the quick conversation, and his hands were balled into fists, raised high as though he were ready for an old-time bare-knuckle John L. Sullivan-type boxing match. "Get the hell out of here, whoever the fuck you are!" he snarled

Ms. Oborn winced. "Lloyd, watch your language!" To Brock, "This is my son, Lloyd Oborn. Mr.—?"

"Molloy."

"Mr. Molloy. We have nothing to say about any of that. We never met this person and we know nothing about him."

"Except he's dead!" Lloyd Oborn said. "Now fuck off!"

"Lloyd," his mother warned him again.

Sheehan had not expected such antagonism; there must be a pretty good reason for it—and he thought he knew what it was. He said smoothly, "Ms. Oborn—Kenneth Pine had just signed a multimillion dollar basketball contract with the Denver Nuggets. Sports fans, and everyone else, are shocked by what happened to him, and want to know who committed such a brutal murder. So my editor sent me to Ohio to dig up some background information. I certainly don't want to upset you—"

"Well, you are upsetting me," she began, until her son broke in with a threat.

"Fuck off before I rip your goddamn heart out!" Lloyd threatened, and Sheehan tried not smiling; he knew he could break half the bones in Lloyd Oborn's body without even working up a sweat.

Brenda Oborn turned and firmly told her son, "Stop it, Lloyd! Just stop it at once! You're acting like a maniac!" To Sheehan, she said, "I truly apologize, Mr. Molloy." She did want him to go away, but her son had been so incredibly rude that she felt compelled to do something—*something*—to make up for it. "Please," she said, reluctance coloring her tone, "come in, won't you?"

Lloyd angrily stepped aside and Sheehan walked by him closely, almost *smelling* his rage. He went through a two-story vestibule toward the back of the house, a gathering room with broad, wide windows looking out on trees and greenery so thick that Bambi and Thumper would appear at any second. Hard to believe this house was less than two miles from busy Summit Mall, the Mustard Seed healthy supermarket, Walmart, the Apple Store, and dozens of other corporate-owned retail shops in Northeast Ohio.

"Something to drink?" Brenda Oborn offered before sitting down. "Coffee?"

"No, thank you." Brock glanced over at Lloyd, whose arms were crossed angrily on his chest as he leaned against the wall— the classic posture for protection. "I don't want to keep you long. I'm so sorry your daughter was involved in a sexual problem at a party attended with a lot of OSU athletes. Is that true?"

Lloyd gasped, and Brenda's lips nearly disappeared. Her ghostly-white face made the brownish-blue bags under her eyes even more apparent. "I suppose they were."

"Your daughter socialized with them?"

"She socialized with everybody—at that party and everywhere

else, too. After—after it was all over, the only one she mentioned was that—that *basketball player.*" She pronounced it as though it were an obscene profession, and obviously would not even mention Kenny Pine's name aloud. "And his friend and teammate, Cody Thacken, too. Thacken didn't hang around much, though, but the other one—" Her breath grew labored. "She told me what happened after that."

"Was Meredith drunk at the time?"

Now she wouldn't answer him at all, and Brock didn't want to have to crane his head around and look for a reaction from the boy. At length Brenda said, "Mr. Molloy, my daughter—took her own life."

"Yes, ma'am, and my sincere sympathies. Did Pine have anything to do with—with that party she attended?"

"You're goddamn right he did!" Lloyd pushed himself away from the wall and moved clear across the room to hunker over Sheehan. "The university covered it up—they had a big-time superstar to protect."

"There's no way to prove it?" Sheehan said. "No witnesses?"

Brenda Oborn said quietly, "No witnesses would talk—none except Meredith. And no one would believe her."

"She went to the police?"

She nodded. "The campus police, yes—and to the local newspapers."

"And she couldn't get anyone to listen to her?"

Brenda pinched the bridge of her nose between thumb and middle finger. "The first thing she did when she got home was to get into a very hot bathtub, and wash away anything the—the rape kit might have found. But she refused to go to the hospital. She couldn't stand anyone touching her—looking at her—or asking her intimate questions." She took an uneven deep breath as though her lungs were working at half-staff. "It took her three days to tell me it was probably *him.*"

"Probably?"

"She said she was so drunk, she wasn't completely positive.

She thought it was him because he spent the entire evening talking with her, dancing with her, and feeding her drink after drink."

"She told the police she wasn't positive?" Sheehan said quietly.

"In many cases," Ms. Oborn said, "rape victims often aren't taken seriously by some police departments—or they wind up being blamed instead of the rapist. Besides, OSU is rich and powerful. To avoid any negative publicity, they shut everyone up."

"You couldn't take this further?"

"We could have," her son said, "but then that scum graduated—a C student! He spent more time shooting baskets than studying—and right away got busted for owning a dogfight ring. When he went to prison, OSU decided it was better to just forget about the rape and move on."

Brenda said, "It was so shocking. That's when Meredith—" She gasped trying to hold in her sob.

"I was the one who found her," Lloyd broke in, "hanging in her closet!" His voice was raspy, quivering. "Well, justice has been done. Three weeks after he got out of prison and signed that damn contract with *your* basketball team—somebody killed him. And I'm gladder than *shit!*"

"Good riddance," his mother said softly.

"She was my big sister," the young man snapped as though his anger was aimed at Sheehan, "and just as I'm standing here, Pine killed her—as if he'd shot her in the head."

Brenda stood and went to her son, putting a hand on the side of his face. "Lloyd—please calm down. Meredith is gone—and now *he* is gone, too. It's all over with. There's nothing more to do. You need to let it go."

He spun away from his mother, stomping out of the room. Sheehan thought he heard him mumble, "Fuck it," but he wasn't sure.

After the furious footsteps on the stairs faded away, there was quiet for almost a minute before Brenda Oborn said, "I'm sorry for all this commotion. It never used to be this way when

149

my husband was alive—or Meredith. We had family dinners often, with vibrant conversations about all sorts of things. We watched movies together on Netflix. Lloyd was happy, ambitious—a star quarterback at his high school. He'd always wanted to follow Meredith at OSU because he adored her—a big sister who always took his side." Her deep inhale used up half the air in the room. "Now you couldn't get him there to save his life. He's enrolled at the University of Akron, but his grades—tops in high school—are slightly below normal. He'd always wanted to be in a fraternity. Now he's not interested. You see, Mr. Molloy, families don't get over a beautiful child's suicide. We live with it—for the rest of our lives. Families are like three-legged stools. They're upright and solid until one of the legs is taken away, and then the whole thing crashes."

She stopped and put her hand over her heart. "The death of this horrible rapist will not bring Meredith back." She moved a few steps toward the doorway, her forehead wrinkled with a confused frown. "Neither will any newspaper stories. I'm going to ask you to leave now. There is nothing more we have to say to you."

Sheehan walked ahead of her to the front door and stepped out onto the pathway. Then she said, "I do have a question myself, Mr. Molloy."

"What would that be, Ms. Oborn?"

"Just wondering," she said, her hushed, gentle tone taking on a sharp edge, "why a newspaper reporter, coming all the way from Denver to interview someone for a story—didn't have a notebook with him—or a press pass."

I should kick myself in the ass, Brock thought as he drove back on Market Street toward the I-77 freeway. He could have bought a spiral notepad for less than a dollar—and sure as hell could have come up with a better movie name than Terry Molloy! The Oborn boy was more furious than anybody he'd met since beginning this crazy odyssey to discover who cut the throat of Kenny Pine. Lloyd might need further looking into.

Akron University, where Lloyd Oborn studied, might be a good place to start an inquiry—but not on a Saturday. Maybe on Monday he would return to Akron and talk to someone who might have a previously unknown scoop on Lloyd—on his rage. As for now, he had another stop to make.

He went further south on the freeway, turning east on I-76 toward Youngstown.

He couldn't remember whether he'd ever been to Youngstown before. He knew no one there, and to his knowledge there wasn't a sister organization like Cleveland's West Side Gaelic Society. Youngstown had, for decades, been under the thumbs of two rival Italian organizations—so he was pretty much on his own.

He wanted to explore further the dogfighting exploits of Kenny Pine that put him behind bars in the first place—and the famous "arena" on his farm, where he killed his animals so brutally, was located in Mahoning County, just outside Youngstown. It was still owned and occupied by one of Pine's former "partners." Did someone in the same business get mad at him, and stayed mad until he was finally released from prison?

He found a motel, not far from downtown. He hated motels—without personality or particular comfort, and without a bar in which to relax with a cocktail before bed. He'd been in enough of them to always check the bed's mattress for signs of bedbugs, or sheets that were possibly unwashed and contained some stranger's dried bodily fluids. When away from home, however, and on sort of a budget, one has to sleep *somewhere*.

Linus Callahan's problem, and those of Maureen Flanagan and of his coworker, Patti Korwin, had set Sheehan's schedule back twenty-four hours. Life often gets in the way of schedules, which meant Sunday was do-nothing.

He hung up his clothes bag, took off his jacket, and splashed cold water on his face before looking at his weary face in the bathroom mirror. He didn't look nearly as exhausted as he felt; his Dorian Gray portrait in the attic, he thought, must look like shit.

When he was younger—when an early grave was a just a laugh to a man in his profession—nothing stopped or frightened him. Now, after a long, dull retirement, the only thing slowing him down was getting easily tired. Was it his diet? He hadn't put on much weight. Were his heart or lungs making it tougher for him to breathe? He didn't know. He couldn't remember the last time he'd seen a health provider for anything.

He dressed in clean clothes, got back in his car, and drove around for a while, looking for a place to get a drink or two before he tried locating another restaurant in which to eat a decent, non-corporate meal.

He found a cocktail lounge on Wick Avenue that carried a halfway decent bourbon when Irish whiskey was unavailable. He ordered the upscale brand, the Maker's Mark, and ignored the local news show on the TV opposite him at the bar, not giving a damn what was happening in Youngstown.

Just as he was taking his first sip, he heard a voice on the television set—familiar but from long ago—and an iron band tightened around his heart. He put the glass down carefully, and as though afraid of what he might see, he raised his eyes.

It had to be her. He hadn't seen her, nor heard her voice since the night they said goodbye when she was in her mid-twenties and he was nearly forty.

"There'll be a big get-together for kids tomorrow at Youngs-town Toyota," said the TV news anchor, smiling to enlighten the world. "I'll be there from noon to two, and we invite you to join us for games, presents, snacks, and balloons."

She was older, of course, still looking great on TV. Twenty years scrawl their own victories and defeats on every face—but Arizona Skye had not changed that much. Her hair, dark as midnight, was shorter now, curled around her neck rather than spilling down to her waist the way it had when he'd fallen in love with her. He recalled mornings when they'd awakened and cuddled, and he'd drape her long hair across his face and, ever so slowly, took lots of time to get out from under. Her clothes now were more appropriate for a middle-aged professional, but her eyes—dark, penetrating, sometimes bubbling with life and sexuality and other times cold as a December moon—had not changed.

"That's it for now," she said into the camera, smiling, "but we'll be back at eleven for late news—and hope to see you then. I'm Arizona Skye. Happy Saturday evening."

Then she faded away to a blast of music and the logo of the local station—too quickly for Brock Sheehan.

Did she move to Youngstown when their torpedoed relationship ended? That was a surprise. Anyone wanting to get away from Cleveland usually settled much further away than a ninety-minute drive.

"What station is that?" he demanded of the young female bartender, who told him the four identifying letters. "Where is it located?"

"How would I know?" she shrugged. "I don't pay much attention to TV unless it's a Steelers game. I think they're in Canfield or someplace—or Poland."

He tried to find the station's address on his iPhone, but it only had two bars, so he downed the bourbon quickly, went out and stood beside his car, and tried again.

Canfield, he discovered. He entered the address into his GPS and checked his wristwatch. It was a twenty-minute trip, at best. Maybe if he drove faster—

Finally, at a few minutes past seven, he rolled into the parking lot of a sprawling, white-painted building over which loomed an enormous radio-TV tower. Sheehan had never been sure what those towers just outside TV stations *did*. Sending out programming to the rest of the world, or receiving it? He didn't care, nor do most people who rarely understand how a light comes on when they flick a switch on the wall, or water spills out of the tap when they twist a handle. He wasn't a tech guy at all, though he'd had to learn from scratch how to care for his boat's engine.

He went inside. A well-dressed black woman sat behind a

desk at one end of a very long lobby, and she smiled as he approached her.

"I'm looking for Arizona Skye," he told her.

"She's not here right now."

"I just saw her on TV, half an hour ago."

The woman nodded. "Yes—she does the six o'clock news and the eleven o'clock news. She doesn't hang around here for the five hours in between. She has dinner—at a restaurant or at home, and comes back at around nine thirty to read up on any breaking news stories for the late show."

"I don't suppose you have her phone number?"

The woman's pleasant openness turned to a frown, and she became more formal—and more annoying. "Obviously we can't give out personal information to strangers." She pushed a pad of white paper across the desk to him. "If you'd like to leave her a note…"

Shaking his head, he went outside and sulked in his car for about ten minutes, knowing that if he scrawled a few words to be delivered to Arizona Skye, the receptionist and fifteen other people at the station would know what it said, and probably gossip about it. Arizona's cell phone wouldn't be listed—she was, after all, a local celebrity. What would he do for the next two and a half hours? Hang out in a saloon? Irish whiskey soothed his soul better than any prescription, but he knew he'd be too hammered when he returned to see her. He drove around looking for a restaurant. The best he could come up with was an Applebee's.

Applebee's. There were more than one corporate Applebee's in every city in America. He couldn't recall being in one before.

He sat by himself at a table, though usually he preferred eating at the bar when he was alone, as there was a bartender or a fellow boozer with whom he could talk. Hunched over a barstool while people bustled around, jostling his elbow and talking loudly in his ear to someone else didn't appeal to him, though the restaurant was fairly crowded. Ten minutes after he left the place, he wouldn't remember what he'd eaten for dinner—only that he'd had one Maker's, neat, to wash it down.

Arizona Skye—an exotic woman with an exotic name. He'd asked her once, and she'd replied that somewhere down the line, several generations passed, there had to be some Comanche in her DNA. That might or might not have been so—but no matter. He would have loved her no matter what her ethnicity.

He had no clue how many women had passed through his life and bed. Most of them he could barely remember. Their faces and names all blended into a shadow-memory, as if awakening frightened and unbalanced from a powerful dream but unable to remember what it was, like vague moving inkblots on an iPad screen.

But not a day had gone by he hadn't thought of Arizona Skye. What he felt for her was far beyond what others call "love." Inamorata? Soul mate? Adoration? Rapture? He could never pick a name for it—and sadly, whatever it was he didn't realize until after she'd left him.

"We can't do this anymore," she'd said, leaning against the door and not even removing her coat that protected her from the March chill. She'd come to his apartment that evening to break it off—and it wasn't easy for either of them.

"We can if we want to."

"Brock—you're a brute."

"Not to you," he said. "I'd die before I hurt you."

She shook her head resolutely. "You're paid to hurt other people. I can't stand that."

"I hardly hurt people at all."

"Hardly? Wow, Brock, Just—wow!"

"Arizona, you knew I've worked all my life for what people around here call the Irish mob. What did you think I was, their interior decorator?"

"I don't know what I thought!" She hugged herself. "I

*thought you were hot stuff when I watched everybody in Cleve-
land stand in long lines waiting to kiss your ass. I knew from the
first minute I saw you that you were big and intimidating.
That's why I was attracted to you. It took me to realize people
wanted to kiss your ass so you didn't beat them up, break their
kneecaps—or worse!"*

*"And I was attracted to you because you're the most beautiful
woman I ever saw. I still think so. I'll always think so."*

*"Stop!" she ordered, never realizing that what he'd said
would turn out to be completely true. "My coworkers whispered
about you at the station when they knew we were seeing each
other. Every one of them warned me that you were a dangerous
man. I chose to ignore it. But there are things I can't ignore."*

"Like?"

*Her eyes were frosty. "You've been arrested four times—for
murder."*

*"I was never charged. Never went to court. How much
importance do you place on false arrests?"*

*"If you never really murdered anyone," she said, "as far as
I'm concerned, you still came too damn close."*

*"What do you want from me, Arizona? Quit my job and be
a road construction guy for the county? A bartender? A high
school wrestling coach?"*

"At least," she said, "I could trust you."

*"You know damn well I've never even looked at another
woman since the moment I saw you."*

*"That's a different kind of trust. I can trust that—but I can't
trust where you are in your life. I never could again."*

*"I'll change my job," Brock Sheehan promised, raising his
hand to take the pledge. "I'll move out of Cleveland—to wherever
you go. You know I adore you—I tell you that twenty times a
day. I'll never stop loving you, no matter what."*

*She shivered, even though she was in his warm apartment.
"I'll always love you, too, for what it's worth." Her eyes welled
up with tears just waiting to be shed, and she turned and put
her hand on his doorknob for the last time. "That's the shitty*

part of it."

A few minutes before nine, he drove back to the TV station and parked in a dark corner of the lot.

Waiting.

Again. The night had turned cooler, and he wished he'd brought a heavier jacket, but he preferred keeping the engine turned off so he wouldn't draw too much attention. He checked his watch at least once each minute, feeling stupid for doing so. He'd always heard the older one gets, the quicker time flies by—but for him, the minutes, the seconds, were endless, and he couldn't make them move any faster.

He figured he wasn't *that* old, anyway.

It seemed like forever, but only twelve minutes passed until a light tan Toyota Camry, looking brand-new, pulled into the lot and parked near the station entrance. The light inside went on for mere seconds as the driver opened the door and got out— but Sheehan knew, more from tightness in his chest and his own heavy breathing rather than one quick look, that this was the only woman whose loving memory had never left him.

He slid out of the car and quickly walked toward her as she headed for her job, and called out as quietly as he could, "Arizona!"

She stopped walking, turned—and sighed. Dark as it was in the parking lot, she couldn't help recognizing the voice, the height, the stance, the walk, and the bulk. She waited until he got within ten feet of her.

"Brock Sheehan." There was no fear or resignation in her voice, no anger. It was just—"Brock Sheehan."

"Surprise, Arizona." He took one step backwards. "My God, you look terrific."

She touched her face absently with her fingertips. "It's all TV makeup. What are you doing here?"

"In Youngstown? I'm on business. I didn't know you lived

here—I didn't know where you were. But I caught you on the six o'clock news, so I wanted to get in touch."

"In the middle of the night?"

"It's only nine thirty." He shrugged. "I didn't know any other way to reach you."

"It's a bad time, Brock—I go on the air pretty soon, and I've got to prepare."

"I know. Can we meet afterwards?"

She shook her head. "You've got to be kidding."

"I'm not making a move on you," he said. "Just renewing an old—friendship."

"I sign off the air at eleven thirty and don't even haul out of here until one o'clock in the morning."

"Well, how about tomorrow?"

"I'm making a personal appearance between two and four at the Toyota dealer."

"I heard you say that on TV. I don't want to be in a car showroom watching you give out balloons to kids. I—it's been such a long time, Arizona. Now that I found you again, I just want to talk. Catch up on things, you know."

"Brock." Arizona waited for at least fifteen seconds, hunching her shoulders against the chill breeze. Then she finished her thought. "After twenty years, what would we have to talk about?"

"Old friends," Sheehan said. "If nothing else."

"Old friends," she murmured.

"More than that. Give me a break, Arizona." He felt his Irish face coloring. "You didn't give me a break all those years ago—maybe it's time."

She remained silent for a while. Then she looked at her watch. "I have to go to work, Brock."

"How about brunch tomorrow? You pick the time and the restaurant. We'll just talk about what we've been doing. No danger. We won't sit there all day. It'll just be—old times."

"Old times." She looked down at her shoes. The wind kicked

up a bit and she shivered. "I must go in! My hair will look like crap by the time I get back on the air."

"Then make an appointment with me now. I won't screw up your newscast. From what I saw earlier, you're pretty good at it."

She shoved her hands into her jacket pockets. She'd never forgotten Brock Sheehan, though god knows she'd tried—but it seemed awkward for them to be meeting again—talking, reminiscing. She wished it was all behind her, yet she really wanted to know what he'd been up to since the day they said goodbye so long ago. Eventually she gave up. She took out a reporter's pad and scrawled the name of an upscale Youngstown restaurant that serves brunch. "Nine thirty in the morning, if you get up that early," she said, tearing the page out and giving it to him. "It's a good brunch, so be hungry." She chewed on her lower lip for a few seconds. "And keep it light, Brock, for Christ's sake."

She spun on her heel and marched into the TV station. Sheehan stood there for quite a while, trying to decipher what she meant—and wondering why he'd looked her up in the first place. It was past time to stir up cold ashes. Yet he'd cared about her life since they parted and she left town quickly, without a hint as to her next destination. He wanted to know.

Wanting to know, he finally thought, was a damn silly thing to do. Of course he knew. She'd told him on that long-ago night.

He returned to his motel, passing a few saloons a little more raucous for him to choose, but in his current mood—and with his thirst for another two or four or six more shots of bourbon—he'd pass out on the floor and wind up in the drunk tank. So he took to his bed in his underwear and watched the eleven o'clock Arizona Skye news, knowing she was more distracted than she had been on the earlier newscast.

He knew she'd loved him, but never understood *why* she didn't love him anymore. Many couples stay together for forty or fifty years, even though each change, because that's the way life is. There are good times and bad times along the way, in any relationship no matter how pure. But if the love is there, the lovers bide their time and wait until things got better.

He didn't know what he did so completely wrong. He'd never struck her or touched her roughly, even in playful moments. He'd never lied to her, which made him reason for the next two decades why cutting off love was the way one would cut off a hangnail. And he'd never touched or flirted with or kissed another woman. He was far too deeply in love with her to even consider that. But he had to cast his lot between her and his job—the family job. That was the choice he had to make.

He wondered if she was seeing someone else now, but he dismissed it out of hand, or *chose* to dismiss it. He had spent the majority of his adult life carefully nursing a heart that was broken beyond repair.

He'd never loved again, never even had the inkling to do so.

Not being much of a news-watcher, he hardly listened to what she was saying, but let what went on in Washington or Beijing or Moscow wash over him like rough waves. When Arizona broke away and introduced the show's sports guy to recite the results of that day's college football, he found himself missing her already, in agony having to wait until the next morning to see her once more, that beautiful face and astonishing eyes in the cheerful light of day—and it saddened him to realize that never before, in his entire life, had he gone to a restaurant for Sunday brunch.

CHAPTER TWELVE

There were many things Brock Sheehan did not miss. He didn't fear for America, for instance, wishing it would be the way it was when he was a kid, despite the current president trying desperately to make everything different. He had few bad recollections of his own—of often being hit by his father, which was completely normal for shanty-Irish families. He had no regrets, either over the tough guys who'd set themselves up as Rory McCurdy's enemies, or of being stabbed on two separate occasions—once in the stomach and once across his chest by a hoodlum punk who had violated the daughter of one of McCurdy's most trusted hangers-on. That was all part of the job.

Arizona Skye was a different story. He had loved her—*really* loved her in the time they'd been together. They didn't live together back then—she had to awaken early to be news anchor on Cleveland's Channel Twelve, while Sheehan was a night person who rarely slept before two or three a.m. They saw each other four or five days per week and every weekend, and went everywhere together.

Their sex was frequent, gentle, tender. It lacked the wildness of Sheehan's earlier years, but it was far more important to him to be in the throes of passion with someone with whom he was totally smitten.

Was she the most beautiful woman in the world? He thought so. He managed to wake up early enough every morning to see her on television before going back to sleep until about nine o'clock—and his heart skipped a beat every time he looked at her, even when he heard her name.

As a noontime anchor, she knew all about things most people did not, and Brock Sheehan's reputation found its way to her desk. Naturally she discovered his toughness, and sort of loved him for it. But when she ascertained that he earned his living by hurting people—the killings had never been proven, but she always wondered—she pulled away from him, making him choose Rory McCurdy over her. Whatever they had together was finished, and she didn't want to see him anymore. Shortly thereafter she quit her job and left town—Cleveland had too many memories for her to deal with. Sheehan had no clue as to where she'd gone—and knew damn well that if he did find her, she'd just shut him out again.

Twenty years in the past—no seeing, talking, or touching—and it ground his guts every day. Now, as he drove to the restaurant for a Sunday brunch before Arizona had to run off to another public appearance, Sheehan was as frightened of that encounter as he'd ever been in his life.

The eatery was fairly crowded, and he cringed inside because he knew private conversation would be close to impossible. Still, he spied Arizona Skye the moment he entered, sitting at a table by the window clear across the room from the brunch spread, sipping from a coffee mug. To him, she was still exquisite, and he didn't notice twenty years of living that had sculpted its way across her face. She possibly weighed ten pounds more than the last time he saw her, but they were good pounds, sexy pounds, too.

She didn't rise to greet him, robbing his expectation of at least a hug. He bent to kiss her and she turned her head—all he reached was her cheek.

"Thanks for meeting me, Arizona. It's been a long wait."

"For old times' sake," she answered as he sat down opposite her.

"You look amazing."

"That's what you said last night—in a parking lot."

"You're even more beautiful in the light."

She lifted one eyebrow. "You lie better in the dark. What are you doing in Youngstown, anyway?"

"Just—business."

She shook her head sadly. "You're still doing that, huh? Hurting people? Twenty years later and you're still a teenager who thinks he'll live forever."

"It's not that kind of business. I've retired, Arizona."

"Spare me the horse shit," she said. "It took me all this time to forget about it."

He tried not to look hurt. "Come on, let's get some brunch. You'll feel better after you eat."

"I just want coffee first." She pointed to a carafe on the table. "Help yourself."

He refilled her cup and poured his own. "Tell me all about yourself."

"Condense half a lifetime over a cup of coffee?"

He wasn't sure why that injured him so badly—but he assumed she hadn't been celibate since her relationship with him, and he didn't want to hear about it. Instead he said, "What brought you to Youngstown?"

She shrugged. "You know I left Cleveland. First I went to Tulsa, Oklahoma as a field reporter—but that got me on the street interviewing people who were too—difficult for me to relate to, I guess. They lived in a big city but they were rural at heart—rural or very hung up with the oil they pumped. Then I got hired in Spokane. Nice enough job. I stayed there five years until I got a better offer—from Buffalo. Good town, great people, but Jesus, it's so cold and snowy there! So when Youngstown beckoned, I figured it was close to my hometown, but not *too* close, and—well, here I am."

Brock Sheehan nodded.

"And here *you* are," she continued, "but I can't figure out why."

"All these years, I never knew you were back here living so close."

"You didn't Google me?"

"I don't Google. I don't own a computer—just a smart phone I don't use it much. I could kill myself for that. If I'd known you were a short drive away, I'd—"

"Come to Youngstown and try to fix things?" Arizona asked. "When something's broken, you can't fix it, Brock. Try sticking it together with duct tape or Super Glue, but it'd never be the same. Broken is—broken."

"I don't think that's true."

"Why?"

"Because I never stopped loving you."

Arizona put her hand to her face and rubbed her eyes as though she had a headache. "I loved you, too, then—or the *myth* that was you, the local legend. Sure, we'd go to dinner together and bartenders and headwaiters and half the people in the joint would fall all over themselves sending over a round of drinks because you were special. That was pretty damn impressive to me for a while—until I found out *why* you were so special in Cleveland."

He took a sip of his coffee—not very good, but it was hot, and that was enough at the moment. She had changed, or at least her attitude had toward him. The coolness, the distance between them had never been there before. A wall had sprung up without either realizing it was there. He had to swallow twice, as his mouth had gone dry.

"You were on Channel Twelve five days a week," he said. "More people watched *your* local news than any other channel in Cleveland. Did it ever occur to you that the fuss was being made over you and not me?"

She thought about that for a moment. "No. It didn't occur to me. I wouldn't break someone's leg just because they didn't offer me a free drink. That's the difference."

"Whatever I do—or did—doesn't change the fact that I've

been in love with you forever."

"Love," she murmured.

"It hasn't changed."

"Uh-huh. And that makes it okay?"

"It could—if you could meet me. Not even halfway—but just be there for me. I can show you I've changed."

"Twenty years without a word passing between us, and suddenly a cup of coffee brings all of that back?"

"It never went away—not for me."

Arizona closed her eyes momentarily. "Brock, I'm not going there. Let's just—eat. Okay?"

She stood and moved across the room to the buffet table. Naturally he followed her, like a naughty puppy begging to be adored. They filled their dishes, but once back at the table, he realized he wasn't hungry at all. He ate half a muffin, only picking at the rest of his food, while she attacked hers like a hyena.

"So I guess you like Youngstown," he said.

"It's okay. It's comfortable. And I grew up with Ohio weather, so I don't worry about snow, or heat, or too much traffic."

"Cleveland is bigger, though—more exciting. Theater, music, sports teams, and the lake."

"Exciting?" She rolled her eyes upward. "Not so much anymore. Besides, I like my job here."

"You can get another job in Cleveland. The TV people would remember you."

"And if they don't," she said, "you're still a big shot who can pull some strings?"

"I'm no big shot," he said defensively, "and I have no strings to pull. I've lived in Vermillion on a houseboat for the last ten years. No one in Cleveland knows me anymore."

She put down her fork. "I know you, Brock—and you're hard to forget. God knows I've tried." Her face changed, grew warmer, more understanding, and she leaned forward, put her hand on his, and squeezed softly. "Brock, I'm seeing someone."

"I figured you were. No woman who looks like you spends her life alone. Do you love him, Arizona?"

"I—care for him. We've been together for more than a year."

"Living together?"

"No. *Being* together."

"Then it'd be no big deal to kiss him goodbye and come back to me," he said. "You really loved me."

"I trust him, Brock—and I changed my whole life because I couldn't trust you."

This time he put his hand over hers. "You know I'd never hurt you, no matter what."

"No. But I couldn't get my head around sitting in a courtroom while the man I loved was tried for murder."

"Arizona—"

"It's no good!" she said, pain in her voice as she pulled her hand away. "And don't ask his name or who he is, because you'll show up one night and wring his goddamn neck! Go home! Do what you have to do in Youngstown and then go back and sit on your boat and fish—or whatever else you do—because it doesn't work between us anymore."

"We'll never know," he said, "until we try."

"The odds on trying and failing are even money. I couldn't stand the thought of failing back then, and I still can't. Let it go, Brock."

They finished breakfast in near silence, and Arizona grabbed the check from the waitress and paid it with her credit card. "I invited you, remember?" she said—and once again he felt humiliated, impotent, and unimportant.

They walked together to her car. Both stood quietly, neither knowing quite what to say. Finally Brock found his voice.

"It was good seeing you, Arizona. Still beautiful. Still—well, you know."

"I know."

Finally they hugged each other, and his hug was tighter, longer, more desperate than was hers. No kiss—she wouldn't

166

have allowed it—but he kept his face pressed to hers, her hair tickling his nose. She still wore the same perfume, and still smelled to him like an angel.

She broke away, turned, and unlocked her car door with a beeper. Then she faced him again, her smile tinged with incredible sadness. "Live a good life, Brock," she said.

He watched her drive away, remembering the last time he'd done so when they were both young, intense, in love, until she called a halt to it and drove off down Clifton Boulevard toward the freeway and to wherever the hell she might be running. A part of him went with her that day.

The rest of him disappeared after her this time.

When he'd arrived in Youngstown the day before, Saturday, he'd had no idea she lived there, no expectation of seeing her again or even the touch of her hand. Now, as he'd felt so many years before when she told him their relationship had to end, his heart was in his throat, and the place in his chest where it belonged was an abandoned hole.

A strange town and a completely empty Sunday stretching before him, that sharp jabbing pain whenever he felt truly lonely reappeared in his gut, reminding him of how royally he'd already fucked up his life.

Lonely.

Since his mid-thirties, he'd always been lonely—shut out by his family, and Rory McCurdy's tight-knit "mob" disgusted with his leaving. His job description had left him with no other friends, and the only love he'd ever known melted away in the middle of the night and vanished without a trace.

Every night since—every desolate, rejected night, like Thanksgiving. Christmas, the Fourth of July, his birthday. All spent alone. Those who profess solitude spend more nights than they'd admit yearning for the company of another human being, especially one they could love. He occasionally had one-night stands. He had physical needs, but they were unsatisfying, because he could never love anyone the way he'd loved Arizona Skye.

He couldn't. Life moves on, as it must, but love—real *true* love—never goes away.

So how to fill the yawning nothingness of the next few hours? A library again, he supposed. According to his cell phone, the main Youngstown Library, downtown on Wick Street, was closed on Sundays, but the one on Glenwood Avenue, not that far from the restaurant, was open from one p.m. to five. That would probably be enough time for him.

For many years he had not been a newspaper reader because whatever else was going on in the world didn't matter a damn to him, but he had little choice of what to do until the library opened. He bought a copy of the Youngstown *Vindicator* from a sidewalk rack—heavier than usual with its many Sunday additions and advertising pages—and spent the next few hours in a McDonald's drinking coffee. Though he hadn't bought a speck of food from Mickey D's for the past thirty years, he had to admit their coffee was among the best anywhere.

At a few minutes before one, he drove to the library. They too had a microfiche—he wondered where that name came from—and searched for the nearby location Kenny Pine had owned and managed when he made a fortune from staging dogfights, but in every article from the time Pine was arrested until he went to prison, they never printed the address.

Then he got an idea. It was a long shot, but what the hell. Out in the parking lot, he dialed the phone number of the TV station where Arizona Skye worked, and asked to speak to the news director.

"I'm just news director on the weekend," Carlo Sordetto told him when Brock Sheehan introduced himself as, once again, news reporter Terry Molloy from the *Denver Post*, and asked for the address where Kenny Pine had staged dogfights and dog executions. "You probably ought to ask the big guy when he comes to work tomorrow."

"I've got to get back home tonight on the red-eye," Sheehan told him. "I've really looked everywhere for that information, and I figured your station would be my last shot. I'm friends with Arizona Skye, by the way. We had brunch together this morning—I asked her, and she didn't know, either."

"Right—Arizona's my weekend anchor. As far as I can remember, Kenny Pine got arrested three years ago, and since then he's only been covered on this station three times. The first time was the day he got out of prison. Next was when he signed his basketball contract—and naturally when he was found murdered. But that happened in Cleveland, so we weren't on top of it as much as the Cleveland stations were."

"And you can't tell me where his dogfight farm is, exactly."

Sordetto said, "Why would the *Denver Post* give a damn one way or the other?"

"We won't print the address," Sheehan said. Lying about being a reporter for the *Denver Post* was becoming easier for him each time. "But I want to see it for myself, get a—you know, a *feel* for what it was like."

"Uh-huh. I'm not sure we ever sent a camera crew down there to film it."

"Sometimes words paint better pictures than TV cameras." Sheehan shifted around in his car seat. "Your station is kind of my last hope."

The editor sighed. "Well, it's Sunday. Slow news day. Okay, then—I'll have one of my interns look it up for you."

"That'd be great." Sheehan took out a pen and his notebook.

"It'll take a while, though. Can I call you back in maybe half an hour?"

"If you don't, I'll call *you* again." He recited his mobile phone number and hung up, rolling down the driver's side window so the fresh air circulated. He loathed waiting.

Slumped in his car in a city he'd never visited, hoping a news director he'd never met at a TV station he'd never watched would call him back with the information that had brought him here in the first place was a particularly personal form of torture.

He'd brought with him the newspaper he'd bought. He'd

read all he'd wanted to of the news, but as empty minutes ticked by, he looked through the ad pages, including shots of beautiful women wearing only bras and panties. Those photos would have been considered immoral, if not downright obscene and illegal, when he'd been a kid.

He also checked sale prices on things he'd never dream of buying. He even read the Sunday funnies—but the Peanuts strip was the only thing that made sense to him.

It was 3:45 in the afternoon before his phone rang in his lap.

"Carlo Sordetto again," the weekend news director said. "My intern took a good look at everything, but we really don't have a specific address for you."

"Shit!" Sheehan grunted.

"Kenny Pine's partner back then was a guy named Monroe Miller, and as far as I know, he still owns the farm."

"How come he didn't go to prison along with Pine?"

"He turned state's evidence against him. He got off with a sizable fine, but he kept the title to the farm. As far as I know, he still lives there."

"We seem to be in a period when it's always someone else's fault."

"Sure," Sordetto said. "But they were more interested in taking Kenny Pine down, anyway—and Miller's name meant nothing to anyone. Nailing Pine created lots more publicity for the county prosecutor, and a stepping stone for him to bigger politics in Ohio. I can tell you where the farm is, though. It's in a little town of Campbell—mostly rural and mostly not rich. It's at the edge of Mahoning County, about five miles from the Pennsylvania border."

"How the hell am I supposed to find it, then?"

"Campbell is a pretty small town, but you can't miss it. I wouldn't be surprised if you drive past it by accident."

"And if I don't?"

A pause. Then Carlo Sordetto said, "Ask somebody."

CHAPTER THIRTEEN

Campbell, Ohio wasn't much to look at—a very small town with a population of less than seven thousand souls, few of whom were out socializing on Sunday afternoon. The only action that Brock Sheehan could see with a naked eye was in and around a gas station that also sold all sorts of merchandise not found in many other stores—jackets and T-shirts marked with not-very-clever sayings, first aid supplies of sorts, a panorama of chips and popcorn, canned food Sheehan wouldn't dream of eating, hot dogs seemingly rolling on a moving grill since three days earlier, wrapped deli-type sandwiches of similar vintage, hundreds of pairs of inexpensive sunglasses, a few paperback books and a vast collection of books on CD-ROM for those more literary road warriors driving the huge trucks and vans parked outside, who stopped here for cigarettes or chewing tobacco or maybe a few cheap toys they could bring home to their kids—whenever they *got* home.

The sun had gone missing and the sky was gray with overhanging clouds as Brock moved from his car to the doorway and went inside. The customers, all male, were porky, middle-aged, and Caucasian, as were the store clerks. Several of them visibly wore handguns at their hips. That was the carry-law in Ohio, and he guessed if someone buzzed along a lonely highway at night and ran into trouble, a handgun wouldn't be such a bad thing to have.

171

He himself was rarely heeled, even on his wildest days. He owned a weapon—Rory McCurdy had given him a Glock for his thirty-fifth birthday present. But except for his rare appearances at a gun range, he rarely took it out of the hidey-hole in which he'd placed it on the boat. When he headed for warmer climes in the winter, as he did each year, he kept it in his suitcase in the trunk of his car until he got to where he was going, and after that stored it under the bed—loaded, naturally. On the rare occasions he carried it, he couldn't shake the feeling of being a very large child strutting around pretending to be the *Fistful of Dollars* Clint Eastwood.

He'd never had to threaten anyone with a gun, as he was reluctant to use it. Big to begin with, his reputation—much of which was myth—was even bigger. Most of what he'd done successfully was to threaten, not hurt. On the four occasions when he went past threats and arm-twists and occasional punch-outs, he did so efficiently, because that was what needed to be done.

He wandered around the store for a while, trying to get an idea of which people would welcome his question and which might draw a weapon against him, just for the hell of it. Not a tough crowd, exactly, as most of them seemed pleasant and decent, but a rural citizenry—upper middle-aged guys working twenty-four-seven all year round with not much room left for idle chatter.

Nevertheless, he had to try.

"Excuse me, sir," Sheehan said, approaching a guy wearing a trucker's hat and thumbing through audiobooks looking for something interesting to listen to, a Smith & Wesson holstered at his waist.

The man looked up. "Howdy."

"I'm not sure I'm asking the right guy—but do you know exactly where it is down here that Kenny Pine ran his dogfight shows until he got arrested?"

The man no longer looked pleasant; whatever Brock said made

him angry. "You one of those people looking for a dogfight? I own dogs, mister, and love 'em, like I love my kids—so I don't have much use for guys who like watching good dogs fighting and killing each other. You understand me?"

"Perfectly, sir, and you're right. I don't like dogfighting, either. I'm with you."

"Then why you want to know where the dog arena is? They haven't had anything going on there since Pine went to jail."

"Maybe," Sheehan said, his tone a bit on edge, "I have other reasons besides watching dogfights."

The truck driver had to consider whether or not he'd start a fight of his own in here—and then decided against it. This stranger with the questions was far too big to throw a punch at, he thought—unless he'd shoot, and then run like hell.

"I'm not from around these parts," the driver finally said. "The only place I know is this place right here—stop for a quick bite, a piss, and on the road again."

"Thanks anyway."

The driver looked around. "See that old feller over there—yellow striped shirt and his belly looks like he swallowed a watermelon whole? I think he's got a farm not too far from here. Whyn't you ask him?"

"Maybe I will. Drive safe, now."

He crossed the length of the store to where the yellow-shirt man was chatting with a few others his own age. "Afternoon, gentlemen," he said.

They all stopped talking and looked at him. They were unsure as to who he was and what they should do about him. He was at least four inches taller than the tallest of them, and obviously unfamiliar to Campbell.

He turned to Yellow Shirt. "You own a farm around here, sir?"

Yellow Shirt nodded. Barely. He had a pistol at his right rear hip, pearl handle like the ones Roy Rogers used to wear in third-rate cowboy movies.

"Then I was hoping you can direct me to the farm where they used to have dogfights about three or four years ago."

"Whattayou want with that farm?" the old man asked.

"Thinking about buying it."

The three men all laughed aloud. Sheehan said, "What's so funny?"

"You gonna buy the Miller farm? Man, you crazy!"

One of the other farmers told him, "You couldn't grow shit on that place. They ain't took good care of it like a real farm for so many years, it's prolly all sand and weeds by now."

"Could be—but I'd like to take a look at it anyway."

"Your funeral," Yellow Shirt said.

"Does the owner still live there?"

"Far as I know. He ain't exactly social—which is fine with us."

"Why?"

"Cuz he's a damn criminal!" Yellow Shirt was getting mad. "Only reason they didn't throw him in jail too was that he squealed on that Pine guy. As it was, they hit him with a fine of twenty-five thousand smackers. It was either that, or they'd take away his farm, too. So now he's broke on his ass, skulking around and not talking to nobody. We don't miss him, neither."

"Sounds good to me," Brock Sheehan said. "I could get that farm away from him for a song. That's how people make big bucks, right? By buying cheap real estate, spruce it up, and sell it for a big profit. Of course, I'm not going to flip it. I'll move in, fix it up for small farming, and settle down for probably the rest of my life." He smiled, which made the trio of old guys happy, too. "Now, this *is* Monroe Miller we're talking about?"

"That's him, all right," Yellow Shirt said, and kind of moved his pot belly off to one side and sighed. "Scum-suckin' shit skunk!"

"Not looking forward to it—but if I can take a few layers of skin off his butt, that'll make my day!"

"Nothin' wrong with that," one of the other men said.

Sheehan said, "Hey—if you guys can give me directions how

to get there—if I talk him into selling it to me—as soon as we get in, I'll invite you all over for dinner. My wife's a great cook."

"Oh, man!" Yellow Shirt reached out and shook Sheehan's hand. "I'll hold you to that deal, my friend."

"Cross my heart," Brock Sheehan said, doing so, "an' hope to die."

He chuckled as he pulled out of the parking lot, heading toward Monroe Miller's farm. His parting shot was one more lie; since getting involved with Linus, not telling the truth was becoming a habit with him. Actually it was a double lie. He wasn't buying the farm from Monroe Miller—and he didn't have a wife who was a terrific cook.

But he planned to squeeze information out of Miller about what had happened when his partner ran the show there—and maybe even find a killer. From what little he knew, there was no love lost between Monroe Miller and the late, great Kenny Pine.

Sheehan was on an off-road, according to what he'd been told. No one had known the exact address, and his GPS wasn't giving him much help. Many of the highways that bordered farms were flat, but now he found himself between two thick, hilly forests, owned by the county and never bothered with. Hunters prowled those woods without a license, hoping to bag some unsuspected wild creature for dinner. Otherwise, not much else went on in there.

Eventually Sheehan came to a place matching Yellow Shirt's explicit description. A driveway led to a beaten-down dirt path winding into the trees and eventually disappearing. A heavy wooden gate had been constructed, wide enough when open to let a large truck come through. Now, though, it had been solidly closed off with two heavy-duty padlocks. A large hand-painted sign with bright red letters had been affixed to the gate: *NO TRESPASSING!!! ENTER AT YOUR OWN RISK!!!* A few of the letters had dripped red paint off the bottom.

Interesting, Sheehan thought—the multiple exclamation points made the message look even more serious.

However, either side of the gate was open and unfenced, meaning anyone on foot could squeeze between the gatepost and the trees and walk right in—even someone as big as Sheehan. He looked around for someplace to leave his car. Though no other driveways were in sight, the grassy apron running along the side of the road looked good enough, even close to being a ditch, as long as it didn't rain. If it did, he'd be hard-pressed to move the car out of the mud.

He had no other choice—he'd come this far, and wasn't about to do a one-eighty and drive two hundred miles home for nothing. So he carefully maneuvered his car into a place where it wouldn't be noticeable when it got dark, then moved back to the gate. Turning sideways, he was able to wedge himself through, and began a trek up the dirt path. He had no idea whether the house and the dog kennels were a mile further in, or just around the next turn.

It grew cooler by the moment, and darker, as the branches of tall trees on either side of the path reached out to each other, forming an impenetrable archway of leaves that were turning color. The dust Sheehan's feet kicked up was clogging his nose and crunching between his teeth. He wished he'd worn work boots instead of dress shoes, and a more rugged coat than the sports jacket he'd chosen for a long-overdue brunch with the woman he'd loved forever and lost—twice.

What was he doing on this dirt road anyway? A hardly remembered nephew had appeared, whining for help, throwing his uneventful life into shambles. He should have stayed home, looking for a more clement climate in which to spend a winter out of the snow where it never got really cold no matter what the month. Instead, here he was in the southeast end of Mahoning County, getting more chilled by the minute as he chased a dog killer who might or might not be the key to the death of a super-star basketball hero the fault of whose demise was somehow being hung around the neck of that nephew.

After walking for ten minutes, he followed the dirt path's

sudden twist into a big clearing that had obviously been churned up and re-sodded. On his right side was a house. On his left, a large red barn and a much smaller one beside it. In the approximate center of the yard was an enormous sawed-off tree stump on which someone probably chopped up firewood for the coming snow season. Lights were on inside the ramshackle house, which was in need of both paint and carpentry work, its front porch bowed in the middle like the back of an old, tired plow horse. From the small barn he could hear dogs barking—big dogs with low, throaty voices.

Monroe Miller still has dogs and still stages fights for money? Sheehan thought he must be out of his mind.

He headed toward the house, but when he got within fifteen feet, the front door opened and Miller came outside. He was close to the same age as Kenny Pine—mid-twenties—but he was already losing his hair, he had a shocking gap where one of his two front teeth had left for greener pastures, and his nose was permanently flattened, probably from a punch administered by a guy twice his size who might or might not have been the heavyweight boxing champion of the world. He wore a camo jacket and heavy khaki pants that didn't cover the fact he was rail-skinny. His work boots were unlaced, as if he'd just thrown them on but didn't take the time to lace them. His Pittsburgh Steelers cap was worn backwards, giving him a dorky look. He carried a hunting rifle announcing he meant business, already truculent over a surprise visitor.

"What's your problem, man? Can't you fuckin' read?"

"Are you going to shoot me?" Sheehan asked.

"I might. You a cop?"

"I'm not a cop—and I have no weapon. Relax, kid, I just want to talk to you."

"'bout what?"

"Invite me inside and we'll have a nice long chat."

Monroe shook his head angrily. "You ain't goin' inside my house."

"Ah, well." Sheehan felt relieved, believing the inside of the home was filthy, strewn with ancient empty pizza boxes, gross porno magazines, and cockroaches, rats and stink bugs galore. He strolled to the tree stump and sat on it. "You own this place all by yourself, Mr. Miller?"

"How come you know my name?"

"I wouldn't have sneaked in here just to talk to a stranger, and it doesn't look like there's much here anybody might want to steal. So just answer a few questions and I'll be on my way."

Miller leveled the gun at Sheehan. "You'll be on your way right now," he said, "or I'll blow a hole in your head the size of a bowling ball."

"I don't think you will—no real reason to. Besides, I was thinking about buying your place. I don't know, though. Now I've seen it, it looks like a real fixer-upper."

"Who said I'd want to sell it?"

"Why would you keep it? You don't have dogs anymore— and it sure as hell doesn't look like you're growing vegetables."

Miller looked defensive. "I got dogs. What are you, deef? Can't you hear 'em?"

"Oh yeah, now that I think of it." Sheehan asked his next question carefully. "Are you still fighting them?"

Miller lowered the rifle—at that angle, if it went off it might blow off Sheehan's foot. "I don't dare. They watch me like a hawk."

"Who? The dogs watch you?"

More annoyed, he spat out, "Naw! The sheriff. He'd cream his jeans if he could put me away."

"He put Kenny Pine away, didn't he?"

"Yeah, but that was cuz I ratted on Kenny—the only way I could stay outta jail."

"Sending your partner over must've pissed Pine off pretty bad."

Miller just shrugged.

"How come he didn't rat on you, too?"

"Cuz." With his free left hand, Miller dug into his ear with his little finger and then examined the wax treasure as though he'd hit a vein of gold before flicking it away. "They come to me first, cuz they'd get more juice out of it if they took down a big sports hero and not some dumb *putz* like me."

Putz, Sheehan thought. Monroe knew more than one language. "So there was no real problem between the two of you?"

"Whattayou mean?"

"Somebody killed Kenny. I'm just wondering if it was you." Sheehan leaned back, one elbow on the tree stump. "He gets out of jail, he makes a couple million bucks off an NBA contract and he decides he's coming after you because it was you put him into the slammer. You argue, things get physical, you grab a knife and cut his throat."

"Right," Monroe said. "Then I load him in my truck so's he could bleed all over my seat, and drive him a hunnert miles up to Cleveland and dump him by the river. Don't be so dumb, man."

"Maybe you were both in Cleveland in the first place."

"Don't you hear good, neither? I ain't seen him since before he went to jail."

"Hard to believe," Sheehan said.

"I give a shit what you believe."

Sheehan nodded, stayed quiet for a bit, listening to the barking coming from the smaller barn. Then: "You still own dogs but don't fight them. Why do you keep them?"

"I pick 'em up from shelters and dog pounds around here for practically nothing—pit bulls, Rotties, bull mastiffs—and then sell 'em to anybody who wants 'em."

"For fighting?"

"For whatever. Make 'em into a pie if they want, and serve it for dinner. I don't care."

"Can I see them?"

"You wanna buy a dog along with buying this farm?"

"You never know."

"Are you in the dogfight business, Mister?"

179

"I'm in—lots of businesses, Monroe. Do I get to see the dogs or not?"

Monroe shrugged, and started off toward the small barn. "Come on, then." He did not put down his hunting rifle, but carried it in the crook of his elbow. Sheehan followed him, kicking up more dust; he'd probably have to throw his dress shoes away.

The barking grew louder as they approached. Monroe said over his shoulder, "These are godawful mean sons a bitches."

"How come?"

"You wanna keep 'em mean—otherwise they don't fight for shit." He took out a key and used it on the padlock. The door swung open with a squeak and he leaned in and turned on a single hundred-watt light in a completely dark room except for one open window at the back of the barn.

Sheehan stepped inside. There were only two dogs in evidence, each in a large cage as big as a citified dog run. One was all black, the other white with big splashes of black markings. Both were male, angry to be locked up in the dark and bothered by their owner and a complete stranger. They both came to the front of their cages, the black one standing tall on his back feet, his front paws against the chain link, his snarl low and threatening.

"Nice dogs," Brock Sheehan said.

"Nice, my ass! Mean fuckers!" Monroe slammed the rifle butt against the cage, and the black dog leaped away, still snarling. When he returned to the chain link again and stood up against them, Monroe picked up an electronic cattle prod propped against the wall, stuck it inside the cage and zapped the black dog near his penis. The animal leaped completely off the ground, yelping in pain, and retreated to the far end of the cage. "See?" Monroe chuckled. "Just keep 'em nasty—an' hungry. That way they get used to pain. They ain't ate nothin' today, either—another way to keep 'em mad."

Sheehan tasted bile. No wonder Linus Callahan got so furious at anyone who gave pain to an animal, just for the fun of it.

"You get off on that, Monroe? Laughing your ass off when you're hurting dogs?"

"Like I give a damn. This sumbitch costs me too much money to feed him. If they don't make money, I put 'em down—just like Pine used to. That's my business—what's left of it, anyway."

"Is there anybody else in the dogfight business around here who hated Kenny Pine's guts enough to kill him?"

"Lotsa people—but that was three years ago. Let's not forget gamblers, too—they spent a fortune in this place bettin' on dogs."

"Why would they hate Kenny?"

Monroe lifted his shoulders and then dropped them. "You don't think me and Kenny ran this place just for the fun of it, do ya? Every gambling nickel spent in here, bettin' on dogs and stuff—and everybody who owned dogs and paid a fee to put 'em up for the fights, Kenny and me took a percentage." He gritted his teeth. "And the big shot gamblers, they took a percentage off of *us.*"

"Gamblers!" Sheehan ran a hand through his hair, trying to put it all together. "Are you saying gamblers really ran this place, and not you and Kenny Pine?"

"There's nothin' in this world exists that ain't run by gamblers, or corporations, or other big money. Don't be an asshole."

"And they skimmed money off the top? What was it? Ten percent? Twenty?"

"What's the diff? Nobody's bet nothin' here for three years or more, cuz the cops watched me so close. Half the money guys think I went to jail with Pine." Now Monroe looked embarrassed. "Besides, they thought this was his place, alone. That's how come they put up the money in the first place. Half of 'em didn' even know I was alive. So—nobody cares anymore."

"Interesting. So maybe some high roller decided to take it out on Kenny, even three years later after he got out of the joint." Sheehan failed to hold back a sneer. "Damn lucky you were just a nobody—just like you still are—splitting gambling money with a superstar. So who was this gambler—or gamblers? I'm sure you know their names—but now I want to know them, too."

Miller's face closed up as though a vacuum had sucked out all his feelings and emotions. "Who you callin' a nobody? You're a shitheel!" His eyes turned to suspicious slits, and his lips nearly disappeared into one straight-line slash across his face. "Why you wanna know? You sneak in here, talkin' about buyin' this farm, buyin' a dog—but all you do is ask questions that's none a your bidness. You work for gamblers, too, and tryin' to pin some murder on me, you lyin' sack a shit?" He took the rifle from the crook of his arm and aimed it at Brock's face. "You wanna send me up for killin' Pine, right? I oughta blow you the hell away, right here."

"I'd hate it if that happened."

"You were one of the gamblers, too?"

Sheehan shook his head. "No, Monroe—I only bet on sure things."

"Oh, yeah?" Now he grew crafty and vicious. "I don't believe you. Nobody's hangin' any crime on me. I been through enough already. But you're trespassin' on my proppity. So if I say you tried stealin' one a my dogs and they chewed you up, that wouldn't be my fault, right?"

"I'm pretty tough—even for a pit bull."

"Yeah?" he breathed softly. "Let's just see how tough you really are."

He took one step forward, changing his grip on the rifle, and slammed the butt into his unwanted visitor's forehead, hard.

Sheehan staggered from pain and shock, stumbling backwards and banging into the chain link. Holiday fireworks went off inside his head, and he squeezed his eyes shut tight, hoping the explosions of light and color and torment would go away. Scrawny and skinny, Monroe Miller somehow packed a devastating wallop.

The last thing Brock Sheehan heard was the black dog near the fence, snarling and barking wildly as if violence really got him going. Then Miller hit him once more with the rifle butt—and that was when all the lights went out.

CHAPTER FOURTEEN

What the hell is this? Brock Sheehan wondered as he struggled his way from the bottom of the ocean to break water and get his first breath of air. A concussion? He'd never had a concussion before. Even before he opened his eyes, he tried to recall whether anyone had struck him in anger since his teen years. He was too big, too tough-looking, and everyone had figured that if they had the urge to hit him at all, they'd have to do it so severely that he wouldn't get up again until they were miles away.

Skinny Monroe Miller wasn't that good with his hands, but pretty impressive with the butt of a hunting rifle.

The pain behind Sheehan's eyes was far worse than an ordinary headache. It felt as if his brain had suddenly grown too huge for the inside of his skull and was madly struggling to get out. Every heartbeat sent agony shooting through him. He was lying on hard, cold pavement, his cheek pressed against it, stinging with the chill. The smell of stale meat, urine, and feces making it difficult for him to breathe at all, he spent a moment gasping for an inhalation.

There was blood all over his face, but he couldn't figure out how badly he'd been hurt, or even where he was. Had someone glued his eyelids shut? It required a prodigious effort to finally open them to look around.

He didn't like what he saw.

He had been tossed inside the cage with the black pit bull,

majestically sitting about fifteen feet away from him, head forward, vigilant, shoulders hunched. Even Sheehan's eyes flickering open made the creature nervous and alert. A far-off thunder within the dog's massive chest made perilous any move from an invader to his territory. Stringy saliva swung from his half-open jaws. He was obviously hungry.

The white-with-black in the cage next to them was at the fence, too, also making subtly terrifying noises deep in his throat.

Not daring any sudden movement, Sheehan worried if these dogs had attacked a human being before. The black pit bull's current owner enjoyed shocking him painfully with a cattle prod, which made Sheehan think this monster would enjoy ripping anyone to pieces—human, canine, or anything else alive.

He groaned from the headache, which got the pittie on its feet and moving closer, the top lip curled upward to reveal a frightening set of fangs. What little Sheehan knew about dogs, other than the Irish wolfhound he'd owned decades earlier, was that barking dogs rarely bite. He understood the black's low, long growls instead of a bark and the half-closed eyes and exposed teeth were signs that things were not going well.

Slowly—very slowly—he raised the top half of his body and supported his weight on one elbow, all at once aware that his wallet had been removed from his rear right pocket. The pit bull crouched lower to the ground and moved a few inches closer—and the growl grew louder.

He rolled over slowly, only his feet and his butt touching the pavement, and looked the dog straight in the eye. He squeezed his own eyes shut for a moment and then opened them again, trying to smile. He'd learned years earlier from a cat-loving female he'd dated for a few short weeks that making that kind of face to a cat was supposed to exhibit friendship and love.

The black didn't seem to appreciate his offer of amity.

Sheehan had to try something else. Speaking very softly, just above a whisper, he said, "Hey, guy."

The dog stopped growling. One eye twitched.

"I want to be your friend. Are you my friend?"

Probably too long a sentence the pit bull would listen to, as he lowered his head and rumbled some more. Brock took a slow, deep breath. Despite the pain in his head, he wanted to be Best Friends Forever with this trained-to-kill animal, at least until he got out of this cage. It was either that, or become an evening meal. "Hey, friend," he said again.

The black emitted an echo of a long-ago storm—not exactly a growl, but definitely a warning: don't make any quick moves. The tail angrily lashed back and forth. It wasn't like tail wagging at all.

"Come here, boy."

The dog didn't move.

"Let me pet you. Come on."

The tail stopped, and the mean, squinting eyes relaxed a little.

"Come on, buddy." He slowly moved his hand in front of him and gently patted the ground. "Come on."

The pit bull cocked his head, trying to figure out what this crazy man was doing.

"What's your name, big guy?" Sheehan whispered. "I bet they never gave you a name—just a number. Right? That stinks the big stink. Everybody should have a name."

The dog had been as close as possible to the ground. Now he raised his body up slightly. The tail, formerly whipping angrily, just moved in a one-quarter wag.

"I'm gonna name you, then." He tried to get his brain working. The only names he could think of at the moment belonged to Irish saints, and most of them Sheehan couldn't pronounce. The anguish of his headache made him recall his years in a Catholic school and the relentless Jesuit priests and monster nuns hammering Catholicism into his head with slaps and punches and whacks across the knuckles with a ruler, along with more Hail Marys and Our Fathers than anyone else had ever been forced to recite. Finally he hit on a saint name he liked, and his voice grew more normal. "I'll call you Conor. Conor. Right, boy? Conor. You like that name, don't you? It's a saint name. You know what Conor means?"

Now the dog was sitting up straight, front legs straight ahead, never taking his eyes from Sheehan's. It wasn't a stare down; it was a bonding moment of sorts.

"That name, Conor," Sheehan said, "means 'hound lover.' Bet you didn't know that, huh? That means you really hate fighting other dogs, because you love them. I love dogs, too." Sheehan's whisper grew even softer. "I love you too, Conor, if you give me half a chance."

He turned his hand palm upward. "Come on, Conor. Give a healthy sniff, find out everything about me, and you'll know I'm your friend." The dog shifted his weight. "Friend, Conor. *Friend.*"

It took nearly twenty minutes. With each word Sheehan spoke, the pit bull seemed less fierce and more relaxed. Now, his black nose twitching, he finally began moving closer to that outstretched hand.

Sheehan suffered waves of lightheadedness, but at least he was already on the ground and didn't worry about falling. The bleeding had all but stopped, and where the blood had run down his face had dried and felt stiff against his skin. He tried ignoring that, and the pain, too—just concentrating on the possible friendship of the huge beast.

He continued speaking softly, saying "Conor" as often as he could, presenting the non-bloody side of his face with its most approachable look, half the time trying to make an ally out of an angry pit bull rather than being eaten alive.

Finally, the high moment of Sheehan's day so far, Conor's nose tentatively touched his exposed palm—icy, friendly, pressure growing until the nose was actually pushing against him, asking for more. He released his held breath and said, "Attaboy, Conor. Good dog. Good dog."

The one window in this barn on the other side of the cage door, high up on the wall, had grown more than half-dark, so

Sheehan realized he'd been in here for a while. Near twilight, it was hard for him to see anything. Slowly he rose up, still murmuring love sounds to the dog, and moved to the cage door.

It was padlocked.

He wasn't going to get out of here until someone came and opened that lock.

He slowly walked around the cage, though there wasn't much to look at. The black sat in the middle of everything, turning his body to keep this strange human in view, no matter what, somehow knowing Brock Sheehan was more ally than abuser. The food dishes in both cages were empty, and the water bowls were only about one-third full, the water dirty and stale. Both dogs had found corners near the back of the cages they'd used to relieve themselves so they didn't have to lie in it.

Eventually Sheehan's unsteadiness made him sit down with his back against the chain link. He wanted to shut his eyes again, but he knew concussion victims should not fall asleep, so he struggled to stay awake and alert.

For another fifteen minutes.

Someone outside the barn was fumbling with the lock. Brock's mind raced, then clicked, and he lay down again, bloodied face up, and pretended he was still unconscious as the door swung open and Monroe Miller stood there, cattle prod in one hand, a bucket of cheap dog meal in the other, his eyes struggling to adjust to the near darkness. He put down the prod, and with the high-powered flashlight he unhooked from his belt he searched the cages, the beam finally falling on his human prisoner. He wondered whether the blood on Sheehan's head, neck, and ear was a result of his brutality, or if the black pit bull had actually chewed on his face.

He set the flashlight on the ground and made his way toward Conor's cage, hefted his handy cattle prod, unlocked the cage door, and stepped inside.

Sheehan did not move.

As Miller walked toward the unmoving man, the pit bull

rose, moved between his owner and Sheehan, lowered his head, and grumbled a protective warning.

"Get away from me, you motherfucker!" Miller shouted, and jabbed Conor with the cattle prod. The growl turned to a painful yelp as the dog scrambled away toward the back of the cage.

But that was all Brock Sheehan needed. Miller was only two feet away, looking the other way. Sheehan drove his right foot up, toe carefully aimed, and smashed into a kneecap, hard enough so that Sheehan heard the bone snap.

Monroe Miller's scream hit a coloratura E above high C and he tipped over onto one side, as the black pit bull advanced on him and was snarling and barking right in his face, and the black and white in the next cage was roaring also.

Brock scrambled to his feet, pulling Miller up from the floor of the cage, and swung his right fist, once, striking him just below his ribs, doubling him over. Then he offered a looping left that caught Miller on the side of his jaw, snapping his head back. When he went down hard and lay completely still, Brock worried that he might have killed him.

"Shh, Conor," he said to the dog. "Easy, boy." He bent down through a wave of agony, stroking the muscular neck, head, and ears as he whispered. Finally Conor—still not sure if that was his name—calmed down and retreated a few steps, nervous and alert, and Sheehan turned his attention to Miller, checking his pulse and breathing. He was still alive—more or less good news.

He straightened up, touching the side of his head where Miller had hit him hours ago, and looked around, taking in everything. His observations, always accurate, told him this was a ghastly dungeon in which to keep any living thing—cold, dark, filthy, and lacking even the decencies of fresh food and water. He smiled down at the dog again. "Let's see what we've got here, huh?"

Fifteen minutes later, pleased with his work, he lifted the dog's dish containing several day-old water and tossed what was left into Miller's face, awakening mean spirits of a soulless warden who sputtered as he realized he was sitting on the cement floor, his hands tied to the chain link, at shoulder height, with the heavy leather leashes he used whenever he wanted one of his dogs out of their cage. At length, he made his eyes focus as Brock Sheehan stood above him.

"Nice nap?" Sheehan asked pleasantly. "Don't answer unless you want to, but we do need to talk, don't we? First of all, though—" and he picked up the cattle prod, jammed it into Miller's armpit, and pulled the trigger. Miller screamed again.

"See how that feels? You get off on using it on this dog here, every day, don't you?" He stooped down to pet Conor's neck again. "The tables are turned, Monroe. This guy just might tear you to shreds for dinner. And why would he do that? Because you do *this*."

He shocked Miller with the cattle prod again.

After he stopped yelling, Monroe Miller whimpered, "Stop. Please. I think my jaw's broken."

Sheehan shrugged. "You'll recuperate—if you're lucky. Schedule your next pussy eating for about a year from now—on the off chance your mouth still works. But we need to talk, Monroe. I was asking questions about this place—and the people who might've had it in for Kenny Pine. But you didn't answer me. Instead you tried to split open my skull with your rifle butt. That's not nice."

"Don't hurt me again! Please!"

"That's up for debate. So here's what we do. I ask the questions. You answer them. If I like answers, that's lucky you. If I don't, well—we'll find out about that when we come to it. So—" He squatted down in front of Miller, cattle prod in hand. "Here we go. I really wasn't bugging you all that much, Monroe. Why did you feel it necessary to club me with a rifle butt?"

Miller shrugged, and Sheehan zapped him in the armpit. "A shrug isn't an answer, is it? So I'll ask again. Why get physical with me?"

Miller had to take a moment to catch his breath. Then he gasped, "You was askin' too many questions."

"So you decided to kill me."

"I didn't kill you!"

"No, you put me in here so the dog would—because you haven't fed him for a long time, you piece of shit!"

"Hey, I'm sorry!"

Sheehan laughed. "You hoped the dog would eat me, and now you're sorry. That deserves another zap, doesn't it?"

"No, *please!*"

"Were you going to bury me out there someplace where you bury the other dead dogs?"

Suddenly Brock tried swallowing down the nausea engulfing him. He waited until it subsided, and his next question came through a partially closed throat. "What else did you do with the dead dogs? Toss them into the woods so the vultures would clean them up for you? Or did you skin them, cut them up, and feed them to the ones that you left living?"

Monroe Miller's eyes bulged with terror, as big and wide as half dollars. "Not alla time!" he screamed again. "Not alla time! Not when we was makin' money!"

He began sobbing. Brock Sheehan said nothing. He just squatted there, wrestling with his rage until Miller's blubbering stopped. Then, almost in a whisper: "You have any idea how much I want to kill you right now, Monroe? And how slow I want to do it?"

The crying started again, so much so that Miller couldn't even get out a "please." Sheehan waited—perhaps for three minutes or so.

"Okay, Monroe, enough. It's time for us to talk again—mostly about gamblers. If those answers suck..." He squeezed the trigger on the cattle probe in front of Miller's face and it crackled and buzzed. "The next one, my friend, isn't going to be in your armpit. I'm going to lay this probe right against your balls and zap—long and hard. Trust me, it won't be fun."

Miller didn't say anything but screamed "Ahhhh!"

"After that, the next one is up your ass—so think carefully before you answer."

"Anything," he sniveled. "Anything. I swear to God—"

Sheehan stood up, looming over Monroe Miller, his right hand gripping the cattle prod, wishing with all his heart that he could use it again. "Okay," he said. "Let's chat."

Brock Sheehan didn't arrive back at his boat in the Vermillion harbor until ten o'clock that evening. He'd stopped at a gas station along the way, one in which one doesn't have to ask for the key to the men's room. He scooted quickly inside to wash much of the dried blood off his face and neck, knowing there'd be a scar between his eyebrow and his sideburns unless he chose plastic surgery to repair it. Well, hell! He was too damn old for cosmetic surgery anyway. He wasn't an actor or a fashion model, so scars didn't mean much to him anymore. However, there wasn't much he could do with his ruined shirt and jacket.

He also spent a few minutes in a supermarket along the highway, too—but no one bothered looking at him strangely on a late Sunday evening. He had his wallet back again after Monroe Miller was more than happy to tell him where it was.

Once he arrived home at his boat and adjusted to his new situation, he wadded up all his bloody clothes and put them in a trash bag to be disposed of. He showered, had a fast drink of Irish whiskey, then a much slower one, and fell to sleep almost immediately.

Awakening at seven thirty a.m., he showered again, fixed breakfast, dressed in his out-on-the-town clothes, and sat on the deck to use the telephone.

"Detective Sergeant Tobe Blaine," the voice loud and clear over the phone.

"Good morning, Detective," he said. "This is Brock Sheehan. Remember me?"

191

"Remember you? You're in my highlight film. What can I do for you?"

"You told me to keep out from under your feet about the Kenny Pine murder."

"So I did. And...?"

"You also said if I had any interesting information, I should give it to you instead of doing something about it myself."

"Are we reliving the magical moments from our last conversation, Mr. Sheehan, or is there something you wanted to tell me?"

"I learned that a lot of people in the dogfight business—specifically the big-time gamblers—were ticked off at Kenny Pine."

"What big-time gamblers?"

"I don't know their names—but I know the ones at the top end are mostly Italian mob guys."

"Italian mob guys?" Blaine's tone got more intense. "Youngstown mob guys or Cleveland mob guys?"

"Sorry," Sheehan said, "I didn't get their home addresses. Italian guys are—Italian guys. That's all I know."

"And where did you hear this crap?"

"I—can't reveal my sources."

Now Blaine sounded annoyed. "How do I know you're not making this up?"

"Call the sheriff's office in Mahoning County and suggest they drop by the farm where Pine used to stage his dogfights."

"What are they going to find there, Mr. Sheehan? Dogs?"

"One dog, yes—and maybe something else."

"What else?"

He hesitated. At length he said, "A big surprise for the sheriff."

"Did you murder someone at Pine's farm?"

"Not that I know of. I did commit a felony, though."

"Really? What's that?"

"Theft."

"Tacky. What'd you steal?"

"A dog."

"I'm not a dogcatcher," Blaine said, her tone edging toward boredom, "and I don't investigate theft. I'm with homicide, remember?"

"Then I'm free and clear, as long as you don't rat me out to the Mahoning police. This just might give you somewhere else to look besides at Linus Callahan." He took a coffee gulp. "His girlfriend of two years was beaten and gang-raped by the guys who were looking for him—and she's throwing him under a bus. Then he got the crap kicked out of him by the same crew. A good friend and coworker of his was beaten half to death and wound up in the hospital—all because you're calling him a 'person of interest.'"

"My fault?"

"It sure as hell isn't mine! You can follow up on this little tip—or not, as you so choose. As for me—I'm out of it. Have a great day."

He clicked off the phone, smiling. He finished his coffee, then went below to his bunk, leaned down, and rumpled the ears of the black pit bull, fast asleep on the multicolored rug at the side of his bunk.

"All right, Conor," he said, "you've slept long enough. Get your butt up so I can feed you and take you for a walk."

Conor opened one annoyed eye and checked out his new best friend forever, Brock Sheehan.

CHAPTER FIFTEEN

It was Monday morning, not quite ten o'clock. Linus Callahan had never been in Metro Health before, the enormous hospital just west of the Cuyahoga River. He had no idea of its vastness. His knee still in horrible shape, he'd had to limp at least half a mile between buildings, wishing he had a cane or thick walking stick to keep him from falling on his ass. He'd moved through huge lobbies and down long hallways, asking questions and getting directions from guards and nurses and hospitality volunteers who didn't know much more about the sprawled-out campus than he did. He carried a large bouquet of flowers while he looked for the room he sought.

Finally, he found it. He stopped in the open doorway for a moment, not knowing whether he should knock.

Maureen Flanagan was half asleep on the hospital bed. She shared the room with another woman, but the curtains were pulled around that bed so no one could see her even by accident if they walked past the open door. The TV hanging from the ceiling was playing some daytime soap opera, but the sound was muted.

Maureen opened her eyes and allowed them to focus. Seeing Linus, she instantly put her hands to her face to hide the damage. Knowing it was hopeless, she said his name quietly, her lower lip twice the size it normally was, and turned toward the wall.

"Hey," he said softly. "How ya doin'?"

"You're not supposed to be here," she said to the wall beside her.

He held out the bouquet, though he was too far away from the bed for her to take them from him. "I—brought you these flowers—to cheer you up, y'know."

She didn't respond, nor did she look at him. Finally she said, "I wish you'd go."

"I care about you, Maureen."

"If you cared about me, I wouldn't be here." She breathed heavily through her mouth. "If you hadn't been such a big shot in the bar with Kenny Pine, none of this would've happened." She put her hands up to her face. "I'll never forgive you for this, Linus—not as long as I live."

Linus didn't know how to answer. His emotional injury was even more painful than his physical ones. He just shook his head, even though her eyes were closed. "It kills me that you—got hurt."

She closed her eyes and shook her head, and there was desperation in her voice. "No talk about it. Please."

"It wasn't your fault, not one little bit of it."

She finally did look at him, as he was standing directly under the overhead light. "They beat you up bad enough," she said. "Why did they bust into the apartment and—do what they did to me?"

"I—don't know. Meanness, I guess. They think I murdered Kenny Pine."

"So do I."

"Jesus, Maureen! How could you believe—?" He leaned back against the wall, fearful of losing his balance and falling. "Shit! So do the police. I can get arrested any time. Those three guys who—hurt you—" He had to use "hurt" because he couldn't bring himself to say the R-word to her. She pulled the sheet and blanket up under her chin and shook her head. She didn't want to hear about it anymore.

"All three of them are in jail," he continued, not paying

attention to her feelings. "That's one good thing." He eased himself into the bedside chair, his broken ribs grinding against each other, and tried not to grunt aloud. "They confessed. My Uncle Brock is a very persuasive guy."

She turned away again. "Go home. Take care of yourself."

"I'm not leaving you alone here. No way." He shifted around to try getting his body more comfortable.

"My mom's coming a little later. She'll be here at around six o'clock."

"I'll wait until then."

Maureen's eyes teared up. "Linus, I'm moving out. I'll stay with her for a while. She's got a key to the apartment, so she'll come by tomorrow and pack up all my things. I can't live with you anymore." She had little strength left, but managed to turn her voice raw, nasty, furious. "Don't argue, don't try to make this right. It's never gonna be right—not ever. I don't want be with you. I never even wanna see you again as long as I live!" Her face reddened beneath the stitches and bruises. "I'll never let another man touch me, ever again." Her eyes darkened. "Either that, or I'll let everybody. Now get out, Linus. Goddammit, *now*!"

He could say nothing more. He left her, found the waiting room, and sat there for ten minutes until he realized he'd been a damn fool for coming there in the first place. Maybe he should have just sent a card, or had the flowers delivered.

He gave the unwanted bouquet to the nurse in charge, and left the hospital—a long walk again. His badly bruised knee with a hairline fracture would torment him for several more days.

Brock Sheehan and his new dog, Conor, returned to his boat from their early-evening walk. It had been more than thirty years since Sheehan had actually walked a dog; back then there was no law forcing dog owners to carry plastic bags with them to clean up messes their pets made outside. He thought about chucking the plastic shopping bag he'd used over the side, but then realized it would mean at least two bags each day floating in the harbor—and that would get every other boater up in arms, especially those that lived aboard. So he deposited the bag in the trashcan at the head of the dock.

"How do you like going for walks, Conor?" he said as they both reboarded the boat. "Good exercise, huh? Well, it's good for me, too."

The dog just looked at him, confused. From earliest puppyhood he'd been ignored or abused—kicked, beaten, shocked with a cattle prod, and savaged by other dogs while a crowd of onlookers cheered. He didn't understand why this new person hadn't hurt him yet. He was still suspicious, even when Brock Sheehan gently rumpled his ears

Fingering the bandage plaster on his head where he'd been hit with a shotgun butt, Brock emptied into a salad bowl one of the inexpensive supermarket dog food cans he'd bought—but reading the small print ingredients on the label and discovering there were more grains and gross chicken parts than meat, he realized this wasn't the best sustenance for a dog, and resolved to shop in a pet store in the morning for food more nutritious. Then he filled another bowl with fresh water for Conor, poured himself a tall Bushmills Black, switched on his old boom box to listen to a CD of Celtic music, and settled into his captain's chair on the deck, facing the setting sun.

The previous day had been one hell of an adventure.

He reached down to scratch Conor's head and neck. The dog's body tensed and quivered, fearing he'd be hurt again, but the sound he made was less of rage than a slight warning. Brock took his hand away.

"Hey, Conor," he whispered. The day before, he'd worried his new dog might kill him. He hoped they would eventually bond, and the pit bull would wind up loving him more than anyone else had in the past two decades.

Love from a dog vs. love from a woman? Not quite the same thing, but it would work as a substitute. He arose and poured himself another drink.

He hoped Linus Callahan's police problems would finally go away. He'd already torn open old wounds with Rory McCurdy because of the flimsy connection of Linus and Kenny Pine, and now being under the microscope of Detective Sergeant Tobe Blaine was a boot in the ass for him. His Arizona Skye brunch had turned out badly, jerking him back to their previous disenchantment—and treacherous meetings with dog abusers George Schmitt and Monroe Miller had kicked up memories he'd tried to stuff away—memories of other brute force—which was how he'd made his living.

All because Linus Callahan was "family," and Brock Sheehan was very much a kinfolk man despite his own blood relatives eliminating him from their ménage as if he were a hot rock.

The CD he'd been listening to finished. He wanted to put on another one—he loved music and solitary drinking on his boat in the evenings—but somehow getting out of his chair, going below to his cabin, and shuffling through music CDs for something that would fit his mood seemed to be too much trouble, so he sat quietly in the cool silence as the twilight turned to night, closing his eyes but not sleeping, just—resting.

That's when he heard footsteps on the dock and Conor immediately rose to his feet, head down, shoulders hunched, short ears pressed back against his skull, humming deep from his gut.

Two men were approaching, one several steps behind the other. The man in the lead was a few years past Sheehan's age, dressed impeccably in a very expensive suit like those worn by top-rung Wall Streeters in New York. Truly handsome and smooth like an old-time movie star who always played the good/bad guy—the flawed-but-beautiful Paul Newman-Alan Ladd type star. The one just behind him was in his forties, wearing an off-the-rack sports jacket, khaki Dockers, and a hideous necktie he'd probably bought for a buck at a resale shop. Sheehan knew instinctively that one was subordinate, the jacket not disguising an underarm shoulder holster that made him lean slightly to his left.

Sheehan stood up. Conor's side pressed against his leg.

"Gentlemen," he said.

"Mr. Sheehan?"

"That's what people call me who don't know me very well."

"I see. May I come aboard?"

"You're both welcome."

The leader said, "He'll stay out on the dock if that's okay."

Bodyguard, Sheehan thought. "If that's what you want—but I won't make you walk the plank."

The man shot his white cuffs so the gold links showed. He looked at Conor. "That's a pit bull, isn't it?"

"You know your dogs."

The man nodded. "I have two Borzois myself. That's another name for a Russian wolfhound."

"I know what a Borzoi is."

"Excellent. Does he bite?"

Sheehan sighed. "He hasn't bitten *me*."

"I don't suppose you'd lock him up before I join you."

"He lives here. You don't."

The man shrugged. "I'll take my chances, then."

"Fine, just don't make any quick moves like you're going to strangle me."

"Not planning on strangling you—or him, either." He stepped aboard the boat and extended his hand for a shake. "My name is Victor Gaimari, Mr. Sheehan. I'm—"

"I know who you are—*Don* Victor." Sheehan shook his hand.

Gaimari looked startled and pleased. "I'm impressed. You live way out here on a boat and you've still heard of me."

"I read the papers." Brock took his handshake. "You know who I am, too—or at least who I used to be—so let's not waste time feeling each other out." He pulled over another deck chair

199

and set it up. "Make yourself comfortable. Drink? I'm afraid all I have is Irish whiskey."

"No, thanks. I'm here on business, sort of."

"Sort of." Sheehan turned and said to the bodyguard on the dock, "How about you? Something to wet your whistle?"

The bodyguard looked blank. Gaimari said, "Johnny doesn't drink on duty."

"He doesn't talk when he's on duty, either?"

"Not much. It makes life easier.' He unbuttoned his suit jacket. "I had a surprise visit today—from a friend."

Sheehan reached down and touched the top of Conor's head, feeling the pit bull quivering. "Down, Conor. Down. That's a good boy." The dog lowered himself onto the deck, still alert, having heard the command before. Sheehan thought he hadn't always been a trained fighter—he'd been someone's pet, perhaps long ago. How old *was* Conor, anyway? "Do we have shared friends?"

"Figure of speech. My office is in the Terminal Tower—I manage hedge funds for other people—and I'm a financial planner."

"I know that, too. I used to get around back in the day, Don Victor. Nothing like you do—but I learn stuff."

"About me?"

"I still keep my eyes and ears open, just so I don't lose my edge. You're the *boss man* of the—Italian business community in Northeast Ohio—ever since your uncle passed away and named you his successor. Have I got that right?"

"Close enough. I'm impressed. You know a lot of people."

Sheehan shrugged. "Even ones who aren't Italian."

Gaimari cocked his head, accepting Sheehan's assertion. "My visitor this morning was not Italian—but knows all about you and your quaint live-aboard life here."

"And what does he know about me? That I'm a great sailor?"

"You're not the American Jacques Cousteau, Mr. Sheehan. Not yet." Gaimari carefully crossed one leg over the other, making sure there would be no wrinkles on his trousers. "And my visitor was not a 'he,' either."

Tobe Blaine, Sheehan thought, gritting his teeth. She must have told him he'd been involved with her investigation. Why? He had no idea.

Gaimari continued, "It regards the unfortunate elimination of one Kenny Pine."

"What have you got to do with Kenny Pine?"

"Other than he's a dead basketball player and an ex-con? Not much—but somebody ratted on the Italian community in Cleveland about Pine's death," Gaimari said. "And that somebody, Mr. Sheehan, was you."

Sheehan's eyebrows climbed toward his hairline. "I never mentioned your name. Not once."

"Then why does my female visitor know all about you?"

"Research, probably. I do a bit of that myself. My nephew, Linus Callahan, is a—person of interest, according to the cops—and I know damn well he wouldn't kill Kenny Pine or anybody else. He doesn't have it in him. He's an animal lover—but that doesn't mean he's looking to eliminate everybody who isn't one. I want to get him off the hook—or at least put somebody else on it. Eventually I wound up in Campbell, Ohio talking to Monroe Miller—Pine's partner in the dogfight business."

"What I've heard," Gaimari said, "is that Miller blabbed to the authorities that sent Pine to prison in the first place."

"He admitted that to me."

"Why would he do such a thing, I wonder?"

"Because the Mahoning County prosecutor was looking for a big name to take the fall—and Pine fit the bill perfectly. So he made a deal with Miller, Kenny Pine went to prison for three years, and the DA is now ginning up for the governor's race next year."

"Fine," Gaimari said, "but who made Miller cast shade on his business partner?"

"He told me some Italian friends in Youngstown suggested he do so."

"Suggested."

Sheehan attempted a smile. "I'm giving you Monroe's condensed version."

"Let me give you mine, then." He looked at his bodyguard, who peered down the dock at who might be approaching, paying no attention to his boss. Then he asked, "Can I change my mind about that drink? It's cooling off now that the sun has gone."

Brock Sheehan stood, and the dog did as well, while Gaimari uncrossed his legs, ready to leap from his chair. "Don't worry about the dog," Sheehan said. "He had a chance to rip off chunks of my body, too. Instead I made friends with him, and—well, here we are."

"Maybe I should make friends with him, too."

Sheehan headed for the bottle. "He just needs one friend at a time. You want this with ice?"

"Neat, please." Don Victor Gaimari put his hand out toward Conor, palm upward, but the dog shied away.

"His name's Conor," Sheehan said. "That means hound lover."

"Cute."

When two drinks were poured and Sheehan returned to his seat, the dog no more than four feet away from him, he said, "Fill me in, then."

"You might not remember," Gaimari said, "that some years ago there were two different Italian—groups—in the Youngstown area. Half of them were hooked into the Cleveland organization and the other half worked under the Pittsburgh guys. That meant they were—friendly competitors."

"Friendly."

"You can call it that."

"Like the Irish Catholics and the Belfast Protestants."

Gaimari said, "My Cleveland people haven't one damn thing to do with dogfighting—or horse racing—or cockfights. We never have. We're more of a high-class company—and strictly on the level. We're all legal now."

"*All* legal?"

Gaimari chuckled. "Well—just like the Irish guys you work for."

"Worked—past tense. I'm retired now—just like your Italian crew."

"Legal ninety-five percent, then."

"I'm not so good at math and numbers, Don Victor, so I accept that."

"Excellent. Whatever happened between Pine and Miller and any Youngstown or Mahoning County Italian organization was not on our wavelength. Therefore, it's the Mahoning sheriff's problem and not mine—and Cleveland homicide cops shouldn't be walking into my hedge fund office to cry on my shoulder."

"I hope the tears didn't stain your pretty suit."

"Very thoughtful of you to ask—but I'm always careful regarding other people's tears. I found out a lot about you before I had Johnny drive me here to see you—your name and your reputation when you were Rory McCurdy's top assistant. I also recall when you were active, you had—confrontations with some Italian people. True?"

"Confrontations? I wouldn't call them confrontations. Differences of opinion. But I'm long retired now. I just hang out on my boat with my dog and my Bushmills Black—and every winter I go someplace south of here where I won't freeze my ass off."

"I go south for a while, too. To Naples, Florida. Ever been?" Sheehan shook his head.

"It's a great town. Half the people there are from Cleveland—and half of *them* are Italian. You can't even walk down the street in Naples without seeing people wearing Browns jackets or Indians ball caps or Cavaliers sweatshirts. It's almost like a home away from home."

"Home," Sheehan said softly. "I don't have a home anymore. Just a homeless guy with too much money to sleep on a sidewalk grate."

"This boat is as good a home as any."

"If you say so."

Victor Gaimari held out his glass. "Well then—chin chin, Mr. Sheehan."

"'*Slainte*, Don Victor," Brock Sheehan said—and they clinked glasses.

CHAPTER SIXTEEN

Victor Gaimari was more than comfortably rich, as were all halfway-intelligent hedge fund managers. His elegant offices were located on the eleventh floor of Terminal Tower, right on Public Square, with a great view of the lake and westward. One junior associate in the firm was kept employed, less for his financial abilities than his talent as an amateur chef, mostly creative Italian dishes. All sorts of movers and shakers in Greater Cleveland hoped and wished they'd be invited for lunch at Gaimari and Associates.

Victor was also the *capo di tutti capi* of the Cleveland Italian mafia. He'd been the acting head for several years while his uncle, Giancarlo D'Allessandro, was the aging mastermind. When the old man grew tired and senile and eventually died, he willed to his nephew his honorary title of "Don," and all his incredible dominance and mastery.

Victor tried to bring the mob into the twenty-first century, but still followed most of his uncle's preferences. The outfit had not actually put out a hit contract for more than seventy years, and even back when they did, they mostly killed off mobsters belonging to other rival gangs—not barbers, dry cleaners, or taxicab owners. Liquor was most often the cause of the shootings and stabbings and cars being wired with bombs, especially when the United States of America was under the ridiculous Prohibition Act. The alcohol bought and sold was either smuggled in from another country, or made in the cellar or back room of someone's local business—and sugar was a main ingredient, which caused the historic Sugar Wars in Cleveland during the 1920s. The four corners of East 185th Street and Woodland Avenue hosted gunfights and killings happening almost weekly, and the local landmark, still called Bloody Corners, is a shrine to the elderly Italians with the longest memories.

Today, mob kingpins strived mightily to be legal and honest, and succeed more often than one might imagine. They still had enormous power in unions, construction contracts, and naturally in gambling, as almost any Italian would eagerly bet on something as minor as how many minutes late the next eastern suburbs RTA passenger train from downtown would arrive. Restaurants and nightclubs in Greater Cleveland run little casinos in their "private dining rooms," and most area bookies had their own businesses thriving. The Italian mob took a slice off the top.

Whatever influence they had now—and frequently used in Cleveland's three legal rival casinos—remained a mystery and was never spoken about by anyone.

Gaimari also swore to protect the legacy of the late godfather by not tampering with prostitution and chemical substances. There were plenty of hookers in town, though, owned by other ethnic crowds—and a plethora of habit-forming illegal drugs in Ohio and almost everywhere in the United States, if not the world.

Now, Brock Sheehan thought, the local mob boss shows up on his boat to find out if he'd been squealed on to the cops for quietly operating a brutal dogfighting operation, which he swore he had nothing to do with.

It didn't take much for Sheehan to figure out Detective Sergeant Tobe Blaine had visited Victor Gaimari to tell him what happened at the Kenny Pine-Monroe Miller farm and who was behind it. He wished he'd never contacted her.

Did she now suspect Gaimari in the Pine murder—or was she somehow involved with him that had little to do with police business and was trying to warn him?

For this evening, anyway, he and Don Victor clinking glasses of *his* Irish whiskey aboard *his* boat made them temporary BFFs. They enjoyed several drinks together, since Victor had a faithful driver with him who never imbibed—at least not where anyone could see him.

So the following bright, snappy morning, Brock Sheehan and Conor headed back to Cleveland and its environs to make a few unexpected appearances.

His first stop was in front of the animal shelter where Linus Callahan worked. He stayed in the car, calling the shelter to ask if Linus could step outside for a few moments, then climbed out of the driver's seat, Conor on a leash beside him so he could sniff around and then lift his leg against one of the trees.

Eventually Linus hobbled out, squinting into the sun. His face showed shining red stitches like Karloff's Frankenstein monster. The bruises from the beating had turned him several hues of Technicolor. Looking like someone else's nightmare, he seemed stupefied at his uncle's arrival, especially with a black pit bull he'd never seen before.

"You brought the shelter a dog?" he said by way of welcome. "Did you find him on the street?"

"Nope. He's my dog now. His name is Conor—with one *n*, like the saint. I just wanted to let you know, Linus, in case of a situation when both Conor and Patton are around. I'd hate like hell trying to break up a fight between two pit bulls. I'll have him neutered as soon as I get around to it."

Linus offered Conor a palms-up hand to sniff. "How old is he?"

"I haven't the vaguest idea."

"Where did you get him, anyway?" He moved his hand up to scratch Conor's neck just below his ear, knowing exactly where pit bulls love to be touched. "We have lots of rescue dogs you could have adopted, right here."

"It's too involved to go into, Linus—except that he was a

prisoner at Kenny Pine's farm, and I rescued him. Impulse of the moment."

"A prisoner?"

"Locked up in a cage where he didn't want to be. I guess I became a dog lover at that very moment, so I took him."

Linus understood perfectly. His feeling for animals had gotten him his job, his own best four-legged friend, and eventually marked him a murder suspect. "What were you doing at Pine's farm?"

"Trying to get you off the police suspect list."

He leaned forward eagerly. "And?"

"I dug up a few things the cops might be more interested in," Sheehan said, "which doesn't mean you're pure and innocent again. Not yet. We're on our way back to Akron to maybe get a nudge in a different direction. Meantime, take care of yourself—and don't forget that poor girl who worked with you. Visit her in the hospital. Bring her some flowers or some candy she won't have to chew. She needs a friend." He turned and opened the rear car door, making a kissing sound to Conor, who jumped inside as if he'd been doing it all his life.

He didn't head for Akron right away. There was someone else in Cleveland he had to see.

Paisley Electronics was in a modern, low-slung building in Solon, a well-to-do community south of the city. Sheehan navigated his way through Solon via Ohio 91, lined with many restaurants, malls, and small businesses tucked into former retail shops. Paisley, though, was on a long stretch of road with other big-time companies and manufacturing plants on either side, close by Stouffer's high-rise headquarters.

Brock left Conor in the car with both rear windows open about four inches. It had been decades since he'd owned a dog, but he knew one did not shut an animal up in an airless car. He also thought no one reaches in to pet a pit bull they'd never seen before, and if they do, it's their own damn fault.

Inside, the receptionist called Cody Thacken to announce his visitor. It took him little time to pop out from his office. He was a leggy six foot seven—not surprising for a guy who'd played Big Ten basketball. When shaking Brock's hand, his fingers went halfway up Brock's arm. According to his graduation date, he was no more than twenty-six years old, but looked older, beginning to lose his hair early—or because he was so damn big and his head was too close to the sun.

"What can I do for you?" he said, his voice low and rumbly as he led Sheehan back toward the rear of the building where he hung out. "You said on the phone you were writing a book on OSU basketball?"

"Everybody writes about Ohio State football," Sheehan told him. "I just want to do something different."

"I've been out of it for more than three years," Thacken said, "so I don't know what I can tell you."

The young man seemed pleasant enough as he sat behind his desk—in a very large chair—and leaned back, relaxing. "So here we are," he said. "Ask away, Mr.—I'm sorry, what was your name again?"

"Molloy," Sheehan said. "Terry Molloy. You played for three years at Ohio State?"

Thacken nodded. "Point guard. I wasn't really a starter. I used to get my minutes, though—about ten per game."

"That's not bad."

"I wish I could've started, but I knew damn well I wasn't that good."

"You played with a real superstar, though."

Thacken looked down at his hands on a desk that was too small for them. "Kenny Pine? Sure. I kind of idolized him—just to sit on the bench and watch him. Amazing."

Sheehan took a small spiral notebook and a pen from his pocket. "Were you friends off the court?"

"Oh, yeah. Great friends. I hung out with him whenever I could. When you're best buds with someone that famous and talented, it makes you feel especially good about it."

"Kind of like some nobody fucking a movie star."

Cody Thacken seemed to find that extremely amusing. His laughter was loud and powerful.

"Speaking of fucking," Sheehan said, "Kenny Pine got into some trouble over a rape incident during his senior year."

Now there was no more laughter, and all Thacken's bodily perspiration seemed to rush to his forehead and upper lip and shine there under the office lights. "There was talk—but no formal charges, because there was no proof. Nobody mentions it anymore," he said, mopping himself with a Kleenex from the box on his desk.

"That was at a party, as I recall."

A nod.

"Were you at that party, too?"

"Yeah. Kenny and I talked to—that girl for a while. She was totally shitfaced after a while. Pretty soon I went looking for the bar—I was gonna bring each of them a drink. She was slurping vodka, by the way. When I came back, they were nowhere in sight. I—got no idea what happened next. But about an hour later, Kenny finds me and tells me we better get the hell out of there. I ask him why but—he doesn't answer me."

"He raped her?"

Thacken shrugged, eyebrows lifted, palms upraised. "Nobody goes around telling people they raped somebody, for crysakes. I couldn't find them for a while—but I didn't look upstairs or in the basement. All I know is he shows up again and wants to leave."

"And?"

"And we left."

"Didn't say goodbye to anybody? You didn't try to find Meredith Oborn?"

"I figure she'd nodded off and was asleep under a table somewhere. The rest of them were either drunk as a skunk or were making out hot and heavy—on the couches, on the stairs, in the kitchen, and who knows where else upstairs or in the basement. It's not the kind of party you drift around to say goodbye, shake hands and tell 'em you'll see 'em around."

Sheehan's eyes narrowed—he couldn't help it. Through his gritted teeth, he said, "The police questioned you afterwards?"

The head bobbed affirmatively. "A few days later, yeah. Campus police. I told them the exact same thing I told you." He tried getting more comfortable in the chair, wriggling his ass and half standing before he relaxed again.

"Campus police? Not Columbus police or the state inspectors? Just campus cops? Sounds like you got off pretty lucky, huh?"

Thacken grinned. He needed an orthodontist, as his teeth were crooked. "You can say that again," he chortled.

Brock Sheehan parked in the garage across from the main Akron Public Library, leaving the rear window cracked again so Conor could breathe fresh air—or as fresh as air could get in an indoor garage.

Once in the library, Sheehan signed onto the microfiche again and checked out sports news from St. Cyril High School for the past four years. The school was in a nice neighborhood, not too far from where the Oborn family lived, and its football team had racked up a more-than-respectable rate recently, thanks to their celebrated quarterback, Lloyd Oborn.

There were photos of Lloyd all over the St. Cyril paper and the *Akron Beacon Journal*, mostly wearing his football uniform, shaking hands with the Fairlawn mayor, the Akron mayor, the principal of the high school, cheering in the center of all his teammates, and one special one clasping the hand of former Browns quarterback legend Bernie Kosar, whose retired uniform number, 19, he had insisted on wearing. Lloyd Oborn was a good-looking kid—always smiling, happy, proud.

Except for one photo, obviously candid and snapped from the sidelines. Lloyd was wearing his helmet in midfield, being held back by his teammates from attacking one of the defensive linemen from the opposing team—though why two human beings

211

would fistfight each other while wearing helmets with face guards Sheehan couldn't understand.

The story beneath the *Akron Beacon Journal* photograph reported that Lloyd had been sacked three times in one game and lost his cool the third time. Well known for his temper even before this, Lloyd had once been benched for two weeks as punishment for starting a fight the year before.

Brock Sheehan wrote down the sportswriter's name: Ezra Hoffman

More than a year later, Hoffman had written another story—this time without any photos: Lloyd Oborn had turned down many football scholarships, which was surprising to everyone. He chose instead to stay close to home and attend the University of Akron—with no mention of his being on the freshman football team.

Sheehan went out to his car, letting the dog out to pee in a grassy swath behind the parking garage. Then he coaxed him into the back seat, fumbling around for a small pack of tissues to wipe the dog drool off his own face and jacket.

Dog love is tough, he thought.

He pondered for at least ten minutes as to what he was going to say. At last he called the *Beacon Journal* on his cell phone and asked to speak to Ezra Hoffman.

"Mr. Hoffman, I'm—Terry Malloy, sportswriter for the *Denver Post*. I'm in town because Denver University is trying to snag some great high school football players around the country. Now I know one of the Akron kids, name of—" and he deliberately paused as though he was checking his notes "—Lloyd Oborn. He had college offers all over the place—schools like OSU and Florida and Notre Dame. But he picked University of Akron instead, and isn't playing football for them, at least not yet. I know you covered Oborn all during his high school years, so can I pick your brain a little bit?"

There was silence for a moment, as if Hoffman was considering his options. Then: "Who did you say you were again?"

"Terry Molloy, *Denver Post*."

"Uh-huh."

"So can I come by and see you?"

"Well—it's awkward here in the newsroom—noisy—but I guess you know all about that," Hoffman said. Then his voice grew seductive; at least it sounded like that to Sheehan. "It's almost one o'clock. We can talk if you take me out and buy me lunch. How's that sound?"

"Okay, I guess."

"Great. Meet me at Eduardo's in about fifteen minutes. Know where that is?"

"I'll find it."

"Just look for me. I'm in my fifties, I'm wearing a tweed sports coat, a yellow shirt, and the ugliest damn purple tie you've ever seen."

Sheehan cruised around looking for Market Street—not hard to find, right in the middle of downtown, parking in a lot next to the restaurant. He warned the attendant who took his money not to put his hand in the slightly opened window to pet the pit bull. "If you get hurt," he said, "you've been warned." Then he slipped him an extra five-dollar bill. "Keep your eyes open and don't let anyone else touch him, either."

The valet parker almost glowed. Extra five-buck tips were rare during a late Akron lunch hour.

Eduardo's was kind of elegant for Akron, and being hustled for an expensive lunch nitpicked at Brock's psyche. He had no trouble finding Ezra Hoffman, though. He could have spotted the purple tie from half a block away.

"Hi, I'm Terry Molloy," Sheehan fibbed again, sliding into the booth opposite the heavyset man already halfway through a vodka martini.

"Get yourself a drink," Hoffman said, and waved at the waiter. Sheehan ordered his usual Bushmills Black.

"I don't think we have Bushmills Black," the waiter said. "What's your second choice?"

A better restaurant, Sheehan thought. Instead he said, "Jack Black, then. Neat."

"And another one of these," Hoffman added, waving his martini glass. Then he said, "So how long have you been in town, Mr. Molloy?"

"A few days."

"You came all the way here from Colorado for this bullshit story about colleges recruiting high school quarterbacks when you could've just picked up the telephone?"

Sheehan felt his throat tightening over the unsubtle insult. "I like to get the—feel of a place I write about."

"Costing the *Denver Post* a fortune."

"It's getting ready to snow in Denver, so—"

Hoffman toyed with his glass some more, then took the rest of the martini down in one gulp. "A guy writes about high school football when Denver has all three major league sports teams, plus skiing and snowboarding and ice skating out the yin yang? I wouldn't think there'd be that much interest in a bunch of seventeen-year-olds knocking each other around on a gridiron."

"You cover high school football."

"This isn't the wild, wild west—it's Akron. Ohio. The biggest sport here is the Soap Box Derby. I'm running my time out until I retire." He cocked his head. "You look like you're close to retiring, too, but you're on a big hot expensive trip to write about kids with acne playing football."

"You do what you can."

When the waiter brought the drinks, Ezra Hoffman ordered a Thai peanut salad *and* a shrimp and scallops entree—the two most expensive items on the lunch menu. Sheehan settled for a cheeseburger with potato chips.

The food arrived. Hoffman said, "So—you could have been a contender, huh?"

"What?"

Hoffman nodded, and then did a pretty accurate impersona-tion of Marlon Brando. "*I coulda been a contender! I coulda been somebody! Instead of just a bum—which is what I am!*"

Brock Sheehan was shocked, feeling like a butterfly that had just been mounted on a pin. He tried not to look humiliated, and failed.

"Terry Molloy." Hoffman shook his head, sipped his new drink, and then laughed. "A Brando movie name. You should just call yourself Stanley Kowalski or Don Vito Corleone."

"Big fan of old movies, are you?"

"That's why god invented DVDs."

"Lots of people are named Terry Molloy. It's not that unu-sual."

"Really?" Hoffman said, boring in for the kill. "Then, tell me this, Terry Molloy from Denver, Colorado. The Akron U football team's nickname is The Zips. Michigan's team is the Wolverines. What's the nickname of the Denver U team?"

Brock Sheehan didn't answer because he couldn't.

"It's the Pioneers, asshole—the Denver Pioneers. You're no sportswriter. I called the *Denver Post* before I left the office and they never heard of you. I don't even think you're from Denver. So before you scoot out of here and stick me with the lunch tab, who the hell are you and why are you giving me this line of bullshit?"

Brock thought about it for at least a minute before he figured at this point there was no further reason to lie. He lowered his voice. "Okay. Straight truth. My name is Brock Sheehan. I live in Vermillion, but most of my family is still in Cleveland. A few days ago, Kenny Pine got killed."

"Everybody knows that. He gets busted for owning and promoting dogfights, and spends three years in the Stony Lonesome. Then he's out, having paid his debt to society, and he's an instant multimillionaire with the Nuggets. Next thing you know, somebody slices open his jugular. Why do you give a shit, and what's it got to do with you?"

"My nephew wound up as the cops' most-likely-to-be-arrested murderer."

The waiter arrived with the food, and Ezra Hoffman wasted no time digging into the Thai peanut salad. Eventually coming up for air, he said, "So is this a standard keep-your-nephew-out-of-the-death-chamber uncle job?"

"It's—family. I never dealt with anything crazy like this before."

"That's such a ridiculous story, it's got to be true."

"It is true," Sheehan said, "except my nephew didn't do it."

"Fine. So an OSU basketball legend gets murdered, and you're down in Akron asking a sportswriter about a high school quarterback who won't play football anymore."

"It's a long story."

"So is *War and Peace*, and I had to read that in college. I hope yours doesn't take longer than me finishing my lunch."

A headache began thrumming behind Brock Sheehan's eyes. He didn't want to go through all the twists and turns one more time to a sportswriter who didn't give a damn one way or the other. He took a bite of his expensive cheeseburger, washed it down with water, and began: "Apparently Lloyd Oborn's older sister was a victim in some sort of sex scandal at Ohio State, and the university busted their asses trying to cover it up…"

Ten minutes later, he was finished.

Hoffman had slowed down a bit on eating his salad, so fascinated with Sheehan's story that he hadn't yet tasted his shrimp and scallops. Before commenting, he downed the rest of his vodka martini and signaled the waiter for another one—his third.

When it eventually arrived, he took a healthy swallow and said, "Sheehan—it sounds like you're looking for a black button in the dark."

"Why?"

"I didn't directly cover Kenny Pine when he was at OSU—but I met him plenty of times and I knew everything about him besides him being a hell of a basketball player. Yes, he was arrogant. Yes, he thought pure rays of sunshine came out of his ass. And yes, he was a major man-slut—a serial fucker. But Lloyd Oborn blaming him for raping his drunkenly unconscious sister at a party and then waiting four years before he kills him for it—that's a long reach."

"Also a reach for Sasha Burton at the Buckeyes' Title 9—but she knows more about sex harassment at Ohio State than almost anyone else."

"I've heard of her. She didn't actually tell you, though, did she?"

"She didn't have to," Sheehan said.

Hoffman planted two elbows on the table. "I covered Lloyd Oborn when he was in high school. Good quarterback—probably do great on some college team. He wouldn't wind up with the New England Patriots or anything. I mean, he wasn't *that* good. He got all A's and B's on his report card, but he had some temper when he put on shoulder pads—and high school kids knew better than to get into fights with him all the time."

"What were his fights about?"

"One of those offensive geniuses thinking Almighty Jesus made a rule saying no opposing team would ever dare sack a quarterback, so that was most of it. He also swung at a couple of his own offensive teammates who didn't protect him the way he thought they should."

Sheehan asked, "Did he ever get furious when he wasn't playing football?"

"I didn't hang around with him. I just wrote newspaper stories about his Hail Mary passes and his running game—which, by the way, nobody ever reads about unless they have a high school kid playing football, too." Hoffman pushed his salad plate away and upended his martini until it was all gone. Then, eyes twinkling, he said, "I'd guess your best bet is to interview the football coach. Meantime, I gotta get back to my desk or the editor will think I fell asleep on a park bench somewhere."

Then he hailed the waiter again, pointed to his untouched shrimp and scallops and said, "I need a doggie bag to take this with me."

Brock Sheehan's nascent ulcer burned as he signed his Master-Card tab. He'd been screwed, royally, as he hadn't known at first he was actually buying Ezra Hoffman both his lunch *and* his dinner.

CHAPTER SEVENTEEN

When Brock Sheehan went inside St. Cyril High School, it was the first time he'd been in such an institution since the day he'd walked down his own auditorium aisle to the deadly slow, anguished strains of "Pomp and Circumstance" to accept his high school diploma forty years earlier. He recognized the smells he'd put up with and contributed to during his adolescence but had never before noticed them. All kids ignored them, too. The odors of adolescent sweat, blossoming estrogen and testosterone, acne medicine, stale cigarette smoke, and unwashed armpits combined into a reminder of days past. He couldn't wait to ask questions and then get the hell out of there.

The head football coach at St. Cyril looked as if he'd been hired by Hollywood casting. Coffee-with-cream skin, two hundred forty pounds of solid muscle on a six-foot-one build, light brown eyes, a head shaved shiny and slick as a billiard ball, and a slightly crooked smile that never appeared on the sidelines during a physically violent game, but often showed in his more private moments. Somewhere in his middle forties, his name was John Zone.

His office was covered with things related to football—photographs, awards, plaques, framed news reports from the *Akron Beacon Journal*, and several championship trophies. On his desk was a nine-by-twelve formal portrait of his pretty wife and two children—both girls—under the age of ten, right next to a half-drunk bottle of Gatorade.

Sheehan's memories rushed back at him in another way, too. Even in high school, he'd been a big, tall guy topping two hundred pounds. The football coach—who also happened to be a Jesuit priest in Catholic school—had pressured him almost daily to join the team, probably as a linebacker if not as a nose guard, positions that were mainly about sudden physical confrontations. Sheehan wasn't that fond of football. He didn't want to hurt other people for the fun of it daily, and didn't want to be injured himself. As a result, priests and nuns were harder on him than on others because he wouldn't play football, despite his being a fast learner.

On this day he sat opposite Coach Zone after explaining to him that the dog at his feet, Conor, was a registered companion dog who rarely got into trouble. That was a small lie, of course, but few people would challenge it.

Brock wondered how such a genial, good-looking guy got stuck coaching in a high school in which most students were Caucasians more anxious to get into a good college to major in hedge funding and become part of the one percent rich than they were in learning geometry and physics, football strategy—and racism.

Still, Sheehan was more relaxed than he'd been in a while. After the awkward and humiliating moment earlier that day when Ezra Hoffman had called bullshit on his lies in the middle of a crowded restaurant, he'd decided that from now on, he'd tell the truth while helping Linus out of a messy situation. He'd always been a lousy liar, anyway. But Coach—sharper than most high school jock tenders—was interested in more than just a real name.

After a few minutes of honest conversation and a few questions about former quarterback Lloyd Oborn, Zone said, "I don't understand why you're here about Lloyd, Mr. Sheehan," Zone said. "Are you a private investigator?"

"Sort of," Sheehan replied.

He smiled his lopsided smile. "That tells me you don't have a license to do this."

"I don't. I'm poking around trying to save my nephew from getting arrested."

"For what?"

"I don't think I want to go into it."

"I see." He leaned back comfortably in his chair, folding his hands across his stomach. "You just ask questions, right? You don't answer them."

Sheehan tried to be as vague as possible. "It's nothing you need to know, Coach. I'm not messing with you, I just hold my cards close to my chest."

"That makes you a mysterious guy. Ever play football?"

"No—that's why I still have all my teeth."

"I wish I still had all mine," Zone said. "So—what exactly does Lloyd Oborn have to do with your nephew?"

"Nothing. But Kenny Pine was murdered a few days ago."

The coach frowned, puzzled. "The OSU fast forward? Then why am *I* talking to you?"

"Ever play a jigsaw puzzle? You don't know what the puzzle is supposed to look like unless you put all the pieces together—all touching each other."

"You do realize Lloyd Oborn graduated from high school this past spring? He doesn't play football here anymore, and though he turned down Ohio State in favor of Akron U, I haven't much followed him since then. I have enough to do taking care of the boys who play for me now."

"I'm not looking to get him in trouble," Sheehan said. "I just need generalities. I know he has a temper, right?"

Zone nodded at Conor, sitting quietly next to his new master, relaxed but always alert. "I hope your companion buddy there doesn't have a temper, either. I like pit bulls—but I don't try making friends with them unless I'm given permission."

"Maybe next time, Coach, He's kind of new. About Lloyd?"

"Fair enough. Lloyd didn't always fly off the handle. I think it started during his sophomore year on my team."

"But he was good."

"*Damn* good. Not good enough to go NFL pro, of course—that happens once in a lifetime to a high school coach, if at all. But he had a great arm, a good sense of the game, and girls loved him."

"He got angry a lot, though."

"Yeah—more often the older he got."

"Because you pissed him off?"

Coach Zone laughed. "You try not to piss off your best quarterback, Mr. Sheehan. I was tough on all of them, and I still am. That's what football coaches *do*. But I handled Lloyd as carefully as I could."

"Why did the anger start up, then?"

"I tried prying it out of him, but I couldn't. He played smashmouth football the same way he got good grades in his scholastic work—because he was mad at something else." Zone ran a hand over his bald head. "Partly because his sister took her own life. That has to be tough to live with."

Sheehan said, "I'm sure. Did you ever ask him about it?"

"I tried to—once. He told me in the locker room to get out of his fucking face—and that's a direct quote. Then he threw a football against the brick wall so hard it busted, and stomped out of practice. I could've gotten him kicked off the team, or suspended—but I just put it aside and kept working with him on his athletic skills."

Sheehan nodded. "You kicked him out of a game, though—I read that in an old newspaper—and kept him benched for two weeks. Why was that?"

Zone said, "I never really found out why he blew his top and went after one of the defensive linemen on the other team. At least he wouldn't tell me. I phoned their coach that evening to talk about it, and he wasn't sure either, but he thinks it was one of his linemen guys saying something about Lloyd's sister."

"You don't know that Meredith Oborn was raped at a party

when she was too drunk to say no, and everybody at OSU knew about it—which is why she eventually committed suicide?"

"I—heard something about it," he replied awkwardly. "Nothing specific, though."

"And you didn't hear that Kenny Pine just *might* have been the rapist?"

Coach Zone looked shocked, right down to his toes. "Jesus, never a single word about that!" Now he leaned forward, both elbows flat on the desktop. "Look, it happened at Ohio State— a lot of miles from here. We high school teachers aren't exactly in the loop on everything collegiate, so I don't think I ever heard Pine's name mentioned in connection with the Oborns." He winced as though a hungry fox had sneaked its way into his guts and was chewing happily on his colon. "If that's true, it's no wonder Lloyd was cheesed off all the time." He looked even more shattered. "And Kenny Pine got killed when he'd only been out of prison for a few weeks. Are you saying Lloyd murdered him?"

Sheehan shook his head. "I'm not saying anything—just asking around, that's all."

Now John Zone stood up, anger beginning to build. "Your nephew is a suspect, too, so you're trying to make somebody else look guilty?"

"I'm trying to get the truth," Sheehan said, also rising. Though much older, he was still bigger, wider, and stronger-looking than Zone—and he'd never in his life lost a fight. "You football coaches piss and moan about a fifteen-yard penalty if it's deserved or not. But this is no game—it's the life of another human being, specifically my nephew."

The coach's aborning irritation melted away, and his body relaxed, shoulders slumping. "I know. I have kids, too. I'm just hoping Lloyd didn't do anything crazy."

"Losing one's temper sometimes leads to bad things,"

Zone bobbed his head. "That's a problem. It's hard for teenagers—especially if they're lonely. The other kids at school thought he was hot stuff—and he had a pretty girlfriend for a while, but he kind of dumped her. At least that's what I heard."

"Dumped her?"

Coach Zone nodded. "Right after his sister killed herself. He said he just couldn't handle it anymore."

"But he could handle football?"

"Football is physical—and violent, even in high school."

"He might have been violent with his girlfriend, too."

"You'd have to ask her that."

Sheehan took out his notebook. "What's her name and where could I find her?"

"Not here anymore. She graduated right along with him. She was a cheerleader. Her name's Rebecca Viskas—but everyone calls her Beck. At least they used to."

"Where's she going to college?"

Zone shrugged. "I didn't know her except to nod at her or say hi once in a while during a football game. I think someone told me—maybe it was Lloyd—that she chose Cleveland State. She wanted to major in political science—or history."

"Really?"

"Yeah. She didn't pick Akron U, or OSU, either. She'd be too close to home—and to Lloyd. So without Lloyd, she's probably lonely, too, just like him." His lips pressed together for a nanosecond as he frowned. "Even without the rest of the loneliness, it's pretty hard for a teenager."

Brock Sheehan shoved his hands into his pants pockets. "Coach," he said, "lonely is tough for grown-ups, too."

He walked Conor after his meeting with Coach Zone, and then drove back to downtown Cleveland. Twilight arrived a few baby steps earlier than the night before, so the sky was already dark. Brock had pretty much stayed away from the city for the past decade. Too many memories he didn't want to stir around like ashes for fear they would flare up and burn something.

A giant outdoor chandelier hung above Euclid Avenue in the

theater district and gloriously lit up each night, an amazing landmark for a city the size of Cleveland. Letters hung large over the intersection welcoming one and all to Playhouse Square. Both the Great Lakes Theater Company and the Cleveland Play House had moved to theaters just around the corner from each other, along with the other storied and remodeled theaters presenting Broadway series and visiting shows all season long, which gave Cleveland the second-largest theater complex in the country, right behind Lincoln Center in New York. Joyful evenings and people on the street having a great time, as superb restaurants and small, fun bars stretched from Playhouse Square to Public Square, so no one ever goes hungry in the neighborhood—unless they hadn't enough money to dine elegantly.

After partly opening his car windows and admonishing the valet to watch carefully over his dog, Sheehan found a restaurant at East Thirteenth Street and Euclid Avenue, called Cowell and Hubbard—the name of the high-end jewelry store that used to be there. Now it was a fine eatery. No reservation, no table, so he ate at the bar, accompanied by three shots, neat, of Bushmills Black. He knew he should be stone-cold sober for what he was about to do next; almost everything else he'd done since his nephew showed up on his boat called for a steady hand and a clear mind. But the tension was steadily rising within him, and the drinks seemed to slow down his hammering heart.

Cleveland State University was a few blocks east of Playhouse Square, in the heart of downtown. Unlike the huge Ohio State location in Columbus, one could walk from one end of the Cleveland State campus to the other in ten minutes. Euclid Avenue, therefore, was always full of college kids, most who had grown up in the city and often still lived at home, though there was affordable new housing in the neighborhood for those who traveled farther afield from their mom's home cooking.

Sheehan got Conor from the car, fed and watered him in the parking lot, and then walked him a block north to Chester Avenue and turned east until he found the relatively new apartment building erected for CSU students. Rebecca Viskas was staying there, as he'd learned earlier that day. He couldn't just call the administrative office at CSU for that information, so he'd contacted Garrett Lavender, Rory McCurdy's attorney, and within half an hour, Lavender had somehow gotten her address for him. He wondered then if that single phone call would cost him another four hundred bucks.

Walking, he worried what to say when he finally talked to her. If he were a cop, there'd be no problem. If a licensed private investigator, he'd have a fifty-fifty chance. But a stranger?

When he finally got there, he circled the block once, thinking hard until he came up with something—naturally another lie.

He entered the vestibule, searched the names next to the signal buttons until he found ACKLEY-VISKAS. Damn! A roommate, he thought. Many college students had roommates, for companionship and to save money. He pushed the button, hoping Lloyd Oborn's high school ex-girlfriend answered, and not anyone named Ackley. Boy Ackley or girl Ackley? He wondered.

"Yes?" A female voice—youngish.

"Hi, I'm looking for Rebecca Viskas."

"That's me."

"My name is Brock Sheehan." That, at least, was the truth. "If possible, may I have about fifteen minutes of your time? I just have a few questions to ask you."

A pause. "If you're selling something, forget it. I'm a college freshman, broke on my ass, who lives on Ramen noodles and potato chips—and I'm not going to Harvard, either."

"I'm not selling anything. We can meet somewhere neutral so I won't have to come up to your place, in case you're worried."

"What questions you want to ask me? Are you some kind of pervert?"

"Hardly. I'm old enough to be your grandfather."

"So you're a dirty *old* man."

He had to chuckle. "Not yet. Look, we can meet in a restaurant or coffee shop somewhere. I won't touch you or talk dirty or want you to take your clothes off. It won't be gross, I promise you—and I'll pay you a hundred dollars for your time." He stopped, took a deep breath, and allowed words to flow out on his exhale. "I want to ask you about Lloyd Oborn."

No answer for a long moment. Finally she said, "I haven't seen Lloyd for almost a year. Haven't heard from him, either."

"That doesn't matter. I'm a headhunter, Ms. Viskas, and I'm working for a big company looking for a paid college intern. Lloyd Oborn is one name they suggested to me because he's a smart, personable guy. But I need to talk to someone who knows him very well. Come on, Ms. Viskas—it's my job. Please?"

Another pause, then a sigh. "Do you know where Rascal House Pizza is on Euclid Avenue?"

Sheehan recognized the legendary pizzeria. He'd eaten there himself on occasion. Not the best pizza in the world, but a good place where college students hang out—and can afford the pizza. He said, "I think so."

"Meet me there in half an hour. How will I know you?"

"I'll probably be the oldest one in there—and I'll have my pit bull tied up right outside. I'm a pretty tall guy—and I'm salt-and-pepper."

Rebecca Viskas said, "Who puts salt and pepper on a pizza?"

In the Rascal House, Sheehan sat at a window, looking out onto Euclid Avenue at the light post to which he'd tied Conor's leash. If anyone went near him, Sheehan would be up and out there within seconds—but then not too many strangers just walk up to pet a pit bull. Students ran around, singly or in pairs, carrying books, eating at pizzerias or Subway or in CSU coffee shops, and enjoying the crisp fall air that would soon turn into a chilly winter—but they all knew a pit bull when they saw one.

Sheehan couldn't remember when he was that young, carefree, and excited to be out on his own in a college full of people his own age from whom he could learn—or could teach.

He was drinking coffee, which had garnered a strange look from the kid behind the counter. People rarely mix pizza with coffee.

Thirty minutes later, two young women entered Rascal House—one black, one white, both very pretty and both looking angry. The dishwasher blonde spotted him right away and marched over as though they were Navy Seals on a kill-or-be-killed mission.

"I'm Beck Viskas," the blonde said, her voice low with a sharp, nasty edge to it. "This is my roommate, Shelene Ackley."

Shelene Ackley's skin was medium beige, but her hair was bright orange and she hadn't dyed it. "This better be goddamn good," she warned.

Beck Viskas extended an upturned hand. "We're having pizza. You're buying."

"Whatever you want," he said, digging into his pocket for two twenty-dollar bills. "Keep the change."

Beck took them and handed them to her roommate, who glared bloody murder at him before moving to the counter.

"What did you say your name was again?" Beck wanted to know.

"Sheehan. Brock Sheehan."

"Give me one of your business cards."

"I don't have one."

"A headhunter working for a big corporation who doesn't have a business card? You're sure you're not a serial killer?"

"Not in a pizzeria, that's for sure."

She slid in opposite him. "You have a driver's license?"

"Sure."

"Let me see it."

"Really?"

"Really. Along with the hundred bucks you promised me."

He handed her his wallet, open so she could see his license. "I guess you *are* Brock Sheehan, then."

He counted out five more twenties and pushed them across

the table at her. "You want to make a note of where I live, just in case I *am* a serial killer?"

"That's right," she said.

He laughed. "Don't worry—I don't plan to murder you. What are you majoring in at CSU? Political science?"

She looked stunned. "How do you know that?"

Garret Lavender did excellent research. "The same way I knew where to find you in the first place—but it's not important." Sheehan said. "I only know you went to St. Cyril High School, you were Lloyd Oborn's girlfriend for a long time and then you weren't. That's it, Beck, and nothing else. I just want to ask you a few questions about Lloyd. Not sexual questions either, if that's what worries you—and then I'll go away and you'll never hear from me again."

"Promise?"

"Cross my heart."

"And hope to die?" she said.

He shook his head. "Let's not go overboard."

Shelene Ackley came back to the table carrying a tray—one large pizza, two paper plates, and two large Cokes. She sat down next to Beck. "Here's the deal," she said. "One wrong word, one bad move, one touch—or even playing footsie under the table with us—and you're going to get a face full of liquid pepper you won't soon forget." She took a pepper spray from her jacket and put it down on the table in front of her. "Am I clear?"

"Crystal clear. Are you Rebecca's guardian angel?"

"I'm her roommate," Shelene said, "best friend, and bodyguard, as you can plainly see. But I'll add guardian angel to the list, and tell everyone it was your suggestion."

Beck took a pizza slice from the tray and put it on her plate. "Let's get going, huh? We both have studying to do."

He sat back, appraising both of them—strong, independent, take-no-crap young women. He admired them. "Okay. Beck, you dated Lloyd in high school, right?"

"We were just friends for a year. Then we started dating—

for two years." Until, she thought but didn't say, he dumped her just before graduation.

"Was he always angry?"

"He was depressed—because of Meredith. Who wouldn't be depressed to come home and find a sister dangling from the ceiling? I tried hard to cheer him up—everyone who knew him did. But he started getting angry."

"What took him that long?"

"Grief doesn't just come and go," she said. "Some people live with it forever. He moped around big time for almost a year, mourning her suicide, and then he got mad."

"Mad? All the time?"

"Most of the time. It was hard. I never knew if he'd be soft and loving one minute and then suddenly become really furious over—well, over nothing at all."

Sheehan didn't want to ask the next question, but he had to. "Did he ever hit you? Hurt you?"

Beck seemed to be biting down hard on nothing, mouth tightened into an angry smile as though she were airing out her teeth. "Not hit me, exactly. But every so often, when he'd gone off the deep end about nothing at all, he would physically— push me away. Hard. Against a wall or something."

"And still you stayed with him?"

"When you're sixteen, your brain hasn't developed enough for you to make good decisions," she said, very confident now that she'd turned twenty years old. "I should have walked away, I guess. But underneath it all, he was a damn nice kid who'd gone through a horrible experience. He worried that something awful might happen to me. He really did care about me—but mostly it ground him up about Meredith."

"Nobody was actually blamed for that rape."

"Not—legally, no."

Sheehan looked at Shelene Ackley. "Is that what you think, too?"

"I'm just a bystander tonight," Shelene answered. "I don't

know much about it. I never met Lloyd. I've only known Beck since last spring we met and decided to be roommates. But we've talked about him a lot. We both talk about our ex-boyfriends, but I broke it off with mine when we both chose different colleges. He's at Michigan State, now, and we both can live with that. Beck, though, was really bummed when her ex stopped dating her."

"I'm still bummed," Beck said, eyes glistening with tears just waiting to be shed. "I mean, when you're in high school you don't figure you're going to spend the rest of your life with someone—but when he rejected me, it hurt. Real bad hurt."

"Did he ever mention who he thought took advantage of his sister?"

She frowned. "We were kids. We didn't know shit about shit. OSU pretty much covered it up—but Lloyd always said it was Kenny Pine."

"Pine," Sheehan reminded her, "went to prison for dogfighting right after he graduated—which means Lloyd was furious with him for almost four years."

"Pretty much, yeah. When someone causes the death of a loved one, 'furious' doesn't just dry up and blow away."

"Furious enough to wait until he was out on the street again and then kill him?"

Rebecca finally took a bite of her pizza slice, not answering until she finished it, washing it down with a gulp of soda. "I haven't seen him for more than a year," she said eventually, "so I can't really answer that. As far as I know—as far as I *feel*— Lloyd Oborn was no killer."

"Nobody's born a killer," Sheehan said, "but anyone can kill if they have to."

"That's bullshit!" Beck snapped.

"You sure of that?"

"How about you, Mr. Sheehan?" Shelene asked pointedly. "Have you ever killed anyone?"

Rebecca Viskas was looking at him very hard, too, which

made his throat and chest tighten up. He finally forced a grin he knew was false, and said, "Not today, no." He wondered in his gut whether that would work.

CHAPTER EIGHTEEN

Brock felt no succor. Talking with Beck Viskas and her feisty roommate, Shelene Ackley, had disturbed him more than he wanted it to while he learned about Lloyd Oborn.

He'd known from the moment they'd met at his home that Lloyd's fit of pique was subcutaneous, lurking just below the first layer of epidermis and ready to boil over. If his mother had not been present to soothe him a bit, Sheehan didn't know what might have happened.

He was fairly certain Lloyd wasn't expert with a knife. No teens, unless they are street drug-peddling thugs, walk around with switchblades unless they've watched *West Side Story* one time too many.

As for the adolescents of yesteryear—well, that was a different story. Especially one young punk that Brock remembered vividly every time he took off his shirt anywhere near a mirror and saw the knife scar that left a straight line from his left shoulder across his chest and down to his waistline.

The kid's name was Aloysius Petkus. Many Clevelanders had names originating in Eastern Europe—more than most American cities—but Brock Sheehan didn't know where this guy's family came from. They must have been serious Catholics, as no parent would call a poor innocent baby Aloysius unless they were honoring a long-dead saint. He vaguely remembered Saint Aloysius was the patron saint of teenagers, but opined that Aloysius Petkus wasn't much of a saint, as he was angry, rebellious, and out-of-control.

He answered to either Alo or Loy, as no one except his mother ever called him Aloysius. He apparently worked hard to change the perception of the name, as he was an out-of-work high school dropout, not only a tall, skinny bully, but also a top-of-the-line philanderer. His name and reputation became well known to Rory McCurdy after he commandeered the virginity and impregnated one Dierdre Coyne, the sixteen-year-old daughter of Aidan Coyne, and bragged about it to anyone who would listen.

Aidan Coyne owned a classy west side store selling all things connected to the Emerald Isle, from clothing to badges, plaques, paintings, photographs, and Irish-themed books, including classics by Sean O'Casey and Brendan Behan, and who was an honored member of the West Side Gaelic Society and met with some of the big shots for breakfast at the then-famous Tony's on West 117th Street two or three times a week.

Dierdre Coyne was sent off in one hell of a hurry to County Mayo in Ireland, so other than her own word, which she was not in-country to share, there was no way to prove Aloysius was the father. She gave birth to a baby girl who was immediately placed in foster care and eventually adopted, and never visited the United States where she had been conceived. Dierdre Coyne did return, but not to Cleveland; she was sent to distant relatives on the west side of Chicago south and west of the vast stockyards that were once the biggest meatpacking center of the USA, an Irish neighborhood that is forever more known as "Back-of-the-Yards."

Aidan Coyne wanted revenge. Murder was what he had begged of Rory McCurdy, but Rory felt the deliberate killing of another human being was undertaken only in the worst circumstances—as, for instance, doing something lousy to him. He also refused Coyne's second request, i.e., Aloysius Petkus being relieved of his testicles, a step even Rory didn't want to consider.

After giving it his most sagacious study, he came up with Loy Petkus's sentence: a severe beating. The assignment was naturally given to the West Side Gaelic Society's number one pain giver, the young Brock Sheehan.

Sheehan had no daughter, and only one sister who would never in a million years get herself involved in such a situation, especially with a non-Irish punk with an attitude. He didn't have a steady girlfriend, either—he played the field. However, if some random date of his became pregnant by him, he'd either buy an abortion ending that pregnancy—a venal sin in the church he no longer attended—or he'd actually man up and marry the girl. Aloysius Petkus had no morals whatsoever, no decency, and not one bit of care for a woman carrying his child. Brock Sheehan agreed with the girl's father, and with Rory as well. The beating was well deserved.

Easier said than done. Aloysius had no regular job, so Sheehan couldn't track him down at work. He knew his address—a two-bedroom house on West 83rd Street between Lorain Road and Madison Avenue in which he lived with his widowed mother. But there's a right way to do things and a wrong one, and Sheehan couldn't exactly beat a fellow half to death in broad daylight, especially in front of his mum.

So he set himself up to watch, and to take advantage whenever he could. Knowing the unemployed loafer would probably sleep past noon, he arrived at midday, parked just down the street from the home, and waited.

And waited.

At about two thirty in the afternoon, Loy backed his own car out from the garage and headed west, toward the high school. Then he hung around, smoking cigarettes, until the school bell sounded inside and an enormous crowd of teens erupted from the main doors and headed off in all directions.

One pretty girl, though, managed to break away from the rest and cross the street to where Loy waited for her. He hugged her, kissed her on the mouth the way actors kiss each other in romantic movies, and escorted her into his car, his hand clasped at the back of her neck as if he'd choke her if she tried to escape. Then they drove off. Sheehan followed them at a distance until they parked on a rarely driven street between Detroit Road and Lake Erie and began making out, hot and heavy and much fumbling with clothes. Brock didn't stick around to see whether or not they went all the way, but parked almost a block away so he could see when and if the car moved.

After about forty-five minutes, the engine fired up and the car turned right at the nearest corner, drove for several blocks, and pulled into the driveway of a similar home in the same neighborhood. The girl got out of the car, looking rumpled, her shirttails hanging outside her skirt, and went up the steps and into the house. The driver rolled down his window, fired the butt of a smoking cigarette onto the home's front lawn, and then backed out fast, laying down rubber.

Returning to his house, Loy left his car in the driveway and went inside. Sheehan checked his wristwatch; it was close to five o'clock. Damned if he'd sit there staring at the parked car for the next several hours, he drove off to a Mister Hero and consumed his sandwich in his own vehicle. He enjoyed potato chips but hated eating them in the car—the crumbs got all over him. He finished them anyway because he was hungry, then headed back to Loy's house.

Just before eight, the kid reemerged, now wearing black Levi's, black sneakers, a black T-shirt and a black leather jacket a la 1950s punk bikers, got into his car, heading south toward the Westgate Mall.

Sheehan sighed, pulling into the mall lot and parking ten cars away from Loy Petkus's space. Malls. Nothing changed—malls were where kids hung out in the evenings and on weekends in what became social centers for those who were too young to spend all their spare time in saloons. He hated the idea of lurking around inside, hiding behind pillars and watching the man he'd been ordered to badly injure as he acted tough with his buddies and made unwanted passes at every young girl who walked by *in a skirt or too-tight jeans.*

Sheehan filled up time by buying himself a Cinnabon. He'd never had one before, and he was amazed at how much he liked it, though worried that if he ate Cinnabons all the time he'd turn into a real porker. Afterwards he moved over to the Dairy Queen stand in the food court and got a black coffee to wash it all down, always keeping one eye on his assigned target, not wanting to lose him. He had no desire to go through this search-and-wait for another entire evening.

The high school girls Aloysius approached would probably get in trouble if they went someplace with him or one of his pals when they were supposed to be home—but a few jotted down their phone numbers for him, to be called at a later date when advance arrangements were to be discussed.

It was near closing time when people began filtering out into the parking lot. When Loy left, Sheehan followed him, approaching as he was unlocking his car. They were almost the same height, he noticed, but he was at least fifty pounds heavier.

"Loy," he called softly.

The kid looked up. Sheehan stuck out his hand. "Nice to see you. My name's Brock Sheehan."

For anyone to shake the hand of a stranger who offers it is almost automatic—but when Loy finally decided to do so, Sheehan took his hand with a steel grip and twisted him around so his right elbow was pressed hard into Sheehan's side. The kid's wrist was bent back almost double.

"Don't yell," Sheehan said quietly to Loy Petkus, who'd sucked in a big breath to carry the scream of pain that didn't materialize, "or I'll break your hand right off your arm like the end of a pretzel stick. Move!"

Together they marched around the corner to another side of the mall building where there were few cars parked and little night lighting. Sheehan moved them into the shadows, let go of his wrist, and threw him roughly against the wall.

"What's the deal, man?" the kid said, his voice sounding like the whine of a six-year-old.

237

"Remember Dierdre Coyne?" Sheehan pinned him with a left hand around his throat. "You knocked her up when she was a virginal sixteen years old."

"I remember her," the boy said through the choke hold. "Not much in the titty department, but she had a nice tight cooze."

"Really? Well, I have a message for you—from her father." Sheehan drove his fist into Petkus's stomach as hard as he could. The kid bounced back against the wall and sank to his knees, clutching his midsection and gasping for the breath that had been knocked clean out of him. Sheehan waited almost a full minute, then grasped the lapels of his leather jacket, pulled him to his feet, and punched him in the same place again.

Loy went all the way down, lying on the pavement, trying to capture even a gulpful of air, making a sound like a vacuum cleaner, wriggling and groaning. Sheehan backed up a few steps and watched him, knowing that two solar plexus punches weren't going to make Rory McCurdy and his pal Aidan Coyne happy enough. He'd probably hit him in the face next.

The victim rolled over on his stomach, grasping onto the wall as he lifted himself off the ground, and when he was on his feet, Sheehan spun him around—and got quite a surprise.

The pain across his chest didn't happen right away. When he looked down and saw his shirt was torn and blood was pumping out, he realized he'd just been slashed by a switchblade knife. He backed up, seeing the shiny blade, now blood-covered, waving in front of the attacker who advanced on him, still having trouble breathing.

"Come on, motherfucker," Loy gasped through the pain. "Come and get it."

He slashed again and missed as Sheehan danced backward and out of the way. He sensed his wound was not deep at all and probably could be stitched up without much problem. Dumb bastard, he thought—if you have a knife and you want to stop somebody, stab—that will end things quickly. Don't slash!

He saw the swipe of the knife coming at him again, and turned sideways, making himself less of a target, and his hand *flashed up to grab the sore wrist—one he'd already bent almost double—and twist it, pushing the kid backwards until he could smash the knife-holding hand against the wall.*

Then with his left hand he put all his strength behind a punch in the face, and his breath hissed as he heard teeth breaking off, the sharp edges gouging his own knuckles. The boy slumped, no defense left in him, and Sheehan had to hold him up with one hand while battering his face with the other—not with closed fists this time, but with vicious slaps, front- and backhanded while wearing a large turquoise ring, bruising, opening cuts, closing one eye.

Finally, when the kid was nearly unconscious, Sheehan stepped back and let go of the jacket, and Loy Petkus slid down the wall to the cold asphalt concrete, half sitting, half leaning, being looked down upon with utmost contempt. There was rage, too, as Sheehan felt blood running down his chest. He never carried a weapon, and now someone had tried to kill him with one, and he couldn't let it go. Moving toward a helplessly crushed Fonzarelli wanna-be and stomped down as hard as he could on Aloysius's right hand, shattering the fingers and knuckles.

When the screaming stopped, Sheehan said quietly, "It'll be quite a while before you'll be able to use a knife again—not with that hand."

Leaving Aloysius sobbing quietly on the pavement, he kept to the shadows as he returned the way he'd come, hoping he wouldn't run into anyone who'd notice the entire front of his shirt was bloodied and his knuckles bleeding, too. Naturally he knew of the doctor who was always on call to fix up those who surrounded McCurdy's crew, and hoped, at half past nine in the evening, that he'd be at home and available. Otherwise, the tall, muscular, and intimidating Brock Sheehan might just bleed to death.

When Sheehan got halfway back to Vermillion, he pulled off I-90 and found a copse of trees just behind the parking lot of an office building; his pit bull had gone too long without a rest stop. He felt guilty about not cleaning up after the dog, or so the law said, but what would he then do with a plastic towel full of dog poop? Drive it the rest of the way home? After all, it was in a stand of tall trees in which no one really walked around, and he couldn't be bothered buzzing through a suburban downtown looking for a trashcan at eleven o'clock at night.

Vermillion was pretty much quiet, especially at the harbor. Giving Conor another short walk for a tinkle, he went onboard, very much wanting a drink. It was too chilly to sit on deck, so he made do with below deck, stretched out on his bunk with his shoes off, Conor alert beside his bed, facing the seven steps in case anyone tried to barge in. Sheehan sipped a Bushmills Black. He needed it.

Lloyd Oborn had a temper, all right—dating back to the suicide of his sister, which was blamed on the late Kenny Pine. The fact that he'd exploded into rage for little or no reason when Sheehan visited his mother was another red flag. He poured a second drink, feeling good about the work he'd put in at the request of his nephew. If he reported what he knew about Lloyd to Detective Sergeant Tobe Blaine, perhaps Linus Callahan would no more be a "person of interest," or at least he'd not be on that list alone.

Had she lived, would Fiona—his bad-mannered, judgmental sister and Linus's mother—feel kindly toward him for undertaking this pro bono investigation that belied any other experiences he'd known? Or would he remain an outcast, an outsider?

Fiona had realized from the start that he'd been the number one guy behind Rory McCurdy, known he was big enough and tough enough to terrorize people into doing what they were told. But when she saw the knife scar on his chest, she realized just *how* involved he was in violence and intimidation and brutality. It was she who had the real trigger-finger temper in their home, and she went over the top. She didn't want a paid bully-boy anywhere near her or her very young son, Linus—so Brock Sheehan was turned away from Sunday dinners, birthday bashes, and the religious holiday festivities and a whole group of Saint's days she'd thought important, get-togethers on which he'd been raised and nourished.

His banishment from his own clan had broken his heart. Yet, he loved strong women. Submissive females who were geniuses in the kitchen and wildcats in bed didn't really attract him. That's why he was fascinated with two young co-eds he'd interviewed earlier that evening—Beck Viskas and Shelene Ackley—both brave and tough, and would stand up beside a best friend and fight tooth and nail for her until the cows came home. He knew he was nearly old enough to be their grandfathers—far too old to even consider either of them romantically, but both Beck and Shelene couldn't help reminding him of Arizona Skye.

CHAPTER NINETEEN

The next morning, Sheehan went back to Cleveland again. Conor was once more happy sticking his head out the car window, the force of the wind blowing back his lips exposing gums and an impressive set of teeth. It was brisk autumn, and as Sheehan drove off the freeway and into downtown, he noted nearly every restaurant, bar, gas station, or small retail store had "Go Browns" signs plastered all over their windows, making him remember that for the most part, Cleveland had always been a happy town, even when their sports teams were not successful. He missed living "right there" where something was always going on. Action was vibrant near the West Side Market on West 25th Street, in and around Public Square, and on East 4th Street, which used to be a tacky block full of ratty wig stores and pawnshops and is now one of the most popping places in Cleveland, with a dozen great restaurants and taverns. The country's second-largest theater district, Playhouse Square, is several blocks east. Ninety blocks further lay University Circle.

Brock Sheehan had accrued many local enemies over his adult life—men with long memories and short tempers, and while he could always take care of himself, being on guard every moment had eventually worn him down.

His harbor berth in Vermillion was more peaceful—right on the shore of the lake. Sunshine. Breezes. Fresh air. He could boast a great view, and the slight, pleasant smell of Lake Erie perch. He didn't have the coterie of friends he had when he was the Irish guy who made everyone step aside. When he thought about it, though, they weren't really friends, but those who pretended to be friends to get on his good side—or better yet, to *not* get on his bad side. Many knew exactly where he'd relocated, but no one called him, sent him a birthday card, offered to make the short drive to have dinner or a few drinks with him and rekindle old times.

Ten minutes before he arrived at the no-kill pet shelter, he called Linus Callahan and asked him to come out front and talk to him. When he got there, he noticed no one had yet replaced the shattered front door, still covered in thick planks of wood. Inside, Linus had told him, was also in vandalized condition, thanks to the rat scum who were now in jail. Unspoken thanks for that should go to Brock, too. The repair would put an extra burden on the day-to-day budget, as the shelter was nonprofit. They spent all the money they could collect caring for abused or deserted animals, and kept their fingers and toes crossed for the kindness of strangers with checkbooks to keep the doors open for just a little bit longer.

Out of the car, Conor relieved himself against a tree trunk, then got busy sniffing every inch of sidewalk in front of the shelter, as many dogs had crossed the threshold since the last rain.

Linus came out, still lame. The stitches on his face against his pale skin glowed pink, along with the shaved scalp behind his ear where the torn skin was sewn together. He didn't shake Brock's hand this time, but instead bent to scratch the dog's ears, groaning a bit from the broken ribs. "You two seem to be getting along okay," he said, straightening up. "What's his name again? Conway?"

"It's Conor. One N." Sheehan looked more closely at Linus's battered face. "You seem to be healing up pretty good."

Linus wrinkled his nose and rubbed at his side. "It's taking time. They can't really mend broken bones—they just tape 'em up tight and hope they come together all by themselves. So I'm out of action for a while."

"Hang in there." He looked down at Conor, who was hoping for more attention. "Sit, boy. Sit!"

The dog sat quietly, his tail still wagging gently. Sheehan said, "What about Maureen?"

Linus frowned—chagrin and despair hovering over his head like a threatening storm cloud. "That's—yesterday's news. She's moving out and going to live with her mother. At least that's what she told me. So I'll be alone again."

"And your coworker who got roughed up? Patti?"

"She'll come out of it—but I think she lost a few of her teeth, too. Goddammit! Such a nice kid."

Sheehan didn't answer him, instead dealing with what he'd learned in the past few days, the weight of it crushing his shoulders. Linus Callahan: number one suspect in a headline-making murder, dumped by the grievously injured woman he thought he loved, giving him up for trouble that he had not caused. After his sister's suicide, Lloyd Oborn ditched his longtime love, too, and turned from an A-student and talented athlete into a mad-as-hell young adult who couldn't hold his wrath anymore. Patti was a kind young woman working at an animal shelter who was beaten within an inch of her life. Jesus H. Christ!

He moved slightly closer to Conor, who leaned his weight against Sheehan's leg. The dog's touch gave him solace, what there was of it. Was *anyone* happy, he forced himself to wonder, who stood fast in a marriage or relationship or a lifestyle for an entire existence? Or had they learned to just shut up and make the best of a bad decision?

Well, that wasn't why he was there in the first place.

Linus said, "You must mean you have news, right? Is it good for me—or bad?"

Sheehan sucked in a deep breath—Cleveland air subtly flavored with the lake perch scent, and smoke and steel from the plants just minutes away. "I've uncovered someone else who might be even more likely to have killed Kenny Pine than you."

Linus moved toward him eagerly. "Who? Who?"

"I can't share it yet. I don't want the police to connect the two of you in any way. All I know is that he had a motive—a much better one."

"A dog lover?"

"Not at all."

"Then what?"

"Linus, I'm not going into this with you, okay? I stopped by to mention it so you might feel a little better."

Linus Callahan blinked. Any use of his facial muscles was obviously very painful. "I guess that's the best I could hope for this morning. What are you going to do about it?"

"Have a late breakfast at The Harp—that Irish restaurant on Detroit Road, because there's a lack of really Irish food where I'm living in Vermillion—and then I'm going to tell the police."

Detective Sergeant Tobe Blaine was out to lunch when Brock Sheehan arrived at downtown headquarters, this time bringing Conor along with him on a short leash. Once again he'd gone through the metal detector, borne a pat down by a uniformed cop, and suffered an elevator ride crowded with miscreants and their sad families on the way to the courtrooms on the top floors, all pressing themselves into the far corners so as not to be to devoured by a pit bull. Ensconced in police HQ, he waited on an unpadded wooden bench opposite the desk sergeant's post, entertaining himself watching those who came in for one reason or another, looking with either appreciation or fright at the dog at his feet. He'd always thought Cleveland a contented town—rock and roll nuts, classical music nuts, sports nuts, theater nuts, lake lovers, beer guzzlers, and joyful eaters. But everyone walking into the police station looked miserable, nervous, or helplessly trapped—as though they had just approached the

Wailing Wall. At least he felt more at ease with Conor as a friend.

Sheehan had never felt scared, despite being hauled into police precincts all the time when he worked for the Gaelic Society, suspected of assault and battery or, worse, murder. Back in those days, even in custody, he was polite, charming, and always at ease. When released, he often shook the hands of the cops who'd locked him up in the first place. He'd had confidence and comfortable arrogance to spare, knowing Rory McCurdy's lawyer, Gowan Scully, would have him back out on the street before the big hand of the clock on the wall ever reached twelve. Oddly, he'd never walked into the main police headquarters downtown on his own—not until Linus Callahan came into his life unbidden.

He checked his wristwatch, wondering if homicide detectives took long lunch hours, and then chuckled quietly. Why get annoyed with Tobe Blaine's tardiness? It's not as if he had anything else to do that day.

For a while he tried matching up the appearance of the people brought in by a cop with the crime they'd committed. Young women in low-cut blouses and short-short skirts and wearing heavy sexy makeup were obviously street hookers—anyone could have guessed that. Men? This young one a purse-snatcher, that one an arrogant gang drug dealer, a third a terrified college kid caught with too much Mary Jane in his pocket? Sheehan felt sorry for that nerdy-looking college boy, certain the cops would make him spend fifteen years in prison down in Mansfield for possession, a candy-ass for any tough guy who wanted him bent over for an hour or a night.

One of the old-time police officers close to cashing in his thirty years—a few years younger than Sheehan, but with a bulging pot belly from too many donuts, and a hairline that had gone so far north that it could have been in the middle of Lake Erie—came in to chat with the desk sergeant and did a double-take at Sheehan.

"Do I know you?" he said, coming over.

"Did I buy tickets to the policeman's ball from you twenty years ago or so?"

"No, no." The cop believed it was a real question. "I know you maybe because the last time I saw you, you were sitting right there on that bench. You didn't have the dog with you, huh? And I think that time you were handcuffed. Am I right or wrong?"

"You're right," Brock Sheehan said, "but it was a long time ago."

"Yeah?"

"Quite a few years."

"Give me a while, I'll come up with it," the cop promised.

"Then we'll both be excited."

The inquiring cop drifted away slowly, scratching his head as he tried desperately to match a name with a face.

Ten minutes later Tobe Blaine came in, going directly to the desk sergeant without looking around. The sergeant mumbled something and pointed at Brock Sheehan with his chin.

"Surprise," Blaine said as she approached Sheehan. "New dog? Congrats. Has your next-door neighbor complained that he barks all night long, and you're either here to turn in your dog for relocation, or you want the neighbor exiled to Siberia? Am I close?"

"Closer than you think, Detective Sergeant. Can we talk?"

"About sports? Movies? Politics? Your sex life? *My* sex life? I'm kind of busy for chatting."

"Chatting about murder?"

Blaine's eyes closed for a mini-second too long. "Follow me," she said, opening them again and heading down the hallway toward her office.

Once they were sitting on each side of her desk, she said, "Well, Mr. Sheehan, you and your dog got my attention. Are you confessing?"

"The last time I confessed, it was to a priest," Brock said through a dry smile, "and I was thirteen years old."

"What did you confess to?"

"I thought you said no talking about sex."

"Sex at thirteen?" She grinned. "Why, you little slut!"

"When you've got the name, play the game. Let me ask you a question, Detective Sergeant."

Blaine said, "I'm the one who asks the questions."

"Just one. You work for the Cleveland Police Department."

"Good guess. Shot in the dark, was it?"

"Can you arrest someone in another city?"

"Not usually."

"How about this, then?"

"Question number two?" Blaine said. "That's cheating."

"How about this person committed a crime right here, in your city—but lives and usually hangs out someplace else?"

"Then that's my case. Even if 'this person' were in Timbuktu—it's still my case."

"I've got a name for you. Lloyd Oborn. Lives in Akron, right off Market Street."

"Never heard of him."

"I thought not. A college kid, goes to Akron U. Upper middle class, nice mother."

"And he has a dog he just loves to pieces?"

"I didn't notice a dog," Sheehan said. "When I showed up at their home, I didn't hear any barking."

"So he iced Kenny Pine—who just spent three years in the slammer for running a dogfight ring? Sounds fishy to me."

"I can't prove it, except that he's got one a hell of a rage going on."

"How do you know that?"

"Because when I showed up at the Oborn home to talk to his mother, he had a complete hissy-fit."

"Hissy-fits make him a psycho killer, huh? What was he so ticked off about?"

"Well," Brock Sheehan told her, "he had this sister..."

It took him ten minutes to tell Blaine the entire Lloyd Oborn story as he knew it—the rape of drunken and barely conscious Meredith Oborn, the suspicion of Kenny Pine as the rapist, the blatant cover-up by Ohio State, Meredith's suicide, and Lloyd's descent into mediocre scholarship and unbridled fury. Blaine had made two pages of notes on her yellow legal-size pad, and when Sheehan was finally finished, she didn't say anything for a while as she perused them, drawing little geometric triangles in the upper corners and filling them in with her ballpoint pen.

Eventually she pushed the yellow pad away from her. "I told you if you fucked around with my homicide investigation, I'd peel off your skin and make a quilt out of it."

"I remember you saying something like that."

She shrugged. "You've robbed me of the chance. The girl was drunk and barely conscious, so even a halfway decent defense attorney would've made mincemeat out of her in court, and she could never prove rape, especially against a sports superstar. The Ohio State University is more secretive than a Washington politician when it comes to the identity of the rapist—if they even *had* one—and we can't ask the girl about it now anyway because she's dead."

Sheehan digested all that. "So?"

"So," Blaine went on, "this kid might not even know for sure that Kenny Pine raped his drunk, half-conscious sister, never mind that he got mad enough to kill him for it. Therefore, I can't take a SWAT-armed backup team with me to a different city and county, and arrest somebody I never heard of until you walked in here ten minutes ago."

"I see—meaning my nephew is still at the tippy-top of your suspect list for slitting the throat of a guy twice his size."

"Tippy-top? That's seriously adorable. Well, Linus pushed Pine—in front of a dozen witnesses."

"A push? I've pushed people trying to get a hot dog and a glass of beer at a Browns game," Sheehan said angrily.

"But they didn't get their jugular vein sawed open twenty-four hours later like Pine did."

The room grew quiet. Then Blaine stood up, walked around her desk, and loomed over Brock Sheehan, making him look up at her. "You decide how this police division should conduct a homicide investigation? Less than an hour after our first meeting, I knew all about you and your no-conviction arrests for assault and battery, including four—*four* arrests on suspicion of murder. Every veteran cop is familiar with your name and your face. You're no plaster saint, Mr. Sheehan, you're a real iconic shitburger."

"I've never been convicted of anything worse than speeding on the turnpike, so I'm cleaner than anyone who's ever sat in this office."

"Another proof," Blaine snapped, "that you don't know your ass from first base."

"Maybe. Does that make Linus Callahan a shitburger, too?"

Tobe Blaine compressed her lips, and hellfire danced behind her eyes. "I call him a shitburger-wannabe," she finally said, "until I know any different. As for you—you are now on my very last nerve. Get the hell out of my office and out of this precinct before I have you thrown into the drunk tank and leave you there for a month."

"On what charge?"

Detective Sergeant Tobe Blaine held both hands up, palms outward. "Threatening a police officer with a vicious dog."

"He's hardly vicious."

"Okay," she continued, "how about getting arrested for being a pain in the ass?"

"I might even plead guilty to that, Sergeant."

"Great. And by the time you're behind bars, I'll think of something better."

Brock was thinking, too, as he and Conor rode the elevator downstairs—and his thoughts angered and frustrated him.

He couldn't blame Tobe Blaine for wanting him off the case. She had a squad of dedicated cops working for her on who killed Kenny Pine.

But he had changed, too, since Linus Callahan approached him asking for help. He'd hardly been aware of his nephew's existence before, but now he realized he was a pretty good kid, and the only relative left who gave a damn about him. A part of his brain, though, wondered if Linus were guilty.

Brock hadn't understood that at first he himself was a bone-deep animal lover and that he couldn't hurt a fly. Now his lonely existence had changed with a newly found blood brother fur baby who seemed to want to go with him everywhere. He always cracked the windows open when he left Conor in the car, not a good idea at the best of times—not in the hot summer—but he wasn't sure if he were to leave a covered-up boat whenever he went anywhere, the pit bull might not be there when Brock arrived back home.

This was bonding, a new feeling that left him rocky on his feet—but it had taken a short time for Conor to become the best friend he had in the world. He'd never really had a best friend before, except for Rory McCurdy who was old enough to be his father. Now he figured he would have cut Kenny Pine's throat from ear to ear himself, because he was on his way to loving all animals like Linus did.

Most importantly, though, for the first time since he left Cleveland and the Rory McCurdy crowd, he had something to do, something that kept him active and searching and on the move.

Now he was double goddamned if he'd let Tobe Blaine kick him to the curb. He needed to be doing something—really *doing* something—for the first time in a decade.

Conor was all over him when they got out of the elevator and back outside. He gave the dog a few minutes to calm down, then clicked on a longer leash and walked with him in the partly cloudy autumn afternoon that would disappear in just a few days.

After Conor paid leg-up tribute to several lamp posts and trees, he and Sheehan burst upon the sprawling formerly called

Mall A, now referred to as Veterans Memorial Plaza, in the center of which is the Fountain of Eternal Life. Sheehan hadn't seen it for the last several years, and had forgotten how beautiful it is. A few blocks from Public Square, many people miss it altogether, and in the brisk trot behind the excited dog, Sheehan once again felt vital and full of enthusiasm.

What does a cop do, he wondered, when a murder is committed in their own neighborhood by someone who lives a good thirty-five miles away in another county—especially when the only clue they have to the killer's identity comes without a shred of proof? Blaine couldn't drive to Akron and serve a warrant on Lloyd Oborn only on the suggestion of a strange man who'd been often arrested but never convicted. And Sheehan couldn't barge into the Akron Police Department headquarters and demand they handcuff a previously innocent kid for suspicion of a murder that took place in Cleveland—one they weren't even aware of unless they read the sports pages.

Brock Sheehan wasn't a quitter, never thought of himself as one. Before quietly resigning from the West Side Gaelic Society, he'd cleaned up all situations he'd started. McCurdy was not owed money by any welshers, wished no enemies malevolent revenge, and had no one selected for a beating for some other reason, so Sheehan was for that moment free and clear, and not bailing out.

When Rory gave him the houseboat as a retirement present, he'd figured he'd have a great old time sailing all over the Great Lakes from his new home harbor in Vermillion, close to the rocking Lake Erie Islands and not all that far by water to the rest of the North Coast and eventually all over the Great Lakes. It hadn't occurred to him that taking a boat trip by himself very much resembled his living alone with no friends, few women with whom he'd wished to spend more than a night, listening to the soft plash of the harbor water against the sides of his waterborne home and digging into Bushmills Black every night. His only lake trips early on—one to Geneva in Ashtabula County, one to

Monroe in Michigan, and a few too many to South Bass Island and Kelly's Island where there was little more to do than get drunk and fall asleep in the sand—were not equated with travel and adventure.

Then, of course, there was dry-docking every November and spending the winter in a far southern or western city that was always too damn hot during a sunny, sticky Christmas season full of rich widows ten years older than he is.

He fished a few scraps of treats for Conor from his pocket, and then walked over to Superior Avenue and an office building he'd visited only once before.

CHAPTER TWENTY

Garrett's long-legged receptionist today wore a shimmering silk lavender jacket over nothing very much, and a white short skirt, her hair once more in a full bun that, when combed out, would probably reach mid-back. Her half-bored, half-angry fashion show runway face had no other expression, and Sheehan figured she even had the same look during amazing sex, standing in the shower, or waking up with a terrible hangover. Her unexpected visitor approached her with a smile—and a pit bull.

"Hi. Remember me? I'm Brock Sheehan."

"I know," she said in a flat tone indicating she didn't give a damn what his name was. She stared at Conor as if he were a warthog. "This place is animal-free."

"Not today it isn't. And you are...?"

"The receptionist," she said tonelessly. "What is your purpose here?"

"I was hoping I could spend a few minutes with Mr. Lavender."

"He works by appointment only."

"As I said, only a few minutes."

She frowned even more deeply, taking longer to decide than a president of the United States pondering whether to press the nuclear button that will blow half the world's population off the face of the planet. Finally she blinked—it was the first time Sheehan remembered her doing so—and pointed to an upholstered chair clear across the reception room. "He's with a client right now, you'll have to wait."

He sat down and Conor draped himself across his shoes. He looked around for a magazine with which to fill his time, but there were none in sight. Probably a good idea, he thought; scattered reading material that was months old reminded him of a vintage barbershop. He preferred looking at the receptionist, anyway, and after a few moments he realized it made her very nervous. That pleased him.

She punched a button on her phone, swiveled her chair around to hide her lips moving, and whispered something he couldn't hear. Did she whisper while having sex, too, Sheehan pondered, or was she a surprise screamer of obscenities? He realized he would never know, but it was still fun to imagine it.

After a quarter hour, the door at the end of a long hallway opened and Garrett Lavender came out, his arm around a young woman, guiding her gently but firmly toward the elevator. Shanty Irish, ginger hair with freckles, brown eyes rimmed with redness and blotted tears, and a bruise on her left cheekbone that was about four days old.

"Now don't worry about a thing, Mary." Lavender's tones soothed her. "You're a good Catholic girl, and you don't want your priest or the church getting mad at you for even thinking about a divorce. Tell you what—I'll talk to Rory and he'll send someone around to speak with Brian to make sure he knows he's not to lay a hand on you ever again—unless it's a loving hand."

"Yes, but—the drinking," she began.

"Now, some people can drink and be okay with it, Mary, and some can't. I assure you the favorite bars he goes to in your neighborhood won't pour anything for him except ginger ale. Rory McCurdy will make sure of that. Just trust me, darlin'."

When they got to the elevator, he pushed the button for her and gave her a hug. If his hand had gotten any closer to squeezing her ass than it did, there would have been major trouble—and no more trust. As it was, she thanked him profusely, sniffled, blew her nose in a tissue, and got on the elevator.

Mary. More than half the Irish women are named Mary at birth, or at least Mary *Something*—like Mary Margaret or Mary Kathleen or Mary Elizabeth, all honoring the Holy Mother. Sheehan couldn't recall any major earthshattering women in any of the other religions named Mary. All Catholic women from the time of Jesus clear through the Middle Ages were horribly martyred, tortured and executed, and then, centuries later, consecrated as saints. He wondered why that was. But this particular Mary had evidently come to Lavender because she'd gone to the West Side Gaelic Society first, as husband Brian? Was that his name?—knocked her around whenever he drank too much, making it a habit. Garrett Lavender wouldn't get out of bed in the morning without checking with Rory, so Brian would be dealt with firmly and Mary will hopefully look back at marital abuse as ancient history—but Sheehan doubted it.

He realized but didn't care that Conor was out of place in an expensive downtown office with a breathtakingly sexy front-desk woman to remind prospective clients how much they must pay the lawyer who always wore three-hundred-dollar shoes and three-thousand-buck suits—and with all that, Lavender was still a variant of what Sheehan used to be: Rory McCurdy's high-paid bitch.

The attorney shot his cuffs before he turned to Sheehan. "You're supposed to make an appointment," he said severely, "or Rory should make it for you." He looked at Conor. "I have a dog myself—one I like very much. He's a miniature poodle. I leave him at home, though. Next time you leave this monster at home, too, or he'll eat my poodle just for the hell of it." Then he moved closer, lowering his voice, even though the receptionist could easily hear him. "What's the deal? Are you in trouble?"

"Not yet," Sheehan answered. "If I were, I'd want to know you've got my back."

Lavender glanced at his Rolex watch. "There's ten minutes before my next client." He started back toward his private office, motioning him to follow. "No coffee this time. No chatting, no sports, and no asking if my gorgeous receptionist has a boyfriend."

"I'd rather have a date with a refrigerator freezer."

"I don't care who you date. Talk fast, Mr. Sheehan."

Seated across from him in his office, Brock told the story as quickly as he could, noting that Lavender took no notes. When he finished, the lawyer sat back in his chair.

"Is that it? Does this fairy tale have a climax?"

"That's the problem. I talked to Detective Sergeant Tobe Blaine earlier today, and not a ripple in the water. I can't do the same thing with an Akron cop who's never heard of me, because I have no proof."

"Then take yourself on a boat ride, get drunk, get laid, and tell your nephew to pound sand, Sheehan. You've done enough."

"My question is—"

"You have a question? A legal-type question?"

"I need your answer to your own question: the fairy-tale ending."

Lavender put his head against the back of his throne-like chair and closed his eyes, as if taking a fifteen-second nap. Then he looked directly at Brock Sheehan and said, "There's only two ways. The first one is to find incontrovertible proof this kid killed his sister's rapist—or someone he *thinks* was his sister's rapist. But without proof it's going to make both of you look like assholes."

"And the second way?"

"You're a pretty intimidating guy, Sheehan—or you used to be. Find a way to make him confess."

"You mean beat the piss out of him until he tells me what I want to hear?"

"Crude—but effective."

"I've been roughing up people most of my life," Brock Sheehan said, "and *that's* the legal advice you give me?"

"Who do you think I am, the fucking Oracle at Delphi? You

257

jumped in on your own just because your nephew whined to you. If you'd come to me first, I would've told you to shine it, to enjoy your retirement. But no, you were in all the way and on the prowl before you checked with the Old Man—or with me."

"I did check with you, Lavender, and it cost me four hundred dollars."

"Well, now I'm telling you to back away—and that'll cost you another four bills."

Sheehan looked at his watch—not a Rolex like Lavender's, but a Folio, whatever that was, that he'd bought at Kohl's in Sandusky for twenty-nine bucks. "A pretty steep price for ten minutes, isn't it?"

"I squeezed you in without an appointment. That makes it four."

Sheehan reached into his pocket and pulled out a roll of bills from which he peeled two fifties. "Four hundred per hour. Fifteen minutes makes it one hundred, and you're only giving me ten of them. Take it or leave it."

The bills lay on the desk across a file Lavender had worked on before Sheehan came in. *MARY GILLIGAN* was printed on the tab—and the lawyer had probably charged her the full amount, no matter how financially stressed she and her beloved but fearsome hubby, Brian, might be. Lavender stared at the bills as though they were from another country. "You know better than to fuck around with lawyers. Don't think I won't report this to the Old Man."

"Really? And he's going to send some tough guy around to beat me up and get the other three hundred?" Sheehan looked at him with abhorrence. "That's what I did for a living, Mr. Lavender. I still do it better than any idiot he could find, or you either—so if some shit-for-brains musclehead comes around and threatens me, I'll rip out his kidney with my bare hands and feed it to my pit bull, here—and then, counselor, I'll drop by here again to collect your kidney, too."

Sheehan stood up and made a lazy exit, Conor trotting

obediently beside him but still on the alert. Through the open door, he saw the lawyer sitting with fists clenched, his cheeks glowing red. He knew Lavender wouldn't follow him, at least not without help, so in the lobby he stopped at the receptionist's desk.

"I don't know your name," he said to her, "but I doubt Lavender is paying you a fortune to sit out here doing nothing just because you're gorgeous. Find a decent job a million miles away from this hotshot lawyer. Then you can hold up your head and let everyone know you're a lot more than the prettiest girl in Cleveland. Have a good rest of your life."

Sheehan walked across the large room and punched the elevator button, leaving the receptionist gaping, wide-eyed and open-mouthed. She wanted suddenly to reply, to have more of a conversation with him because for the first time, despite his age and his gruff exterior, she realized how attractive he was, how forceful, how—large. By the time she came up with anything to say to him, the elevator door had opened and shut, and Brock Sheehan had gone out of her life forever.

He walked at a swift pace through a midafternoon autumn breeze, Conor beside him, heading from Garrett Lavender's high-rise office building near Public Square to the garage across from the Police Department, getting madder by the moment. So what if he got in trouble for continuing his search for an open door Linus could walk through to freedom? Hell, how much trouble *could* happen to him when he wasn't committing any crime? For fifteen seconds he ruminated on Garrett Lavender, and then dismissed it. He'd learned to take care of himself in every circumstance. He wouldn't stop now.

Beating a confession out of Lloyd Oborn wouldn't stand up in any court—and would land him in the hoosegow for assault and battery. He'd be better off wheedling a confession out of him. He looked skyward in frustration. Wheedling was not one of his strong points.

He headed back west over the Detroit-Superior Bridge to the main headquarters of the West Side Gaelic Society. After all these years, he was used to independence, but he wanted to be certain no one watched him before he got sucked further into a homicide gig he shouldn't have undertaken in the first place.

He walked Conor up and down the block a few times, and was about to put him back in the car when the door to the Society opened and Niall Grogan Junior stuck his head out.

"Mr. Sheehan!" he said, his eyes brimming with excitement. "Geez, back again!"

"Back again. I'd like to see Rory."

"Sure, I'll tell him you're here."

"Wait till I put the dog back in the car…"

"No, bring him in. Mr. Rory loves dogs."

Sheehan frowned. All he remembered of McCurdy and dogs was the Old Man saying Sheehan's own Irish wolfhound from decades ago was "one big son of a bitch." However, if Niall Junior invited them both to come in…

It was chilly inside. The Old Man had not yet switched from cool air to heat, and the building was so ancient that nippy breezes blew in through the cracks and crevasses around the window frames. Niall seemed to want to pat Conor, but was uncomfortable with pit bulls, so his hand just hovered until the dog simply decided to ignore him.

Niall went into the inner office and shut the door, and it obviously took him more time than it should have to announce Sheehan's visit to McCurdy.

The Old Man was behind his desk. This time there was no hello, either—just a hacking cough before he finally said, "Why bring a dog in here? Is this a present for me? I don't want no present. I don't want no goddamn dog."

"Just introducing you to my new friend, Rory. His name is Conor. Like the saint."

Rory studied the animal. "Saint my ass. He's a pit bull, right? Is he a fighter?"

"I don't know. He probably fought. I rescued him a few days back."

"I thought you told me your nephew iced the basketball player who used to run dogfights for money."

"My nephew didn't ice anybody," Sheehan said. "I'm trying to find out who did. Remember?"

"I got a good memory, Brock." He rested his chin on his chest for a bit, and might have gone to sleep, but eventually he looked up. "I remember every lousy thing you ever did."

"The lousy things I did were on your order."

"Maybe." He wiped one corner of his mouth with his thumb. "But your heart was never in it."

Brock took one of the visitor chairs and Conor sat quietly at his side, pressing his leg. "It was a job, Rory, and I did it the best I could. I never failed, not even once. I was completely loyal to you, too."

"Then why did you leave me?"

"It wasn't the old days when people worked at the same company for a lifetime for a ceremonial retirement dinner and a gold watch. Today, when a guy hits middle age, it kicks him right in the nuts that he didn't want to be a hedge fund genius anymore. So he quits his job, lets his hair grow, and spends the rest of his days doing what he'd secretly always wanted to do, like taking photographs of little kids doing their ballet recitals or having first communions."

"You take pitchers of little kids now?"

"Now? I'm investigating a murder."

McCurdy's back stiffened, chin jutting out an extra inch. "What are you, a cop?"

"No police department would have me."

"Then what are you coming around here again for?" he roared, slamming his palm hard on the desktop, making his cell phone jump. Conor, ears flattened against his head, immediately rose to his feet, rumbling softly. He was uncomfortable with yelling—less so with banging on furniture.

"I just left Garrett Lavender's office," Brock said, putting a hand firmly on the top of the dog's head. "He's a royal pain in the ass."

"What do I care what you and him talked about?"

"I'm asking you, flat out, if he can be trusted."

"*You're* the one who can't be trusted!" McCurdy bellowed, pointing a skeleton-like index finger. "Just now, you fucked Lavender out of three hundred dollars!"

"He called you about it already? How many times a day does he ring you up, Rory? Does he ask permission whenever he needs to scratch his ass? He's a money-grubbing little prick! I was with him for a few minutes, and all he gave me was boilerplate bullshit. He's your lawyer, not mine."

"He is my lawyer," Rory McCurdy said, icy fury flashing from his eyes, "but you are not one of us, and you haven't been for years!"

A shocker that struck Brock Sheehan mute for half a minute, trying to catch his breath. Eventually he managed to say, "I'm as Irish as County Mayo, and you know it. I gave you twenty years of my life." His mouth had gone bone dry, and he wished he had a bottle of water with him. "I did everything you asked me to—good, bad, or indifferent. I never questioned it, never asked *why*. I just did it."

"That's a wind-up doll," Rory said, "not a man."

"Then how come you said I was the son you never had?"

"Because I wanted you to marry my daughter—but you fucked that up, too."

"I didn't love her, and I told you that. I liked her a lot. I still like her. We were friends—but you don't marry somebody you 'like a lot,' and get stuck with it for the rest of your life."

"Sure," the Old Man said, "and just *look* at the rest of your life. It's shite! You're completely alone! Nobody loves you, nobody likes you, you turned your back on your friends and haven't made any new ones, and you're high and mighty on a thick pile of dirty money and an expensive houseboat so you make sure nobody else comes near you."

"You gave me that houseboat as a retirement gift, remember? Why did you do that if you're so pissed off at me?"

McCurdy wiped his hand across his face as if he were brushing away cobwebs, and then heaved a deep, heavy sigh. "You were my right hand, Brock. I always knew when there was something not so good to you, not exactly kosher, as the Jew-boys say. It couldn't be helped, though, cuz you were the one I could count on. Sure, it was a going-away present." He closed his eyes. "Nobody around could take your place. Nobody. It was like getting a divorce, or losing a child. This whole place has been half-cocked for the past ten years. So I'm kicking myself in my white Irish ass every goddamn day and hating myself for giving you that boat."

"You can have it back if you want."

"I'm in my nineties! What would I do with a houseboat?"

"Just what I do. Sit in it. Read. Drink. Nap. Suck up all that fresh Lake Erie air."

"No more boat? Where would you live?"

"The whole world," Sheehan said, showing McCurdy an imaginary world globe with his two hands. "Maybe in Ireland."

"Good riddance to you, then! And don't come back. I mean it. If you come back here, you come back to work, just like always. And if you come back and not work for me—" Rory drew himself up as high as he possibly could while being swallowed up by an executive office chair that made him appear a wrinkled child sitting on the throne of England. "Then," he continued, "I'm going to kill you."

CHAPTER TWENTY-ONE

Sheehan tried contacting Lloyd Oborn through the University of Akron campus, but to no avail. A perfect stranger could not just march into the administration office and demand to know the time and location of a student's class to whom he was not related. Probably Detective Sergeant Tobe Blaine would just flash her badge, and doors would open wide—though she had no authority in Akron and wouldn't make the trip to arrest Lloyd just on Sheehan's hunch.

He recalled, though, that Lloyd had been home during the day the first time they met. Maybe the kid didn't have a dorm close by, but lived at home with his mother.

As he headed east on Market Street past enormous shopping centers on both sides of the street, the painful reality pricked at him that if he'd just stayed on the freeway for another few miles, he could have hooked up to I-76 that would quickly take him to Youngstown and to Arizona Skye—one last shot, he thought, one serious conversation about how much he'd always loved her and how his life had never been the same, never been as good as their time together. It might change her mind. At least it would get her to think about it.

Avoiding life imprisonment for his nephew, though, seemed more important than his heart, which had been broken for so long that he'd come to accept it. He doggedly continued toward the Oborn home. It was early enough in the afternoon that Lloyd might still be at school. He parked around the block with a good view of the driveway of the house, leashed up Conor for a quick pee stop at one of the bushes on the front lawn of someone else's residence, and then hunkered down in his car to wait.

The autumn hues were seriously appearing, the best time for enjoying the colorful season before all the leaves fell. The small tree in Oborn's front yard had grown vividly red, branches rustling in the breeze. It wouldn't be long before all over the neighborhood there would be a truckload of work for everyone to rake the fallen leaves and put them at the curbs so the town's huge vacuuming vehicles could suck them up and dump them somewhere to either be burned or smushed up for composts.

Conor was peacefully asleep, his chin on Sheehan's lap, when he jerked his head up quickly, having heard the sound of a car pulling into the driveway across the street even before Sheehan had.

Lloyd Oborn had parked next to his front door and was getting out of the car—a dusty three-year-old Toyota Corolla—when Brock and Conor approached him. In his right hand was a briefcase obviously chock full of textbooks, papers, a calculator, and a laptop computer. In the other hand were his car keys. His sneakers were dirty white Adidas, his jeans the expensive kind that nicely sculpted his ass, his hair as if he'd combed it with his fingers. A pair of sunglasses looped over the neckline of his sweater.

He stopped short, his fearsome scowl deepening—but apparently a frown was the only expression Sheehan had ever seen on him. "Christ," he muttered. "You again? You mean you haven't finished writing that goddamn book yet?"

"Just a few more questions for you," Sheehan answered.

"Go ask 'em somewhere else. I still got nothing to say to you."

Apparently they didn't teach perfect grammar at the University of Akron. "You get mad easily, don't you, Lloyd?"

"I get mad at assholes coming around my home asking me

265

questions."

"The world is full of people who ask questions. Otherwise nobody would ever learn anything." He pointed at Lloyd's briefcase. "I imagine you've got a ton of books in there that are getting you to ask questions every day."

"Here's a question, then. Why are you bothering us? We've had enough grief without having to put up with your shit!"

"Maybe I'm trying to help you."

Lloyd Oborn scoffed, "You wanna help? Keep away from me. Keep away from my mother. Don't ever come back here again." Then he glared at Conor with contempt. "And get your fucking dog off the lawn."

"He already did what he needed to. He'll be okay now."

"Don't you get it? Conversation *over!*"

"I know how angry you are—and I don't blame you. I'm just wondering, though—how much research did you do after your sister's attack?"

"What are you bullshitting about?" Lloyd snarled. "I know what Meredith told me. That was enough."

"Are you certain Kenny Pine was the one who took advantage of her?"

"Who the hell else would it be?"

Sheehan said, "There were many guys at that party. Maybe Kenny was the only one whose name she knew, because he was famous."

"She didn't mess with overpaid jocks!" Oborn growled. "She was too smart for that. She didn't even like sports. I bet somebody had to tell her who Pine was, and that he was a big deal superstar."

"You sure of that?"

"She told me Pine did it!" he screamed, spit flying from his lips. "She told me!"

"She also told you she was drunk. You've been drunk, haven't you, Lloyd? Didn't you ever wake up with a hangover and didn't quite remember what you said or did the night before? If she was plastered, maybe she couldn't remember what happened to her."

Lloyd's chin came jutting out, ready for a fight. "What are you saying? My sister was a drunken slut?"

"Not at all. Just trying to get the facts straight in my head."

"Oh yeah?" Lloyd Oborn's eyes grew smaller and meaner as he studied his visitor and the dog. Something wasn't making sense to him. Finally, "What kind of book are you writing, anyhow? It's not sounding like college athletes."

"I'm not writing a book at all. I'm trying to find out who killed Kenny Pine."

Now the kid was puzzled. "I don't get it. You're a cop?"

"No."

The mean suspicious look returned. "Are you a friend of that motherfucker?"

"Never met him. Never saw him play basketball, either."

Now he was loud and angry again, and took two steps closer to Brock, ready to pick a fight. "Then whaddya want with me?"

Conor, who stood to the left of Brock Sheehan, stiffened, ears laid all the way back. A grumbling in his throat indicated he was not a happy dog.

"You're angry. You loathed the guy who assaulted Meredith, and that incident eventually led her to taking her own life. But you can't go around killing people out of revenge after they did three years in prison."

"He did jail time for killing dogs! Not for raping my sister!"

Brock told him, "I sympathize with that—but I need you to man up. When you're in one of your rages, did you murder Kenny Pine? Did you cut his throat from ear to ear?"

"Fuck you, man!" Lloyd screamed. "Get out of my face!"

He took one step forward and swung the heavy briefcase right at Sheehan, who was taken by surprise and didn't move out of the way fast enough. The buckle on the front of it caught him exactly where Monroe Miller had clubbed him with the rifle butt. He stumbled backwards, trying to keep from falling. Blood once more spilled over his left eye and down his face.

Then Lloyd hit him again, this time on the side of his head, and he sank to one knee.

The pit bull, however, had other ideas. He charged forward, ripping the leash from Sheehan's hand, leaped up at Lloyd and sank his teeth into the crook of his shoulder, snarling and growling. The boy, screaming in pain, fell on his back, trying vainly to push Conor away. But once pitties bite, whether animal enemy or human, they don't let go.

Dizzy and bleeding badly, Sheehan made an effort to get up but couldn't quite make it. He croaked out, "Conor! No! *No!*"

It didn't work.

Lloyd's shrieks, however, alerted his mother inside. Brenda Oborn rushed out, bellowing at the top of her small voice, hoping to chase Conor away. All she'd grabbed on her way out, though, was a polka dot umbrella, with which she battered the dog around the head and shoulders. But Conor wasn't about to stop.

With great effort, Sheehan clawed his way to his feet and lurched to the wrestling match that was Lloyd and Conor. He managed to get hold of the dog leash and pulled gently but firmly. "No, Conor. No. Come! Sit, Conor. Sit." He reached down, petting the dog's head while he tugged on his collar as Brenda smote fiercely with the umbrella, even hitting Sheehan on the side of the head once. Conor shook the front of his body and shoulders back and forth as if he might behead the poor kid.

Finally, Sheehan tugging Conor's collar made him let go. The boy stayed where he was on the ground, whimpering, his sweater already torn and blood-soaked. Sheehan knelt beside him, taking Lloyd's right hand and moving it up to his shoulder. "Hold on right there, Lloyd," he said, "and press as hard as you can to stop the bleeding." He looked up at Lloyd's mother. "Call an ambulance—right away!"

Still in high fury, she started to say something, and Sheehan snapped, "Now! We'll discuss all this later. *Move!*"

Brenda blinked once and then dashed back into the house. Sheehan took up the dog leash and led Conor back to the street, bloody mouth and all, making him jump into his car's back seat. Closing the door, he leaned against the car and brushed his hand all over his face to feel how much he'd bled.

Now he knew he was in trouble with the police—or more precisely, Conor was in trouble. It's rare that a dog of any breed is allowed to live after attacking a human. Conor had defended him, as any loyal dog would, but Brenda, with a son whose neck had been ravaged, would eventually flog her revenge into a frenzy, and the dog catcher—did they still call them dog catchers in Ohio?—would drag Conor off to the pound with a chain loop at the end of a stick around his throat, and gas him to death by morning.

That's not going to happen, Brock Sheehan thought, no matter what. Conor had defended him with courage, and he wouldn't let anyone hurt the dog.

If he could get back to Vermillion, to several banks at which he had accounts, he could draw out all his money, hook up his boat to a trailer hitch, drive east until he hit the coast, then sail south, maybe to Carolina, or even loop around Florida and into Texas and the Gulf of Mexico, and set up a new life, because neither Brenda Oborn nor her son knew his real name. If they remembered at all, they thought he was Terry Malloy.

Few knew who Brock Sheehan was. Linus, Rory McCurdy, and the Gaelic Society would keep their mouths shut; they knew *omerta,* the code of silence, as did their Italian counterparts. Garrett Lavender wouldn't give away his name unless offered four hundred dollars. Tobe Blaine would eventually find out that the Terry Molloy being blamed was actually Brock Sheehan, but she wouldn't go looking for him all over the country.

Brenda knelt beside her son, her fingers pressing on the neck injury to stanch the blood loss, sobbing loudly, her face the color of white chalk. She didn't look at Brock. She didn't dare to. At the moment her only thoughts were of Lloyd; the abhorrence for man and dog would kick in later, he thought.

He couldn't blame her. The worst pain in the universe was a

parent outliving their child, and losing her second kid would destroy Brenda Oborn beyond repair.

Brock's own guilt was disturbing him more than letting Conor attack the kid and nearly tearing his throat out.

The screaming, crying, and barking had alerted some other nearby homeowners. Still working hours, it was mostly women and children who came out from their houses to watch the melee. There was nothing more compelling to onlookers than someone being hurt or killed in an accident—much better than a July 4th parade with cotton candy and popcorn and watery homemade lemonade.

He opened the back car door slightly, reaching in and soothing the still-excited pit bull with strokes of his hand. "Don't worry, Conor," he crooned into a twitching ear. "Nobody will hurt you. I'll make sure of it." He scratched under Conor's chin, getting Lloyd's blood under his fingernails, and the dog wagged his tail furiously, murmuring softly and whining as he looked up into Sheehan's face.

"Nobody," Sheehan repeated in a near whisper, "will ever hurt you—ever again."

When the EMS ambulance arrived eight minutes later, so did three police cars, which meant six uniformed Akron cops were wandering around the lawn trying to look efficient. One of them, noticing the blood all over Sheehan's face and shirt, insisted that he go with the EMS guys to the hospital, probably thinking he'd been dog-bitten as well. If Sheehan argued with the cop, more questions would be asked, so he promised he'd drive his own car to follow the ambulance. He wouldn't like sharing a squad car with two uniforms and his own pit bull, nor did he think he'd be safe riding in the ambulance with the Oborns. Neither he nor Conor would be welcomed.

Brenda had told the police her son was attacked by a dog, but made no mention that the very same dog was sitting in the back seat of Sheehan's car. That made Brock wonder.

Lloyd was immediately taken into the ER, his shoulder still

bleeding. A kindly nurse gave Sheehan a wad of gauze and a few ice cubes to press onto his forehead, but no doctor looked at him until an hour and a quarter had passed. Nine stitches later, he was back in the waiting room, hoping to speak with Brenda Oborn when she finally emerged from where her son was being treated.

She spotted him immediately and came right over, sitting next to him on one of those uncomfortable chairs. Her lips were pressed together, but she didn't look furious. More—upset.

"How's Lloyd?" he said to her.

"He's getting sewed up and shot with all sorts of antibiotics and disinfectants. He'll be all right, but they said the scar on his shoulder will fade but not go away."

"I'm sorry. When my dog saw him hit me in the head with that heavy case, he went into action. Pit bulls are like that— loyal as hell."

She said, "I won't press charges, if that's what you're worrying about."

Sheehan was too stunned to thank her. After his barbarous misadventures in the employ of the big-time Irish godfather and the self-styled mission he'd fashioned for himself to escape the law's relentless examination, he was certain he'd be jailed for all that he'd done in the past several days.

Brenda Oborn interrupted his ramble down memory lane. "You're thinking Lloyd killed Kenny Pine, aren't you?"

He breathed a sigh of relief. "Lloyd is angry about what happened to Meredith, and I can't blame him. I wanted to talk to him some more." He gently fingered the gauze just to the left of his eye. "He didn't feel like talking."

"I'm sorry he hit you."

"Not the first time I've been hit," Sheehan said. "Not even the first time this week. Conor—that's my pit bull—was trained to be a fighter, if training dogs means treating them cruelly and indecently and making them mean. He's loyal and affection- ate—but always answers violence with violence. It's how he was brought up."

"How long has he been with you?"

He hesitated. "Not very long."

"I'm afraid, then, both you and your dog wasted your time."

"Why is that?"

She licked her lips; her mouth was obviously dry. "Because Lloyd did not kill Kenny Pine."

Distressed, Brock Sheehan attempted an understanding smile. "How would you know that, Ms. Oborn?"

She squinted, trying to prevent tears from flowing but only partially succeeded. Her eyes were red and watery. She inhaled half the air in the room and then let it out slowly before saying, "It's because I was the one who did it."

From the time he was old enough to walk and talk, Lloyd Oborn had adored his older sister, Meredith. She was the nicest, sweetest, prettiest girl in the world to him, and she made sure he got every bit as much attention from her parents as she did. When he was only six years old and getting into a hassle with an older kid from down the block, it was Meredith who barreled out of the house, fists knotted, bellowing, "Don't you dare hit my brother!" and laying the bad guy flat with one roundhouse right to the nose. She was Lloyd's hero—up until the day she died.

All during her high school years, it was Lloyd, still in the higher elementary grades, who watched over her, vetted her girlfriends and her male dates, and hardly let a day go by without telling her how pretty she was and how much he loved her. He never realized that at a certain age it would get very embarrassing.

He himself was a high school sophomore when Meredith packed up to move south to Columbus and enroll in The Ohio State University. He didn't cry, pout, or become overly emotional, but called her at least once a week, Skyped with her occasionally, and sent her tweets, notes, paper clippings, postcards, and news of his own life. He would hate to lose touch with her.

And then she came home—broken. She wouldn't talk to him about it—he was only sixteen—but she confided in her mother, and Brenda quietly told Lloyd about the rape while Meredith stayed up in her room, sleeping sixteen or seventeen hours a day. Lloyd went temporarily insane, naturally, and Brenda worked hard to keep him from allowing his head to explode. When she finally calmed him down—it took more than an hour—she repeated the story Meredith had told her. As a pretty freshman, she'd been invited to a house party slightly off-campus, was fed several drinks she was unused to, and spent much of the evening talking to two guys from the basketball team, Kenny Pine—a senior who'd become an American stand-out player hoping to be drafted by one of the NBA teams—and his friend and teammate, Cody Thacken. They were both eagerly flirtatious, but Meredith just wasn't interested in them that way.

The last thing Meredith told her mother she remembered was Kenny Pine going off to get her another drink. Then she passed out, and woke up about two hours later with a throbbing headache, on a sofa in the basement of that house. Her skirt was up around her waist, her ripped panties thrown on the floor next to her, blood and semen dripping from her vagina and her anus. Both Kenny Pine and Cody Thacken were gone from the scene. She staggered up to the living room and found one of the other young women she knew slightly from her Physical Geography class and begged to be driven home.

Back in her dorm she had a bout of vomiting, after which she got into the hottest shower she could stand and cleaned herself off as best she could, both inside and out—stupid, perhaps, but she didn't watch Law and Order SVU, *so knew nothing about rape kits anyway.*

Two days later she approached Sasha Burton in the Title 9 coordinator's office and told her Kenny Pine had raped her while she was unconscious. The dean of women was called in, and eventually the vice president in charge of student affairs, but after repeating her story to all of them, she had to wait several days until they notified her there was no way she could prove her accusation, and it was Kenny's story against hers.

That's when she cleaned out her dorm and went back home to her family. A few months later, no longer able to sleep and forgetting how to smile, she found a rope in the garage and tied one end to the sturdy rafter in her bedroom closet and the other around her neck, and jumped off a high stool on which she'd been standing.

Lloyd found her later that day when he came home from school.

After her funeral, her mother became quiet, moody, and very sad. Her brother stayed angry, sullen, and quick to lose his temper. He threatened to find Kenny Pine and kill him, but sixteen year-olds rarely carry out such a threat.

It was difficult for both of them that a week after Pine's graduation from OSU, he was arrested for operating a dog-fighting organization on a farm in Mahoning County he owned for profit, along with his more-or-less silent partner, Monroe Miller. Terrified of being incarcerated, Miller squealed to the cops, to the assistant district attorney, and again on the witness stand during Pine's trial about his particularly brutal treatment of dogs that weren't "winners" bringing in high bets, crowds, and big money gamblers. Hanging them alive, drowning them with his two hands or electrocuting them was a gross turn-off to hear and contemplate for the jury, and Pine rapidly was sent from the defense table to prison in Mansfield for three years.

When finally released, he was immediately approached by several NBA teams desperate for a superstar, and eventually accepted an invitation and signed a contract for several million dollars per year by the Denver Nuggets.

And then...

"I couldn't stand it another moment," Brenda Oborn told Sheehan in the hospital waiting room, sitting on the edge of her faux leather chair, her voice quivering as she rubbed her hands together. "Pine being paid a fortune—after what he'd done? Revolting! I even hired a private investigator from Toledo to shadow him for a while and report where he hung out—mostly in Cleveland, his birthplace. I gave the investigator a made-up name and paid him in cash—I guess he was a sneaky kind of private eye, because he said he wasn't licensed. Then, I told Lloyd I'd be away on business for a few days, and that didn't seem to upset him. The next day after he'd gone off to his classes, I took a very sharp knife from my kitchen counter, drove to Cleveland, and waited under the bridge, just across the street from the Flat Iron Cafe—that place has been around in The Flats for over a hundred years." She waved her hands high in the air as though they were actually crouching under the big bridge. "Anyway, he didn't show up that night, so I rented a room at the Holiday Inn Express, and hung around outside the Flat Iron for four more nights until he finally arrived. He stayed in that bar for half an hour, and when he came out and went to his car, I walked up to him."

There were other people in the waiting room, too, and Sheehan glanced around to see if anyone could hear her, as Ms. Oborn was speaking in a normal tone, not trying to whisper. But people in a hospital emergency waiting room are too busy thinking about what might be happening to those they'd brought here in the first place, so paid attention to no one else.

"I knew that since he signed up with Denver," she continued, "he loved for strangers to tell him what a great man he was— and even though I'm an old lady he wouldn't be interested in, we started talking. I lauded the hell out of him, fluttered my eyelashes, told him how proud I was of him that he became a major athlete at Ohio State and finally got picked up by a big pro team—and then when he was relaxed, I thanked him for even talking to me, congratulated him one more time, hugged him around his neck—and ripped open his throat with my kitchen knife. The last words he heard in his lifetime were from me. *This is for Meredith Oborn.*'"

She slumped, her back pressed against the hospital waiting room chair—but she'd stopped wringing her hands.

"I got back to my hotel, late," she continued, "so no one saw I was covered in Pine's blood. I put all my bloody clothes, even my underwear, into a paper sack, and in the morning I tossed them into a Dumpster in an alley about three miles from the hotel."

Brock Sheehan kept quiet for more than a minute, his mind racing. Eventually he said, "Are you telling me the truth, Ms. Oborn? Or are you confessing to a crime your son committed just to keep him out of jail?"

"I suppose I would—if he'd done it. Behind all the outrage and the mood swings, Lloyd is a sweet, kind boy who might have thought about getting revenge for his sister—but never did anything about it. No, he's a good person. If he'd killed Kenny Pine, he'd have admitted it from the beginning. It was *me*."

CHAPTER TWENTY-TWO

Three days later, Brock Sheehan was back on the deck of his boat, late afternoon, another of his Irish cable-knit sweaters over a turtleneck shirt to battle the nearly cold lake breeze, listening to classical music on WCLV, and sipping his first Bushmills Black of the day, neat. Conor had taken to sitting beside him, learning to relax from fear and enjoy his new life a bit more each day.

Brock, a few years shy of sixty, was age-fretting, thinking there were larger dog breeds than pit bulls—Rottweilers, Saint Bernards, Irish wolfhounds—but still predicting that within another five years, the big strong Conor on a leash would drag him on his face at a jaunty pace on the sidewalk.

He was sad that, besides his new dog, he hadn't made a true friend in the decade since he left the Rory McCurdy crowd, and even when he'd been at the center of it, he really didn't have Friends-with-a-capital-F. He'd had hangers-on who adored him, or were afraid of him, or bowed and kissed his ring because he was a big deal in the west side Irish mob and they figured if they draped themselves all over him, some magical starshine might rub off.

So now, after less than a week of knowing him, Conor had dropped most of his suspicion and turned into BFF—his best friend forever.

"Haven't you, big guy?" Sheehan said aloud, stroking the dog's shoulders with his soothing fingers. "You're my Number

One Buddy. You know what Chinese people say, don't you? If someone saves a man's life, they're responsible for him for the rest of their days. So I'm your problem now, kiddo—you kept Lloyd Oborn from killing me. From now on, if anybody talks mean to me, you'll just eat 'em for breakfast, won't you?"

The music on the radio changed, and he leaned forward and turned it up louder, better to hear Aaron Copland's "Appalachian Spring," in his opinion the finest American classical music since "Rhapsody in Blue." He half closed his eyes, feeling the musical spring breeze dancing its way through the mountains, and seeing the rugged trees and great stretches of pure blue sky, even though he'd never been anywhere near Appalachia, mountains, or hardly even a tree.

After his dragged-out adventure getting Linus Callahan off the police hook, it was time to relax. Linus said Tobe Blaine phoned and, without explaining, told him he was officially exonerated, and that took the weight of an enormous boulder off Sheehan's own shoulders.

The angry Canadian wind whipped in from the lake. Sheehan needed to dry-dock his boat as soon as possible and find warmth and sunshine for the winter—maybe Nevada this time. Not Las Vegas, which was tacky and tawdry behind all the glitz and glamor. Maybe somewhere outside Reno, "The Greatest Little City in the World." He sank his neck lower into his sweater and reached for his drink. "Appalachian Spring" was playing so close to his ear that he didn't hear footsteps approaching on the pier.

Finally looking up, Sheehan saw Detective Sergeant Tobe Blaine on the dock near his boat, in jeans and a slim brown leather jacket. With her was a man approximately the same height and build as he was. Sheehan flashed quickly what might happen in a fistfight between the two of them, both on the edge of upper-middle age, but neither Blaine nor her date looked antagonistic.

When they boarded the boat, Conor was at once on his feet,

his head straight out from his shoulders—not aggressive, but very much the guardian.

"It's okay, Conor," Brock said soothingly. "Sit, boy. Sit."

Conor hunkered back on his haunches, but wouldn't lie down while visitors were present.

"Hi, Mr. Sheehan," said the visitor beside Blaine. "I'm Milan Jacovich—Tobe's companion."

Sheehan got out of his chair and shook Jacovich's hand. "I've heard of you for years," he said. "Private eye."

"I've heard of you, too."

Sheehan sighed. "I'll bet you have." He turned to Blaine and asked, "What is it this time, Detective Sergeant? Am I under arrest and you brought a friend along to make sure I came quietly?"

"If I arrested you," Blaine said, "I wouldn't need a chaperone. No, Milan and I are spending a three-day weekend relaxing in Sandusky, so we're in the neighborhood. I hope you don't mind we stopped by."

"Not at all—now that we're friends."

"But I have to talk to you about something, if that's okay."

"Sure," Sheehan said, "I can get more chairs."

"We'll stand. We won't be here that long. Brenda Oborn told me enough about the crime scene—exactly where Kenny Pine was, how he was cut, how he fell—and she even handed me the murder weapon all wrapped up in a plastic freezer bag— her own kitchen knife. She said she killed Pine because three and a half years earlier he'd fed her teenaged daughter Meredith some sort of Roofie or other illegal drug, and then raped her— which led to Meredith's suicide. Her lawyer told her she'd plead guilty by reason of temporary insanity."

"So his death had nothing to do either with basketball or with his cruelty to dogs."

"Spot on," said Blaine.

"The temporary insanity plea doesn't bother you?"

"Pleas and trials are not my job."

"I'm glad it gets you off Linus Callahan's back, at least. He was going bananas thinking he'd spend his life in prison for something he didn't even do. Congratulations, Detective Sergeant Blaine. Good collar."

"Thanks."

Sheehan turned to Blaine's lover. "Did you bring about this arrest, Mr. Jacovich?"

Milan gave a half shrug. His shoulders were wide and powerful like Sheehan's, though he was slowly losing his hair. "I didn't even hear about it until it was all wrapped up. Tobe rarely shares her cases with me."

"And vice versa," Blaine said. "Brenda turned herself in voluntarily, but she first confessed to a *Denver Post* reporter by the name of Terry Molloy. Ever hear of him?"

"I don't read the *Denver Post*."

"Of course not," Tobe Blaine said, nodding more sagaciously than was necessary. "You're a Cleveland guy."

"No, I'm a Vermillion guy—which is where we both are right now."

"Exactly." She shivered slightly against the wind and lowered her chin onto her neck—as if that would protect her from the chill. "According to Brenda Oborn, he was a big guy—just like you."

"Lots of big guys like me, aren't there? Even like Mr. Jacovich, here." Brock half smiled at Milan's nod of appreciation.

"Right again. Well—I wish I knew where to find this Terry Molloy guy. I want to thank him."

"He was probably just doing his duty."

"Uh-huh. Terry Molloy probably still unloads Irish whiskey on the Hoboken docks—just like in the movie—back working on the waterfront?"

Brock Sheehan bent and scooped up his drink for one last swallow to hide his flaming cheeks. Blaine and Jacovich were obviously enjoying the game. "Detective," he said, "I wouldn't be the slightest bit surprised."

"Yeah, right. Well, about Kenny Pine—during my investigation after the fact, I dug up some crap about him." She moved over and leaned against the deck rail. "A cop smells out secrets better than somebody's uncle." She looked sideways at Milan Jacovich. "Or even a private eye—if you get my drift."

"This isn't a contest, Tobe," Jacovich said.

"The hell it's not. I even managed to find out who was doing the bartending at that on-campus party the night Meredith Oborn ran into trouble."

"How did you manage that?" Sheehan asked.

"Through one of my best pals—a homicide detective down in Columbus. She tracked down two frat guys back then who poured a lot of booze to earn extra money."

"Three years ago?"

Blaine said, "It was easy for my friend to find. She called some frats until she found the one in which the sainted brothers weren't quite as filthy rich and obsequious to everyone. They named names, and the first name she called sang like Luciano Pavarotti." She didn't bother hiding her grin. "Back then, if you went to OSU, you damn well knew who Kenny Pine was. You're both tall men, but Pine and Thacken were both six foot seven, which is harder to forget than you guys—and their games were on TV all the time."

"Okay. So?"

"So the barkeep on that fateful night—his name was Samuel Wenderhaft—remembered that at the beginning of the party, Kenny visited the stand-up bar a lot—along with his teammate, Cody Thacken."

"And a hundred other guys, too," Sheehan said.

"Around mid-party, when both of them were talking to Meredith Oborn across the room," Blaine continued, "it was Pine alone who visited the bar next—and asked for two beers and a vodka. Wenderhaft—he didn't spend the whole evening staring at Pine, he was too busy pouring—noticed Pine wandering around with those three drinks in his hands as if he were looking for someone—maybe Cody Thacken and Meredith Oborn."

"Did he find them?"

"Who knows? But less than one hour later—that's his estimate, anyway—he saw both basketball players get the hell out of there in a hurry."

"Not Meredith?"

"Not right then. Half an hour after that, Meredith was practically stumbling out the door being helped by another girl—Wenderhaft didn't know her name. But Meredith Oborn looked swacked, rumpled, her clothes half on as if she'd dressed in a hurry—and her eyes were red and puffy."

"She must have complained to the school for a damn good reason," Sheehan mused, looking at his wristwatch and then at the darkening sky. "What's this about? Don't you two want to get to Sandusky to begin your big weekend?"

Blaine's voice became louder and sharper. "Come on, Mr. Sheehan. Meredith spends all evening talking to these two big handsome, hunky athletes—even though she probably never heard of Kenny Pine before the party started. She somehow gets hit with a solid Mickey Finn that knocks her all but unconscious. All she remembers after that is waking up with ripped clothes and her virginity gone with the wind. So she waits a few days and then reports to the Title 9 office at OSU that Kenny Pine sexually violated her."

"OSU had no real proof other than he said/she said," Sheehan observed, "so they shut it up, especially because Pine was a superstar. Almost every university in the country does things like that to avoid a scandal. Remember Penn State a few years back?"

"This one might have, too," Blaine said, "if Pine hadn't gotten arrested and drawn a three-year prison sentence for dogfighting. Then, bingo-bango, he's out on the town for three weeks, he signs an obscenely rich contract with the Nuggets—and then Meredith's mommy cuts his throat."

"Better late than never."

Tobe stood up, looming over him to make him realize she

wouldn't need a backup to arrest him if she wanted to. "Really? Well, give this some cogitation, since you didn't speak to that bartender and I did—at length. Sure, Pine flirted with Meredith. He always hit on pretty girls, including your nephew's significant other. By midevening, she was almost comatose by whatever chemical got into her system along with the booze. But according to Samuel Wenderhaft, it was Pine who came to the bar for more drinks—and the one who lost track of both Cody Thacken and the girl for more than an hour, after which Pine rushed Thacken out of that party as if the Temperance movement just arrived with religious songs and hatchets—to break the barrels and dump out all the booze."

"Why didn't he mention this to the police when Meredith first reported it?"

"First, nobody asked him to. So I'm thinking, and I can't prove it—nobody can. The rape didn't happen in my territory, not even in my county." Tobe patted herself on the stomach, and said, "My gut tells me Brenda Oborn might have murdered the wrong man."

After Detective Sergeant Blaine and her boyfriend disembarked the boat to begin their romantic Sandusky weekend, Brock Sheehan sat on the deck, flummoxed, drinking Bushmills Black until it became downright cold out there. Then he and Conor repaired below, but even in his bunk Sheehan couldn't go to sleep, tormented by the homicide cop's parting remarks.

Kenny Pine had been a lowlife snake, especially when it came to the abuse and brutal execution of helpless animals. He'd paid dearly for it, though, with nearly three years of his life given to the state of Ohio and told when to wake up, go to sleep, when to eat, when to shit, when to exercise, and when to sit and watch a boring, nonviolent movie like the cartoon *Cars*. To animal lovers like Linus Callahan, and even for Brock Sheehan, three years was not enough. Murder, though, was a bit much.

It may be that Pine supplied MDMA, the ecstasy drug better known as "roofie"—but according to Wenderhaft, he didn't enjoy the benefits, and spent the rest of the party looking around for his intended target of the evening, Meredith Oborn, and his non-celebrity teammate, Cody Thacken.

Which meant that Thacken probably committed the rape of a young woman too chemically wasted to know the difference.

And Kenny Pine paid the ultimate price.

Sheehan awoke the next morning as hung over as he'd been in decades. He spent a long time under a hot shower, then turned the water to cold, made a whole pot of coffee, and drank half of it before he had anything to eat for breakfast.

He was troubled—and wasn't sure why. Linus, who had dragged him kicking and screaming into a homicide appraisal in the first place, had been exonerated, which meant he'd completed the mission to which he was assigned. The rest of it—hell, it had nothing to do with him.

He leaned down and thumped the ribs of Conor, who rolled over on his back and exposed his belly to more pats and scratches, groaning with happiness, which made Sheehan feel better. He would shed no tears for the death of Kenny Pine, and just one or two drops for the woman who thought she was avenging her young daughter's demise and might spend a good hunk of her life behind bars.

Sheehan wondered just how good Brenda's defense attorney might be. Hoping for a plea of not guilty by reason of temporary insanity? He was no lawyer, but under these particular circumstances, that sounded pretty good to him.

It wasn't Brenda who made him nervous and agitated. The guy who really got away with it and skated off without a scratch was under his skin—and it stayed there for the next three days, long enough to make provisions for dry-docking his boat, packing what he'd need for the next several months in a more temperate climate and atmosphere and renting a storage unit in Vermillion for the next five months. Then he booked a room in the town of Sheffield at the west end of Cuyahoga County for two more nights in a motel that welcomed pets.

The skies were beginning to darken earlier, so on his last day in town, he timed getting out to Solon when twilight was already turning the world dim. He waited quietly in the parking lot of Paisley Electronics, Conor in the back seat resting his head on the console.

It was about ten minutes past six when Cody Thacken came through the building's front door carrying a briefcase and an umbrella. He moved leisurely toward a two-year-old Cadillac Escalade, jet black in color, parked nowhere near close to the entrance for someone important like a vice president or sales manager. Sheehan followed the car out of the lot, eventually heading toward one of the Heights suburbs.

"Stay calm, Conor," he almost whispered, touching the pittie's head gently with his palm. "Any time now we'll be heading west for the winter. You'll like it there, it's pretty and warm. Be patient."

Conor hummed happily.

Thacken arrived in Cleveland Heights half an hour later at a nice, white-painted Cape Cod colonial home on one of the side streets, the garage not connected to the house but back off the street and more or less out of sight, especially since the sky was almost dark. Thacken turned into the driveway and headed back to the garage, pushing a remote button to open the door. Brock parked at the curb, leaving Conor inside, and walked back toward the garage, still open. Thacken was collecting his briefcase and leaned in to snag his umbrella as his visitor walked up behind him.

"Hello, Mr. Thacken," Brock said.

Cody Thacken jumped, startled, and banged his head on the top of the car door.

"Who the hell are you? Oh, wait," he said, squinting one eye in partial recognition. "I remember you. You're the guy writing the book. We talked in my office."

"Right," Sheehan said. "Glad you remembered me."

"What are you doing here?" Thacken's tone was edgy and annoyed. "I don't like strangers coming to my home. If you have any more questions about my life at OSU, make another appointment at my office. I'll talk to you then—if I can."

"Married?"

"No."

"Cohabiting with someone?"

"No, but that's beside the point."

"It's smack-dab right *on* the point. Do you remember a guy named Samuel Wenderhaft from that party you were at with Kenny Pine? The one where a pretty young freshman girl was fed some Ecstasy and got raped and sodomized in the basement."

"There were a hundred people at that party—and it was almost four years ago. I can barely remember it. So I don't remember some Samuel Whatever-his-name-is?"

"He was one of the bartenders."

Thacken laughed without any mirth behind it. "Who looks at bartenders?

"He looked at you," Sheehan said, "and at Kenny Pine looking for you, but you and Meredith Oborn were missing in action."

"All right, what's your deal, pal? Is this some sort of blackmail?"

"Just seeing if you have balls enough to tell the truth for the first time in four years." Sheehan backed him up against his car. "You put the blame on Pine because you knew OSU would shut up tight as a drum to avoid a scandal. You both skated, free and clear. Then he got busted for animal abuse and went to prison for it. Don't worry—I can't turn you in if I wanted to. You're one lucky son of a bitch—because after he got out of the slammer, somebody murdered him for raping that girl. He was innocent of that. You were the one that did it, and you damn well know it."

"Back off, man," Thacken growled, pushing Brock Sheehan

away with his finger. He was five inches taller and thirty-some years younger, and wasn't about to put up with the older man's accusations. "So I fucked her. So what? I never before got something *first* that Kenny Pine wanted, and I was goddamn sick of his—*seconds*. She was more than halfway out cold, so she wasn't even aware of it—and I had fun. So no harm done."

"No harm? A few months later, Meredith hung herself. That harm is significant."

"You better get out of my face, you old fart, before I hurt you—real bad."

Sheehan said, "Real bad, huh? You mean like this?" And he drove his fist deep into Cody Thacken's stomach, doubling him over and sending him to his knees, gasping for breath. The punch traveled no more than six inches, but it came from Sheehan's hips, not his shoulder. He'd done it before, enough to make it count.

He grabbed a handful of Thacken's hair, pulled him to his feet and hit him again, feeling a rib or two crack beneath his knuckles. Then a left hook into the side of his ear knocked him sideways onto the floor.

By the time Sheehan tired of it all about three minutes later, he'd flattened Cody Thacken's nose, knocked out three of his front teeth which so badly cut his tongue that he might not ever talk properly for the rest of his life. He also blackened Thacken's right eye shut and gushing blood, and his ear was bleeding, too. Then he cracked another couple of ribs—just for the hell of it

While he was still half conscious, Sheehan spoke very softly into his good ear. "That's for the rape," he whispered. "On the chance anyone will ever look at your face again without shuddering, remember if you slip any woman a Roofie and use her while she's out cold, I'll know about it—and I'll come back and finish the job. Understand?"

Thacken moaned, and Sheehan slapped him smartly on both cheeks. "Tell me you understand, Cody, or I'll work on you until you do."

Nobody could have understood what Thacken said through his damaged mouth.

Before leaving, Sheehan made his goodbye speech. "Is this the worst thing that ever happened to you? Look on the bright side—you could have been Kenny Pine."

CHAPTER TWENTY-THREE

Heading west toward Reno—man and dog. Sheehan packed light, not knowing when he might return. After so many long drives in his life, Sheehan thought he'd be used to it, especially crossing flat Kansas—but the paved highway droned on beneath his car forever, with hardly a tree in sight to get his attention. Two thousand miles was a lot shorter to drive when he'd been forty than it was now that he was close to sixty.

"How about you, Conor?" The dog raised his head and twitched his ears to a name he'd already accepted. "Bored already? How old are you, anyway? Are you two years old? Six? Eight? How many candles on your next birthday cake?"

That thought eased its way into a depressing moment or two. If Conor was in the middle of his existence, a dog his size doesn't have a long life expectancy—and he might be gone sooner than Sheehan expected.

It would be even worse for Conor if Sheehan died first. Few would adopt an aging pit bull, even a neutered one. Sheehan believed he'd writhe in Purgatory forever knowing Conor would be stuck in a second-rate shelter and live out the rest of his days in a cage.

He rumpled Conor's ears. "I'm damned if you outlive me and wind up in doggie hell. I'm going to hang around for decades."

He tried getting worries to fly away. After ten minutes he pulled off into a "rest stop" and bought a Mountain Dew with ice, and a bottle of water costing twice as much as a McDonald's coffee. He took Conor out of the car, along with the dog's water bowl, and the two of them found a bench on which they could enjoy their beverages.

Spending several months wherever he might wind up would be different than on his boat in Vermillion. He was sick of being lonely. Maybe there'd be people to meet and befriend, and fun places to go and things to do besides Nevada casinos and whorehouses.

His sudden relationship with Linus Callahan, made him re-evaluate his life over the past ten years. Violence had destroyed the tender love and caring of every Sheehan in Cleveland, and disrupted his romance with Arizona Skye. Perhaps his new relationship with Linus would change some of the rest of it, too.

Was there something different in Reno, or in another place that would suit him better? Friends who'd never know what he once did for a living—out of the way with people who said hello and often stopped to chat about nothing in particular?

He finished his Mountain Dew and looked down at Conor, who'd happily slurped up half of the water. "Come on, Conor." Ever since the dog's arrival, Sheehan got used to talking to him as if he were human. "Let's try for someplace in California instead— if an earthquake doesn't pitch us into the ocean. Not San Francisco—too damn expensive—and not Los Angeles with its la-la show business crap. Maybe someplace up north a ways, right by the water."

He stood up, and the two moved back to Sheehan's car, where he spread some road maps across his lap, running his finger slowly up the rugged coast along the rim of the Pacific, studying and figuring.

"This might be an extra day in the car, buddy. Think you can make it?"

Conor wriggled all over.

Then his finger wandered from California on the map to another state right next door, Arizona.

Arizona. His finger brushed over a place that was not huge, but more of a town or just a village? He didn't know, but he liked its name, and he envisioned himself in a small cottage on a high ridge overlooking the desert. Maybe there was a half-way-decent city close by—maybe a half hour's drive—where there might be a good restaurant or two, even one that served Bushmills Black. If he liked it a lot, he could sell the houseboat long-distance and not give another single thought to Vermillion or Rory McCurdy or any of the rest of it.

He stared at the map for some time. Then he folded it up and put it into the pocket in the door. His arm circled Conor's big head and he pressed his cheek against the dog's, hugging him tightly.

"There's got to be some really pretty women in Arizona," he whispered. "Maybe even another one named after her state. You think?" The tail wagged furiously, making whacking sounds each time it hit the back of the seat. "You with me, buddy?" he said, letting go of the muscular neck. "You think maybe we should take a quick look at some little town in Arizona?"

Conor put his paws on the man's shoulder and licked his face.

Brock Sheehan took a big breath and expelled it slowly as he curled his fingers around the steering wheel. "Then fuck California," he said, and turned on the engine.

LES ROBERTS came to mystery writing by winning the very first "First Private Eye Novel" Contest, which gave him his literary start. *Sheehan's Dog* is his thirty-second published book. Prior to that, he worked in Los Angeles for a quarter of a century, writing and/or producing more than 2500 half hours of network and syndicated television. A Chicago native, he has lived for the past 31 years in Northeast Ohio.

On the following pages are a few
more great titles from the
Down & Out Books publishing family.

For a complete list of books and to
sign up for our newsletter,
go to DownAndOutBooks.com.

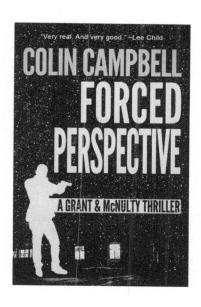

Forced Perspective
A Grant & McNulty Thriller
Colin Campbell

Down & Out Books
December 2021
978-1-64396-241-2

Jim Grant enlists Vince McNulty's help to invite criminals to audition as movie extras. The plan is almost derailed when McNulty and Grant protect a girl from an angry biker but the plan is successful. Mostly.

Except the sting is a dry run for the main person Grant wants to arrest; a crime lord movie buff in Loveland, Colorado. A sting that won't be nearly as successful.

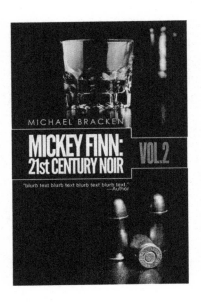

Mickey Finn: 21st Century Noir
Michael Bracken, Editor

Down & Out Books
December 2021
978-1-64396-242-9

Mickey Finn: 21st Century Noir, Volume 2, second volume of the hard-hitting series, is a crime-fiction cocktail that will knock readers into a literary stupor.

Contributors—Trey R. Barker, John Bosworth, Michael Bracken, Scott Bradfield, S.M. Fedor, Nils Gilbertson, J.D. Graves, James A. Hearn, Janice Law, Hugh Lessig, Gabe Morran, Rick Ollerman, Josh Pachter, Robert Petyo, Stephen D. Rogers, Albert Tucher, Joseph S. Walker, Sam Wiebe, and Stacy Woodson—push hard against the boundaries of crime fiction, driving their work into places short crime fiction doesn't often go, into a world where the mean streets seem gentrified by comparison and happy endings are the exception, not the rule.

Razing Stakes
The De La Cruz Case Files
TG Wolff

Down & Out Books
February 2022
978-1-64396-245-0

Colin McHenry is out for his regular run when an SUV crosses into his path, crushing him. Within hours of the hit-skip, Cleveland Homicide Detective Jesus De La Cruz finds the vehicle in the owner's garage, who's on vacation three time zones away. The suspects read like a list out of a textbook: the jilted fiancée, the jealous coworker, the overlooked subordinate, the dirty client.

Motives, opportunities, and alibis don't point in a single direction. In these mysteries, Cruz has to think laterally, yanking down the curtain to expose the master minding the strings.

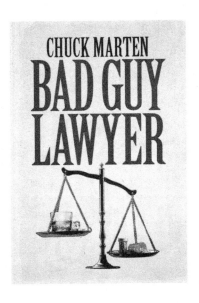

Bad Guy Lawyer
Chuck Marten

Down & Out Books
March 2022
978-1-64396-249-8

The only time Guy McCann stops talking is when he's downing scotch. Guy was a hot-shot attorney for the West Coast mafia until he got cold feet and split town, earning a target on his head. Now he's lying low in Las Vegas, giving back-room legal advice to second-rate crooks while pining over his old girlfriend Blair, a working girl with a razor wit and zero inhibitions.

When Blair is committed to a psychiatric ward, Guy is drawn back to the dangerous underworld of Los Angeles. Next thing he knows, Blair has escaped from the hospital and Guy's former mafia associates are on her trail, with Guy caught in the crossfire.

Made in the USA
Monee, IL
06 December 2022

19840034R00184